Charles Leonard Marsh

Opening the Oyster

A story of adventure

Charles Leonard Marsh

Opening the Oyster
A story of adventure

ISBN/EAN: 9783744747868

Printed in Europe, USA, Canada, Australia, Japan

Cover: Foto ©Andreas Hilbeck / pixelio.de

More available books at **www.hansebooks.com**

"With a hoarse cry the one whom Ned had struck . . . made a dash at us with a knife." — *Page* 292.

A.C. McCLURG
AND COMPANY
CHICAGO 1889

OPENING THE OYSTER

A Story of Adventure

By CHARLES L. MARSH

"Why, then the world's mine oyster"
MERRY WIVES OF WINDSOR

CHICAGO
A. C. McCLURG AND COMPANY
1889

COPYRIGHT
BY A. C. McCLURG AND CO.
A.D. 1889

TO YOU, READER,

Who enjoy a simple straightforward story, this Book is dedicated. It will teach you nothing. It conceals no new theories. If it can help you to while away pleasantly a few idle hours, or make you, for a short time, forget the cares which more or less wear upon all of us, it will have reached its aim, and will have done for you what it has done for

THE AUTHOR.

CONTENTS.

CHAPTER IX.

CHAPTER X.

CHAPTER XI.

CHAPTER XII.

CHAPTER XIII.

CHAPTER XIV.

CHAPTER XV.

CHAPTER XVI.

CHAPTER XVII.

CHAPTER XVIII.

CHAPTER XIX.

CHAPTER XX.

CHAPTER XXI.

OPENING THE OYSTER.

CHAPTER I.

PHILADELPHIA, April 9, 1877.

DEAR TOM, — I am disgusted with you. I loathe and despise you. I am equally disgusted with myself that I should be weak enough to write to you again. Have n't I wasted pens and paper upon you some dozen of times within the last year? Have n't I wheedled and coaxed you? Have n't I belabored you with the thorniest sarcasm? Have n't I tickled you with the most delicate irony? Have n't I cursed you in the choicest ecclesiastical style? And have you ever answered one word?

Are you grown into a book-keeping machine? Have you no interest in anything above a trial balance? Is your ambition palsied? Is your hope departed? Are your friends forgotten? *Are you alive, or are you dead?* If the former, I suppose you are still plugging over Rabelais. Then "borrow the mouth of Gargantua and answer me all these questions in one word."

Just reflect a little on the past. Three years ago we graduated together. Remember the plans we laid out; the glorious times we anticipated! *Eheu fugaces!* You have become a stick of wood, an office-stool, a miserable appendage to a third-class counting-house! And I, alas! worse yet, — I am a teacher in a young ladies' boarding-school! Lawn-tennis! croquet! flirtation! frivolity! flum! Pah! how I hate it all!

You are growing morose under your disappointment, psychically squint-eyed, nursing and brooding over your melancholy, hatching out a rope for your own neck. I am getting weak in

the upper regions, silly, with intervals of frantic desperation.
I am frantic now, — have been so for weeks ! Have resolved
to cure myself, — and you too ! Don't sneer. I am serious.
I must and will have your co-operation. I charge you by all
that you hold sacred, meet me in New York ! Dinner at
Delmonico's ! Bottle of Roederer ! Half a day of life ; then
I 'll tell you ! Write and appoint a day. Fail not ; or, by Heaven !
I will come from my den and tear you from the clutches of the
leech ledgers that are sucking the life-blood from the only friend
I ever had.

I await your reply by return of mail.

Yours, etc.,

E. G. MARKHAM.

The above letter was received by me on the morning of
April 10, as I sat at my desk in a Tremont Street office in
Boston. In obedience to the impulse of the moment, I wrote
the following reply : —

DEAR NED, — After your very able diagnosis of my malady,
and the wholesale abuse you have heaped upon me, I shall
deem apologies on my part superfluous. It is true I have been
growing somewhat morose and misanthropic. Disappointment

and dissatisfaction have become so habitual to me that somewhat of their poignancy is lost. I have become in a measure contented with discontent. Writing letters, talking to people, making new acquaintances, have grown odious. I manage to endure the office through the day, and spend the night with my books and music. Not that I have any definite aim in my studies; I am merely dipping into everything, — dabbling in science, fooling with half a 'dozen languages, writing occasionally (solely for my own amusement), becoming in fact a melancholy recluse.

Your letter has revived me a trifle, though I am half inclined to hate you, as one who has roused me too rudely from a dreamy morning doze. However, I will humor you to the extent of going to New York. A dinner at Delmonico's has n't the same attractions for me that it once had, but for the sake of old times I will endure it. I shall enjoy jeering at your latest extravagance, and squeezing the enthusiasm out of you by the pressure of remorseless logic. My dear fellow, have n't you gotten over that unfortunate habit of building uninhabitable air-castles? Must I play the physician again for your benefit? My medicine was always bitter, but you generally admitted its wholesome effects after the dose had taken hold.

And *you* think to cure *me* with your soda-water prescriptions! Old boy, my head has grown too steady to be affected by carbonic acid, or even by the fumes of alcohol.

Nevertheless, don't be down-hearted. I will listen to your scheme (how glibly that word glides from your pen !), and will let you down easily. Look for me in the Brevoort House on the 13th inst., at 3 o'clock P. M. Until then you can hug your delusion, and I will post my books, and read my Rabelais that you affect to despise.

Yours in spite of your follies,

THOS. S. JACKSON.

On the 13th of April, 1877, at 6.30 P. M., we sat down to a memorable repast. A Delmonico dinner requires no description, but my friend Ned Markham does.

> "He was six foot o' man, A 1,
> Clear grit an' human natur;"

straight but supple, the king of the gymnasium, the most scientific boxer, the hardest hitter, the best jumper, the sunniest tempered and most popular man in college, but with a brain full of queer nooks and corners, wherein found lodging the strangest theories and the most extravagant desires.

"Ned," said I, as he leaned back and smiled expansively at the shrimp salad, "that chest has more inches than custom accords to school-teachers. I see you have n't altogether forgotten Indian clubs."

"Well, no, Tom," he replied; "there 's no fatty degeneration here, whatever you may say about intellectual ditto. I can put up the hundred-pound dumb-bell to-day as cheerfully as when we graduated, can clear my eleven feet at a standing jump, and hold a brimming glass as steadily as John B. Gough himself."

"Not a glass of this Carte Blanche, my boy," said I. "Pity your head is n't as steady as your hand ! When are you going to leave your romancing, and settle on something worthy of you?"

"I like that from you ! Shall I take to book-keeping? Tom, I have settled on something, and I enticed you over here with a view to settling you on that identical something ; but be patient a little. You need mellowing still. A few more glasses, and you will begin to be recognizable. It takes some washing to clear out three years' dust."

"All great Neptune's ocean would n't wash the cobwebs out of your brain !" answered I. "But come, deliver yourself of this *ridiculus mus.* I have sworn to treat it tenderly."

"In about an hour's time you will be in condition to listen to reason. Till then, 'eat and drink —'"

"'For to-morrow we die'?" interrupted I. "In other words, Ned, you are naturally and chronically drunk, and you want to reduce me to your level by artificial means."

"On the contrary, your blood has been getting thicker and muddier and more stagnant for the last three years, and is only now beginning to course once more at a proper gait. I have spent long hours in studying your case, and my treatment will infallibly benefit you."

An hour passed in this idle banter, when Ned suddenly straightened himself and said : —

"Attention ! Waiter, hard crackers, Stilton cheese, and a

bottle of Chambertin ! Now, my dear pupil, you will pardon me if I proceed with you in the Socratic method. Oblige me by answering my questions without comment, and suffer me to draw you to the conclusion."

" I am ready, O Socrates ! "

" If you had abundance of money, so that the necessities and even the luxuries of life were assured to you, how would you first employ it ! "

" By renovating my wardrobe, O Socrates ! "

" Good ! And then ? "

" And then ? Well, I think I would invite my friend Ned Markham to make the tour of the world with me, so as to keep his mind occupied with strange scenes, and prevent his absurd crotchets from coming to the surface and making him a stumbling-block to his friends."

I noticed a peculiar twinkle in Ned's eye as he answered :

" Excellent ! Bravo ! Thanks for your benevolent intentions ! But as you have no money to spare, and see no prospect of acquiring any, you are forced to forego what you would consider your greatest enjoyment ? "

" Unfortunately, yes."

" How do you make a living now ? "

" By keeping books for a Boston firm."

" How much of a living do you make ? "

" As good as seventy-five dollars per month will secure."

" Could you keep books for any other house equally well ? "

" With some slight introduction to another kind of business, undoubtedly."

" What else can you do besides book-keeping ? Name all the accomplishments you possess, which in any possible circumstances might be turned to account to increase your income."

" Your question is weighty, O Socrates. It requires consideration. Any office work would come to me naturally enough. As for teaching, I could tackle any of the ordinary branches, and some few extraordinary ones, music for example. I might play an organ passably, blow a flute in a variety theatre orchestra, act as accompanyist, sing tenor in a village choir, write a little for a third-rate newspaper. I might perhaps do something in the way of chemistry, — assaying or analyzing. And, finally, I could probably, after some practice, chop wood or shovel dirt with the best Paddy of them all. Are my accomplishments vast and varied enough for your mystic purpose?"

"How many languages do you know?"

"Am tolerably well acquainted with the English, have a smattering of Greek, Latin, French, and German, and less than a smattering of Spanish and Italian."

"Capital! Why, you are a famous fellow! How is your health?"

"Quite good, thank you, physically."

"No hereditary disease hanging over you? Lungs all sound? Digestion good? Organs unimpaired?"

"So far as heard from."

"Suppose you were set down this moment in — say Calcutta, without a cent in your pocket; what would you do?"

"What would I do, Love? Do like that other young man in Calcutta, whose mouth was too utterly utter; I would sit on a stile and continue to smile till I fell back a corpse in the gutter."

"No levity, young man; and don't murder machine poetry in that way. It 's bad enough when quoted correctly. In all seriousness, now, what would you do?"

"In all seriousness, O Socrates, I suppose I should try to find some way to earn a living until I could get home."

"Where is your home?"

"Well, I am accustomed to call the place where I reside, my home."

"Yes, from habit, and the lack of any better term. But if you were compelled to leave your nine-by-ten room in a Boston boarding-house, you would n't really feel very homesick, would you, now? Tom, we are practically alone in the world. The only near relative you have is a brother who lives some five hundred miles away, and whom, I 'll venture to say, you have n't seen once in the last three years; and my only relative is a father so taken up with his experiments and inventions that I feel like apologizing for my existence whenever I come in his way. We could both drop out of sight for the next five years and leave scarcely a ripple of regret. Now, we are bound to each other by ties much stronger than any relationship. We are both full of longing for excitement, adventure, travel. We have plenty of resources, except the vulgar resource of money.

If we stay where we are, we have no prospect of being any better off. What hinders us from starting out to see the world, going where we please, working our way, and perhaps finding that fortune which will never come if we fold our hands and wait for it?"

"Ah, indeed!" said I. "And let us advertise ourselves as the two orphans, the celebrated tramp brothers, the two biggest fools on earth; and we will say to the public, 'You behold here, gentlemen, two idiots, who, having fairly good positions, with salaries sufficient to support them comfortably, deliberately started out and turned their backs on fortune, sulkily refusing

the piece of cake offered them because they could n't have the whole dish.' And the public will say: 'All right, my little boys! Go hungry for a while, and by and by you will come back and beg for your little mouthful, and cry for your school-teaching and your book-keeping.' Ned! Ned! has all this preliminary flourish served only to usher in such rank absurdity as this? Truly, your intellect has degenerated."

"Tom," said he, not in the least disturbed, "suppose you keep the position you have. How much better off do you think you would be at the end of five years? Candidly, now."

"It's not likely that I shall have an independent fortune. I might possibly have some slight increase of salary."

"And suppose I were to say, 'Come with me; let us work our way to forty of the principal cities of the world, and if we succeed in doing so within five years, I will guarantee you five thousand dollars'?"

"Then I should say, 'O Crœsus, take thy five thousand dollars and disport thyself therewith. Such a travelling companion will be much better company than my poverty-stricken self.'"

"Here, you incorrigible sceptic!" said Ned, flinging me a document that he drew from his pocket. "Read and realize."

I spare the reader the legal redundancy of this contract, for such was the paper that I now examined. It stipulated that the party of the first part should leave New York on the first day of May, 1877, without any money or valuables, with merely the clothes that he wore, a single change of underclothes, a few specified toilet articles, a revolver and thirty cartridges, and a flute; that on or before the first day of May, 1882, he should return to New York, bringing with him documentary evidence of his having visited forty of the principal cities of the world, the names of the cities being mentioned in the contract; that during his absence he should write and mail to the address of the party of the second part one hundred letters descriptive of his travels and his adventures, each letter to be of at least the length of two columns of the weekly illustrated newspaper published by said party of the second part, and to be accompanied by two sketches illustrative of said letter, and forty of the said one hundred letters to be mailed, one from each of the said forty cities.

Upon the return of the said party of the first part, after having successfully performed his part of the contract, the party of the second part hereby contracted and agreed to pay him the sum of ten thousand dollars.

The contract was signed by Edward G. Markham as party of the first part, and by a prominent publishing-house of New York as party of the second part.

I read this weighty document through, and then looked at Ned in speechless astonishment. He was drumming on the table with a spoon, and watching my face expectantly.

"You see I mean business, old boy," said he. "Have been working this thing for months. Have had some slight dealings with that paper before. Written one or two squibs and made a few sketches that have been graciously received, though they never brought me much money. And then I know one of the staff quite well. You see a wide-awake paper can create a good deal of interest in an undertaking of this kind. It says to the public, ' Here 's a fool going to knock about the world without any money, and tell you how he gets along. Watch him.' The public gradually gets interested. ' Wonder where he is now! Holloa! letter from Peking! There he is! Not a penny in his purse! How will he get out of that ?' A series of fairly good letters would attract attention all over the country. People would begin to bet on me against time, bet on where the next letter would come from, etc. Well, I await your profound opinion."

" I am utterly dumfounded," said I, "that you should have gone so far, and only now come to tell me of it."

"My boy," answered he, "don't you think I know you by this time? If I had consulted you before, you would have made a *reductio ad absurdum* of the whole thing in short order. The only way to secure your co-operation in anything is to have matters prepared beforehand, and then say, ' Here! the boat 's all ready to start ; jump aboard, or you 'll get left!' I felt sure you would n't desert me at the last moment ; but if you really refuse to go, Tom, why, I shall have to stick it out alone, that 's all, though that takes the romance out somewhat."

" I 'm afraid you won't find much romance in it," said I. " But, romance or no romance, you sha' n't go alone ! Here 's my hand, O foolishest of mortals, and we 'll sink or swim together ! "

" I knew it ! " shouted Ned, joyfully. " Come to my arms, my Fidus Achates ! " And before I could utter a remonstrance, he had me in his arms and was dancing round the table.

" Now let Fate put us in her darkest pit," said he. " We two together will soon find daylight."

" Two more glasses of Burgundy will put us both under the table," answered I ; " and instead of our finding daylight, daylight will come and find us. Let 's adjourn, and renew this discussion to-morrow."

" One moment," said Ned, filling the glasses ; " one more

toast.   In this wine, rich and red as the blood in our veins, we
pledge ourselves that if that blood shall continue to flow for
the next five years, we will be true to each other and to our
enterprise, — sharing as brothers all the hardships, the sufferings, the pleasures, the gains, and the losses that may result,
and allowing no impediments however dreadful, and no attractions however alluring, to turn us for an instant from our devotion to each other and to our undertaking ! "

"Amen ! " said I.   A clear musical note rang from our
glasses as they touched ; we emptied them in silence, and so
to bed.

"Ned," said I the next morning, sitting up in bed, "I have
dreamed a dream.   'I would not spend another such a night,
though 't were to buy a world of happy days.'   I have been
round the globe a dozen times, and crocodiles 'with gently
smiling jaws' have embraced me, and turbaned Turks have
pounded me with champagne-bottles ; and when I called on you
for aid, you became a Chinese idol and leered at me."

"And now," said my friend, springing from the bed, throwing
back the blinds, and waving his hand dramatically, "behold
that flood of sunlight, and know, O friend of my soul, that
as the dark shadows of the night flee before the splendor of
yon refulgent orb, so shall the dangers and hardships of our
enterprise flee before dauntless resolution and never-failing
hope ? "

"Champagne and Burgundy ! " groaned I.   "Turn in again,
my boy.   You 're as drunk as you were last night."

"And just so drunk shall I remain," replied he, "till I come
back to claim that ten thousand ! "

"And if we fail — " I began.

"'But screw your courage to the sticking-place, and we 'll not
fail ! ' " was his prompt rejoinder.

After breakfast, and an hour's discussion over our cigars, we
separated, to arrange our affairs and make the necessary preparations for our great tramp.

On the 29th of April we met again in New York.   I had
succeeded in making contract with a Boston newspaper to pay
me five thousand dollars upon my successfully performing the
same items as those enumerated in Ned's contract, except that
my letters were not to be accompanied by sketches.

We were similarly equipped in all points. Stout high shoes, suits of the most durable Scotch goods, blue flannel shirts, hats verging on the sombrero style, made up our costume. We had each a revolver and cartridges, a light haversack, containing a change of underclothes, needles, thread and buttons, a flute, matches, paper and pencil, and a few necessary toilet articles. Stamps, being equivalent to money, were barred out. We were also provided with large knives, and pocket-books containing, among other documents, a collection of letters of recommendation "To whom it may concern," signed by various individuals and firms, prominent or otherwise. Brierwood pipes and Durham tobacco completed our accoutrement.

"How much money have you, Ned?" said I.

"About twenty dollars."

"And I have eighteen dollars. We can easily dispose of that between now and the 1st of May, and be ready to start with clear consciences and empty pockets."

"I called on my respected progenitor," remarked Ned. "Found him in his shirt-sleeves, surrounded by a lot of wheels, pulleys, and cranks, — himself the biggest crank of the lot ! — working on some electrical absurdity or other. 'How are you, Governor?' said I. 'Holloa, Ned!' says he, as calmly as though he saw me last night instead of last year. 'Going away for a few years, father!' 'That so? Well, take care of yourself, and drop me a line now and then.' He let go of his pulley long enough to shake hands, and I came away. A trifle rough, is n't it? But then, I suppose it 's just as well."

"Your queer head comes to you in a right line of descent, does n't it, Ned?" said I.

"Here 's something I drew up as a kind of reminder," said he, presently. "I have another copy, and if you like we 'll sign in duplicate, and each keep a copy."

The paper read as follows : —

"We the undersigned pledge ourselves to fulfil to the best of our ability the ensuing articles : —

"1. We will leave New York on May 1, 1877, and visit as rapidly as possible, and in such order as may seem expedient, the following cities : —

"*In North America;* Halifax, Quebec, Chicago, Mexico, and San Francisco.

"*In the West Indies;* Havana.

"*In South America;* Lima, Buenos Ayres, and Valparaiso.

"*In the Sandwich Islands;* Honolulu.

"*In Africa;* Cairo.

"*In Asia;* Peking, Canton, Calcutta, Bombay, Teheran, Damascus, and Jerusalem.

"*In the Japanese Islands;* Tokio.

"*In the Philippine Islands;* Manilla.

"*In Europe;* Athens, Rome, Naples, Florence, Venice, Paris, Marseilles, Madrid, Granada, Lisbon, Cologne, Berlin, St. Petersburg, Vienna, Copenhagen, London, Edinburgh, Dublin, and Constantinople.

"*In Australia;* Melbourne.

"2. We pledge ourselves to let no individual advantages or attractions influence us to abandon or delay the accomplishment of the project contained in Article 1.

"3. We agree to do all in our power to assist each other to the utmost in our undertaking, to travel together as much as may be possible, and to preserve our brotherly feeling in any circumstances that may arise.

"4. All pecuniary gains that may accrue to either or to both of us during the performance or as a result of the completion of this enterprise shall be equally divided between us, and similarly all losses shall be borne by both equally.

"5. Neither of us will make any engagement to marry during the performance of this undertaking."

"That 's all correct!" said I. "But why did you insert the last article?"

"Not on my own account, you may be sure!" replied Ned. "One of the very things I am seeking to avoid, is the frippery of female society. But Heaven knows what temptations your callow youth may be exposed to among the dark beauties of Spain or the gay daughters of France."

"I will sign that article as cheerfully as all the rest," said I; "but for your own sake, I warn you, Ned, strike it out. It 's not in you to keep out of love for five years."

"Bah!" said he, and seizing a pen wrote his name at the

bottom of the paper. I placed my name below it, and we filed the documents carefully among our other papers.

"And now," said Ned, "what shall be our first objective point? As we are young in tramp life as yet, perhaps we had better go west for experience. What say you to Chicago?"

"With all my heart!" answered I. "Probably the walking is better in that direction than it is toward the east."

"Chicago it shall be, then!" said he. "And I allow six weeks as an outside limit to reach there. So, as all preliminaries are settled, let 's give ourselves up, for two days, to a last enjoyment of civilization."

And we did.

CHAPTER II.

A MAN at any given moment of his life is the product of two factors. The one, constant, or invariable, is his natural self, that which he was at his birth; the other, and generally the more important factor of the two, ever varying in value and so ever changing the product, is that with which he has come in contact in life, — his experience. And as it is impossible for a man, even in reflection, wholly to eliminate the factor of experience and realize what he is in his natural self, so it is also impossible to take away a part of this experience, and shutting out the life of the last month, year, or decade, summon his past self again before the eye of consciousness.

With a mind thronging with the tumultuous memories of the five years now gone, — years of adventure, of danger and hardship, of wrestling with Fortune at close hugs, — I can but faintly recall the feelings with which I set out from New York on May 1, 1877. The events are as fresh in memory as though they had occurred yesterday, but the brain that examines them has been moulded on the anvil of Time by the trip-hammer of Experience.

It had been agreed that we should take our departure from a certain point in Jersey City. Punctually at half-past seven o'clock on the morning of May 1 we were at the appointed spot, where we were joined by some three or four friends and acquaintances, and a representative of each of the newspapers that were to receive our valuable contributions.

Many a good-natured scoff and jeer was hurled at us, but we bore them all with a conscious or assumed air of superiority, as men who remembered the saying, "He laughs best who laughs last."

One of our friends produced a bundle of cigars which he handed to Ned with the remark: "Make the most of these, boys; they're probably the last 'High Lifes' you'll ever smoke — unless," he added with a grin, "I meet you strolling down Fifth Avenue within a week, which I fully expect."

"We will smoke them with grateful thoughts of the giver," replied Ned, "and will reciprocate a little later. Tom, make a memorandum to send George a box of 'High Lifes' as soon as we reach Havana."

"Many thanks!" answered our friend; "but long ere that box reaches me I shall be where cigars will have ceased to be of interest, even though fresh from Havana!"

"'The good die young'!" said I. "But you will live to have many a smoke at our expense, and to drink a glass of welcome with us on our return."

A few minutes later we were fairly launched on our five years' cruise, swinging along the road to Newark, with courage in our hearts, stout canes in our hands, and emptiness in our pockets. The world was all before us where to choose, and we proposed to make a thorough survey of it before choosing.

It was a beautiful spring morning. The sun looked cheerily over our shoulders with a smile that seemed meant to assure us that he at least would be with us in all our wanderings; that, come what might, he intended to see this thing out to the end. The passers glanced curiously at our sombreros and hurried on their way, little children eyed us shyly from behind fences or paused in their play to shout; but we strode steadily onward, looking neither to the right nor the left.

At one o'clock we had passed through the streets of Newark, crossed the ridge at Orange, and paused to rest under a clump of trees about fifteen miles from New York.

We had taken the precaution to provide ourselves with picnic provender in the shape of sandwiches, hard-boiled eggs, etc., enough to last for three or four meals, also with a tin pail and a pair of small tin cups.

So now, reclining on the soft turf, with the beautiful landscape before us and the blue mountains in the distance, we lunched, and smoked our cigars, and stretched our legs with a mighty sense of freedom.

Ned was in a poetical mood.

"O wretched, struggling humanity!" apostrophized he, "toiling, from feeble infancy to blear-eyed old age, like coral insects, that others may mount higher on the accumulations of your lives, know ye not that one warm embrace of Nature is a greater happiness than all the weary work of your generation can achieve?"

"It seems to me," said I, "that every day, as I pored over my ledgers, there came visions and faint premonitions that filled me with vague longings; and this bright landscape, this invigorating air, and the glorious freedom from responsibility, all come with a double sense of completeness and satisfaction, like the fulfilment of that incessant craving that has haunted me so long."

After an hour's rest we pursued our way, a little more leisurely than in the forenoon, with feet that began to suggest the presence of pebbles in the road, and legs that betrayed a growing inclination to shut up like jack-knives. Still we kept resolutely on, neither liking to be the first to call a halt.

Slowly the sun sank before us, and the shadows of the mountains crept up to meet our weary footsteps. The level rays gradually slanted upward, — a moment, — the last red rim disappeared. The day was done. We had met the twilight.

"That farm-house below shall be our quarters for the night," said Ned. "How are your spirits now?"

"'I care not for my spirits, if my legs were not weary!'" I answered.

A last half-mile down the hill, — we washed our hands and faces in the brook that flowed across the road, and seated on the wooden bridge, with our feet dangling over the water, supped and smoked in serene contentment.

"The barn looks more hospitable than the house," said I. "What say you to a nest in the hay?"

"Afraid to face the music, eh! my boy?" answered Ned. "All right; the barn's the thing!"

The shadows were growing deeper, and the night was fairly upon us as we approached the barn. Keeping out of sight of the house, we clambered in the window, groped our way to the stairs, and soon reached the upper regions and the hay.

Scarcely had we nestled out a bed for our tired bodies, when the sound of footsteps and voices was heard approaching, and at the same moment bright rays of light shot through the cracks beside us, and crept slowly up the opposite wall to the rafters above. The heavy door was pushed back, and a flood of light came up the stairway.

"Better bring it into the kitchen, Jim! Ye can't see to fix it out here!" said a voice; and a rattling sound followed, like taking a harness from the wall. Then silence for a moment, and then another voice, presumably Jim's.

"Guess the d——d thing's past fixing, anyhow; but we'll try it."

The heavy door was pushed into place again, the light disappeared from the stairway and reappeared through the cracks; slowly, as the steps and voices died away, it crept down from the roof to the opposite wall, lingered an instant, and was gone.

The frogs down in the brook sang their drowsy song, a cricket somewhere in the hay piped up bravely for a moment and then was silent, the horses munched and stamped beneath us, and I fell asleep.

I awoke shivering, poked the hay from over me, and sat up. The dim gray light of early morning was shining through the cracks of the barn, and my breath rose in steaming clouds around me. With a mighty effort and a shiver of cold I stood up — and dropped down again. Each leg weighed a ton. Every bone in me was a separate instrument of torture. My muscles were powerless to move, but all-powerful to ache.

Ned, curled up in the hay, with his head resting on his arm, slept as peacefully as if in the most luxurious bed. I looked at him, and groaned in utter misery. Instantly he popped up like a Jack-in-the-box, and opened his eyes.

"Holloa!" said he, cheerily. "Daylight! What's the matter, Tom? You look like Marius in the ruins of Carthage! Is your doll stuffed with sawdust?"

"My legs are!" answered I, grimly. "Get up, and let's see you walk!"

Ned promptly got upon his feet — and collapsed as I had done. We looked at each other, and broke into a simultaneous laugh.

"Oh, that's nothing!" said he, in a moment. "Slight stiffness of the joints from unusual exercise yesterday, and numbness from a chilly bedroom. Remedy — a little extra will-power, and — I have it! Will you take the prescription if I set you the example?"

"In an evil hour," said I, ruefully, "I placed myself under your treatment for the next five years, and suppose I must submit to your doses."

"Then follow me, and do as I do."

In the next two minutes we had scrambled and rolled down the stairway, out at the window, and were running at full speed toward the brook, Ned a rod in advance, and I straining every aching muscle to keep up with him, feeling as if I were running on stilts. In another two minutes we had reached the brook, stripped off every stitch of clothing, and were splashing and gasping, puffing and swearing, in the icy water.

If any one wants to realize the very acme of physical torture, let him walk thirty miles, sleep in a barn, rise at five o'clock, and after running at full speed quarter of a mile, plunge naked into a meadow stream, and all on the chilliest kind of a spring morning!

We endured it for about a minute, then rubbed each other dry with rough towels, and hurried on our clothes.

"Not cold now, are you?" asked Ned.

"Tingling with warmth!"

"Nor stiff?"

"Can walk fifty miles to-day! Your remedy is efficacious, but — don't prescribe it often!"

"And now to breakfast!" continued Ned. "Trot out that coffee, and we 'll finish the treatment."

We filled our pail at the brook, and proceeded to a clump of woods at the other side of the meadow. Here we kindled a fire and made coffee, settling it with a couple of snails that we unearthed from beneath a log. We drank it in true frontier style, without sugar or cream ; but the finest *demi-tasse de café noire* never was enjoyed with a keener relish, or produced a more beneficial result than this muddy compound that we drank from our tin cups.

The last remnants of provisions made up our breakfast.

"This noon we must earn our dinner, or go hungry. The campaign is fairly opened."

So saying, Ned drew a roll of maps from his haversack, and selecting one, spread it out before us.

"We are now about here," continued he, indicating a point with his pencil, "in the wilds of New Jersey, about fifteen miles west of Orange. The road we are following ought to lead to Dover."

"*En avant,* then !" said I. "Dover, or bust !"

After an hour's tramping along the dusty highway in the cool morning air, a farmer's wagon overtook us. We hailed it, and tumbled in without ceremony. Ned sat on the seat and chatted with the driver, and I squatted behind.

We passed several villages, looking fresh and pretty in the morning light ; the mountains in the distance began gradually to change from blue to green, and at last, as we reached the brow of a hill, the spires and chimneys of Dover and the silver stream of the Rockaway River lay before us.

At Dover we took to our legs again, and continued toward the northwest, through a pleasant, hilly country, past the southern shore of Lake Hopatcong, surrounded by its trim villas, and at noon walked boldly up to a farm-house and thumped on the back door.

A middle-aged woman, with a vinegary aspect, showed herself, and surveyed us from head to foot.

"Good-morning, Ma'am," said Ned. "We are on our way to Port Jervis, and have got out of money. We don't want to beg a dinner, but if there 's any work to be done about the place we should be glad to earn one." All this was said with Ned's most ingratiating smile.

"We 've nothing for you," said the woman.

"No odd jobs about the house?" continued Ned, with the same bland countenance. "My friend here is a carpenter."

"No, nothing !" And the door was shut and bolted.

"There 's something peculiarly horrible about a carpenter," said I. "I 'm obliged to you, Ned, for adding such a desperate profession to my list of accomplishments."

"An ill-natured woman," said Ned, reflectively, "is an excrescence on the fair face of Nature. A regular scab, — the more you pick at it the worse it becomes !"

"A new experience for you to be treated that way by the sex, is n't it, old boy?" said I. "Never mind ! You are in search of experience. Don't fail to appreciate it ! That kind will probably benefit you."

"'Faint heart never won fair' — dinner !" replied he. "We 'll try that house on the hill."

The house on the hill was a neat, white farm-house, with green blinds, standing somewhat back from the road. An old man was leaning over the fence, smoking a pipe. He nodded good-naturedly as we approached.

"Nice weather !" said I.

"Wal, yes !" answered he, looking round at the clouds as if the idea were a new one to him. "Pretty fair weather ! It 'll do ! Where ye bound for, boys?"

"Just taking a little walk through the country," answered Ned.

"Where 'd ye come from?"

"From New York."

"Well, I swan ! From N'York ! Come afut?"

"Yes, we came afoot."

"Well, I swan ! Came afut ! from N'York !"

"Yes," said I, "and we 're a little hard up ! If you have any work to be done, we 'd be glad to earn a dinner."

"Little hard up, eh? Well, I swan ! sh'd think ye was hard up, to come from N'York afut ! Want to work, eh? What can ye do? Got any muscle?"

For answer, Ned looked about, and seizing the heavy gate with one hand, lifted it from the hinges and held it out at arm's-length, then put it gently back in place again.

The old man's astonishment was prodigious. He went up

and lifted the gate with both hands, then surveyed Ned from all sides like some new kind of machine, then ejaculated, —

"Well, I swan to man!"

Presently he continued, as if recovering himself : —

"Boys, there 's some wood in the shed wants sawing and splitting! Let 's see how you tackle that!"

We tackled it. I sawed, and Ned split. The old man stood by and watched the blows of the axe with long-drawn breaths of admiration, and an occasional "swan!"

In twenty minutes the job was done, and we went in to dinner. Ned was in capital spirits, and soon had the farmer's wife and his buxom daughter gazing at him with admiration equal to the old man's. At the close of the meal we contracted with our worthy host to stay and assist him for a couple of days longer, for our board and a dollar a day apiece.

The two days were quickly gone. The work was not too laborious, and the evenings were passed in playing flute duets and singing songs for the edification of the family. On the morning of May 5 we set out on our tramp once more, bearing with us the best wishes of our employer, the longing glances of his fair daughter, five dollars in cash, and provisions enough for three good meals.

"Tom," said Ned, as we turned the hill and lost sight of the farm-house, "all funds are in common. Suppose you exercise your book-keeping proclivities, and keep track of the earnings and expenses."

"Agreed," answered I. "And you can keep as accurate a record as possible of all distances travelled, on foot, by wagon, boat, or other conveyance."

In the course of the forenoon we reached Waterloo, just as a freight-train was pulling out to the north on the Sussex Railroad.

"Jump on," said Ned; "it 's just as cheap to ride."

So we clambered up behind, and coolly sat down on the steps of the caboose. In a few moments the door opened, and the conductor appeared.

"Now, then," said he, gruffly, "get out of that! We don't run this train to carry tramps!"

"Don't get excited," said Ned. "We 're no tramps. Here, have a cigar. How far do you run?"

"About nine miles," answered he, somewhat mollified by the cigar. "To Newton. I can't let you ride, boys. It 's plump against orders."

"Oh, we 'll get off before you reach Newton," said Ned. "Light up your cigar. There 's more where that came from."

"Well, come inside then," said the man.

So we went inside the caboose, rode comfortably till near Newton, then jumped off and walked into the town.

From Newton we trudged on to Branchville, the terminus of the road, and thence struck out for the mountains.

Steadily uphill we walked, the road becoming rougher at every step, the houses ruder and more scattered. Dead giants of pine-trees, scorched by the lightning or the forest fires, stood all about us, and at last we entered the forest and still mounted upward over a path strewn thick with rocks and stones of all sizes.

Soon we were in a narrow defile between two dark walls of rocks, and the path became level. A mile farther, and suddenly the sun, which had been hidden by the mountains, burst full upon us, about an hour above the horizon.

The road began to descend, and after a few minutes' rapid walking we had emerged from the pass, and stood on the west side of the mountains. A broad valley lay below us, dotted with villages and farm-houses, and the Delaware River wound close at our feet.

"To-morrow," said Ned, "we dine in Pennsylvania."

A few miles down the road a solitary barn offered a lodging for the night, and in the morning a boy and a scow landed us on the Pennsylvania shore at a cost of ten cents, which I entered in my account-book as the first expense.

Through the picturesque scenery of northern Pennsylvania we worked our way westward, sometimes drenched by the rain, sometimes lifted on our way by passing wagons, often stealing rides on freight-trains, ever onward toward the west.

Occasionally we worked for a day or two on a farm, resting our legs and replenishing our pockets, and once we stopped half a day for repairs. A secluded spot away from the road and a clear sparkling brook tempted us.

We bathed, washed our underclothes and put on our extra ones, and then while our washing was spread out on the grass to dry, Ned sketched and I wrote up notes of the trip. In the evening we built a roaring fire and camped by its side, enlivening the hills and meadows with the pastoral echoes of our flutes. We had played together a great deal in college, and now, having no notes, we amused ourselves by recalling all the airs we had ever played or heard, and picking them out on the flute, Ned extemporizing a second part. It was only a pastime, but we felt as if it might some time be of value to us.

We acquired a good deal of facility in stealing rides on freight-trains. Box-car or gondola, it was all one to us. We managed to stow ourselves away and escape detection almost always; and many a weary mile flew by and many a moment of our precious five years was saved in this way.

Some time we lost through want of familiarity with the roads, and wrong information. It amazed us to find how ignorant the country people were of the regions immediately surrounding them. On one occasion we were trying to reach a village, whose name I have forgotten, but which was set down on our map directly in the route we were following. The road branched off in several directions, and we hailed a rustic mending a fence, and inquired the road to the village in question. After mature deliberation he informed us that it lay down the road to the right, and was about twenty miles away. Accordingly we trudged off to the right for a mile, till, wishing to assure ourselves once more, we asked the same question of a man who was at work in the field. To our inexpressible disgust he told us we were on the wrong road, that our village lay about fifteen miles to the left. He was so positive on this point that we turned back and set off to the left. A half-hour's walking brought us to a sudden bend, and our new highway led straight back toward the east.

"Confound it!" said Ned; "this road will take us back to New Jersey."

We turned around again and returned to the main road, and asking no further questions kept on to the west.

A wagon overtook us, and we were glad of the chance to climb aboard.

"Why, that village," said the driver, "is straight ahead about ten miles! That's where I'm bound for."

With these varied experiences, pleasant or provoking, we made our way to Honesdale over the gravity road to Carbondale, across country to Tunkhannock, and thence, riding all night on a freight-train, reached Elmira, in New York State, on the 10th of May.

Keeping most of the time on or near some one of the many railroad lines running north and northwest, we passed through the pleasant farming country of western New York, our experience scarcely varying from that already described, until on the 18th of May we entered Buffalo, and saw the blue waves of Lake Erie stretching away to the horizon.

My report as treasurer showed that we had earned since leaving New York, $9.50; had expended $1.35, leaving a balance of $8.15.

Ned's distance-book gave the following approximate figures: Total distance travelled on foot, 201 miles; in wagons, 38 miles; and on freight-cars, 207 miles; all together, 446 miles.

Feeling reasonably well satisfied with our achievements, we supped at a small restaurant for fifteen cents apiece, and took cheap lodgings for the night. The evening and part of the next day were spent in writing our first letters.

In aiming at Buffalo we had had in mind the water communication between that city and Chicago; so the next day we proceeded to make a systematic tour of the docks, interviewing captains and sailors, and by evening had secured the privilege of working our way to Chicago as deck hands on the freight steamer " Portage."

The events of the first few days from New York have been described so minutely, and so much remains to be told of what was then in the future, that I pass over somewhat rapidly our life on the " Portage." The work was hard and the fare was not luxurious; but by this time we were inured to hardship, and got along famously. A few casual displays of Ned's muscle soon dissipated any inclination on the part of the crew to jeer at our freshness.

The trip was made without any remarkable occurrences or adventures. A little rough weather on Lake Huron produced a temporary disgust with life on my part, but the gale subsided, and my stomach soon resumed its naturally modest behavior.

On the morning of May 24 we came on deck to gaze at a beautiful prospect. The eastern horizon was obscured by a mass of crimson and golden clouds, through which the rays of the rising sun shot far across the water. Not a breath ruffled the tranquil face of Lake Michigan, which literally glowed with all the shifting hues of the rainbow.

All around us lay a dozen or more vessels of different kinds, their sails flapping idly against the masts. Three or four tug-boats were puffing fiercely through the water, trailing long columns of black smoke behind, and sending the regular pulsations of their machinery to our ears from a distance of five miles or more.

To the west lay a long, low shore, rising gradually into bluffs toward the north, and, sleeping in the distance, its lofty spires and the round dome of the Exposition Building glistening in the rising sunlight, lay the city of Chicago.

We steamed in past the solitary crib, up the filthy stagnant river, through the swinging bridges, and moored at last to the Union Steamboat Company's dock, on Market Street.

" City number one," said Ned, as we stepped ashore. " Mr. Treasurer, how about finances? "

" I have to report $6.20 in my possession," replied I.

" Good ! " answered he. " That 's enough to start on."

" The first thing to be done," said I, " is to secure our credentials."

We repaired to the mayor's office and obtained from him two papers. stating, over his signature, that two young men, calling themselves Edward G. Markham and Thomas Jackson, presented themselves at his office on the morning of May 24, 1877, bearing letters, etc.

In a cheap lodging-house on West Madison Street we engaged a room for the day and night. Here we deposited our haversacks and other superfluities, and started out to look for something to do.

" If we can find work," said Ned, " it will probably be worth while to stay in Chicago for a month or two, until we are a little ahead financially, before moving farther west."

We separated, agreeing to meet in the evening at our room.

Up and down through the principal business streets I trudged, trying at nearly every door. Sometimes I met with a gruff dismissal ; at other places I was treated with some courtesy, and went so far as to show my letters of recommendation ; and once or twice I was asked to call again.

There was nothing accomplished, nothing actually attained,

when, late in the afternoon, I stumped up the narrow stairway to our den.

Here I found Ned seated at the window, scratching away at his note-book.

" Well? " said he.

" Nothing ! " answered I.

" Ditto ! " was his reply.   " Then there 's no other way but to keep at it until we strike something."

We supped at a small restaurant on wheels, and then strolled across the bridge, up Clark Street, and over to the North Side.

" Ned," said I, " would it be a sinful extravagance to indulge in a glass of beer? "

" We 'll try and stand it, if it is," he answered.

We entered a beer-saloon, sat down at one of the tables, and called for two beers. A raised platform at the farther end of the room supported a piano.

" You have music here sometimes? " said I to the proprietor.

" Yes, we has music. The man vot plays, she is sick dis night."

"Do you want to hire a substitute?" continued I. "What do you pay for an evening's performance?"

"You can plays?"

"Yes."

"You plays me once tunes, and I tells you vot I pays."

"Come on, Ned!" said I. "Musical talent to the front!"

I opened the piano, and banged away through the "Blue Danube Waltzes." Then I switched off on to "Larboard Watch," and Ned and I sang through the two verses of that time-honored duet, while the tables began rapidly to fill up with a motley crowd of men and women. When we paused, quite a round of applause greeted us. The proprietor was pleased.

"Dot is goot!" said he. "You plays better as de odder man. You plays and sings to eleven o'clock, and I pays you each ein dollar."

We banged and howled away through our whole *repertoire*, and when we took our two dollars and our departure, agreed to play three evenings in each week at two dollars per evening.

"Six dollars a week, at all events," said I.

The next day we pursued our researches, and at night Ned had secured a position as assistant book-keeper and general office-man in a wholesale house on Lake Street, and I was a clerk in the P. F. W. & C. R. R. freight office at Madison Street Bridge.

Ned was to receive seventy-five dollars per month, and I, forty-five.

Our life in Chicago was begun.

CHAPTER III.

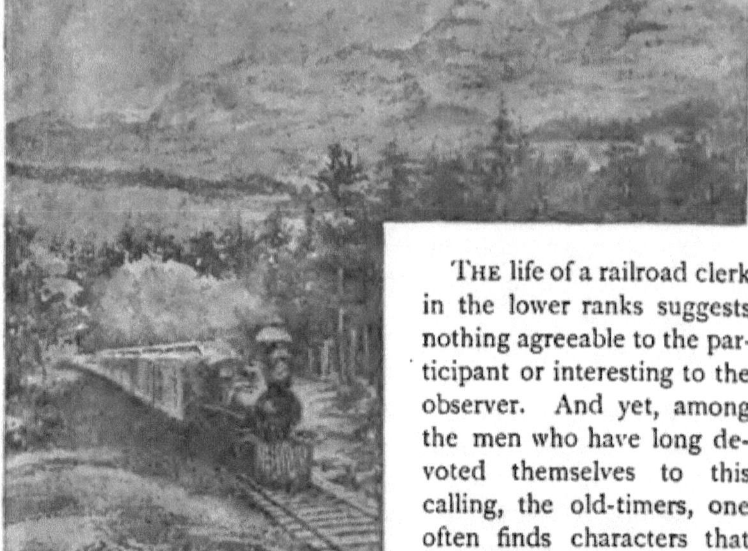

THE life of a railroad clerk
in the lower ranks suggests
nothing agreeable to the par-
ticipant or interesting to the
observer. And yet, among
the men who have long de-
voted themselves to this
calling, the old-timers, one
often finds characters that
are sadly instructive. The
broken-down merchant ; the
man whose reputation has
suffered, whether rightfully
or wrongfully, and who is
deprived of the resources of
social influence or credit ;
the reckless "ne'er-do-weel,"
whose habits have barred him from advancement in other call-
ings, — all of them men too honorable or too timid to seek their
living in more questionable ways, — crowd at last into that
" limbo " of commercial life, a railroad office, to draw the scanty
pittance doled out to them by a wealthy but soulless corpora-

tion, and to hide their sorrows or their short-comings among the ranks of its thousand employés.

It is curious to observe the strange fatuity that often possesses young men who come to the city to seek work. There seems to be for them a certain *éclat* surrounding the very name of "railroad," that makes it more attractive than other lines of business. It is associated in their minds with dignity, independence, unlimited passes, and the authority of position. They enter upon the work with an ardent impetuosity that carries their gaze through the mists of intervening years, and shows them their future selves, surrounded with the pomp and importance of high official position, or rolling across country in the indolent luxury of a director's car. Alas! fond hopes! Ground down by the pressure of steady, interminable work, with never a word of appreciation or encouragement, surrounded by the heavy atmosphere of dull, ambitionless drudgery, the young railroad clerk's enthusiasm soon evaporates, and at last he catches the monotonous cadence of the link step that he must keep, — not too slow, lest the man behind push too hard ; not too fast, lest he tread on the heels of the one before.

Rarely, very rarely, there is a young man of such stubborn and dauntless perseverance, that after years of unflagging effort he fairly breaks from the ranks and rises to a position of prominence, where he meets with a fair remuneration for his toil. And even then the man can look back, and in the light of experience perceive that the same amount of energy and talent turned in a different direction would have yielded him four times the harvest he is now reaping.

Like all novitiates in the railroad business, I was set at once to making out expense bills. From eight o'clock in the morning until six, seven, and sometimes eight or nine in the evening, my pen flew steadily over the same weary ground ; and never in all my experience as an expense-bill clerk did I leave the office with the work completed. How the rest of it was done, I knew not, nor cared to know. I was fully conscious of having earned my twenty-three days' salary, when on the 19th of the month, in company with a long procession of other employés, I marched up to the pay-car to sign my name and draw my slender stipend.

To my astonishment and disgust, I received only six dollars.

I would have expostulated, but the supercilious clerk waved me aside, and handed the pen to my successor. Afterward, one of the boys informed me that on the 19th of each month we received our pay up to the close of the preceding month. So I had been paid for four days' work.

Such vexations, however, were powerless to disturb my inward serenity, for I felt that this was only one of the shifting scenes of the panorama, and that in a month or two I should be speeding far on my western way, a free man once more. Nothing is utterly unendurable when the end is in sight.

Ned, in his position as book-keeper, got along famously, and soon became a favorite with his employers and his fellow-clerks, as he always did.

Three evenings, and a little later, four evenings in each week, we devoted to our pseudo-musical performances in the beer-saloon. At odd moments we brushed up our German, and began to talk to our fellow-boarders in their native tongue.

Nearly every Sunday afternoon we took a stroll in Lincoln Park, wandering up and down the beach, and breathing the fresh breezes of Lake Michigan. It was a precious relief from smoke and dirt and the smell of sauer-kraut, and from the Stygian odor that sometimes was wafted from that notable section called Bridgeport.

"Tom," said Ned one day, "Chicago seems to me like a lubberly, overgrown boy, abounding in muscle and vigor, longing to be considered a man, but lacking in the true power of a man, — the power that makes itself felt without childish display. Its tone is essentially provincial, like a huge sprawling village, like an untutored rustic suddenly fallen heir to a fortune."

"Still," answered I, "that intrepidity of enterprise that makes Chicago in some respects the most remarkable city in the world, covers a multitude of short-comings. It is true, the Chicagoan's pride in his city is apt to take the direction of dimension, of quantity rather than quality. He talks of the number of miles of boulevard, of the acres of parks, of the thousands of pigs that can be killed in a minute, even of the number of beer-glasses that can be emptied in a day. If a hall is to be built, it must hold a vast number of people; were a commemorative painting to be made, the question would be of the size of the canvas; a public musical festival must employ an impossible number of instruments and voices. But all this is in keeping with the grand, whole-souled nature of the people. They can never do anything by halves."

"No," said Ned; "even in the matter of fires they must outdo all the rest of the world!"

"How delightful it is to be an irresponsible tramp!" remarked I. "A tramp has the privilege of a minister. He can fire his criticism at the air, and launch his denunciations over the heads of the multitude, knowing that no one will take the trouble to stand up and answer him."

So the days glided by pleasantly enough until the great strike occurred, that for a few weeks paralyzed the business of the whole country. No freight could arrive or leave, cars were destroyed, and the boys in the railroad-offices had for once an easy time.

The difficulty was soon adjusted, however, the men returned to their work, and the manifests poured in on us poor fellows with redoubled volume.

On the evening of July 27th, as I came upstairs after paying the ninth week's indebtedness to our landlady, Ned remarked:

"Tom, I 've had enough of Chicago; have n't you?"

"I 'm at a loss what to put in my next newspaper letter," answered I.

"What do you say to a start on the 1st of August?"

"With all my heart; but how and where?"

"How do we stand financially?"

"Liabilities, nothing; assets, including all outstanding accounts, $212."

"Now, time is money to us. We can buy two second-class tickets to San Francisco for one hundred and eighty dollars. Allowing for the few dollars we can earn here before leaving, and the moderate expenses of the trip, we can count on arriving in San Francisco on the 6th of August, with about thirty dollars in our pockets."

To men in our position, a journey of twenty-five hundred miles was a matter of ten minutes' discussion. We decided to go.

Our method of travelling had one advantage that we did not fail to appreciate. We had no baggage to look after. We were free from *impedimenta* of every kind. There was no packing and checking of trunks, no leave-taking. We had simply to buy our tickets, put our hands in our pockets, and saunter down to the train.

At about noon on the 1st of August we were seated in a C. B. & Q. smoking-car, steaming slowly along the lake shore, looking our last on the busy streets of the great metropolis of the West.

Among our fellow-passengers we noticed two Chinamen, a pleasant looking German with his fat *frau* and his four dirty children, and in the corner a tall, well-dressed man with iron-gray mustache and slouched hat, and something distinctively military about his appearance. The rest of the passengers were men and women of the lower classes, uninteresting in appearance and unsavory in odor.

We had soon left the city far behind, and were rolling over the flat green prairies of Illinois, sweeping past little suburban villages, — Riverside, pretty as a park, with its picturesque water-tower and long dilapidated hotel, La Grange, Downer's Grove, — till we pulled up at Aurora, thirty miles from Chicago.

Ned had been making the acquaintance of our German neighbors, and already had the four children climbing all over him, investigating his pockets, while the mother smiled and scolded alternately. We had brought a huge basket of provisions aboard, and Ned handed out doughnuts to those voracious infants in a way that alarmed my frugal mind.

From Aurora, the train rattled onward through broad prairie farms, past towns and villages, and at eight o'clock in the evening crossed the great Father of Waters into Burlington, two hundred and seven miles from Chicago.

The rain was coming down in torrents as we made preparations for our first night on the cars. Two seats turned together afforded a Procrustean sort of bed, to which Ned's long legs in vain strove to accommodate themselves. The other passengers stretched out in various positions, the children lay around loose, silence and a stifling atmosphere suggestive of unwashed humanity gradually settled over the interior of the car. Without, the rain lashed the windows, the wind howled, and the train rushed swiftly on its way across the State of Iowa.

For hours I twisted and turned, trying desperately to delude myself into being comfortable. Ned, supremely unconscious of space, or the lack of it, snored cheerfully in my ear. At last I too drifted into the land of dreams.

A violent pull and scratch on the nose, a thump on the shins, and a sudden crushing weight as if the roof had fallen, were the greetings that saluted my dawning consciousness. Instantaneous visions of wreck and ruin, collisions and smash-ups rushed upon me, as I clutched out wildly and opened my eyes. My fingers seized something soft, and held on, while simultaneously a fearful scream rang through the car, and my eyes looked full into the terrified, enraged face of one of

those detestable Dutch brats, who was seated astride my prostrate form, and whom I held firmly by the hair. It was broad daylight, and two of the wretches had been coolly clambering over me, catching hold wherever it was convenient, eager to get at their beloved Ned.

"Ned," said I, stroking my distorted nose, "there is a limit even to my patience, and if you like this sort of thing, you may have it all. Henceforth, please sleep on the outside."

We went out and stood on the platform. The sun was shining brightly on a green, rolling prairie, rising into bluffs toward the west. The train passed a farm-house, and a girl on the steps, with broom in hand, and white handkerchief over her head, paused to gaze after our rushing flight.

The military man with gray mustache, whom we had observed the day before, stood on the platform, looking off at the flying landscape. Without noticing us, he suddenly began, in a loud voice : —

" ' Beatus ille qui procul negotiis — ' " Then he paused, and Ned instantly continued the quotation, —

" ' Paterna rura bobus exercet suis.' "

The man turned and looked at us with an expression of astonishment, as if perceiving for the first time that he was not alone, then extended his hand toward Ned, and said : —

" My dear sir, permit me to thank you, and to shake hands with you. The rarity of meeting a man on a Western railroad train, able to refresh one's memory with a line of Horace, is such as to justify a desire for further acquaintance. Allow me to introduce myself."

Thereupon the gentleman handed us a card whereon we read, " Captain John Chambers, New York."

After the ceremony of introduction, we had some further talk with our new acquaintance, and discovered him to be, according to his own account, a man of some property, and an inveterate and untiring traveller, and according to our observation, something of a scholar, and a thoroughly courteous and refined gentleman.

The conversation resulted in our joining him in a cup of delicious coffee, which he manufactured in a spirit-lamp heater of his own, and in his sharing with us a breakfast from our capacious lunch-basket.

The captain was very talkative, full of anecdotes of his travels, and interlarding all his conversation with quotations from Horace. He had been to San Francisco three times, and he proved as valuable, and far more entertaining than a guide-book. Before we reached Omaha, he had so won our confidence that we told him of our enterprise and showed our contracts.

" I can understand your feelings, gentlemen," said he. " It is the old story of discontent, — ' Nemo quam sibi sortem seu ratio dederit,' etc.; you know the rest. Were I a younger man, I should ask to be admitted of your company, ' and let the bonds of love hold three.' As it is, I must have some of the comforts of life, though not too many.　I am used to travelling in the smoking-car, and making my own little cup of coffee ; but for roughing it in good earnest, or tramping among the mountains, — alas !　'Vitæ summa brevis spem nos vetat inchoare longam.' "

At Omaha we boarded the U. P. train, and were soon fairly launched on the great Nebraska plain.

Long monotonous ridges rolled away before us to the distant horizon, clothed with bunches of dry, yellow grass, and the sad artemisia, or sage-bush.

Occasionally a solitary farm-house loomed into view for an instant, like a rock in the ocean.　Towns and villages, with the inevitable saloon in the foreground, seemed to rise out of the prairie to meet us.　All the afternoon there was nothing of interest, nothing to attract attention, in the landscape.

" These dry tufts of grass," said the captain, " are as nutritious as hay, and once supported vast herds of buffaloes that roamed these plains from the mountains to the Missouri River."

" Think of *walking* through a country like this, Tom," said Ned, " and feeling every night as if we were in the very place we left in the morning ! "

" Take my advice," said the captain, " and do all your walking, so far as possible, in a hilly or mountainous country. Twenty miles of mountain-climbing will not be so fatiguing as fifteen miles of desolation like this."

The sun set, red and smoky, and rose again on the same dreary prospect.　Toward the middle of the forenoon our German friends disembarked, bag and baggage, assisted by Ned. The captain and I stood with our hands in our pockets and looked down upon Ned while he gallantly handed out boxes, bags, and bedquilts, shook hands with the old folks, and kissed the dirty children all round.

" I like to see a man so ready to befriend others," said the captain.　" It gives one confidence in him, shows him to be a right-hearted sort of fellow."

I looked up inquiringly, but the captain was watching Ned with a quiet smile, and did n't notice me.

" ' Integer vitæ scelerisque purus.' " said he presently, and returned to his seat in the car.

At about eleven o'clock we caught our first view of the mountains, — a faint blue line of rounded peaks, about a hundred miles away.

Ned was wild with enthusiasm.

"Moderate your excitement," said our new friend; "you will be disappointed. Remember, we have been steadily ascending all the way from Omaha, and are now nearly six thousand feet above sea-level."

Slowly those distant peaks lifted themselves before us, the bleak, barren rocks and rugged outlines became more and more distinct, and at half-past one we had circled round the city of Cheyenne, and came to a stop.

An extra engine was attached to the train, and we pulled out with a consciousness of beginning to ascend.

Vast sand-heaps and huge granite bowlders, with now and then a long snow-shed, shut out the view of the mountains; but suddenly they burst upon us again, stretching far away to the south, peak after peak crowded and piled together, some cold and blue, others touched by the afternoon sun into hues of crimson and purple and gold.

To the north rose the gloomy, barren outlines of the Black Hills, — giant masses of granite, with a few stunted pines fringing their bases.

Suddenly the train stopped at a little collection of frame buildings.

"Come out!" said the captain. "We are now at Sherman, the summit of the Rocky Mountains, the highest railroad-station in the world."

There was nothing suggestive of the top of a mountain, except the clear, cold air. Around us extended a barren plain strewn with colossal bowlders of granite.

"Nevertheless," said our guide, "this is the backbone of the continent. When we start again, it will be down to the Pacific."

As the train left Sherman, we witnessed the strange effects of erosion on the weather-beaten rocks that stood and lay about us. Every weird, unnatural form that the imagination could conceive found its counterpart in some one of the hideous, barren monsters of sandstone and granite. Once or twice we passed straight through a vast ridge of solid rock that had been hewn and blasted out to give passage to the railroad.

Soon the Red Buttes came in sight, — dome-shaped masses of bright-red rock, standing at the right of the track. We swept onward, down to the great Laramie Plain, a thousand feet below. The wild peaks of the Medicine Bow Mountains appeared, and late in the evening we looked down at a river winding in the moonlight below us.

"That 's an old friend," said the captain, — "the North Platte, the river we caught a glimpse of four hundred miles back, and that escorted us all night across the Nebraska plain."

The morning found us in the Green River country of Wyoming. Perpendicular walls of bright-green shale rose in every direction, and the Green River worked its foaming way through narrow gorges, down to the great Colorado Cañon.

Suddenly the Uintah Mountains rose before us, and we saw in the distance the supernatural architecture of the *Mauvaises Terres*. "Tower and town and battlement," massive temples with long rows of lofty columns and carving more delicate than that of a Corinthian capital, mediæval fortresses with frowning portals and gloomy arches, the rich tracery of Moorish palaces, all seemed to our distant view as complete as if designed by the hand of man.

At Hilliard, numerous charcoal-furnaces appeared, and the train passed under a huge trough raised on trestle-work, and extending far up the mountain-side.

"A lumber-flume," explained Captain Chambers, "and an unusually large one. The wood is cut at a mill twenty-four miles distant, and two thousand feet higher up the mountain, and is floated in this flume all the way to the furnaces at Hilliard."

Our basket of provisions was nearly exhausted, and when the train stopped at Evanston, we joined the throng and partook of a dinner of delicious trout fresh from their mountain streams.

Then away again, over a breezy country to Wahsatch, through a long, gloomy tunnel, and down into Echo Cañon.

To the north, close beside us, rose a wall of dark-red rock ; to the south, rugged sloping hills, through whose clefts we caught momentary glimpses of the distant mountains. The Weber River foamed and dashed beside us.

A sudden sharp turn, and we were in a bright, cultivated valley, sweeping through the green meadows toward a dome-like rock of glowing red that rose a thousand feet at the entrance to Weber Cañon. Past it we dashed, and roared onward between perpendicular walls of bronze green a thousand feet in height. Far above the noise of the train was heard the seething, angry roar of the straitened river.

Again we emerged into the sunlight, and green fields, and orchards, bending beneath their loads of apples, peaches, and pomegranates, smiled upon us for a few moments, and then we plunged into the darkness and gloom of Ogden Cañon.

At six o'clock we entered the basin of the Great Salt Lake, and stopped at Ogden, 1032 miles west of Omaha, and the terminus of the Union Pacific Railroad.

As we stepped from the cars, Ogden presented a most picturesque scene. The platform was thronged with people of all classes and nationalities. Immigrants trooped along with their bags and bundles; ladies and gentlemen promenaded arm in arm ; Chinamen in purple frocks, with their long pigtails dangling behind, talked and gesticulated wildly ; rough-looking miners glanced at us suspiciously from under their slouched hats ; close around us lay the trim gardens and regular streets of Ogden, and far above towered the mountains, their summits white with eternal snows, and seeming to overhang the little town.

"All aboard !"

We clamber to our places in the smoking-car of the Central Pacific Railroad, and are off for San Francisco.

At a curve of the road we come in view of the bright-blue waters of the lake, and looking back gaze once more at the giant mountains, their snowy foreheads glistening under the last rays of the setting sun, and Ogden nestling like a bird's-nest at their feet.

We settle back in our places with a sigh of satisfaction, the rails sing beneath us, and the twilight slowly and imperceptibly melts into moonlight.

Suddenly Ned exclaimed : "We are in the middle of the lake ! "

On every side stretched a wide white surface, broken into little ripples that sparkled in the moonlight.

"It was once, undoubtedly, the bed of the lake," said the captain ; "at present, it is the great alkali desert, the dread of immigrants. Many a poor mule or ox, and not a few unfortunate men, stifled and blinded after days of weary tramping through the fine, acrid dust, have at last lain down to die, and mingled their white bones with the white powder of the desert."

Early in the morning we stopped at Wells, a green oasis in the desert, where some twenty or more springs of cool, sweet water gave life and fertility to the unpromising ground.

Then away again over the desert, past dreary little saloon stations, and at last into the grand scenery of the Sierra Nevada.

Sometimes crawling around narrow ledges, thousands of feet above the roaring streams below, sometimes for mile after mile under snow-sheds, plunging into cañons and emerging into bright valleys, we rattled on through the mountains.

The scenery here was much pleasanter than in the Rockies. There, there was nothing but bare, bleak rocks, with here and there a stunted pine striving to cling to the nakedness. The grotesque and forbidding aspects of nature predominated.

But here in the Sierras the mountains were clothed far up to the snow line with green, waving forests. Giant pine-trees and majestic oaks mingled their dark foliage with the lighter hues of other forest trees, and the blessed green, the softest of nature's hues, gave rest and satisfaction to our eyes.

Early in the morning of the 6th we rounded Cape Horn, creeping along a narrow ledge at a sharp curve, and looking down two thousand feet of sheer descent to the bed of the American River below. Then over a long trestle-bridge into Colfax, down the valley to Sacramento, and from there to San Francisco, arriving at about eleven o'clock on the 6th of August.

We shook hands cordially with the captain, feeling that we owed much of the enjoyment of the trip to him.

"Which way shall you go from here?" he asked.

"Wherever the way is opened," answered Ned. "Probably across the Pacific."

"'Cras ingens iterabimus æquor,'" said he. "Well, I wish you all success, gentlemen. It is barely possible that I may run across you again in the course of my travels. At all events, I am heartily glad to have met you, and allow me to add that I am very glad to have found you other than I expected."

We turned to ask his meaning, but with an inscrutable smile and a wave of the hand he was gone.

CHAPTER IV.

THE captain's last remark was a puzzle to us, and we finally gave it up, dismissing him from our minds as an amiable sort of crank. Life was too short, and our work too urgent to allow us time to discuss every oddity we encountered. Some way of living in San Francisco must be discovered, and we must look out for some means of crossing the great ocean that rolled its thousands of miles of heaving billows across our western path.

We took a small room at three dollars per week, and scoured the city for work, getting our meals at restaurants.

On the third day, I accepted with becoming modesty the lofty position of driver of a city delivery wagon, at fifty dollars per month; and on the day following, Ned set out to try his luck as a drummer-up of city trade for a large wholesale house, his salary to be a commission on his sales.

In the evenings and on Sundays we visited the docks and the shipping-offices, looking out for a position on some western-bound vessel.

It was discouraging work. We were a little loath to go before the mast as common sailors, and on the steamers there seemed to be no positions that we were capable of occupying. We were brought to a standstill, — at least for the present.

San Francisco pleased and at the same time disgusted us. The early mornings were lovely, the air soft and balmy ; but about the middle of every forenoon life became a burden. The cold, searching wind, laden with moisture from the ocean, and with sand from the barren peninsula, swept incessantly through the streets, chilling the very marrow of our bones, and forcing us to spend much of our time in picking the gravel from our eyes.

We became thoroughly familiar with the city, explored the length of Sacramento Street, and took a cursory view of the every-day life of the Chinese.

"We shall see enough of them in their native country," said Ned.

" If we ever get there !" added I.

Several times we walked out to the Cliff House, and watched the seals sporting in old ocean. At Woodward's Gardens Ned was fascinated by the grizzly bears.

"It's too bad," said he, "that we must leave California without having a brush with one of those fellows in his native wilds !"

"I would n't be distressed on that account," said I. "A brush from one of those paws would effectually spoil your five years' trip."

As a salesman, Ned was a prodigious success. He possessed just the requisites of character. Never discouraged or intimidated, always good-natured and plausible, and gifted with unlimited ability in the talking line, he soon won the affections of his employers, and began to reap an income of about ten dollars a day.

"You see, Tom," said he, "this ' absurd scheme,' as you called it, has already given me a pleasanter employment and a far better income than that dreary teaching."

A little later, the firm sent him out on short trips into the surrounding regions, and he was more and more impressed each day with the glorious country he had passsed through.

We had begun the study of Spanish, and in the evenings, when working over our conversation-books, Ned would suddenly break out into raptures about the glorious mountains, or the delicious, invigorating air of the San Joaquin valley.

" I tell you, Tom," said he once, " we can't leave California without a trip into the Sierras ! "

" The prospects are," I replied, " that we shall have ample time for a good many trips, before we get a chance to leave California."

" I have it ! " continued he, presently. " There's no absolute necessity of our going west from here. There are other cities to be visited on this continent. Why not work our way south to Mexico, cross to Havana, and from there to Europe? That will give us a chance to spend the winter in the South, and at the same time see something of California."

" A good idea ! " said I. " That's more feasible and more agreeable than crossing the Pacific before the mast."

This was on the 15th of September, and we had been at work in San Francisco something over five weeks. During the next few days Ned succeeded in making arrangements with his firm to let him go as far south as Goshen, in the San Joaquin valley, selling as many goods as possible on the route, they to remit him whatever balance was due on his arrival there.

Not knowing what sort of life we might have to encounter after leaving the railroad, we equipped ourselves with a pair of heavy blankets apiece, a rifle and double-barrelled shot-gun, and a pair of canteens, and set out on the 23d of September, with stop-over tickets, for Goshen.

Our labor, or rather Ned's labor, had been profitable, and we found ourselves at the start with $225 in our pockets, and a chance of making a little more on our way south.

" Prospects booming ! " as Ned remarked.

Our trip to Goshen was marked by no incident worthy of relation. We stopped at many of the towns on our route, and succeeded in selling some goods. On each side of us the mountains were an unfailing source of delight, and we found the air deliciously soft and clear, in spite of the dust and heat.

At Goshen, on the 29th, Ned received a remittance of twenty-seven dollars from his firm, together with letters of regret at his departure, and of recommendation to possible future employers. With blankets strapped on our backs and guns over our shoulders, we walked to Visalia.

" And to-morrow," said Ned, " for the mountains ! "

"With all due deference, most noble captain," said I, "I should really like to inquire what you expect to do in the wilds of the Sierra Nevada? Our course should lie due south; but you propose to move toward the east."

"Just for a little taste of mountain climbing, Tom," he answered. "These foot-hills are all covered with roads and trails, and we can easily work our way through to the southeast."

I had grown accustomed to regard the whole enterprise as Ned's particular project, and to leave the details of management and direction to him; so in this case I made no further objection.

In the morning he slipped out, and returned presently with a pocket thermometer, a compass, and a long Mexican *riata*, or lasso.

"What under heaven are you going to do with that thing?" I asked.

"Quien sabe?" he replied. "It struck me we might find it useful, so I bought it."

Before leaving Visalia we provisioned ourselves with several pounds of bread and crackers, salt pork, coffee, tea, etc., and a fresh supply of tobacco. We still had our old tin pail and cups, that had come all the way from New York with us. Ned carried his long lasso wound round and round his blankets and fastened in front.

"Mighty convenient if you should want to use it!" said I.

"It 'll do there well enough for my purpose," was his answer.

As treasurer, I carried the cash, which amounted to $240, in a belt worn inside my clothes, while Ned, beside his other weapons and accoutrements, had a hatchet stuck in his girdle. At half-past nine on the morning of September 30th, we set out for the mountains.

The road that we followed soon led us into the depths of the forest. Stately pines stood all about, sending down their drowsy, sea-like voice from far overhead, and forming long, umbrageous aisles, through whose distant vistas we could see here and there a stray gleam of sunlight. The path was pleasant, and though steadily ascending, never steep or rugged. The air was pure and soft, faintly suggestive of distant flower-fields, and rich with the resinous odor of the forest.

After three or four hours the road became steeper and the

"The road that we followed soon led us into the depths of the forest."
Page 55.

trees more scattering, and suddenly we came into the clear sunshine. We were on the summit of a ridge of the foot-hills.

Behind and below us lay the great forest we had just traversed, — a sea of verdure, stretching in billowy folds to the south, north, and west. The level plain of the San Joaquin valley, with villages, meadows, lakes, and streams bathed in the warm, hazy air of September, was behind us, and still farther back the forest crept up higher and higher, till it died away in the blue peaks of the Coast Range, closing the view to the west.

A few miles to the north we discerned a clearing, and a thin, blue column of smoke stealing up from what appeared to be a mill. Four or five gigantic trees rose from an opening in the woods, and towered for half their height above the throng of their comrades.

To the east lay a valley, partly wooded and partly open meadow, in which we caught here and there the gleam of water.

Beyond, in wild, stormy succession, rose the massive bases, the scarred cliffs, and above all, the sharp, white, sky-piercing peaks of the Sierras.

Great rocky spurs were thrust far out into the valley, one of them reaching almost to the hill on which we stood. We could partly trace the outlines of deep clefts and rocky cañons, and here and there, far up the mountain-sides, lay detached fields of snow. With such a landscape before us, we sat down and munched crackers and cold corned-beef.

"You see," said Ned, "we can easily follow this ridge far up among the mountains ; and then, with all the world spread out before us, can pick our way down through the gorges on the other side."

"*Et après ?*"

"*Après ?* Away across the plains to the city of the Montezumas !"

The road began to descend, entered the forest again, emerged into a meadow where my shot-gun brought down a brace of grouse, again dived under the pine-trees for a short distance, and then suddenly, as if giving up the effort, veered straight away toward the south. A narrow trail led up over the rocks to the east.

"There lies our path!" shouted Ned, and sprang up the trail, I following close behind.

Four or five miles farther, a little spring bubbled out from beneath the granite rock and flashed away through the trees to the valley below. We sat down and drank long and deep, then filled our canteens and resumed our climb.

After a long afternoon of steady toiling upward through the forest, we came out at nightfall upon the bare rocks by the side of a ruined cabin, and a trough reaching far up the mountain, the relics of a deserted mining-camp. Here our trail ended, and here we made ready to pass the night.

A few sturdy blows and kicks demolished the decaying front of the cabin. We cleared out the room inside, and spread the floor thick with evergreen boughs, and with the logs and timber of the front made a glorious camp-fire that lit up the whole of the rude interior. Then, unawed by the presence of that grim row of white-crowned monarchs, we brewed a pail of tea, roasted one of our grouse, and feasted to our stomachs' content.

The firelight grew brighter as the daylight died. A chill, frosty air crept down over the rocks, and curling up snugly in our blankets we were soon fast asleep.

The morning witnessed another argument in which as usual I yielded the point. Ned was determined to keep on, climbing in some way straight through the mountains, and in spite of my misgivings, we finally set out.

Our shoulders were chafed and sore from the straps of the blankets, the air was chilly and raw, but we struggled bravely upward, working diagonally toward the point where the spur that we were on appeared to unite with the main chain.

It seemed an interminable distance. At the start, we thought it about an hour's walk, but three hours of rough climbing brought us apparently no nearer our goal. The sun came up, and its rays began to be intensely hot. The rocks, worn smooth and polished by the frosts and storms of centuries, reflected the heat and glare like metal. Often we sat down to rest, but never longer than a few minutes.

Toward the middle of the forenoon we reached a wide field of snow, covering a crevasse in our path. We tried it cautiously, found it hard and firm, and marched boldly across.

It was long past noon, and we had been walking some eight hours, when we reached at last the elevated point we had aimed at, and looked beyond. The rocks sloped rapidly down for a hundred feet and came to an end. Beyond, there was — nothing ! We crept to the edge and looked over a sheer descent of perpendicular rock ending, a thousand feet beneath us, in a bank of glistening snow, that sloped abruptly toward a sheet of ice. On the other side of this frozen pond another snow-drift reached to the foot of a wall of rock directly opposite, and as high as the one on which we stood. The cañon seemed about quarter of a mile wide.

" No thoroughfare ! " said I.

We turned to the right, and followed the edge of the precipice to the top of a jutting crag that shut out our view toward the south.

A half or three quarters of a mile away, this vast cleft in the mountains came to an abrupt end. A third wall of rock joined the one opposite to us almost at right angles. The ridge on which we stood sloped toward this terminal cliff, meeting it some hundred feet lower, and forming a notch which gradually widened and sank toward the west, till it expanded into a precipitous ravine, bounded on one side by the perpendicular wall that reached as far as we could see toward the west, and on the other by the sloping spur whose summit we had attained. The only escape seemed to be by retracing our steps for miles to the west.

" If we could only manage to scale that southern wall," said Ned, " we could reach the backbone, and from there easily find our way down one of the ribs to the east.

" If the present difficulty could only be adjusted, no others could possibly be of any importance. Nothing ever troubles you beyond the moment, does it, Ned ? "

We followed the edge of the precipice down to where it joined the terminal wall. Far beneath us lay the snow, filling the end of the gorge, and piled up to within five hundred feet of the top.

" We 've no business down there, any way ! " said Ned.

Above, the cliff rose about one hundred and fifty feet higher, seamed and cut by deep crevices, and bearing here and there projecting ledges.

The top was covered with loose bowlders and overhanging rocks, apparently just ready to fall.

Ned scrambled upon a ledge, and running out gazed up the cliff.

"We can do it!" he sung out. "There is another within reach just above, and beyond that another! Are you good for a climb?"

I looked at him without answering. He seemed to have no thought for the fearful abyss that lay behind, into which one backward step would plunge him. Presently he came back and sat down beside me.

"Tom," said he, "I know you think me a hare-brained idiot, with a courage born only of recklessness; but just listen to me an instant. You and I were both thoroughly-trained gymnasts in college. The actual efforts required to scale that cliff are no more than we have put forth a thousand times in the old gymnasium at home without once thinking of failure. Why should the mere fact that five hundred feet of empty air are beneath us make them impossible now? Surely you don't mean to tell me that a mere idea, the lurking shadow of a possibility, is enough to unman *you!*"

"My nerves are as steady and my pulse as regular as your own, my boy!" answered I. "If you are determined to go up that wall, why, go ahead! I follow."

"Good!" said he. "Now you talk!"

We got upon the first ledge, walked out, and laid down our blankets and guns. I glanced for an instant over the edge of the precipice, and involuntarily shrank back.

"None of that, now!" said Ned, cheerfully. "No tempting of fate! Never look down when you can look up. There lies our goal!" And he pointed to the beetling brow of the cliff.

Then, reaching to the next ledge, about seven feet higher, he drew himself up and scrambled safely over. I handed up the guns and blankets, and easily followed.

Again we went through the same manœuvres, and a third time, and now found ourselves on a parapet about four feet wide and some thirty feet above the ridge we had left. Here we sat down to rest and take a pull at the cold coffee in our canteens, then up again to business.

The ledge we were on ran for some distance horizontally, then sloped irregularly upward. We followed it to the highest point and looked up for the next. It was pretty high !

"Can you reach it?" asked Ned.

"Just !" replied I, standing on tiptoe.

"Wait a moment !" continued he. "Let me go first !"

As he reached the ledge, I started to pass up the blankets.

"No," said he; "unroll my blanket and toss me the lasso !"

I did so, and he continued : —

"Now, keep your place till I climb to the next ledge. There is n't room enough here for two."

I saw him clamber up about six feet higher, and in a moment the lasso came dangling down to where I stood.

One by one the different articles were fastened on and hauled up the cliff, and I followed in safety.

We had now made about sixty feet, or something more than one third of the whole distance. This last halting-place was of considerable width, reaching back into a deep crevice or cavern in the face of the cliff, but was only about ten feet in length. Directly above, the wall was smooth and unbroken for a distance of at least twenty feet. Somewhat to one side, and about eight feet above us, was another narrow ledge, but too far to be reached even by Ned's long arms.

We looked back down the fearful path that we had travelled, and for the first time realized that to retreat was impossible ! Many of the ledges jutted out over those beneath them, so that to hang by our hands and drop would have been simply to fall straight down some five hundred feet to the snow below. I looked at Ned. His face was pale and his lips tightly compressed. One hand was torn and bleeding from contact with the rough rocks.

"It 's late, Tom," said he, "and we are tired out. This crevice is wide enough to bunk in, and to-morrow will bring a way of escape."

All the afternoon we had been working in the shadow, with our faces to the gloomy rock, and now for the first time we noticed that the sunlight had left the rocks and snow beside us, and only lingered on the tops of the highest peaks.

We were thoroughly tired out. The difficulty of breathing

in this rarefied atmosphere had made our exertions doubly exhausting.

With little more conversation, we ate our scanty supper, unrolled our blankets, and crawled in under the shelter of the overhanging rock. Here we lit our pipes, and, like a couple of disconsolate owls, sat and gazed out on the wild scene before us.

The last flicker of sunlight died away from the white peaks, and almost instantaneously the dark vault of heaven was crowded thick with glittering stars, shining with a clear frosty brightness. Our thermometer on the ledge stood at thirty degrees.

Suddenly a cracking, thundering noise sounded over our heads, and a rock more than five feet in thickness, loosened by the sudden frost, came crashing down from the brow of the cliff, struck the ledge on which we sat, and bounded off into the gulf beneath. The thunder of its descent was repeated in echo after echo, reverberating back and forth among the gloomy cliffs, and before the last murmur had died away, another huge bowlder let go its hold farther along the cañon.

Another, and another followed, and the air was filled with a deafening roar. It seemed as if the solid mountains were rushing down into the valleys. A bewildering and helpless feeling of dread oppressed us as we sat motionless, — waiting.

Soon, however, the last echo died away, and an absolute, deathly silence succeeded. A person accustomed all his life to the murmur of earth's thousand inarticulate voices, unnoticed though incessant, has no conception of what silence really is. Only on the top of a lofty mountain or in a balloon can one find entire cessation of sound, silence that seems to beat upon the brain in rhythmic waves, perhaps the pulse-beats of one's own life, that only then become perceptible.

We wrapped our double blankets around us and nestled close together on our rocky couch. That night will never be erased from memory. The bitter cold, the hard unyielding rock, the realization of our terrible position, and the dread of the morrow banished sleep from my eyes. For an hour neither spoke. At last Ned said : —

"Tom, are you awake?"

"Yes."

" How high do you think we are ? "

" It can't be less than ten thousand feet."

" Try to get a little sleep, old boy. We need that more than anything."

" All right ! "

I suppose I must have dozed a little now and then, though it seems impossible in looking back. At all events, it was very early in the morning when we were both on our feet.

The faint light gave a weird and ghostly look to the dark walls and white fantastic peaks around us. We were stiff and sore and horribly cold, — and with reason. The mercury indicated seventeen degrees. The coffee in Ned's canteen was a mass of ice, and a grouse that we had not yet roasted was as hard as the rock on which it lay. My canteen had fortunately been covered by the blankets, and its contents were still liquid.

There was not much talk at breakfast, but a certain gloomy looking up at the cliff above and down into the vacancy below.

As we finished our slender meal and rolled up the blankets, Ned said slowly : —

" I thought of a way out last night. It 's risky, but the only escape, so far as I can see."

" What is it ? " asked I, indifferently.

" Are you strong enough to bear my weight on your shoulders ? "

" Certainly."

" Well, then, if one of us is n't long enough to reach that next ledge, two of us are."

" Why, man ! It 's twenty feet above us."

" Not that one. The other, — at the side ; come and take a look at it."

The nearest point of the shelf in question was about two feet beyond the extremity of the one on which we stood, and about nine feet higher. Winding the lasso around his body, Ned said, " Are you ready to try ? "

" Whenever you are ! " I answered.

I kneeled down while he placed a leg over each of my shoulders, then slowly rose to my feet and moved along to the extreme end of the ledge. Clutching one hand in a cleft of the rock, I stood firm while Ned raised himself till his feet rested on my shoulders.

"Now lean a little to the left," said he. "Can you reach it?" I asked, after a moment. "Not quite. About an inch more."

Suddenly I felt myself relieved of the load. For an instant I stood with head bent, gazing into the dark abyss, which in the dim gray light seemed absolutely unfathomable. When at last with a faint shiver I raised my eyes, Ned had his knees on the shelf above, and was just in the act of climbing over. In another moment the end of the lasso swung within reach of my hand.

Piece by piece our *impedimenta* were hauled up and the lasso dropped down for the last time.

"Fasten it tight under your arms," sung out the voice over my head. "Now! Are you ready?"

"Haul away!"

I felt a steady strain around the chest. The rock dropped from under my feet, and for a single instant I was swinging over that fearful space. The next moment I had grasped the ledge and was drawn safely over.

"Hurrah!" shouted Ned. "We 're out of that fix."

Two hours more of terribly hard climbing brought us to a parapet from which we could seize the summit of the cliff and look over.

A surface of hard, icy snow, pierced here and there by projecting rocks, sloped upward, steep as the roof of a house, to the base of a rugged cliff a hundred yards above. At a point some distance to the left, this new wall was cleft down to the upper edge of the snow by a wide notch through which we caught a glimpse of the sky, faintly glowing with the light of the rising sun.

"From that point," exclaimed Ned joyfully, "we can look down on the plain to the east of the mountains!"

Cautiously testing the steadiness of the rocks, we clambered over the brow of the cliff, and sitting with feet braced against a solid bowlder, strapped the packs on our backs and tied ourselves together with the long lasso. Then, using the guns as alpenstocks, we began the ascent.

It was fearfully slippery, and only by slow, careful steps could we advance at all. So intently were we obliged to watch our footing, that we inadvertently became separated almost to the length of the cord that united us, when suddenly I felt a sharp tug at the waist; my feet flew up in an instant, and I was flat on the steep, icy surface, and sliding downward. Ned had slipped, and in his fall had pulled me down with him.

The shot-gun, jerked from my hand, went skimming down the slope and shot far over the precipice, but I did n't think of the loss. I was sliding faster and faster, desperately trying to dig in hands or feet, twisting over and over, already fancying the dread sensation of falling. I saw Ned for an instant writhing and struggling like myself, sliding swiftly toward the brink, and then, just as I thought the end had come, there was another violent tug at the lasso. I was swept rapidly over the ice toward the left, and before we could either of us realize what had happened, we were clasping each other desperately and were lying still. The lasso had caught at its middle on a projecting rock, and the force of our motion had swung us round together.

Keeping the line taut we drew ourselves up, hand over hand, until we could grasp the rock.

There was not a word spoken. We were both panting with excitement and exhaustion, and I at least could not have spoken had my life depended on it. Ned clutched his rifle with one hand and the rock with the other, and lay motionless.

At last I stood up, my knees quivering under me. The level rays of the sun, peering through the cleft above, struck full in my eyes.

Keeping our rock of salvation behind us, we crawled slowly up the slope to the base of the cliff above and worked our way to the opening.

Alas! no level plain greeted our weary eyes. Only another sharp slope of ice and snow, the opposite side of the ridge terminating abruptly in another precipice about seventy-five feet below, and beyond, a stern wilderness of rocky cañons, jutting crags, and precipitous walls crowned by a second range of snow-clad peaks higher apparently than those on whose ridge we stood.

We were in the very heart of the Sierras. On every side the view was bounded by massive towering mountains, thrown wildly together, rock above rock, peak over peak, seeming to offer no possible outlet.

Ned braced himself against the cliff and held on to the end of the lasso, while I slid down and looked over the precipice. It was not quite perpendicular but ragged and broken, affording an easy descent to a wide ridge of rough bowlders and débris, partly covered with snow, that sloped away to the south, skirting the base of the cliff as far as I could see.

The warm rays of the sun were beginning to thaw the snow, and innumerable little rills trickled down over the ice and fell from the precipice with a sound like tiny bells.

I crept along to a safe place and shouted to Ned to come down, which he did with more alacrity than grace. Twenty minutes later we had clambered safely down to the rocks and snow, and for the first time in twenty-four hours could stand erect, and move about without danger of falling into an abyss.

The bright warm sunlight put new life into our hearts as we walked and jumped gayly down the rugged causeway to the south, and when at last a cleft in the opposite slope of the cañon began slowly to unfold before us, we hurried on for hour after hour full of eager anticipation.

As we came to a point nearly opposite this new gorge, we saw a clump of low pine-trees fringing the base of a mountain at the northern side. With a cry of delight we scrambled down the loose rocks that rolled away under our feet, crossed a narrow, cracking sheet of ice, and flung ourselves exhausted but happy on the soft turf beneath the trees.

It was an unspeakable delight to get back once more to something that had life, however weak and struggling. All about us delicate little Alpine flowers shyly held up their blue and red petals, gaining a whole world of beauty and tenderness from contrast with their stern and wild surroundings.

How we rolled and stretched our weary limbs on the soft turf! How eagerly we strove to persuade ourselves that now our bitter struggle with the mountains was almost over! The promised land, that wide glorious plain that should offer us an easy access to the south, now seemed close within reach.

"Holloa!" shouted Ned, suddenly. "Look at the sun!"

It was far on its western way, and in half an hour would drop behind the great barrier that we had crossed. We could form no idea of the number of miles we had walked since morning. In our eagerness to escape, to find some point that offered an outlet, hunger and thirst and exhaustion had been alike forgotten.

A blazing fire and a warm supper soon made us completely happy, and never have I slept better than that night.

Very early in the morning we set out to limber up our benumbed and aching limbs in exploring this new cañon that opened toward the east. All day long we clambered and tramped up and down over loose bowlders, snow, and ice, sometimes between walls that approached so closely as barely to admit of passing, then through wide amphitheatres formed by sloping spurs and crags of the mountains. In one of these we were forced to camp, with no material to build a fire, and a freezing atmosphere about us.

On the forenoon of the next day we came to where the gorge terminated in a lofty cliff rising directly across our path. Fortunately the sides of the cañon were here sufficiently sloping to enable us to climb up a few hundred feet to a rugged plateau, covered thick with snow and rocks. Two or three miles over this rough platform brought us at last to a point from which we could look down to the east of the Sierras.

Steep precipices, barren rocky hills, low mountains fringed here and there by stunted pine-trees, terminated far below us in a wide white plain, stretching away to the dim horizon, and glowing in the intense rays of the sun. Ten thousand feet beneath us lay a little lake, glistening like a sheet of burnished metal.

With a cheer we began the descent. Sliding down banks of frozen snow, jumping like goats from rock to rock down long, steep slopes, letting ourselves drop from ledge to ledge over precipices, we scarcely paused, until late in the afternoon we stood on the soft white earth of the plain close beside the lake. As we looked back at the point we had left, away up in the sky above us, it seemed incredible that we could have come in safety from so fearful a height.

We were dripping with perspiration, and our legs were numb with weariness. The air was deathly still, and as hot as the breath of a furnace.

Scorched and panting with thirst, we turned eagerly to the inviting waters of the lake. I dipped up a cupful and greedily gulped it down. It was salt and bitter as the ocean.

At that moment all the suffering of the past five days seemed accumulated and concentrated into that disappointment. The fearful position to which our recklessness had brought us, swept over me with an appalling vividness. Alone on this wide desert, the gloomy inaccessible mountains towering to the sky beside us, the thermometer at 115 degrees in the shade, and not a sign of drinkable water over all that wide expanse !

Suddenly Ned shouted, "The canteens ! "

We eagerly seized them, and the tepid remains of coffee that we had carried since morning tasted like the sweetest of nectars. Then spreading our blankets on the sand, we lay down to twist and turn in aching weariness and drowsy forebodings of the morrow.

Faint rays of light were shooting up from the horizon, and the lofty snow-peaks were rosy with the dawn, when we staggered to our feet, and after a wretched breakfast of dry crackers and corned beef, set out over the plain.

Skirting the mountains, we tramped wearily toward the south.

The soft earth sank under our feet, and the hateful artemisia brushed its withered leaves against our legs. The sun cleared the horizon at a bound, and slowly mounted higher and higher in the cloudless sky.

How longingly we gazed on those white peaks that but yesterday had filled us with such horror! Oh for one little lump from those terrible ice-fields that we had trodden underfoot with such eagerness to escape!

Higher and higher rose the sun. The horizon rippled and quivered with heat, and great scorching waves swept over us, blinding our eyes and producing momentary spasms of dizziness.

We kept bravely onward, knowing that the time was short. To give up meant certain death. We must find water or die.

Two giant spectral figures rose from the plain beside us, escorted us for a mile or two, then vanished as they came. Sometimes visions of shady bowers, cool, transparent lakes and sparkling streams tantalized us for a moment with their loveliness, then rose from our sight in fleeting mockery, and away before us stretched the burning desert, pulsating and throbbing with the fiery sunlight.

At last the sun reached the mountains, cast one farewell withering glance upon us, and dropped out of sight.

Faintly reviving, we plodded on in the shadow. As we paused to rest for a moment, Ned placed the thermometer on a ledge of rock; it stood at 120 degrees. Without a word we rose to our feet and staggered on.

Suddenly I saw a line, whiter than the surrounding desert, that stretched parallel to our course and some distance farther out on the plain. I turned and walked toward it.

Ned called out: "Are you mad, Tom? We must keep near the mountains."

I waved my hand to him and kept on.

The white line was a trail across the desert, with the marks of wagon-wheels and the prints of horse-hoofs, half obliterated, in the sand. I sat down and waited for Ned to join me.

"It must lead somewhere," said he. "We may as well follow it."

The road led to the south, following the course of the mountains ; but after an hour's walking we could still see nothing before us but the same dreary plain, the distance growing dim and uncertain in the gathering gloom.

My foot struck something hard and round, half buried in the sand. I stooped and unearthed a human skull. It seemed to me that the discovery caused me no horror, no dread lest our fate might be like that of the unfortunate traveller whose mouldering remains lay at my feet. I felt only an indifference to what might happen ; a longing to be at rest, even beneath the sand of the desert.

In half an hour, Ned, who was some distance in advance, paused for me to come up. Wofully strange and hollow his voice sounded as he said : —

"We can't stand this any longer, Tom ! We must lie down somewhere and try to rest."

We crawled to the side of a rock and lay down, supperless and waterless, to chew the bitter leaves of the sage, and dream of death and the horrors of a hell of eternal thirst.

At four o'clock on the morning of October 5th, we were once more plodding with swollen lips and burning throats along the same white trail. Something in the dim distance began gradually to take shape before us. Our steps grew more rapid, and our breath came deeper, yet neither dared to speak the hope that was dawning within him.

At last there was no longer any doubt. As the light grew stronger, we saw a cluster of trees, an oasis in the desert. The first rays of the sun found us stretched at full length on the soft grass beside a spring of cool, sweet water.

The oasis was about five acres in extent. Four springs bubbled out of the earth, forming a little stream that the thirsty desert absorbed a few rods beyond. The cool shade of the trees, the rustle of leaves, and the twitter of birds put new life and courage into our hearts, and a couple of hares that Ned succeeded in shooting with the rifle, formed a very agreeable change in our bill of fare.

All day we loitered and loafed, bathing in the cool stream and rolling in the grass, and the next morning were ready to brave the desert again.

With roast hare in our haversacks, and canteens filled with water, we set out once more along the trail. The chain of

mountains here took a wide sweep toward the west, and became lower and more broken. Detached ranges and isolated
peaks began to appear to the south and southeast.

For five hours we walked steadily. The heat was becoming
unbearable, and we saw no signs of water or any settlement.
At last Ned stopped, and said : —

"This trail was evidently not intended for pedestrians; the
stations are too far apart. We must take to the mountains
again."

Selecting an opening that seemed to offer an easy access, we
were soon clambering upwards, over rough dry bowlders, now
and then catching a whiff of a breeze from the west.

After a long afternoon of hard climbing, we camped at night
by the side of a rushing stream that swept through a narrow
gorge toward the west.

We slept unusually late the next morning, and the sun was
high up among the trees before we had our pail of coffee prepared. After breakfast, Ned scaled the cliff to see what view he
could get toward the west. I watched him till he disappeared
round a jutting crag, and then sat down to write up my
notes.

Our camp was on a wide, grassy platform above the bed of
the stream and extending along its bank for some distance.
Back of this platform, as well as on the other side of the river,
rose rugged uneven cliffs a hundred to two hundred feet in
height, fringed along their summits by overhanging trees and
at their bases by a thick growth of bushes. Here and there on
the banks of the stream grew scattering clumps of oak and
evergreen trees, and under a spreading oak-tree, about fifteen
feet from the base of the cliff, we had pitched our camp. Here
I sat cross-legged on a blanket, busily writing in a note-book.

The dash of the river drowned all other noises, and it was
some time before I looked up. When I did raise my eyes, the
first object they encountered was a huge, unwieldy beast
shambling along at a short distance down the cañon and coming straight toward our camp. There was no mistaking its
identity. I recognized a larger counterpart of our friends of
Woodward's Gardens. It was the "Old Man of the Mountains," the dreaded grizzly.

I looked up the path that Ned had taken. He was not in

sight. The rifle was leaning against a rock some distance away, and there was no possibility of reaching it before Mr. Bruin could reach me.

Cautiously keeping out of sight, I drew back among the bushes at the base of the cliff. As I did so, something cold and flexible wound itself around my wrist. With a momentary shudder at the thought of serpents, I brushed my other hand over it, and found only the long lasso which had been thrown carelessly over a branch of the tree the night before. One end hung among the bushes, the other, with the noose, dangled on the opposite side of the tree. With one hand grasping the revolver, I lay still and waited.

Old Bruin came slowly along, snuffed and grunted around the embers of the fire, swallowed at one mouthful the remains of our roast hare, licked his chops with a growl of satisfaction, and nosed his way toward the tree.

As he came nearer, and I realized his tremendous proportions, and saw the gleam of the long white teeth, I instinctively drew closer to the cliff. My movement brought the other side of the tree into view, and I saw the end of the lasso, the noose spread wide open, hanging about a foot from the ground. In obedience to a sudden impulse, I reached out and seized the end that hung near me.

The ugly brute came close to the tree, snuffed at the blankets, and pulled them up with his immense paws. I was trembling so with excitement that I actually feared the movement of the bushes would betray me.

With a quick shake of the head the bear dashed the lasso to one side. As a natural consequence it came back and struck him on the snout. Angrily growling, he turned and made another lunge at it, and — yes! that was what I had hoped for — he thrust his head far through the noose. At the same instant I sprang with all my weight on my end of the lasso, slapped it round a stout sapling that grew close to the cliff, and fastened it with a running knot. The bear was caught fast by the neck!

Then the ball opened! The roars of rage, the struggles and tugs at the lasso were fearful. I trembled lest it should give way; but the tough rawhide, strong enough to stop the headlong flight of a wild bull on the plains, showed no signs of breaking. The tree in the bushes waved back and forth, lashing the cliff with a noise that was heard far above the dashing of the stream and the roars of the infuriated bear. At one moment a fierce tug bent it far over, and then as the bear relaxed his hold for an instant, it flew back, pulling his forefeet from the ground.

In the mean time I was dancing about at a safe distance, pouring in shot after shot from the revolver, with no more apparent effect than if they had been so many paper balls. In my excitement I had utterly forgotten the heavier weapon, when suddenly a voice shouted from above : —

"The rifle, Tom ! the rifle ! where the devil is the rifle ? "

I looked up, and saw Ned hurrying down the rocks, and at the same moment I grasped the rifle. An ounce ball in Bruin's head at short range settled the business. The struggles grew weaker, and by the time Ned joined me, the terrible beast was hanging quietly with his forefeet in the air, a lifeless mass.

"Old boy, I congratulate you ! " shouted Ned, as he wrung my hand. "That 's worth all the trouble we 've had for the last week ! But I swear, I wish you 'd seen yourself, as I saw you ! I was coming leisurely along the ledge, when I heard a furious roar followed by a succession of shots. You may guess how I hurried ; and when I rounded the corner, there you were, the pair of you ! Of course I could n't see the lasso ! Lord!

Tom! You looked like a travelling showman! I never saw a bear trained to manifest so much courtesy. He bowed, and waved his paws with the grace of a windmill! And you — Well, Tom! I never supposed you could execute a *pas seul* with so much spirit! A hand-organ would have made the show complete!"

The beast was almost nine feet in length, and nearly as much round the body. It took our united efforts to pull the lasso up far enough to loosen the knot from the tree. We hacked out the terrible claws, over five inches long, and strung them on a piece of fish-line.

"To the victor belong the spoils!" said Ned, as he flung the grotesque necklace over my head.

It was nearly noon when we set out again. Four or five miles farther down the cañon, our grassy platform began to grow narrower, and at last the water rushed swiftly between precipitous walls of rock, forcing us to climb up about fifty feet to a wide ledge, along which we pursued our way.

A dull, distant sound, faintly perceptible amid the noise of the water beneath, gradually increased as we advanced, until it became a roar like prolonged thunder. The air seemed to tremble around us, and suddenly at a slight bend in the cliff we came upon a cataract a hundred feet in height, over which a thin mist of spray hung like a veil.

Below the waterfall the cañon widened again, and green banks appeared, bordering the stream. We sought in vain for a place to clamber down. The cliff descended below our ledge, one hundred and fifty feet, to the grass and bushes beneath. Even our invaluable lasso was not long enough to be of service here.

Our canteens were empty, and we began to be thirsty, in full view of the sparkling water.

All the afternoon we kept on along the ledge, till toward night we were able to descend to another, about fifty feet lower, but still far above the river. At dark we were forced to camp on the ledge as best we could, without water or fire.

The next morning, utterly worn out, and desperate with thirst, we stopped at a point where the ledge descended about twenty-five feet. Some slight irregularity in the wall below, and a bush or two growing out from its face, induced me to attempt to climb down. Grasping the edge with both hands, I lowered myself and felt about with my feet for a support.

Suddenly something began to give way above. I clutched frantically upward, striving to get a fresh grip. The rock which I had hold of was loosening under my weight. Ned's wild cry rang in my ears, and for an instant I saw his face pale with horror as he sprang forward, and then — rocks, trees, and water swept before me in inextricable confusion, my stomach seemed to rise bodily into my mouth, and, like a thick blanket suddenly cast over my head, came silence and darkness.

CHAPTER V.

OME of us can recall times when we have lain in bed day after day and night after night, the exhausted system faintly struggling against the fever, when the brain throbs with swift pulses, when everything in the room, even the face of our dearest friend, seems strange and unfamiliar, when it requires steady, conscious effort of will to keep the mind clear in our waking hours, and when the sleep that is half slumber and half swoon is crowded with dim and direful phantasms trooping in dread procession through the credulous mind unchallenged by the slumbering will.

And how terrible is that moment which we call "awaking," when the vague spectres of the other world are mingled and confounded with the realities of life, and the mind rouses itself by slow, laborious effort, to select and admit those perceptions that come from without, and to hold back the throng that are pressing from within !

Those who have experienced anything like this can realize something of my feelings upon the return of that life which I had vaguely felt was leaving me. A drowsy sense of pain, gradually becoming distinct and terrible, a struggle to conect my scattered senses, to remember where I was, a few detached memories linked inextricably with ludicrous or horrible visions, at last concentrated themselves, like rays of light to a focus, in the conviction that I had fallen.

I opened my eyes, and they rested upon Ned, sitting on the grass beside me, and watching me with anxious face. A pail stood near, and my head was dripping wet.

Summoning all my strength, I managed to articulate the word "Water!"

In an instant a cup was at my lips, and I was gulping down sweet, refreshing draughts. Then, feeling somewhat revived, I sat up and looked about at the landscape that turned slowly round and round before my dazed sight. I was dreadfully sick, and my head throbbed with intense pain. However, by a great effort I twisted my mouth into the semblance of a smile.

"Do you feel better, old boy?" asked Ned.

"I begin to feel alive again," I answered. "Guess I 'm all right!" and I made a movement to stand up.

The attempt resulted in an excruciating pain in my right leg, and a sudden collapse upon my back again.

"Ned," I groaned, "my leg is broken!"

There was no doubt about it. One of the bones of the right leg was broken below the knee. With set lips I endured the torture while Ned examined it, and then for the first time noticed that my right hand was bound tightly in a handkerchief stained with blood.

"You caught a bush on your way down," explained Ned, "and that probably saved your life."

"I might as well have lost it," said I, dismally. "The loss of a leg in this wilderness means pretty much the same thing!"

"Not a bit of it!" answered he. "Pluck up heart, my boy! The man that can scale the Sierras, tramp the desert, and lasso a grizzly, is n't going to be discouraged by such a trifle as a broken leg!"

"How did you get down from the cliff?" asked I.

"That inevitable lasso!" he replied. "You wondered what under heaven I was going to do with it, and this is the fourth time it has saved our lives!"

I glanced at the cliff. There hung the lasso, dangling from

the ledge far above, and reaching to within about thirty feet of the ground.

"I dropped from the end of it!" said Ned. "Without it. I believe the whole seventy-five feet would n't have kept me! I thought you were dead, Tom!"

My injuries consisted of a broken leg, a hand severely torn and lacerated by the bush I had grasped, a big lump on the back of the neck, and sundry bruises and contusions on the arms and shoulders.

"Bad enough!" remarked Ned; "but, Tom, it might have been infinitely worse! This last week convinces me that we are not destined to be starved, drowned, devoured, or dashed to pieces, and that we shall accomplish our trip successfully!"

"Then I fear I shall have to be carried through it!" answered I, ruefully.

"And there 's no better fellow than I to do it," said he, "and no better moment than now to begin. We must get out of this!"

He lifted me, and I clasped my hands about his neck. The broken leg dangled helplessly, causing intense pain, but I ground my teeth together, and kept back the groans. The rifle was on the ledge above, and the lasso hung out of reach; so leaving them both behind, and holding me in his strong arms as tenderly as if I were a sick child, Ned strode manfully over the soft grass, following the course of the stream down the ever-widening cañon.

Puffing under his burden, he still kept up a running fire of small talk, striving desperately to cheer my drooping spirits and to keep up his own. I heard but little of what he said. The pain and exhaustion were so great that it required undivided attention to retain the consciousness I had just recovered. Occasionally a groan escaped in spite of me, and then he laid me gently on the grass, brought water from the stream, and bathed my aching head. Then after a few moments we travelled on again.

Suddenly, in a half-drowsy condition, with my head resting on Ned's shoulder, I felt him pause and draw a long breath.

"Tom! Tom!" said he, "look up! We are saved. Here is the Earthly Paradise!"

I raised my aching head, and gazed for an instant on a scene too beautiful to be real. It seemed like one of the changing visions of delirium, like a treacherous mirage that would vanish in a moment.

We had reached the opening of the cañon, and looked out on a valley surrounded by green sloping hills that here and there rose into low mountains. The rapid river that we had followed so long, expanded into a wide, peaceful stream, winding through the meadows and disappearing between the hills beyond. A white road entered the valley from the north, gleamed out at intervals through the trees, and was lost in the southern mountains. Clumps of wide-spreading oak-trees were scattered over the park-like surface, and on one side we saw the regular rows and dark-green foliage of an orange orchard. Cattle and horses browsed quietly on the meadows and hillsides to the south, and near the centre of the valley, gleaming through the thick foliage, was a white ranch-house, with barns and outbuildings in the background.

A gentle breeze, sweet with the breath of a thousand flowers, sighed in our faces as we descended into the meadow.

I saw a figure on horseback move out from behind the house, and then all became a blank. The constant pain, the jarred and maimed condition of my body, the sickness and exhaustion from our long jaunt down the cañon, had at last overcome my will-power.

When consciousness returned, I was lying on a sofa in a large, cool room, neatly furnished, and delightfully suggestive of home and rest. Ned stood beside me, and a kind-eyed matronly woman of about forty, with a face that to my sick and weary heart seemed the sweetest on earth, was dressing my wounded hand. Two or three children were looking on with wide eyes, while a gray-haired man, bending over me in his shirt-sleeves, examined my leg. Ned's voice was the first thing I heard.

"Well, doctor, what do you make of it?"

"Oh, not so bad!" replied the man. "The fibula is broken, and there's some inflammation from its being left so long without setting. We can fix him up without any trouble; but it'll be some months before he'll feel like climbing mountains again."

The ranch was the property and residence of the speaker, a Dr. French, who had given up his practice in the East some ten years before, and had settled in California with his family.

We had emerged from the mountains a little to the north of San Bernardino, and must have walked about two hundred miles in the ten days since leaving Visalia.

The broken leg was set and the lacerated hand dressed and bandaged, and under the influence of a drink that the doctor prepared, I soon sank into a deep sleep, with Ned sitting on one side and Mrs. French on the other.

I opened my eyes quietly without speaking, and they rested on Ned, still sitting in the same place. But Mrs. French was gone, and in her place sat a girl of about eighteen years, dark

as a daughter of the East, and beautiful with that soft, rich beauty that belongs to the brunette. I might have fancied myself a Mohammedan, awaking from the sleep of death and welcomed by a glorious houri to the Paradise of the Faithful. A long, heavy curl of jet-black hair hung gracefully over one shoulder, and the softly-glowing cheeks and full, snowy throat were close to my face as she leaned forward, gently fanning me.

In the half-light that came through the closed shutters I lay and watched her till the hardships and dangers that still thronged my memory, the ice-fields and barren cliffs, the scorching sun of the desert, began to mingle strangely with Arabian-Nights visions of gorgeous Eastern palaces, white-robed maidens, and tinkling fountains. In another moment I would have been asleep again, when Ned said : —

"Let me take the fan ; you must be tired."

"Oh, no," she answered ; and then in a minute, " Poor fellow ! how soundly he sleeps ! "

I moved a little, and Ned said : —

" Feel better, Tom ? "

" Much better," I answered. " Such comfort as this would revive the dying."

" Tom," continued he, " this is Miss Margaret French, the daughter of our kind host. She has been fanning you for the past hour."

" I am very grateful to you, Miss French," said I. " I understand now what has given me such delightful dreams. It was hard for me to realize when I awoke."

She colored a little as she replied, —

" I rather think papa's medicine has had more to do with your dreams than my fan ; but I am really glad you feel better, Mr. Jackson. And now I presume two such comrades as you will want to discuss the situation, so I will excuse myself."

" We should be glad to have your advice, Miss French," said Ned ; but she shook her head, smiling, gave me her hand with unaffected ease and frankness, and left the room.

Ned gazed after her until the door closed, and then turning to me, he drew a long breath.

" Tom, I 'm awfully sorry you broke your leg ; but — is n't she glorious ? "

" I trust there will be no other fractures to chronicle," said I. " Such a woman as that would have no difficulty in breaking two hearts while one leg was being mended."

" You 're not going to fall in love with her, are you, Tom ? " said he.

There was such an unconscious emphasis on the "you" in this question, and such a momentary shade of anxiety in Ned's face, that I broke into a laugh.

" Don't be alarmed, my boy," said I. " I am *hors du combat* at present, and I should never enter the lists against you, even if I had two legs to stand on."

" I might have expected that thrust," he replied. " Of course you had to misunderstand me. I have been afraid, ever since we started, that you would fall in love with some girl and spoil the trip."

To this subterfuge I deigned no answer, but continued to laugh quietly. Ned gave two or three uncomfortable hitches in his chair, then surrendered and joined in the laugh.

"Well," said he, "I confess I am a little touched. It's nothing; won't last overnight. I thought I was proof against all women, but I never dreamed of such a one as this; or rather, yes, I have dreamed of such a one, but never hoped to see her."

"Be careful, Ned," said I. "Keep tight hold of your heart-strings. Remember your failings. Learn to look upon this fair goddess as something to admire, but by no means to love."

"None of your pedestal utterances," growled he. "Before a month is over you'll be desperately in love with her yourself. I know you. She'll sit and sympathize with you, and you'll pour your picturesque philosophy into her unsophisticated mind, and begin to flatter yourself that you are moulding her into that extraordinary ideal that you used to prate about. and by-and-by — "

"And by-and-by," interrupted I, "she'll surprise me by falling in love — with you. But really, Ned, it strikes me we are repaying the doctor's hospitality in a very unjustifiable way, disposing of his daughter's affections. She's probably already engaged to some enterprising Californian."

The entrance of Mrs. French put an end to our talk. She brought me a supper, the best I had tasted in many months, and I ate it with a relish that proved my stomach at least to be in excellent order.

Ned joined the family in the dining-room, and after a short time they all came in together. The cool evening air breathed in at the open windows, the moonlight stole through the leaves and mingled with the lamplight, as the doctor and I lit our cigars, and Ned began the story of our adventures, commencing with the supper at Delmonico's. The children (two girls and a small boy) listened in open-mouthed astonishment; and when Ned reached our hardships and sufferings in the mountains, I could see the increasing interest on the faces of the older listeners.

Our beauty sat near the table with the lamplight shining full on her face, and I watched her with a speculative interest as she leaned forward gazing intently at Ned.

"And now," said the doctor, when the story was done, "I suppose you've had enough of it!"

"Ask Tom," replied Ned.

"So far as I'm concerned," said I, "I see no reason to back out. We've got along much better than I anticipated, so far."

"Well, you have the right sort of grit," said the doctor, "and, I shouldn't wonder if you came through all right."

"And you'll have a nice long rest before you start again," said Mrs. French; "that is, if you can make yourselves comfortable here."

"'Comfortable!'" echoed Ned. "My dear Mrs. French, I'm only afraid we shall be too comfortable. We shall grow like the Lotus-eaters, and forget our ambition and all the rest of the world;" and immediately I saw him steal a look at the fair Miss Margaret.

"But it seems to me, Mrs. French, like a good deal of an imposition for two tramps to come and take up their abode with you for a month or two," said I.

At this there was a chorus of expostulations, and Miss Margaret said : —

"Mr. Jackson, if you had to live here all alone for a year or two, you'd understand how glad we are to have any one visit us. Even," she added with a smile, "two tramps."

"Perhaps we can make ourselves useful," said Ned. "Our partnership is a union of mind and matter. Tom has the brains, and I have the muscle. I shall enjoy working outside, and Tom can act as private tutor to the children."

There was a slight commotion among the youngsters at this, and the oldest of the little girls said, —

"Maggie teaches us now; but she don't know much!"

"You shall have my sympathy, Mr. Jackson," said Margaret, "if you undertake the task of teaching this family; but I warn you beforehand that California children are a good deal like California colts."

"I want you gentlemen to understand," said the doctor, "that you are my guests so long as you choose to stay here. Of course, if Mr. Markham likes to amuse himself by riding about the ranch with me, I shall be very glad of his company and his assistance; and if Mr. Jackson cares to interest himself in helping the small fry with their studies, we shall all be very grateful, especially their mother. Do just as you feel inclined, and you will please us all. And now," continued he, "I think my patient would be better off in bed."

Ned and the doctor carried me upstairs, where in the luxury of a soft bed I soon forgot all the sufferings of the past. Ned turned in beside me, and in a few moments quiet reigned throughout the house.

From this time for a month I kept my room. The children came up every morning, and I gave them lessons in the elementary studies and in French. Margaret joined us in the latter, and I found her bright and quick, and already quite a French scholar. She had been to school in the East, and for several winters in San Francisco, and she told me the doctor had promised to take her abroad in a few years.

Ned was out all the morning, and his war-whoop, as he rode up to the house, was the signal for our lessons to end. In the afternoon, Maggie and he made little sketching-trips about the valley. I watched the progress of this intimacy with considerable interest, and had a chance to fire many a shaft of satire at Ned, all of which he bore with imperturbable good-humor, still persisting that there was nothing serious in his attentions.

The doctor had a small but well-selected library, and I passed much of the time in reading, as well as writing and studying Spanish. In the evenings, Ned and Maggie, and sometimes the whole family, adjourned from supper to my room, where we held high discussions and laid out our future plans of travel.

Sometimes when I was alone the sound of the piano came from the room below, and Ned's big bass voice blending with Maggie's soft contralto. She was not an *artiste*, this little California girl, but she loved music, and she played and sang as if she felt every note; and the result was that her audience, stretched out with a broken leg, felt and enjoyed it too.

So with all these diversions life was not very monotonous; and yet I was heartily glad when in about a month I was able to get downstairs and stump about a little with a pair of crutches. Then I began to give the children music-lessons; and in the evenings we had regular concerts, — quartets in which the matronly Mrs. French sang soprano with all the gusto of a prima donna, solos in every style, and piano and flute duets unnumbered. As I look back over the five years' trip, there is no period that memory lingers over so fondly, no time so filled with quiet, careless content, as the three months that we passed at the hospitable ranch of Dr. French.

The weather was glorious. The sun shone perpetually, and yet there were frequent soft breezes to temper the heat. Fruits of every kind — oranges, peaches, grapes, and pomegranates — ripened in unending profusion.

The ranchmen were mostly Indians, with a few Mexican Vaqueros that looked after the cattle and horses. I never tired of watching the skill with which these fellows managed the *riata*. From my seat on the piazza I could look off over the plain to the south, and see the picturesque riders, with their wide, jaunty straw hats, moving about among the herd, singling out an old bull, and bringing him to the ground with an unerring whirl of the lasso.

This sort of thing pleased Ned immensely, and he set about learning the art. He had made a trip up the cañon with one of the Indians, and had succeeded in recovering our lasso and rifle; and we could distinguish him every morning, careering about on his mustang, and handling his long lasso about as skilfully as an inexperienced angler handles his fly. He succeeded once in lassoing the horse he was riding, and once the noose came back and narrowly missed his own neck. Nevertheless, he assured us he was improving, and we charitably believed him.

Sometimes Maggie would bring her work and sit with me on the piazza. She was a bright and ready talker, generally perfectly self-possessed; but now and then I could detect traces of an earnestness that seemed to belong of right to those dark Southern eyes.

One scrap of conversation I remembered afterward, because it seemed to have a bearing on the events that followed.

In some way our talk had drifted to the subject of crime and criminals, and I had expressed disgust at the slow, uncertain course of justice that characterized criminal prosecutions in most of our States.

"Of course, Tom," said she (we had long ago dropped the formality of titles), "I agree with you that a guilty man ought to be punished; but think how dreadful it is when an innocent man is made to suffer because appearances are against him! Think of the disgrace of being arrested, and made to stand a public trial for some horrible crime, even if you are acquitted! And then the horror of feeling that your friends and everybody will be half-inclined to think you were guilty, after all!"

Her earnestness pleased me, and just to continue the discussion, I answered: —

"After all, Maggie, I don't know but it's better that an innocent man should suffer now and then, than that a guilty one should escape. Of course it's rough on the individual; but we have to sacrifice ourselves sometimes for the good of the majority, and it's much better for you and me and for all of us, that, whatever happens, crime should be surely and speedily punished! If I were on a jury, I should be inclined to give society the benefit of the doubt, in spite of legal maxims to the contrary."

"Tom, you can't believe anything so horrible!" and the dark eyes flashed gloriously. "Think if your dearest friend — if

Ned, for example — were accused of some crime, would you stand by and see him punished, just for some theoretical idea about the good of society? Why, if all the world accused a friend of mine, and I believed him innocent, I would stand by him and befriend him to the end of my life!"

"I should be willing to be accused of murder, Maggie," said I, "if I were sure you would defend me so zealously! I think Ned would commit the murder."

She colored a trifle at this, and went away smiling, and I smoked my cigar, and wondered for the hundredth time if she really cared anything for Ned.

Some days after this, Maggie excused herself one afternoon from her usual ramble with Ned, and he came and sat with me. It was evident to me that the young man was more deeply smitten than he was willing to admit. Somehow Maggie seemed to creep into almost all his conversation. I had one shot left, however, that I had been reserving for a last discharge; and now, in the middle of one of his harangues, I calmly drew a paper from my pocket and read: —

"'*Article* 5. Neither of us shall make any engagement to marry during the performance of this undertaking.'"

Then I folded the paper, replaced it in my pocket, and gazed sorrowfully at the landscape, as if I regretted the situation, but felt there was nothing more to be said about it.

There was silence for a few moments, and then Ned said:

"Well, what of it? You 're not much of a grammarian if you see any trouble in that article! I don't propose to marry during the performance of this undertaking, nor do I propose to make any engagement to marry during that time. But that does n't prevent my making an engagement during the undertaking, and being married after it is accomplished. You see the time specified refers to the marrying, and not to the engagement."

"Oh!" said I.

Then I took out my paper again, wrote a few words, and read: —

"'N. B. By special request of E. G. Markham, Article 5 is understood to mean just the opposite of what it states.'"

"Now, stop right there!" said he, extending his hand deprecatingly. "There 's no occasion for you to rake out all your confounded sarcasms !   I own up, I love her ! and — I believe she 's rather fond of me ! " and with that he pulled his hat over his eyes and stalked off toward the mountains.

About five o'clock, to my surprise Maggie came in.   I did n't know she had been out of the house.   She smiled and nodded in a rather constrained manner, and hurried upstairs.

Presently Ned appeared, striding over the meadow at a great pace, threw his hat on the ground with a gesture of despair, and sat down beside me.

He looked so worried and distressed, that I at once leaped to the conclusion that he had rushed off with his usual precipitance, declared his affection, and met with a graceful snub.

So I braced myself for the arduous task of consolation, and began, —

" My dear Ned — "

" Now just wait," said he, " till I tell you all about it.   After leaving you, I strolled over to the edge of the meadow, and down along the hills to the south, keeping most of the time in the woods.   Suddenly I came out into a little grove near the road, and there was Maggie holding an earnest confab with a big, broad-shouldered Mexican who had just dismounted from his black horse.   I was so dumfounded that I stood like an idiot, not knowing whether to back out or to step up and face the music.   In a moment, Maggie caught sight of me, and I never saw any one appear so embarrassed in my life.   She turned deathly pale, staggered back, and looked as if she would like to run.   Then she seemed to collect herself by an effort, and introduced me to Don José Miguel, about as ill-looking a rascal as ever went unhung ! He had a dark, Spanish face, and heavy, black mustache, and a villanous scowl that looked as if his greatest pleasure was to commit murder.

" I thought I had to be polite, and held out my hand ; but he only nodded in a surly kind of way, and toyed with the handle of his revolver as if he had half a mind to shoot.

" Maggie tried to say something about Don José not understanding English (I heard them talking something mighty like it as I came up), but her voice trembled, and there was evidently the devil to pay somehow ; so I made up my mind I was *de trop*, and came away.

"Now, will you have the goodness to tell me what you make of that for a yarn?"

"Well," said I, "to an unprejudiced observer it looks very much as if our demure and innocent-looking Juliet had a Romeo, and not a very creditable one either!"

"Damn it, Tom! I can't believe it; but—"

"But you must!" answered I.

He scowled at the floor for a moment, then picked up his hat and went in.

After a short season of reflection, I resolved on a bold move. There was a mystery somewhere, that was evident; and for Ned's sake I wanted to get a little more light on it. So I grasped my cane and limped into the house.

The family were just sitting down to supper. I took my place opposite Ned and Maggie, and mentally took notes of the behavior of both.

Neither spoke to the other. Ned, usually a perfect rattle-box at the table, was as silent as a graven image. He calmly filled his wine-glass with vinegar, and poured the doctor's excellent claret over his lettuce. Maggie unrolled her napkin and spread it in her lap, in less than a minute folded it again and replaced it in the ring, then instantly took it out again, and gazed around the table to see if any one was watching her. She caught my eye, grew scarlet in an instant, and began to eat at such a rate that I feared for her pretty throat.

"Doctor," I began presently, "you don't have many visitors here, do you?"

I felt a sharp dig on my pet shin, from Ned's insufferably long leg. Mentally cursing him, I still kept my eyes fixed on the doctor.

"No," said he, pleasantly, "you have seen what a solitary life we lead here, Tom. There can't have been more than two or three callers since you came."

I cleared my throat for action.

"And who," said I, speaking very distinctly, "is this gentleman, Don José Miguel?"

You know how you feel in a heavy thunder-storm, in the moment between that vivid glare and the crash that you are sure will follow. That's the way I felt after my seemingly innocent question. The silence was appalling. Ned was biting his lips and scowling at the window. Maggie held her head so close to the plate that her face was invisible. Mrs. French was pale as a sheet, and looked ready to burst into tears. The doctor's face was fairly savage.

Gertie, the elder of the little girls, a genuine little tease, broke the stillness by proclaiming in a shrill, triumphant voice, —

"Aha, Miss Maggie!"

What more she might have said remained unspoken. The maternal hand was promptly laid over her mouth.

Maggie left the table and went upstairs, her handkerchief to her eyes.

My heart smote me at the devastation I had wrought.

"The *gentleman* you speak of," said the doctor, slowly, "has seen fit to annoy us occasionally in the past. This is the first time in several years, Mr. Jackson, that his name has been spoken at my table."

Of course I apologized profusely; pleaded my ignorance of any unpleasantness, and my regret at having been so ill-advised. The doctor bowed gravely, and we tried to proceed with the meal; but appetites were apparently all satisfied, and we soon left the table.

I stumped upstairs to our room, feeling like the small boy that dropped a match in his father's hay-loft just to see what it would do. Ned followed me, and closed the door.

"Now, spare your wrath," said I. "I only wanted to find out something for your sake. There's a skeleton in the closet, and I tried to get sight of a bone."

"And a devilish nice mess you made of it!" answered he.

Just then we heard the doctor's voice from below, calling, "Maggie!"

"Yes," came the answer, and in a moment Maggie went downstairs.

Our windows and those of the room below were wide open, and in the still evening air we could hear voices, and occasionally catch a few words. The doctor talked long and earnestly, sometimes with considerable severity in his tone and then apparently pleading and beseeching Maggie to promise something.

Then we heard Maggie's voice, broken and tearful at first, and afterward with a decided ring of determination and defiance. At last the doctor said: —

"Well, Maggie, it's evident that we can't change your feelings; but so long as you remain in my house I shall insist on your regarding the happiness of my family. That is all!"

Then we heard him step out on the veranda, and Maggie came upstairs and locked herself in her room.

Ned had sat all this time with his feet on the window-sill, smoking a cigar.

"Are you satisfied, Ned?" I asked.

"Don't talk to me now, Tom," replied he. "I want to think."

So I lit the lamp and took my Spanish conversation-book, and Ned smoked in silence for half an hour longer, then heaved a tremendous sigh and went to bed.

In the morning he was still dismal. Maggie did not appear at breakfast, and her mother said she was suffering from a head-ache. The doctor's efforts at cheerfulness were very violent, but far from successful.

At dinner, Maggie came down, with eyes that showed traces of some pretty steady crying. She smiled and tried to talk a little, but Ned was glum and unapproachable.

After dinner she waited about on the veranda until Ned marched off toward the woods, and then, evidently not caring for my society, retreated upstairs again.

The next day the programme was much the same until after dinner. Then Maggie approached, just as Ned was on the point of leaving, and said timidly, —

"Ned, won't you please go sketching with me this after-noon?"

"Why — certainly — " he stammered; "that is, if you care to go."

"Well, I do, — very much;" and she hurried in and brought her hat and sketch-book.

I watched them sauntering across the meadow, about two yards apart, and reflected with myself that as two substances may often lie close together for an indefinite time until a slight shock or jar throws them into violent union, so two young people may sometimes live together for months without understanding their own feelings, till some disagreement that has to be cleared up, will launch them into each other's arms.

Having thus chemically philosophized, I repaired to the sitting-

room, and proceeded to constrain the small but rebellious Ger-
trude to her practising.

At about five o'clock my interesting couple loomed into sight
again, no longer walking six feet apart, but as near together as
free use of the lower limbs would permit.

They came up chatting and laughing as gayly as if no cloud
had ever dimmed their horizon.

" Let me see your sketches, Maggie," said I.

She blushed, and glanced at Ned.

" Not now, Tom," she replied. " I must go and dress for
dinner ; I know I look like a fright."

" Your curls do look rather disordered — " began I.

She waited to hear no more, but flew into the house.

Ned stood still for a moment, making a series of gestures, intended, I suppose, to convey the idea of happiness too great for
utterance ; then he came over, grasped my hand with a grip like
a dentist's forceps, and ejaculated : —

" Tom. it 's all right !"

" What 's all right? Confound you, let go of my hand ! You
kicked my broken leg the other night, and now you want to
squeeze my sore hand to a jelly !"

" Oh, I forgot your sore hand !" said he. " Beg pardon ! It 's
all right, you know ; that 's all fol-de-rol about her being in love
with any one else. She loves me ! I tell you, Tom — " And
thereupon his imagination " shook itself free from the face of
the yarth," as Uncle Remus would say, and soared aloft for ten
minutes into those realms of poesy known only to youthful
lovers. When at last he paused to take breath, I said : —

" I suppose she told you all about Don José Miguel !"

His face fell a trifle as he answered : —

" No, she did n't tell me anything about him, but she said it
was all right, and I need n't be jealous of him ; and she begged
me not to ask her about him, — and what could I do?" he
continued, waxing somewhat warm. " Did you think I was going to doubt her then? What do you take me for?"

" Well, I did take you for a man of some discretion in such
matters, if in nothing else ; and here you go and fall head over
heels in love with the first pretty girl we meet, and when her
sweet red lips say, ' Ned, I love you ; that is n't a dog, it 's
a bumble-bee !' you answer, ' All right, darling ! I always

thought it was a dog; but if you love me and you say it 's a bumble-bee, why, I believe it is a bumble-bee ! ' "

"Oh, you confounded sceptic ! " answered he. " If the angel of the Lord were to come down and assure you that a woman was just as sweet and pure as she pretended to be, you 'd say, ' Excuse me, I saw her look sideways at a man once, and I must have absolute, convincing proof that she is n't secretly in love with that man before I can trust her.' "

" Never mind, Ned," said I, laughing. " I was only teasing you a little. I congratulate you from the bottom of my heart, and there 's my hand — Lord ! did you squeeze Maggie's hand that way? Does she know she 's engaged herself to a mangle ? "

" Hang it, Tom, I always forget your game paw ! Come, let 's go in to supper."

That very evening Ned stated the case to the doctor; told him that he loved Maggie, and that she returned his affection ; that he must finish his expedition, and that when that was accomplished, he would like to come back, buy a ranch with his earnings, and settle down with the doctor's daughter ; that is, if the doctor had no objections.

Our worthy host grinned occasionally during this harangue, and when it was ended, he remarked : —

" Well, Ned, I don't think there 's any immediate cause for alarm at a lover who proposes to rush away from his sweetheart for four years. If you both have the same minds at the end of that time, I shall be heartily glad to see Maggie your wife."

So that matter was happily settled, and thenceforward the spooning was unbroken and unrestrained.

But by this time my leg was sufficiently cured to support me without a cane, and we began to talk of our departure. I felt sorry for Ned ; but he faced the music manfully, and we finally decided upon the 20th of December for a start.

The doctor made us quite a little speech, expressing his enjoyment of our visit and his gratitude for the assistance we had rendered him, particularly alluding to my efforts as an instructor, and finally wound up by presenting us with a pair of fine saddle-horses fully equipped, a double-barrelled shot-gun and complete set of camp utensils, and provisions enough for several weeks.

We took an affectionate leave of the family, Ned and Maggie at last ended their private farewells, and about nine o'clock on the morning of December 20, 1877, we rode forth from the doctor's hospitable ranch, and took the road for San Bernardino.

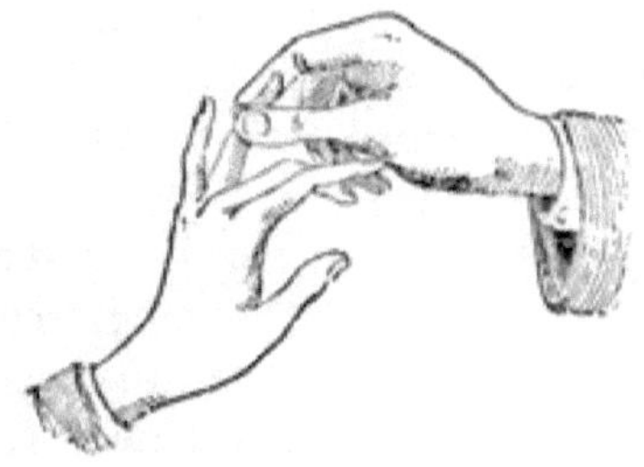

CHAPTER VI.

IN a few minutes we had reached the brow of the hill at the southern end of our Happy Valley. That scene is before me now in memory. The green meadows, the white ranch that had grown so dear to us both, the figures of our friends standing before the door, — we gazed for an instant, fired a salute, waved our hats, and then in a moment the three months' oasis in our years of desert was gone, and we were alone again.

We rode quietly on the way to San Bernardino, between lofty hills and green fields of Alfalfa. Though regretting to leave the kind friends who had helped us so materially, there was an inspiration in the clear morning air that filled me with new enthusiasm. I began to hum old college songs and tattered fragments of operas, but for a long time there was no response from Ned. His soul was not entuned to music, unless it had been a funeral dirge. But he could never resist the contagion for long. I began to hear curious subterranean rumbles of bass, and finally, as I struck into the stirring martial duet from "I Puritani," he fairly opened his mouth, and the pent-up volumes of bass rolled forth with increasing fervor to the end of the three verses.

"By Jove!" shouted he, when we paused. "This is glorious, after all, Tom! I can't afford to have the blues. 'Carpe diem,' as Captain Chambers would say. Come on! Less time in that mile ! " And spurring our horses, we broke into a gallop and pulled up a mile farther on the route.

We reached San Bernardino by noon, rested a couple of hours, and purchased some stout boots. Our old shoes had been completely demoralized by the Sierra rocks, but we had managed to keep the rest of our apparel in tolerable repair, and though somewhat worn, we decided to make it last through Mexico.

Then away again over the road to the southeast, past villages where Indians and Chinamen were loafing about before the low houses, across narrow streams and irrigating ditches, over broad patches of barren plain, through bits of forest and mountain passes, till we camped at night near a wooded hill where a stream trickled down over the rocks.

When we dismounted and were picketing our horses, I found myself so lame that every movement was torture. I was forcibly reminded of our first night in New Jersey. Ned, who had been riding every day for three months, was as fresh and limber as in the morning. He laughed at my misery.

"You remember the remedy," said he; "there 's the brook ! "

So I took a plunge in the cool stream, and felt somewhat better ; but no position was comfortable until I settled into the saddle again the next morning. By another night I was completely inured to a life on horseback.

On the 24th we reached Dos Palmas, purchased some oats, and struck out along the narrow trail toward Fort Yuma.

" ' Away, away, my steed and I ! ' " exclaimed Ned, as we trotted out upon the desert waste. " Eighty miles of this, Tom ; it 's well we 're not on foot ! "

" If we have only eighty miles of desert to cross on foot before we get through, we shall be mighty lucky ! " answered I.

" And where will be our camels and our mules, our elephants and our dromedaries, in the mean time ? " asked he.

" And where will be our gold, that will procure such luxuries ? " answered I. " We 're not quite so financially independent of space as Jules Verne's Englishman was."

" All the more credit to American wits to succeed without the gold," said he.

" Now," said I, " another week ought to see us in Mexico.

I suggest that we employ the time in brushing up our Spanish. We shall not be distracted by the beauties of the landscape."

"And you are afraid that when we reach Mexico we will be distracted by the beauties of its daughters. All right; let us be prepared for the conflict."

So I produced my conversation-book, and we fired off questions and answers during the greater part of that dreary three days' ride.

And a desolate country it was. The same sombre waste of sand and sage-bush that we had encountered east of the Sierras stretched away before us, glowing under a sun that even at this season was intensely hot.

On the night before Christmas one of the horses got loose, and we celebrated a " midnight mass " in capturing him. This was the only event that enlivened those first days.

Still, with the Spanish, our songs, and our discussions, we managed to pass the time well enough, until on the afternoon of the 26th we saw the wide muddy stream of the Colorado, and the low buildings of Fort Yuma.

Crossing into Arizona, we kept on along a road running nearly east, through a country quite as disagreeable as that we had just traversed. Occasionally small Mexican and Indian villages appeared, and gradually the broken ranges of hills and blue mountain-peaks began to rise in the south and east.

" Look out for your scalp, my boy ! " said I. " We 're nearing the hunting-grounds of the gentlemanly Apaches. Those brown curly locks of yours would prove an irresistible attraction."

" I think we could show a clean pair of heels to any Apache mount," answered he.

And in fact the value of the doctor's gift had increased in our estimation since we started. The horses had proved tough, serviceable beasts, and capable of a speed that made us feel pretty safe so long as we were not taken unawares. However, we saw no Apaches, at least none on the war-trail ; and although some of the Indians that we passed looked covetously at our blond top-knots, we were unmolested, and on the 30th of December crossed the line into the State of Sonora, in Mexico.

After a two days' ride through a rocky country, on New Year's day we entered a village of low adobe houses on the bank of a river. Naked children paused in their play to gaze at us, and we hailed a big Mexican, reclining at full length on a bench before his door.

"Hola, señor!" said Ned, in Spanish. "What town is this?"

The worthy citizen glanced from under his sombrero and grunted, "Caborca."

"And is this the river Asuncion?" asked I.

"Si, señor."

"And how far are we from Hermosillo?"

"Quien sabe?"

"Which is the road to Hermosillo?"

"Quien sabe?"

"And are you an ignorant, lazy jackass?" inquired Ned, this time in English.

"Quien sabe?"

After trying four different citizens of this enterprising town and receiving the invariable "Quien sabe?" for an answer, we at last found an Indian, who upon promise of a silver quarter agreed to show us the road to Hermosillo.

With some fears that our munificent reward might have tempted the mind of Nature's nobleman to "assume a virtue though he had it not," and send us off on the wrong road, we nevertheless followed his directions, and were rejoiced to find them confirmed at our next halt.

The country became more hilly as we advanced, and we met mule-trains with loads of ore, and occasional droves of cattle. Soon we began to detect symptoms of fertility and tropical suggestions in the landscape, and on the 5th of January, winding down a road between the foot-hills of the Cordilleras, we entered Hermosillo.

"At last," said Ned, "I begin to have a genuine 'foreign-clime' feeling."

"What a devilish long time it takes an American to get away from home!" said I. "Imagine with what pride we shall tell the rural inhabitant of some eight-by-nine European country that we travelled four thousand miles before reaching the boundary of the United States!"

Hermosillo is quite a city, and some of the streets presented a very business-like aspect. The wide plaza was set with orange and evergreen trees, and from the verandas and balconies of surrounding houses the dark-eyed señoritas, lounging with their cigarettes, cast shy glances at "los Americanos" as we rode slowly by.

A hundred miles over a dusty stage-road brought us to Guaymas, on the Gulf of California. The rays of the setting sun came across the rippling waters, bathing in their rich glow an island that slept in the offing, and lighting up the masts and spars of a dozen sailing-vessels that lay in the harbor, as we rode down the "Calle Principal," and pulled up at a hotel kept by a Frenchman.

For a dollar apiece we secured supper and lodging. We blessed the supper, but cursed the lodging. For at the supper we had oysters alive, and fresh from the waters of the gulf; and at the lodging we had another kind of life about us, — a life that made us long to lay down our own.

"It 's a bad hotel for transients," said Ned. "The nourishment one takes at an evening meal all goes to the support of these small permanent residents. The art of ' bleeding a traveller ' never attained such perfection elsewhere."

Except the flavor of the oysters, nothing pleased us in Guaymas, — a sandy, dirty town, with not a tree in or about it, and no fresh water save what is brought on the backs of mules from far inland, where some river ignominiously fails to cross the waste of sand that borders the gulf. We would gladly have shaken off the dust of our feet as we left the town, but — we could n't.

Then, as we journeyed on to Alamos, we came upon fertile valleys, where broad streams rolled toward the west, and ranchos and haciendas became more frequent. We stopped once to watch some Indians ploughing.

"There 's a primitive, rural simplicity that would delight the heart of Captain Chambers," said I.

The plough consisted of a sharp stick fastened to a piece of timber hewn from the tree. In the road stood a cart with wheels made from the round ends of a log.

Sometimes from the summit of a ridge between two valleys we caught glimpses of the sea, and ever to the left lay a rough forest region, mounting higher and higher to the table-land, and crowned by the blue Cordilleras.

We shot hares and game birds, sometimes camped under our mosquito-bars, and sometimes stayed overnight at a hacienda, where the dogs were legion, the children were naked, and the bed was a hammock on the veranda.

But the air was always soft and delicious, the sunshine never-failing, and our health and spirits strong and steady.

Alamos, El Fuerte, Sinaloa, Culiacan, — these were the principal towns on our route, and we passed them all without a stop. Again the sea glittered before us, and on the 24th of January we trotted into the busy port of Mazatlan.

On a bluff, some fifteen hundred feet above the bay, was a dilapidated fort with a few rusty cannon projecting from the openings, a pompous and childish defiance of the enemies of the town.

"I should really feel sorry for the fort," said Ned, "if a half-dozen ironclads should begin to amuse themselves with it."

"Probably the good citizens of Mazatlan regard it as a second Gibraltar," answered I.

As we rode down the gutter that occupied the middle of the street, we could see a California steamer lying in the harbor. The dock was thronged with a busy crowd of custom-house officials, sailors, and passengers.

We entered a store that bore an English sign, and found the proprietor an American from Boston, who greeted us cordially, and offered us some Mexican cigars. We inquired the best road to the capital.

"Well," said he, "the way I generally take is by Tepic and Guadalaxara ; but if you don't care for a little rough riding, and enjoy fine scenery, go straight across the mountains to Durango. But be sure to go armed."

"That's our chronic condition," answered I, producing a revolver.

"You probably would n't be interfered with," continued he ; "but in Mexico, and especially on the Durango road, there 's always a spice of danger. Have you much money?"

"About two hundred dollars."

"In paper?"

"No ; gold and silver."

"Then I 'll show you the best way to carry it. I was robbed twice before I hit on this method ; but the third time the Greasers only found two dollars out of the five hundred that I had with me."

At his request we brought in one of our saddles, which he ripped up at the lining. Then rolling our coin in a compact mass, except about ten dollars that we reserved for present needs, we deposited it in the saddle and sewed up the lining again.

"Now, wherever you stop overnight," said he, "take your saddles into the room with you. That's an ordinary precaution, and won't excite suspicion."

We thanked the gentleman, and mounting our horses, set out to reach the presidio of Mazatlan before night.

As we rode through the streets there was much to attract attention. The buildings have a quaint, Moorish appearance, and the gay *sarapes* flung carelessly over the shoulders of the passers, the graceful figures of cocoanut-palms, with the bright sunshine over all, seemed like a presage of the glories of the East.

At the old presidio we stayed overnight, and in the morning plunged into the depths of a tropical forest, following the road toward the mountains.

Giant trees towered beside us, forming a dense network of leafy branches far above our heads, and excluding every direct ray of the sun. Only a dim diffused light illumined the narrow road, and revealed for short distances the wild tangle of luxuriant vegetation that formed an impenetrable barrier on either side.

> "Growths of jasmine twined
> Their humid arms, festooning tree to tree."

Here and there slight elevations revealed the presence of decaying tree-trunks, but there were no visible signs of decay. Life — rich, luxuriant, steaming life — was everywhere, and the fall of a forest monarch seemed to call into existence myriads of new plants, that buried the unsightly corpse in a grave of green leaves and brilliant flowers. The air was damp and still.

"Pah!" said Ned, throwing off his coat. "This is like an overheated greenhouse."

"What a picnic it would be for Prof. P——," said I. "The old botanist would be fairly crazy."

"Be thankful he 's not here," answered Ned. "This narrow trail would be blocked in five minutes — with sesquipedalian names."

"Do you notice what a different effect this forest has on the feelings, from the effect of the Sierra forest?" I asked.

"Too much ozone, I suppose," replied Ned. "A tropical forest is depressing and enervating, while the pine forest of the North has an invigorating, tonic effect. Let's get out of this stifling air as soon as possible."

We urged our horses to a sharp trot, and hurried on through the sweltering atmosphere.

Flocks of brilliant paroquets flew screaming across our path. great unknown birds swept silently from their mid-day perches, and occasionally a snake started up in the road and glided hissing into the bushes. In the afternoon we began to ascend, and emerging from the forest, the path wound upward before us for a mile, to the summit of the first terrace, or step, of the *Tierra Templada*.

"Do you see that projecting rock where the road seems to come to an end?" asked Ned. "Don't look back until we reach there."

So we toiled up the steep ascent, and reining in our horses by the side of the rock, looked back toward the west.

The great forest lay below, vast and silent, the topmost twigs just vibrating with a gentle breeze that stole past us from the mountains. Low hills and fertile valleys, white haciendas gleaming through their embowering foliage, here and there a palm-tree outlined against the clear blue of the sky, away on the verge of the horizon the dark spot of Mazatlan with a graceful smoke-cloud hanging motionless above it, a thin, blue, quivering line that marked the shore of the sea, and the tropical sunlight, flooding and illuminating everything with its golden splendor, — such was the scene that lay spread out before us. We gazed for ten minutes without speaking.

"It's worth the whole trip from New York," said I ; and regretfully we turned our horses' heads toward the mountains.

Along a rough, stony road we moved slowly toward a small rancho that stood at the farther edge of the plain, a mile distant. A dozen yelping curs rushed down the path to meet us, and an old man. rising from his seat on the veranda, with vociferous shouts and angry gestures called off the dogs, and then stood, hat in hand, to bow us a welcome as we rode up.

"Can we stay here to-night?" asked I, in Spanish.

"Si, Señor." And unsaddling our horses he led them to the corral, and then ushered us, bearing our precious saddles, into a low, brick-paved room, where the half-dozen naked children stared, with fingers in their mouths, and a slatternly woman paused in her cooking to courtesy us a greeting.

After a supper of tortillas, roast hare, and Chili Colorado, we sat on the veranda and smoked our Mexican cigars with the old man, and watched the twilight creeping up the mountain-sides, until the splendor of the highest peak was swallowed by the devouring gloom. We had improved considerably in our Spanish, but I noticed an occasional smile flitting across the old man's face as we wrestled with some difficult expression.

We talked of the United States, and our host listened in childish wonder as we told him of the miles of railroad, the gigantic business enterprises, and the freedom and safety of an American citizen. It was a restful evening ; and when we curled up in our hammocks under the clear, starlit sky, Ned remarked : —

"I'm afraid this is the 'heyday' of our travels, Tom. Such comfort as this can't last much longer."

The next morning we were riding up the narrow, rocky path, zigzagging back and forth, higher and higher, until suddenly the road seemed to leap across to the next mountain ; only a narrow ridge connected the two, and along the summit of this ridge the road appeared suspended in mid-air like the famous sword-bridge that leads to the Mohammedan paradise. On either side, the rocks descended almost perpendicularly to depths from which the gaze shrank back appalled. Through the thin blue haze that mounted upward we could dimly see valleys and forests, and foaming torrents whose roar crept to our ears as a faint, far-away murmur.

"Here we have it," said Ned. "This is the famous 'Devil's Backbone,' — *El Espinaso del Diablo.* String up your Sierra nerves, Tom, and follow."

Dismounting, we led our trembling horses across the narrow path, and thence rode onward deeper and deeper into the heart of the mountains. Sometimes along narrow ledges where a single false step would have plunged us down to the rocks a thousand feet below, now mounting painfully upward, and now cautiously descending, we were everywhere in the midst of grand and awful scenery.

" How delighted one of those old Pharaohs would have been to set up an obelisk like that in his door-yard!" remarked Ned.

The mountain to which he pointed was a tremendous column of granite, a thousand feet in thickness at the base, and tapering gradually upward to an apex that seemed to pierce the clouds.

At night we camped beside a stream in the valley east of the first range of the Cordilleras.

Day after day we rode toward the east, through the same wild scenery. Here and there we came to villages lying snugly in the valleys or perched on mountain ledges. Sometimes we met troops of peasants with loads of fruit on their backs, supported by a strap across the forehead. We had no adventure worthy of record until the fifth day from Mazatlan.

About an hour after noon, on the 30th of January, as we rode quietly along a mountain ledge in single file, suddenly the sharp crack of a rifle sounded just ahead of us. Immediately a second and a third explosion followed, and the rocky walls and peaks that before had awed us by the majesty of their silence, caught up the sounds and hurled them back and forth from cliff to cliff, until the three distinct explosions we had heard were mingled in a roar like a whole battalion of musketry. Piercing this fearful uproar, as we gazed about for an

" A startling scene was suddenly swung into sight." — *Page* 106.

instant, there came a sharp cry of distress, and the words, " Help ! Murder ! "

About ten rods in advance of us the cliff projected in a huge, beetling crag that hung far over the path and cut off the view of all that lay beyond. At this cry for help we urged our horses forward, eager to render assistance to what seemed to be a fellow-countryman in danger. I was riding first, and as my horse rounded the jutting crag, a startling scene was suddenly swung into sight before me.

A rough, rocky slope lay ahead, thickly overgrown with scrub-oaks and chapparal. Close to the cliff that still formed an inaccessible wall on the right hand, the road wound down the rather steep declivity in a direction nearly at right angles to the one we had been following. About twenty yards distant, in the middle of the road, was a group of men and horses. One man lay in the dust, flat on his face, with arms outstretched, and motionless. Two others who had dismounted were busy at the saddle of one of the horses, and two more were engaged in a hand-to-hand struggle on horseback. Of the men thus grappling, one had lost his hat, and his red hair stuck out wildly in all directions ; the other was a powerful Mexican, with heavy dark mustache, and sombrero pulled down over his eyes.

All these details were flashed into my brain in an instant, and almost simultaneously I heard an exclamation from Ned, who was close behind, followed by the crack of his revolver, and a sharp *whing* as the bullet sped past my ear. The dark Mexican reeled in his saddle, and letting go his hold of the other man, clapped one hand to his cheek, then suddenly wheeled his horse and darted off into the thicket, followed by the two others, who had now remounted. The red-haired man was left alone with the prostrate form in the dust, and the riderless horse that was cropping the leaves by the roadside.

For a moment the stranger glanced at us as if in doubt whether he had to face new enemies, then dismounting, bent over his fallen comrade. He turned the body over and lifted the limp, powerless arm, that fell back lifeless in the dust. Then he tore open the flannel shirt and eagerly placed his fingers over the heart. Mournfully shaking his head, and taking no note of our presence, he began talking in a low voice, and with an accent that unmistakingly proclaimed him an Irishman.

"Ah, Micky, Micky," said he, "ye poor, poor lad! Would n't ye spake to me now? Just wan word! Will ye tell me it 's a liar I am, and ye 're not dead at all? Sure 'n' ye would n't be jokin' wid me now, would ye, Micky? Tell me I 'm an old fool to be thinkin' ye 're killed by a dhirty Greaser. Micky! Och! he can't spake at all; and whativer in the worrld 'll ould Dan do now? And what 'll I be sayin' to the poor mother at home, when she asks me for her bye? And you that was the fine brave lad, and the thrue friend to me through it all! Sure 'n' I can't stand it at all;" and he bowed his head in the dust.

A strange sickening feeling crept over me as I looked at those two figures, — the one stretched out motionless in the stony path, a thin stream of blood trickling down from a bullet-hole in the forehead; the other bending over him and swaying back and forth in the intensity of grief. This was our first experience with death, and it caused me feelings that I had not taken into account in any imaginings of what lay before us. During those few moments, all the romance, the excitement of adventure faded from my mind, and left only a homesick longing for the old desk in Boston.

Presently the Irishman started up and began again in a louder voice: "Micky! Maybe ye can hear me, if ye can't spake to me. I tell ye I 'll have a revenge for this day's work if iver I come convanient to that bloody scoundrel José Miguel!"

I started at the sound of this name, and glanced inquiringly at Ned. He nodded in answer to my look. I coughed slightly, and the Irishman turned, as if he had forgotten our presence. He rose, drew his sleeve across his eyes, and advanced to meet us, extending his hand with a rude courtesy. He was beginning to address us in Spanish, but Ned interrupted him, saying: —

"We are not Mexicans, but Americans, my friend. Speak English."

"The Lord be praised, then," answered he; and then continued, as he shook us both warmly by the hand: "Ye 'll pardon me, gentlemen! What with the poor lad lyin' dead there, I was forgettin' that it 's me own life ye 've saved this day."

We dismounted, and I said, "Do you know this José Miguel?"

"I niver set eyes on the dhirty scoundrel barrin' a week ago, when Micky and me was drinkin' with him and his gang friendly like in Durango, beyant there. And Micky, he was always a bit free, poor bye! and what wid the strong drink settin' him up a thrifle, he was showin' some of the gold, and — but wait a bit," continued he, and stepping to his comrade's horse he examined the saddle. In a moment he turned away again, shaking his head. "It's gone," said he; "divil a rap left. Four thousand dollars, gentlemen, the fruit of me ten years' work, — all gone in a minute, to fill the bellies of them nasty Greasers. It's hard; whin all's said and done, it's a hard blow."

"How were you carrying it?" asked I.

"We had it all stowed safe inside Micky's saddle, and niver a man would iver suspicioned it, but for Micky's foolish talk in the saloon."

"Well," said Ned, "we're going to Durango; you'd better go back with us. There's a chance you may get some trace of the gang."

"Did you recognize Don José, Ned?" I inquired.

"At the first glance," answered he; "and hereafter any one may recognize him by my mark on his cheek."

"And do yez know the scalawag?" asked the Irishman.

"We saw him in California," replied I.

"'T was a good shot ye made at him," continued our new acquaintance. "I wish to God it had been a thrifle closer."

"It's a wonder I hit him at all," replied Ned. "It was only a snap shot."

We buried the murdered man by the roadside, digging a shallow grave with our hatchets, and covering it with a pile of stones.

Over the rude monument thus erected, the Irishman placed a wooden cross, — another memorial added to the hundreds which like milestones, speak to the traveller on these wild Mexican highways, of his increasing distance from the regions of law and order.

Packing our baggage on the horse that Micky had ridden, we all three continued on our way to Durango. A gloom had fallen over us, and Ned in particular was very silent. I knew of what he was thinking, and wondered what effect this new knowledge of Don José's character would have on his feeling for Maggie.

As we rode along, our new companion told us his story. His name was Dan O'Connor. He and his friend Micky Donohue had left their homes in the west of Ireland some ten years before. They had shipped as sailors on an English merchant-vessel trading to South American ports, and after five years' experience in this and other ships, had finally saved enough from their wages to start in a small cattle-business in Buenos Ayres. With varying fortunes, occasionally sending small remittances to their friends, they had finally resolved in the fall of 1877 to take their whole proceeds, amounting to some four thousand dollars, and go back to Ireland, with the intention of bringing their mothers and sisters to America.

Having business in San Francisco, they had come to Vera Cruz, and were on the way to Mazatlan to take the California steamer, when they fell in with a party of Mexicans in Durango. With sailor-like freedom they had caroused and boasted of their success, and Micky, somewhat under the influence of the fiery Mexican drinks, had made some indiscreet disclosures. The last important event in their history was the attack of their former acquaintances and our appearance, in time probably to save the life of Dan.

We grew very fond of our new friend. He was a genuine specimen of a good-hearted, rollicking Irishman, and his experience in knocking about the world had enlarged his views, and enabled him to give us many a bit of advice that proved serviceable afterward.

We journeyed on together, keeping a wary eye out for another attack, but were unmolested; and on the 4th of February we came out on the rugged plateau, in one corner of which stood the city of Durango.

It proved to be a dreary, dirty town, and as we rode through the unpaved streets, eyes and noses alike suffered from the surroundings.

At a saloon where a bottle and glass hung out for a sign, Dan pulled up and dismounted. We followed him inside, and waited while he interviewed the proprietor. The latter remembered seeing Dan and his companion drinking with some Mexicans, but disclaimed any acquaintance with the party, and had seen none of them since.

"I knew how 't would be, byes," said Dan, turning to us. "If he knows he won't tell, and if he don't know he can't tell, so there ye have the whole of it."

We tried a drink of pulque, the national beverage, but neither Ned nor I could stand more than a swallow of it ; and even Dan, who claimed to drink everything, pronounced "poolky" a "thrifle too haythen" for him.

Outside the saloon we held a council.

"Dan," said Ned, "you don't want to go to San Francisco now. Why not keep on with us? We 're going to Havana, and then across to Europe. You can work back to Ireland that way."

"Divil a bit of the grane sod of ould Ireland will I see now, and me as empty-handed as the day I left it ; but I 'll just go on wid yez to Havanny, and then skip down to Bwanes Ares and thry if me friends 'll help me start in the cattle agin."

So we left Durango, and set out for the south, with nearly seven hundred miles of mountain and plateau to cross before reaching the capital.

Travelling early in the morning and resting during the heat of the day, we could average nearly forty miles with comfort to ourselves and no great fatigue to our beasts, although Dan's horse was rather inclined to lag behind.

Not unfrequently we could hear our friend a few rods back, reasoning in a crescendo style of argument, beginning with a plaintive expostulation, such as, "Come, now, could n't ye step up a bit, and not be disgracin' me wid yer laziness?" and ending with a wild whoop, and a dig of the spurs that brought "Old Bones" clattering over the stones with ears laid back, and a look of desperation in his eyes.

The scenery was an endless succession of beautiful pictures, varying from fertile valleys where the sun was hot, and the loaded orange-trees swung their fruit within reach of our unscrupulous hands, to lofty mountain-passes where the wind was bitter chill, and the bare, volcanic rocks, with here and there a dismal cactus, were our only surroundings.

Occasionally we stopped overnight in the towns through which we passed. More often, where the location was inviting, we slept under the stars, and our bright camp-fire added an extra touch of weirdness to the wild scenery about us. The weather was always magnificent, and the nights clear and cool.

As we entered a little village near Leon, one evening, a party of young men and girls were enjoying a dance on a platform erected in the village plaza. We joined the group, and after some conversation, Ned and I produced our flutes and took our places with the orchestra, which consisted of a violin and two guitars.

The music was a wild, monotonous air, full of abrupt pauses and minor runs, and we had some difficulty in catching the tune. At last, however, we got the swing of the time, and were greeted with great clapping of hands.

Dan, after frantic efforts to understand the mysterious figures, finally gave it up in despair, and executed a genuine Irish jig, swinging a shillelah over his head and whooping at every caper, to the delight of the spectators.

Of all the cities that we visited on our route to the capital, none seemed so interesting as Guanaxato. It lies in the very heart of the mountains. Standing in the plaza, the only spot of level ground in the city, one gazes up in all directions, as from the arena of an amphitheatre. Winding roads, twisting back and forth, creep up the rocky slopes between crowding houses, past tall steeples, and under the spreading foliage of orange and lemon trees, until far above the last picturesque cottage one sees the barren rocks and solitary cactus of the mountain-side still reaching up toward the sky.

" Byes," said Dan, as we stood and looked about for an exit, " have yez e'er a bit of a balloon wid yez, till we sail out of this hole ? "

Through a narrow ravine between the mountain walls we made our escape, and kept on toward the south.

At Queretaro we drank to the memory of poor Maximilian, whose schemes for the regeneration of Mexico were so abruptly terminated by his cruel death.

" 'T would have been betther for the Greasers av they 'd let him live," remarked Dan.

Queretaro boasts of quite a business in the manufacture of cigars, or cheroots, from tobacco grown in the surrounding country. They have a peculiar, pungent flavor which we learned to like.

On the 25th of February we suddenly emerged from the mountains upon the great plateau of Mexico, a wide, level plain, surrounded by lofty peaks, among which the massive figures of Popocatapetl, and his wife of the unpronounceable name, rose pre-eminent. The twin lakes glistened in the sunlight, and the great city, with its white-walled buildings, its spires and towers unnumbered, lay between.

We rode through the crowded market-place, where women with cigarettes in their mouths sat under canvas awnings and sorted fruit or plucked fowls, where children rolled among the vegetables, and gayly-dressed Mexicans sauntered with their hands in their pockets, down through a long business street bright with the display of a thousand varieties of wares, where señoras and señoritas reclined in their carriages and fastidiously examined the piles of goods held on the arms of attentive salesmen, through the beautiful plaza set with thousands of shade-trees and surrounded by the imposing fronts of cathedrals and public buildings, and pulled up at last before the hotel Iturbide.

" Is n't this rather high for our purse, Ned?" said I.

" Let 's have one taste of Mexican style," replied he. " I 'm a trifle tired of tortillas and cheap grub."

No sooner were our quarters assigned to us, than Ned rushed off to the Post-Office, whence he returned, radiant, with a whole armful of letters from Maggie. He had written to her from nearly every town on our route, and had given her a glowing account of our rescue of Dan, without, however, any mention of Don José's name. In the last of her letters she was very bitter in her denunciations of the bloodthirsty men who had attacked Dan. Ned read this passage aloud, and looked inquiringly at me. Understanding his thought, and wishing to cheer him, I said : —

" I feel sure, Ned, that she does n't know anything of Don José's real character."

" So do I, Tom ; and I have promised to trust her, and not ask about the matter, but — it worries me."

However, the letters consoled him wonderfully, and the shadow seemed only temporary.

In the evening I picked up an old copy of a New York illustrated paper, and behold! surmounted by a startling heading, was Ned's letter that he had written after leaving the Sierras. While we were looking at it a gentleman approached, and hearing our conversation, introduced himself as a Mr. L——, of New York. He assured us of the interest with which he had followed the accounts of our wanderings, and said that since reading this very letter he had made a bet of five hundred dollars that we would accomplish our undertaking.

As we were talking, others approached, and we found ourselves the heroes of the hour. Champagne and cigars were ordered, and Ned, Dan, and myself were the objects of quite an ovation.

Of course, we had to relate all our adventures, and then to listen to as many routes of future travel as there were gentlemen present.

"But we have given up that sort of thing," said Ned. "We have learned that man proposes, and the state of the treasury and the opportunity of the hour dispose. It 's much easier to trim our sails to the breeze that blows, and not to fret too much about the direction of it."

"Have you no plans, then, beyond Mexico?" asked some one.

"Oh, yes," replied I. "We shall go from here to Havana, and beyond that, all we can see is Europe. The particular port we arrive at will be determined by the vessel we get a chance to sail on."

We spent the following day, the 26th, in taking a hasty view of the scenes of interest in and about the capital, and in mailing the twelfth letters to our respective journals. We had done most of our writing with lead-pencils at odd moments on our route, a page or two at our noon halts, and now and then a scrap on horseback. Ned's sketches were some of them genuine reproductions of the scenes we had visited, and not a few wholly the offspring of his vivid imagination.

In the evening, when we returned to the hotel, I recollect that Dan and I had to unite our forces in an argument with Ned. The latter was possessed of a devil in the shape of an insane desire to get to the top of every high mountain we encountered. He had set his heart now on climbing Popocatapetl. Dan was utterly unable to understand such an inclination.

"Phwat in the divil would yez be doin' on the top of ould Popo?" he inquired. "Sure, 'n' I think the resate of thim letthers has unsettled yer moind, Ned, me bye. If ye go, it's meself that 'll set quiet here in the hotel Itterbeedy wid me cigars and me cocktail, and speculate on the folly of human indavors."

At last Ned was persuaded, though unwillingly, to abandon the project, and we made our preparations to start for Vera Cruz on the following day.

The distance from Mexico city to the Atlantic is about two hundred and fifty miles, and marked by all the peculiar beauties of Mexican scenery.

We descended by gradual stages, from the climate and productions of the temperate zone, down to the tropical regions of the *tierra caliente*.

The scenery before reaching the lowlands is full of startling beauty and grandeur. The mountain-passes, the sudden, wide stretches of landscape that break upon the view with all the tropical wealth of color, are enchanting.

When we came in sight of the volcano of Orizaba, rising like an immense sugar-loaf seventeen thousand feet from the plain, I involuntarily uttered an exclamation of delight; but Dan stopped me, waving his hand mysteriously at Ned, who was plodding along wrapped in dreams of Maggie.

"Whisht!" said he, "he's slapeing. Don't speak till we 're past the mountain, or the divil 'll be in him again."

On the 3d of March we came in sight of the level coast plain, and for the first time in ten months saw the blue waves of the Atlantic. The old walled city of Vera Cruz was in view, a pinkish spot on the edge of the horizon, and beyond we could see the fortress of San Juan D'Ulloa, and two or three vessels riding at anchor near the shore. On the following day we entered the city, and at once set about disposing of our horses.

After several visits to dealers, we decided to have an auction, Dan agreeing to officiate as auctioneer. The horses Ned and I rode had proved themselves exceptionally fine beasts, having made a journey of over twenty-two hundred miles without the slightest injury to themselves. We finally knocked them off for ninety dollars apiece, including saddles.

The expense of our trip through Mexico had been $48.50, so

we found ourselves now in possession of $371.50, or $131.50 more than we had when we left Visalia to enter the Sierras.

Dan, after a great deal of Irish-American-Spanish eloquence, succeeded in getting a bid of thirty-five dollars apiece for the horses that he and Micky had ridden. He chuckled as he pocketed the money, and remarked to us, —

"That 's the very same Micky and me paid for them whin they was new."

Without waiting to explore Vera Cruz, we purchased tickets for Havana by the steamer that was to sail the next day. A "norther" was blowing down the coast as we went aboard, and the vessel was cutting up all sorts of capers at her anchorage, filling my stomach with direful forebodings of the future.

However, on the next day the wind moderated to a pleasant breeze, and the four days' trip to Havana was a delightful change after our three months in the saddle. We arrived in safety on the 9th of March, and took up our quarters in a small hotel not far from the docks. The fourth city of our pilgrimage was reached.

CHAPTER VII.

AR-REACH-ing views of harbor thronged with shipping, of picturesque low-lying hills and fortress - crowned heights, and streets so narrow that one must squeeze against the walls to let the hurtling vehicles go by; buildings painted in the most brilliant hues of red, green, blue, and yellow, and streets ankle, nay, knee deep with mud and filth; flowers and fruits blooming and ripening in tropical profusion, and a stench going up to heaven, the combined and concentrated extract of all earth's vilest odors; careless, happy indolence, a true lotus-eater's indifference to all ambitions, in the movement and speech of every man one meets, and yet all about one the rattle and jingle of volantes, the shrieking of steam-whistles, the shouts of drivers and the songs of gangs of negroes, — an incessant din beside which the busiest American city would seem silent; gayly-dressed ladies sweeping past in their flying two-wheeled carriages, their long skirts streaming in the air on each side, or perhaps in the next half-hour the same ladies peering with their great dark eyes from behind the prison-like bars of their windows, — such, in brief, is

Havana, a city of contradictions, the most charming and the most detestable town that human art has ever placed on the bosom of Mother Earth.

After a long day of sight-seeing, of dodging volantes, smoking good cigars, and talking bad Spanish, Ned and I returned to our room with certificates of our actual presence in Havana safely filed among our other papers. Dan had declined to accompany us, preferring to spend the day among the shipping, in hope of securing a passage to Buenos Ayres. As we entered the room he met us at the door, one finger on his lips, and the most comical expression of wonder in his eyes.

"Whisht!" said he in a whisper. "Don't spake, or he 'll hear yez!"

"Who?" said we, in unison.

"Now, can't ye wait a bit, and I 'll tell yez. Byes, I 've thravelled in Europe, Asia, Africa, and Ameriky, let alone one thrip to Australy. I 've heerd ivery language, barrin' a few haythen ones; but divil saze me if I iver heerd a jaw-breaker like what that chap in the room beyant is sayin' to himself. Whisht! There now! Will yez listen to that?"

At the instant, a sonorous voice in the next room began, —

"'Mæcenas atavis edite regibus — '"

That was enough! With a simultaneous roar Ned and I caught up the line, —

"'O et presidi' et dulce decus meum!'" and Ned continued, without a break in his voice, "Are ye there, Captain Chambers, oh?"

A moment, and the door opened, to disclose the stately form of the captain himself, bland and calm, smiling as if surprise were the farthest emotion from his mind.

"Welcome to Havana, comrades!" said he, as he grasped us each by the hand. "Have you put a girdle round the great earth so soon? I left you in San Francisco, with minds intent on far Cathay."

"But the coast line has deflected us," I answered, "and we are now refluent."

"The American continent is certainly spacious enough for most men's vibrations, though I believe you were pledged to more remote wanderings. But come," continued he, "make me acquainted with your companion here. To judge from his ejaculations, my innocent Horace has somewhat amazed him."

"Faith, 'n' I niver thought to hear English spoken wid that tongue of yours," said Dan, as he shook hands with the captain.

"And now," said our new-found friend, seating himself, "I am consumed with curiosity to hear your adventures. How a journey to China can result in arrival at Havana, must needs prove interesting."

"But you have n't explained your presence yet," said Ned. "What brings you to the tropics so opportunely?"

"My friend," answered the captain, "you know that I am erratic. I was seized with a longing for Havana, — and here I am. There, you have my whole story. And now for yours."

"Wait a bit," said Dan; "business before pleasure." And thereupon he proceeded to tell us how he had found at the docks an old friend in command of a vessel bound for Buenos Ayres; how easily he had persuaded him that he needed an extra hand before the mast.

"And, byes," continued he, getting more excited, "that is n't the best of it. Ye 've got to go wid me. Captain Jones has a fine cabin, wid the most illegant accommodations for several passengers, and he says he 'll take yez to Bwanes Arys for forty dollars apiece, board and lodgin' thrown in. Come, now ! Yez have to go there sometime, — yez 'll niver have a betther chance ; and he sails to-morrow. And, be the Powers !" he continued, his brows contracting, "that dhirty rascal, José Miguel, came to him a week ago looking for a passage to Bwanes Arys, and went away again because the captain did n't sail soon enough."

There was silence for an instant. I happened to be looking at Captain Chambers, and fancied that he glanced up quickly at the sound of that name. Perhaps I was mistaken. At all events, the captain inquired in the most matter-of-fact voice :

"And who may José Miguel be?"

"A good text for our adventures," answered Ned. "But what do you say to South America, Tom? Why not do up the continent all at once, — Buenos Ayres, across the pampas to Valparaiso, up to Lima, and then good-by to the New World? The scheme likes me well."

"'A bird in the hand—'" said I. "Probably, as Dan says, it's the best chance we shall have. I cast my vote for South America."

"I have never visited Buenos Ayres," remarked the captain; then, turning to Dan, "Do you suppose your friend could accommodate three?"

"Faith, and we'll make him!" responded that worthy; and thereupon we all set upon the captain and easily persuaded him to accompany us to Buenos Ayres. Then while we regaled ourselves with choice "Henry Clays" fresh from the factory, Ned went over the old story of our adventures. The personal incidents of the narrative, the close relations of Ned and Maggie, were omitted from the account, and José Miguel made his first appearance on the Mexican highway, where we rescued Dan from his attack.

"And the next time we see that gentleman," Ned remarked, in conclusion, "there will be wailing and gnashing of teeth."

"And a divil of a walin' it'll be if I'm around," supplemented Dan.

We went down to supper, the captain calm and thoughtful, Dan jubilant, Ned engrossed with reawakened memories of Maggie, and I, as usual, forming the chorus and speculating about the other actors.

The good ship "Mary Anne," of New Bedford, Mass., Captain Jones, after ten days' anchorage in the harbor of Havana, finally spread her sails on the evening of March 11th, and got under way for Buenos Ayres, bearing an addition to her previous society in the shape of four individuals, known respectively as Daniel O'Connor, able-bodied seaman, Captain John Chambers, independent gentleman, Ned Markham, and Thomas Jackson.

It would scarcely be interesting to dwell in detail on the incidents that relieve in some slight degree the monotony of a six weeks' voyage on a sailing-vessel. They are always nearly the same. Tremendous excitement over the capture of a shark, great interest in the flying-fish, dismal backing and filling in the "doldrums," sailors' yarns spun under the witchery of a tropical night at sea, awful impressiveness of the fact that we were actually crossing the line, the sublime majesty of the Southern Cross (only specially sublime because it is the

Southern Cross), now and then a short gale of wind that upset the chairs and tables, and ditto my stomach, the wonderful beauty of a ship at sea, the excitement, mostly confined to Ned and myself, when, after four weeks of trackless ocean, we one day sighted the shores of Brazil, — all these things are intensely interesting to one who enjoys them for the first time, but have been so often described as to need no more than a passing mention here.

Our quarters were very comfortable, if not quite so "illegant" as Dan had promised us. We improved our superabundant leisure in studying the ropes and spars, and making ourselves as familiar as possible with the duties of a sailor, against a time when we might have to take a similar trip without the eighty dollars that insured our present comfort.

It was only after considerable practice that I could venture up the rigging, and "lay out" on a swinging yard above the boiling sea. Climbing the Sierras was bad enough; but the Sierras did not dance and pitch in all conceivable ways, as the ship did. However, before the trip was over, both Ned and I felt as much at home hanging on by our eyelids at the end of a swaying pole as we did on the firm planks of the deck.

Captain Chambers remained much the same, — calm, courteous, and impenetrable. I began half-unconsciously to weave a warp of mystery about him. Who was he? What was he?

One thing I discovered in spite of his reserve. He was very anxious to reach the end of the voyage; else why was he so elated when the wind was fair, and we were flying through the water with every thread of canvas drawing, and why did he walk the deck and gaze so gloomily at the sea and the sky when we were rolling idly in the dreadful doldrums?

"Nonsense!" said Ned, in answer to a remark of mine; "every one feels the same way. You do yourself."

We had been sitting on deck for several hours when this conversation took place. It was nearly eleven o'clock at night, — one of those supremely beautiful nights found nowhere but in the tropics. The great ocean that stretched away on all sides to the dim horizon was sleeping a quiet, peaceful slumber, and its long-drawn breaths lifted us so gently that the motion was barely perceptible. Our little vessel was the centre of a vast, glassy surface, glowing in the intense light of a full, tropical moon. Here and there a fish coming to the air left a momentary trail of brilliant, phosphorescent flashes behind him. The only sounds we could hear were the occasional faint creak of a spar, the low voices of two of the watch spinning yarns at the other end of the vessel, and the regular, military tread of Captain Chambers as he paced the deck at some distance from where we were sitting. The smoke of our cigars rose straight into the rigging above, and drifted this way and that, nestling in the folds of the idle sails.

"No, Ned," said I, "such a man as Captain Chambers claims to be, — a mere *dilettante*, whose whole time is passed in wandering aimlessly about the world, — does n't betray such feverish anxiety to get to the end of a journey, to arrive at a place where he has absolutely nothing to do. There is something hidden under that calm, indifferent courtesy of manner. His travels have an object ; and his trip to Buenos Ayres was not the result of the chance that threw him in our way, — if chance it were."

"Of course," answered Ned, "you always scent a mystery in the behavior of every man that does n't gush like a schoolgirl. Come, now ! What elaborate romance have you developed for our harmless friend the captain ? "

" I know of no romance. I have only been speculating about a history that I believe is very unusual. But it eludes me. We seem destined to encounter mysteries, Ned, — female as well as male."

We smoked for a long time in silence. I was thinking of a thousand things, — of the eventful year that was nearly gone, of the impenetrable future, of the old office in Boston, of the strange dreams of foreign lands that had filled my boyhood, of the moon, — of everything and of nothing.

Suddenly Ned disturbed my reverie by saying with a rather forced laugh : —

"Well, have you solved the female mystery ? "

"No," answered I, yawning, "I leave all female mysteries to your more capable hands."

"Now, don't draw back in your shell, Tom ; tell me honestly, for once, what you think of Maggie, and of that Miguel matter. Never mind my feelings ; I want to know what your real opinion is."

Ned spoke rather loud. Was it my fancy, or did the captain pause for an instant in his walk?

"Ned," said I, "you ask me not to spare your feelings. Then you mus' n't be angry if I put the case in what seems to me a common-sense light. A young lady, very beautiful, and (pardon me) extremely fond of admiration, is sent away to boarding-school at the age of fifteen. She goes into society in New York, and undoubtedly meets some people whom her family would not altogether approve of. In a year and a half she is suddenly taken from New York and sent to the other end of the continent, — to San Francisco. A year later she comes home, and for six months is kept in the seclusion of a California ranch.

" 'Two young men drop down providentially into her little world, and one of them, a very good-looking and (pardon me again) susceptible fellow, betrays in every movement and look his profound admiration of this young lady. She is pleased ; of course she is delighted. This is what she has been accustomed to, and long-enforced abstinence has whetted her appetite.

" But another mysterious being appears on the scene, — a dark, handsome villain such as boarding-school young ladies always rave over. This especial villain is one whom the young lady has met before, how many times only they themselves know. She makes a secret appointment with this José Miguel, and when surprised with him in the forest is thrown into the most violent alarm. As soon as the family hear of his having been in the neighborhood, they are all in consternation. Everything has apparently been planned to keep these two apart. The father spends a whole evening in reasoning, expostulating, entreating her never to see this man again. He finally threatens to disown her if she persists."

" But, Tom — "

" One moment ; wait till I am through, and then show me where I am wrong. The young man begins, in spite of his devotion, to distrust this girl that has secret meetings with Spaniards of questionable character. He shows an indifference of manner that is very striking after his previous attentions. The young lady is piqued. Whether she loved this youth or not, she evidently wished to have him love her. Her pique disarms her, and betrays her into admitting a love for him, or perhaps the determination to have his love makes her seem to yield that she may really conquer. With the usual pathetical promises they separate for four years.

"Ned, my boy, you asked me to tell you exactly what I thought. You know that it pains me to say this as much as it does you to hear it; but — the common-sense world would agree with me."

"The common-sense world be damned!" and after this outburst Ned lapsed into a gloomy silence.

At last he rose, and pitched his cigar far out into the water, where it made a flashing, undulating circle in the shining surface.

"Tom," said he, "I forgive you. You know not what you say. How can you? True love is as far above the grovelling paltry dictates of common-sense as that moon, sailing so grandly through the sky, is above this helpless, loitering ship. Do you think, in your wisdom, that you know Maggie better than I? Did you hear her tell me that she loved me; that I might trust her as I would my own soul; that *no one* should ever come between us? Tom, I shall trust her and love her in spite of everything, until I know with absolute certainty that I have been deceived; and then — "

"And then?" said I.

"Well," with a sudden laugh, "then it will afford me great satisfaction to be kicked. Come, let 's turn in."

"Wait a moment, Ned," said I; "I have done what I could to cure you of this love, that I believed would bring you only unhappiness. Now that you have declared so strongly your determination not to give it up, I should be a cheap sort of friend if I tormented you any longer. I honor you for your trust, and henceforth you will find me an ardent champion of the young lady that you have chosen. I believe that my impressions were wrong."

We grasped each other's hands in the moonlight.

As we turned to go, I suddenly thought of Captain Chambers. He had disappeared. Looking about, I perceived a dark figure seated on a coil of rope near the mast, and close to where we had been talking. It was Captain Chambers, apparently fast asleep. At the first touch he started.

"By Jove!" said he, "I did actually go to sleep. I had been

thinking for some time of the advisability of going below, but I could n't tear myself from the chaste embraces of the goddess above there, —

> ' Phœbe silvarumque potens Diana,
>   Lucidum cœli decus — ' "

He walked aft, and paused by the man at the helm.

" Do you believe that he slept here for an instant? " asked I.

" Pshaw, Tom ; what do we care whether he did or not? " replied Ned.   " You are trying to fathom some mystery of his ; why should n't he have the same privilege with regard to us? He 's welcome to all he heard."

The big. hearty voice of old Tim at the wheel sounded distinctly in the silence, as he said to Captain Chambers : —

" Lord bless you, sir !   Do you see that bank of clouds down there on the port-quarter?   Long before you turn out to-morrow she 'll be flying through the water like a duck through a puddle."

So we turned in.

After making his calculations at noon on the 24th of April, Captain Jones informed us that we were at the mouth of the Rio de la Plata, and about two hundred miles from Buenos Ayres.   We had had on the whole a very prosperous voyage, having encountered nothing like a storm, and only lost two or three days at the line.

" If we get in without one of those plaguy pamperos," said Captain Jones, " it 'll be the best run I ever made."

But that " plaguy pampero " was waiting for us.   About three o'clock in the afternoon, the wind, that had blown steadily from the northeast all day, suddenly gave out, and a dead calm succeeded.

Captain Jones was worried and anxious.

" We 're going to catch it ! " remarked he, as he passed us ; and we saw him gazing long and earnestly through his glass, toward the west.

As we watched the horizon, a low dark cloud began gradually to creep up and spread slowly over the sky.   Soon the order was given, —

" All hands take in sail ! " and in an instant the drowsy vessel became a scene of activity.   Orders were given with amazing rapidity, men and ropes were flying about the deck, and above the shouting and the creaking of blocks and spars, a low distant moan crept to our ears from far across the breathless water.

The dark cloud mounted higher and higher, torn frequently by jagged lightning, and the dull, incessant roar became louder each instant.

Captain Chambers, Ned, and myself stood in a sheltered place and watched the approaching storm. Dan rushed past us, waved his hand, and shouted : —

" It 's the divil's own, byes ! "

A light breath of air fanned our cheeks.

" There she comes ! " shouted Ned ; and in a moment the water began to leap into little foam-crested wavelets. A thick pall of darkness settled over the ship, accompanied by a misty, drizzling rain, and the wind became terrific. We were obliged to hang to one another and to the ropes, to prevent being blown overboard. The ship plunged and groaned, the cordage rattled, and the double-reefed mainsail flapped and strained as if about to be torn from the bolt-ropes.

The storm spoke with all the tones of an orchestra. Below and underlying all was the dismal, portentous moaning of the trombones and bass-viols ; the appalling strokes of the waves upon the vessel's sides were like the thunder of the drum ; and above our heads the wind whistled and shrieked and howled through the rigging with the sound of a legion of violins, flutes, and piccolos gone mad. It was a veritable " Ride of the Walkyries," without rhythm.

And the sea ! Every one has heard of waves " mountain high," but only when one clings to the deck of a reeling, pitching vessel, and looks *up* at those stupendous masses of inky water beside which the whole ship seems like an atom, sees those huge, formless monsters leaping and chasing, spitting at each other over his very head, — only then does one realize what the expression means.

And yet in spite of the terror of the situation I found myself interested in watching my companions. All conversation was out of the question. Ned stood clutching me with one hand and Captain Chambers with the other. His face was pale, and his gaze wandered restlessly up into the rigging, back and forth over the ship, and out into the boiling waste around us ; Captain Chambers was as calm and unruffled as ever, only his eyes seemed glued to one point, straight out toward the west. Occasionally his lips moved. What was he saying, I wondered. A sudden lurch of the vessel swung me round in front, so that his mouth came close to my ear. I caught the words, " Shall find him in spite of — "

At last, worn out and drenched to the skin, we crawled with infinite precaution to the companion-way, and rolled down into the cabin.

In a few moments, Captain Jones tumbled down after us, looking like old Father Neptune himself.

" A bad night, gentlemen ! " said he, — " a bad night ; but the old ' Mary Anne ' rides like a bird. You 'll join me in a glass to her health ; " and we were all glad of a pull at the flask of whiskey that he offered.

" Now, I advise you to turn in," continued he ; " the worst is over, and you 'll find all right in the morning ; " and he disappeared up the ladder again.

The next day verified the old tar's prediction. The storm had disappeared, and though the waves were still very high, the sky was clear, and with a fair northeast wind the ship was leaning over and ploughing merrily through the waves toward her destination.

"Good-morning, gentlemen," said Captain Chambers, approaching with his military salute. "This is an improvement. If the wind holds, we ought to sup in Buenos Ayres."

"How long do you expect to remain there, captain?" I inquired.

"Oh, until some other place occurs to me. I never loiter very long in one town."

How eagerly we watched for the first glimpse of land! Long after Dan told us we were already in the river, we strained our eyes in vain. At last a low reedy shore gradually rose into sight to the southwest, and at five o'clock, on the 25th of April, we dropped anchor opposite the city of Buenos Ayres.

It was a grand sight from the river. Covering a wide expanse of plain, with picturesque towers rising here and there among the lower buildings, the magnificent dome of the cathedral and the massive theatre standing out in bold relief against the sky, the city was far superior to anything we had looked for in benighted South America.

Captain Chambers, Dan, Ned, and myself landed together and ate a thoroughly good dinner.

"Now," said Ned, as we rose from the table, "you and I, Tom, have no time to lose. A South American May is a North American November, and this is the 25th of April. We have a thousand miles of plain to cross, and beyond that the Andes. To attempt to pass a high mountain range in the middle of winter would be madness. Ergo, we must be in Mendoza in two weeks."

"Faith, then," said Dan, "there 's only one way ye can do it."

"And how 's that?" I asked.

"By post-horses. Ye go from here to Rosario by the steamer, then in the saddle from post to post, changing horses ivery dozen miles or so. It 's the divil of a way to thravel, and av yez ain't tough it 'll kill yez, but ye can cover a hundred miles a day."

"We 're tough enough," said Ned, "but how much will it cost?"

"About seventy-five dollars, all told."

"'Tom, how about funds?'"

" Balance in treasury, $238.50," replied I.

" And we 've reached a pass now where new clothes are not a luxury but a necessity," continued Ned, holding up his arms to show the tattered condition of his coat. " The first thing, then, is to go with Dan to look up his friends, secure our papers, buy something to cover our nakedness, and to-morrow we take the steamer for Rosario. Not, Tom?"

" Agreed," answered I.

As we prepared to leave the hotel, Captain Chambers held out his hand.

" I shall spend the evening and to-morrow in looking about the town," said he, " and shall hardly be apt to see you again."

" I shall only say *au revoir*, Captain," said I. " I have a presentiment that fate will bring us together again in some quarter of the globe."

" I sincerely hope fate will be so kind to me," he answered, and so we left him.

" A quare divil, that captain," said Dan. " Seems loike there 's something in his moind all the toime."

" Put me down for a false prophet, Ned," said I, " if we don't meet him again within two years."

We secured our papers from the United States consul, engaged passage for Rosario on the steamer that left in the morning, and then went the rounds with Dan among his cattle-dealing acquaintances. He was welcomed like one risen from the dead ; and when his story was told, offers of assistance, positions, and salaries were plentiful. It was easy to see that Dan was a favorite among the guild.

Then under his guidance we visited a large clothing establishment, where for forty dollars we procured a couple of stout, serviceable, though not altogether elegant suits, and an extra flannel shirt apiece.

Dan was jubilant as we returned to the hotel, and the only thing that seemed to sadden him was the thought of our early departure. For himself, his prospects were all that could be hoped for. We promised to keep him informed of our movements, and he agreed to let us know of his success.

" And, Dan," said Ned, " if that José Miguel should happen to turn up, don't fail to let us hear what becomes of him."

" Faith, 'n' I 'll tell yez that same ! " he answered ; and his expressive gesture indicated what he intended should become of him.

The captain was gone when we reached the hotel. He had departed, leaving no trace behind him.

The next morning, after a few finishing touches, we mailed our newspaper letters, and Ned as usual addressed one to Miss Margaret French. After a hearty farewell to Dan, we embarked on the steamer and puffed slowly up the river to Rosario, which we reached about noon the next day.

Guachos and horses were abundant, and we soon engaged a picturesque-looking fellow and three half-wild horses, and prepared once more to live in the saddle.

What do I know of the nine hundred miles of pampas that we crossed in the next ten days? My brain whirls at the recollection of that wild, incessant gallop.

We made from ten to twenty miles at a stretch, then, dizzy and benumbed, we dropped to the ground, hastily swallowed a few mouthfuls of beef and gulped down a few cups of water while new horses were being saddled, then up again and away, faster and faster, until our horses were reeking with sweat, and their sides, pierced by our spurs, were dripping with blood.

The cattle stared sleepily or scampered wildly before us, our guacho guide shrieked in our ears, the sombre, boundless plain whirled its endless monotony before our dizzy eyes as we swept on our way toward the west. All day long we were urging our horses to their utmost speed, and not unfrequently tired a dozen mounts in as many hours.

How we ever stood the fatigue is a mystery.

At nightfall we dropped down anywhere, slept soundly on our saddles, and by daybreak were up and away again with renewed vigor. I believe that the constant diet of beef and water was the only thing that enabled us to endure the killing exertion.

The evening of April 30th found us at Rio Cuarto, quite a thriving Spanish settlement ; and having been gone from New York just a year, we roughly balanced our accounts to see what had been accomplished.

My book showed that our total receipts during the year had been $769.50, and our expenses $590.35, leaving balance on hand, $179.15.

"And the distance-book," remarked Ned, after some calculations, " says that we have travelled approximately 13,300 miles, divided as follows : On foot, 380 miles ; in wagons, 38 miles ; by railroad, 2,457 miles ; by water, 7,950 miles ; and on horseback, 2,475 miles."

During the year we had visited five of our forty cities, and had written fifteen of our hundred newspaper letters.

As we passed the central portion of the great plain, the ground became more rolling, and thickly wooded. Soon we were unmistakably mounting to greater altitudes, and at last the grand range of the Andes appeared, with its eternal snow-capped peaks. We reached Mendoza on the 7th of May, having covered the nine hundred miles from Rosario in ten days, at an expense of about eighty dollars.

We were in capital spirits, and strong as oxen. It seemed as if no exertion could ever fatigue us.

Ned, as usual, was exultant at the thought of scaling the mountains ; but the governor of Mendoza, upon whom we called, would have dampened the ardor of any one less reckless.

" It is absolute madness to attempt the passage of the Cumbre at this season," said he. "The winter storms are liable to begin to-morrow, and in that case you would be infallibly lost. You must wait in Mendoza until October, at least."

We laughed at the idea.

"What!" said Ned, "come nine hundred miles in ten days just for the privilege of sleeping here for six months! Your Excellency does n't know us. We shall pass the Andes though the snow were forty feet deep!"

The old man smiled courteously.

"But you will find no guides willing to accompany you," said he. "Our arrieros are not like you North Americans."

"Guide or no guide, we shall go!" answered Ned. And we left the worthy governor holding up his hands in pious horror at the madness of these Northern savages.

However, as his Excellency had predicted, it was no easy matter to secure a guide. One after another they shook their

heads in dismay at the proposal. Money seemed to have no charms for them. It would be certain death, they said.

At last a young man called Jesu Maria reluctantly admitted that there was a bare possibility of our getting over alive. After that we had no great difficulty, and finally succeeded in inducing him to guide us across the Cumbre and down to San Felipe, he furnishing five mules, and we providing supplies for the party, sufficient to last for two weeks. We promised to pay him sixty dollars when we reached San Felipe.

On the morning of the 8th of May we left Mendoza, mounted on the backs of three fine-looking mules, and leading two others laden with our provisions, guns, blankets, and other bag-

gage. We carried heavy ponchos, or cloaks, and green goggles
to protect our eyes from the glare of the snow.

The whole population of Mendoza seemed to have turned
out to witness the departure of the madmen who were about to
tempt Heaven with their presumption, and many dismal predictions followed our little cavalcade as we rode down the
valley and out of sight of the town.

CHAPTER VIII.

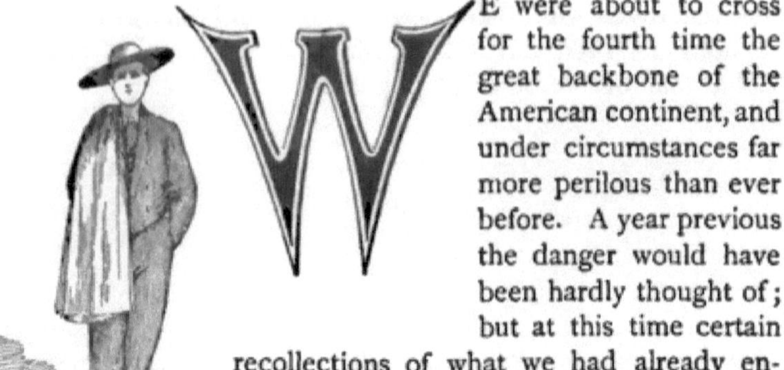

"The Arriero."

WE were about to cross for the fourth time the great backbone of the American continent, and under circumstances far more perilous than ever before. A year previous the danger would have been hardly thought of; but at this time certain recollections of what we had already encountered in the mountains filled me with rather dubious presentiments.

Our guide, the youthful Jesu, had the appearance of a man being led to execution. It was evident that he appreciated the danger at its full value.

" I 'm afraid we shall have trouble with that fellow, after all," remarked Ned, as he trotted up beside me. " By the way he crosses himself and mutters *Aves*, I judge him capable of a sudden fit of remorse for his unparalleled bravery. He may desert us when we need him the most."

" If he shows symptoms of a ' break,' one of us must guard the rear," answered I.

" Hola ! You Jesu !" shouted Ned. " How many storms did you say there had been this season?"

" Three, Patron," answered the guide.

" And how deep do you think the snow is?"

A shrug of the shoulders, and the inevitable " Quien sabe?" was the only response ; and our arriero returned to his beads with renewed fervor, as if the mention of snow had reawakened his religious zeal.

Travelling all day over a rough road, through forests of low thorn-trees, late at night we reached a small collection of huts; and while the guide prepared supper, Ned and I cleaned and loaded our guns, long unused.

In the morning, at four o'clock, we were roused by Jesu, who had breakfast prepared and the mules saddled.

A cup of coffee warmed us up to work, and we set out to reach Uspallata before night. The road became rougher, and we entered the " Paramilla," a region of barren hills, excessively monotonous and uninteresting. Toward evening, however, we descended the last slope, and passing through a cultivated country, with fields of Alfalfa that reminded us of California, we entered Uspallata at about eight o'clock in the evening.

We had been travelling nearly north, so far, edging up toward the mountains gradually and shyly; but on the morning of May 10th we set our faces toward the west, and began to move forward directly upon the enemies' works.

Up and down, over long bleak ridges, through narrow gorges, we followed the course of the Rio Colorado, a foaming torrent that comes from the very heart of the mountains. It was wonderful to note the skill and precision with which the mules placed their hoofs exactly in the only safe places. Sometimes the road, a narrow ledge of rock, seemed absolutely to overhang the roaring stream beneath.

It was hard, painful work toiling up to the first great ridge, but at last it was reached, and we paused to look about. A sublime and beautiful scene lay behind us, but a grander one was before. There, beyond a succession of valleys, rocky hills, and low ranges, lay the stupendous mountain-wall toward which we were travelling. Away up on its heights, flanked by sharp, towering peaks, was the Cumbre Pass. Around and below the summit all was dazzling white.

" Do you see, mi Patron ! " exclaimed the guide, pointing with trembling finger. " The snow ! We shall be lost ! Let us return ! " and he was turning his willing mule about; but Ned seized him roughly by the arm and wheeled him toward the west again.

" See here, my Jesu," said he savagely, " there is the Cumbre

Pass. We are going over that pass, and *you are going with us !* We shall hold you to your bargain ! Commend yourself to the Virgin, for the road to Mendoza lies through Chili ! Now, *Vamos !*"

The fellow looked badly frightened. Ned's Spanish was execrable, but there was that in his manner which told the youth to look out for worse storms than even those of the Cumbre.

We trotted down the rugged slope and continued our way toward the mountains. The scenery was magnificent, but by no means alluring. Rocks and snow, desolation and danger, surrounded us. Dark gulfs opened at our feet, and inaccessible precipices rose beside us. The track wound to the right and the left, around huge bowlders, down short declivities, and up

long and steep ascents, carrying us higher and higher, nearer to
that terrible pass. The sharp wind blew full in our faces. It
began to be bitter cold. Patches of snow appeared beside the
track, gradually becoming more frequent and deeper. until at
last the mules were sometimes wading through drifts several
feet in depth.

The sun had dropped out of sight, and the shadow of the
Cumbre had enveloped us, when we reached the Punto de
las Vacas, where a *casucha,* or house of refuge, had been

erected. It was a rude stone hut, with an opening some seven
feet above the ground. The steps that originally led to this
aerial door had fallen away or been burned for firewood long
ago, and the place looked wofully dilapidated and inhospitable.
Still, this was to be our lodging for the night, and we accepted
its grim shelter very thankfully. The cold wind had been a
severe trial to our faces, grown accustomed to the soft breath of
the tropics, and we lost no time in clambering up the rough wall
and letting ourselves down into the interior, where the uncertain light of a candle that Jesu produced, revealed the luxury
of our apartment. It was just what the outside promised,
— a bare, bleak room, with a snow-drift reaching half across

from the opening; but at least it afforded a shelter from the wind.

"This is not quite regal," said Ned, holding up the candle and peering into the corners. "Still, with a fire, we shall do well enough."

Undoubtedly, with a fire; but where was the fire to come from? The only combustible material we could find, after a prolonged research, was a few charred sticks that had failed to support the life of previous fires. These served us, however, to make a cup of coffee and to warm a slice of beef, and then we nestled together in one corner, wrapped in our double blankets and ponchos, and left the wind to whistle outside, and the poor mules to rub themselves against the lee side of the hut, and nose about for a few dried blades of grass.

All the next day we toiled slowly onward and upward through the snow, seeming to get no nearer to our goal. Grand and terrible it rose before us, away in the distance, and yet appearing close within reach. At night we slept in another casucha, which the guide told us was only a few leagues from the base of the Cumbre.

May 12th dawned clear and cold, and Jesu was in good spirits for the first time.

"The Holy Virgin is with us!" he said. "We shall get over, but we must hasten. The wind will begin by ten o'clock, and the storm may come with it."

"Forward, then!" said Ned. "For the Cumbre!"

The road was terrific. No track was visible in the snow, and a succession of steep ridges, flanked by precipitous ravines, had to be traversed. Huge bowlders obstructed the way, and our route zigzagged back and forth, at each turn rising a few yards higher.

Soon after we left the casucha, my mule began to limp painfully; so, dismounting, I threw the bridle over her neck, and with Ned's rifle on my shoulder started ahead. Picking my way carefully up and down the rocks, and keeping the Cumbre in sight as much as possible, I could trudge through the snow much faster than the laboring mules could follow.

I had perfect confidence in myself, and was so interested in the wild and startling scenery, that I scarcely thought of my companions. It was only after an hour or more that, on glancing behind, I saw that the others had disappeared. I sat down on the summit of a little ridge and waited, expecting momentarily to see them appear on the next elevation behind.

Around me lay a waste of snow and rock. Nothing soft or pleasing met the gaze. All was cold and hard.

Presently a vague mistiness began to spread over the landscape. Objects that had been clear and distinct became blurred and seemed far away. "Snow blindness," thought I, and proceeded to put on my green goggles. But I had suffered no pain, had felt no disposition to close my eyes or to rub them, and even with the glasses on, the same dimness affected my sight.

Suddenly I saw that my poncho was covered with a fine white powder. I started up in alarm. It was snowing! The air was filled with innumerable fine powdery flakes, falling so thickly as to resemble a light mist.

I looked toward the mountains. Where was the pass, — that mighty wall that we had watched so devoutly for two days? It was gone. Its summit and the peaks that rose beside it were covered and obscured by a dark mass of cloud, that rolled swiftly onward from the west, and crowded tumultuously down the mountain-side.

And now the storm began in earnest. Huge flakes came rushing thicker and faster, and in an instant the mountains and all the world were shut out, and I was alone on that desolate ridge, surrounded by a whirling, driving storm of snow and ice.

I turned about in every direction, striving to pierce the snowy gloom. The wind came in fierce gusts, driving sharp fragments and pellets of ice in my face, and as I sat down to cling to the rock, my poncho was caught by the furious gale and ripped up the back like paper.

Gradually the wind seemed to subside, and at last I could stand up with safety. Then I shouted again and again, listening breathlessly each time. The snow fell steadily and silently before me, and no answering call came back. I fired the rifle, but the report sounded dead and muffled, and I knew it would not reach far in that impenetrable storm.

Then for a few moments courage forsook me, and I plunged into the drifts, and rushed madly down the ridge, calling incessantly, and feeling as if I must outrun the storm and gain the open air.

Suddenly came a dread thought! Which side of the ridge was I descending? Was it toward my companions, or away from them? I stopped short, and tried to remember how many times I had turned before leaving the ridge. Which way was I facing when the storm began? Which way did I turn after losing sight of the mountains, — was it left or right? How many times did I look back toward the Cumbre?

For some fifteen minutes, it seemed to me, I stood motionless in the snow, racking my brains to recall in their order every thought and impulse that had brought me to my present predicament. I remember that I constantly repeated aloud, "Patience! Patience! Keep cool! Don't cry out before you 're hurt!"

At last the suspicion grew into conviction, that I had gone down the western side of the slope, toward the Cumbre. But now a new difficulty arose. When the thought first occurred to me that I was going the wrong way, had I paused just as I was, or involuntarily turned about and then stopped? It seemed as if I could remember wheeling round. I looked for footprints. Every trace of them was obliterated. The snow was knee-deep already, and coming thicker all the time.

"But while I am standing idly here, my friends are out in the storm searching for me."

This thought put new life and new recklessness into me, and I began again to plunge madly into the drifts and call at the top of my voice. Suddenly a loose stone rolled from under my foot, and I fell backward in the snow, and in the next instant my heart gave a great bound and stood still. Before me the solid footing came to an end, and the myriad flakes of snow drifted steadily and silently down into an uncertain vacancy. I had fallen on the very brink of a precipice.

Benumbed with cold and stupefied by exhaustion and fright, I wearily retraced my steps. The air seemed to grow colder, and the wind, rising again, drove the storm full in my face, coating eyelids and whiskers with sleet.

"The wind comes from the west," thought I. "I must be moving toward the mountains."

So about again and on for a few moments, and then the storm seemed to meet me again.

Utterly worn out and discouraged, I stopped to rest by the side of a huge rock, and creeping round to a sheltered place, sat down and waited. In a few moments I lay down, and the last thing I remember is drowsily pulling the end of the torn poncho over my face to keep off the drifting snow.

I started up suddenly, with a feeling of suffocation. I could scarcely breathe. The weight of the mountain seemed on my chest. I was snowed in, literally buried.

Forcing the poncho up by main strength, I managed to pack the snow above my face so as to enable me to sit up and breathe more freely. I was quite warm, and but for the closeness and darkness of my prison, would have been very comfortable. However, I began most valiantly to dig out.

On one side was the rock and on the other a soft yielding mass into which I plunged, using the butt of the rifle as a shovel. An hour of unremitting labor, and a tunnel some twenty feet long, brought me to the surface and to the open air.

It was night. The storm was over. Close beside me rose the massive wall of the Cumbre, the moon, nearly at its full, hanging above a dark peak to the north. I stood up to the waist in snow, and behind was the immense drift that had buried me.

A white, silent wilderness lay around me. Gleaming and sparkling fields of snow reflected the frosty light of the moon, and the long, clean-cut shadows of jagged peaks and curiously shaped rocks stood out in striking contrast to the dazzling white. Here and there I could see a darker shadow, the mouth of some tremendous chasm that still yawned unsatisfied. The wind had completely died away, but my nose and ears soon began to testify to the severity of the cold.

Wiping the lock of the rifle, I put in a fresh cartridge and fired it in the air. Instantly a joyful shout answered me, and soon two dark figures appeared on the ridge to the east. After a few moments of floundering through the drifts, Ned and I were locked in a very fraternal embrace.

"Why in thunder did n't you answer us before?" asked he. "We 've been on that ridge, for the last hour, shouting and firing signals."

"I had retired to my chaste and feathery couch," replied I, pointing to the drifts, "and the quilt got pulled over my ears."

At the first sign of the storm, Ned and the guide had turned back to the casucha, calling to me, and supposing that I was close behind them. Then they had passed the day in shouting and firing the shot-gun, and at night, when the storm ended, had set out to find me. It was now nearly midnight, and I must have slept about ten hours under the drift.

Plunging back to the casucha, we found the poor mules shivering in the snow, their ears showing a very dejected droop. After some impromptu refreshments had been served, Jesu proposed that we set out at once to return to Mendoza.

"If I hear you say Mendoza again," said Ned, with the most impressive solemnity, "I shall hurl you into the first chasm we reach! I am what the North Americans call a 'slugger,' and I have been obliged to leave my country for having killed eleven men by blows of the fist. Do not provoke me any more, but get your mules ready and proceed. We shall be on the other side of the mountain before daybreak."

With the guide carefully selecting the way, we began again to work up toward the Cumbre, tramping a path in which the mules followed single file. It was dangerous as well as laborious. Many crevices and deep, narrow chasms were entirely bridged by the snow, and once the ill-used Jesu disappeared from sight, uttering a faint cry as he went down. We had to pull him up by main strength from a deep pit, to the edge of which he clung with both hands.

The final climb up the face of the Cumbre was terrific. Slipping back at every step, sometimes flat on our faces in the snow, sometimes stepping on loose stones that sent us headlong into the drifts, occasionally having to go back and urge on the frightened mules, we puffed and floundered and strained under high pressure, until we reached the summit just as the faint rays of the morning were beginning to shoot up from far behind us.

It was a breathless sight to look back in the uncertain mingling of moonlight and daylight, from an elevation of over twelve thousand feet, out upon the wide, silent sea of the pampas. But we had no time to admire it. The summit of the pass was comparatively free from snow, swept clean by the wind that even now blew fiercely in our faces.

We hurried across, and leaped gayly into the drifts on the other side. The road was not so steep as on the eastern slope, but for that very reason the snow was deeper. It was high noon before we reached the first casucha on the Chilian side. But we were joyful in our success, and the thought of the danger and hardship we had surmounted amply compensated for the fatigue. A few leagues more, and we should be out of reach of cold and snow, in the perpetual summer of the Pacific coast.

As we rested here and refreshed ourselves, we had an opportunity to admire the magnificent scenery. Away beneath us to the north lay the Lake of the Incas, a deep-set tranquil sheet of water from whose shores the perpendicular cliffs rose for thousands of feet in unbroken grandeur. To the east lay the snow-buried valley we had just traversed, bounded by that defiant wall that we could now survey with a calm superiority. To the west was a succession of ridges and valleys, fading away in the limitless distance below.

The poor mules found a little fodder on a bare spot beside the casucha, and after our usual hearty meal of beef and coffee, we were ready to start again.

Gradually, as we descended, the snow disappeared, and at last the track was clear. We trotted merrily over the rocks, down, down, past the tremendous cliffs at the Ojos de Agua, and following the course of a dashing torrent, stopped for the night at a copper-smelting establishment, and made ourselves at home in one of the huts that surrounded it.

As we sat around the fire and smoked, we talked as usual of our future plans.

"This is the 13th of May," said I ; "if all our travelling could be as rapid as the trip from Buenos Ayres, we should be sure of the prize-money."

"Let 's see," answered Ned, blowing out a huge cloud of smoke. "We shall have to face the music in earnest now! Funds low. Have you had rough and tumble enough to feel ready for a ' 'fore-the-mast' experience?"

"Ready for anything!" answered I. "I think if we were stuck on a log in the middle of the Pacific we could hoist my dilapidated poncho on the end of a walking-stick and sail into Melbourne without a mishap."

"After Valparaiso, we must make Lima," said he. "We ought to be in Lima by about the 1st of June."

Before the close of the following day we were down in civilized regions, staying overnight at the flourishing little town of Santa Rosa. A wide, macadamized road, through cultivated fields, vineyards, and peach-orchards, brought us to San Felipe at about noon on May 15th.

We paid the courageous Jesu his well-earned sixty dollars, and left him and his mules meditating together on how they were to pass the winter in Chili. Of one thing we were quite satisfied, — they would not return to Mendoza before spring.

Then, feeling somewhat like cats in a strange garret, we took our seats in the railroad-car, and were whirled down to the coast by steam, reaching Valparaiso in the evening. We had swung across the continent for the third time, and once more the mighty Pacific barred our farther way toward the west.

The next day we clung to our little room in the hotel. Since leaving Buenos Ayres, the only writing we had done had been the few notes hastily jotted down in our journals at the end of each day's ride. Two readable letters of specified length had to be mailed in Valparaiso, to say nothing of a document of unspecified length which Ned felt called upon to mail to a young lady in California.

In the morning we intrusted our labors to the post, called upon the American consul, who entertained us most hospitably for an hour or more, and gave us his autograph, and then we repaired to our room again for a council of war.

The results of our debate were briefly these : Money in treasury, eighteen dollars, not sufficient to pay fare to Lima. Must either try to work our passage, or stay in Valparaiso until we could make another "raise." Resolved unanimously to adopt the former alternative.

Valparaiso is one of the principal ports of South America, a city of sailors emphatically. In the lower town, and in certain quarters, one encounters almost nothing but rough, half-clad seamen of every nation in the world. Some of the vilest dens to be found in any city on earth are crowded together along the narrow streets, and resonant with the profanity and vulgar songs of drunken carousers. Much of the city, however, is quite attractive ; and up on the plateau, where most of the well-to-do merchants and the wealthy foreign population reside, there are many handsome residences and well-kept grounds.

The harbor is filled with vessels from every port in the world, and it seemed an easy matter to Ned and myself to find a ship bound for Lima.

At about eleven o'clock we descended the stairway that led from the upper town down toward the docks, and paused on one of the piers to take a look at the shipping. Two men hurried past us, coming from the town, and one of them hailed us.

" Holloa, you fellows ! Are you English, Dutch, or Spanish? Do you want a berth?"

"Guess again, captain," said Ned. "We 're Americans, and we do want a berth."

" Tumble in lively, then, boys. I 'm short two hands, and I 'd as soon have Yankees as any one."

"Well, but hold on a bit, captain," continued Ned. "Let 's start fair. We 've never shipped as sailors."

"What the devil are you talking about, then?" said the man, angrily. "Perhaps you 'd like to ship as captains ! "

"Don't get excited," said Ned ; "give a man a chance to explain. We 've never actually been before the mast, but we 've been passengers on a sailing-vessel, and spent all our time in studying up the business.

"That 's a rum go !" answered the captain with a sneer. "When and where did you make that practice-trip of yours?"

" Left Havana on the 17th of March, and arrived in Buenos Ayres on the 25th of April; ship 'Mary Anne' of New Bedford, Captain Jones."

"What year?"

"This year."

The captain fairly snorted: "It must have been a fast-sailing steamer that brought you round! In Buenos Ayres on the 25th of April, and looking for a berth in Valparaiso on the 17th of May! Do you want me to call you a damned liar?"

"If you do, you'll get kicked off the dock," answered Ned, quietly.

Strange to say, the man didn't seem angry, but rather pleased.

"Well, how did you get here?" he asked.

"Came across!" answered Ned.

"Across what?"

"Across the continent."

The stranger's bushy eyebrows went way out of sight, and his face was the very picture of scorn as he replied: —

"A thousand miles of pampas without a railroad, and the Andes in the month of May, and all in three weeks! How deep was the snow?"

"A matter of four feet or so," replied Ned. "Captain, I know that sounds like a big yarn, but we have proofs of having been in Buenos Ayres on the 25th of April. However, that doesn't matter. We're here now, and we want to ship. We're tough, have seen hard service, and if you want a couple of hands, I'll guarantee you'll be satisfied with us. We don't care what you pay us if you only go to the right ports."

"What proof have you of having been in Buenos Ayres?"

Without answering, Ned drew out a bundle of letters, and selecting one marked "Buenos Ayres" handed it to the captain. The latter unfolded it, and read: —

BUENOS AYRES, April 26, 1878.

On this day appeared in my office a young man calling himself "Edward G. Markham," of Philadelphia, U. S. A., and requested me to certify to his presence in this city, which I do with pleasure.

[Seal.]   (Signed) ——— —— ———,

U. S. Consul at Buenos Ayres.

"That's correct," said the captain, looking at us with increased interest. "You're a rum couple, any way. Who are you, and where do you want to go?"

"We're a couple of fellows travelling about the world on our muscle and our wits, and just at present we should like to go to Lima."

"By gad! I think by the trim of you, you've more muscle than wit. I like your looks, though, boys, and I'd like to give you a berth. But Lima! Lord! My ship's the 'Falcon,' of Portsmouth, one hundred and one days out, and bound for Honolulu, Manilla, and Melbourne. If those towns are in your line, why, come along; I'll give you a fair show, and pay you what I think you're worth."

"What do you say, Tom?" said Ned, eagerly. "Honolulu, Manilla, and Melbourne. That's a big lift!"

"And Lima?" inquired I.

"Oh, we'll have to take our chances on getting back there somehow."

"All right!"

"Captain," said Ned, "we'll go with you. How soon do you sail?"

"Just as damned quick as I can get aboard. I've wasted fifteen minutes palavering with you chaps, now."

"Well, give us ten minutes more to get our traps from the lodging-house there, and we'll join you."

"Hurry up, then. I'll wait fifteen minutes for you, and then, good-by."

We flew up to the hotel. Ned scratched a line to Maggie, and I one to Dan, telling them to address us at Melbourne, and we were on the dock again in eight minutes. The captain was waiting, watch in hand.

"Good!" said he. "I like to see a man a little better than his word."

A six-oared gig was lying at the end of the pier, with four sailors lounging about. They straightened up as we approached.

"What are you going to do with those guns?" asked the captain.

"Going to give them to you to look after until we reach Melbourne," answered Ned.

"Good! I'll give you a receipt when we get on board.

Now, then, boys, shove along there, and give these fellows an oar. Let's see ; what are your names, — Markham and — "

"Jackson," said I.

"Now make her fly, Mr. Smith," said the captain, seating himself.

The man whom he addressed, and who had been with him on the dock, took his seat, and gave the order to "Give way !"

I suspected that we were to have a hard run, and my suspicions were verified. The ship was about three fourths of a mile away, and after the first quarter the movement became more rapid till we were on a spurt at the very top notch of speed. But they had mistaken their victims. Ned and I had pulled in too many races to be flurried or disturbed by a little dash like this. The man in front of us puffed and strained and splashed, but we took the water firm and steady as clock-work. I saw the captain smiling as he watched us. When the vessel was reached, the four sailors, including the stroke oar himself, were puffing like porpoises ; but if we had choked to death, neither Ned nor I would have betrayed any exhaustion.

As we stepped on board, the captain spoke to a man who was walking the quarter-deck.

"Get the ship under way at once, Mr. Williams," said he ; then, turning to us, "Markham and Jackson, report at the cabin."

The captain took his seat in the cabin, and we stood respectfully before him.

"Boys," said he, "my name's Captain Johnson, of the ship 'Falcon.' I've been captain of one vessel or another for the last twenty years. I've had sailors of every nation and of every kind, but I'll be damned if I ever had two fellows like you !"

"What's the matter with us?" asked Ned.

" Hold your jaw till you're spoken to. I've taken a kind of fancy to you two fellows. — Came across from Buenos Ayres. — Letter from the Yankee consul. — Hm ! — I 'll tell you what it is, boys, I never meddle with any man's business. — Hard enough to look after my own. — Hm ! — If you like to tell me something about yourselves, perhaps it might be a good thing for you."

Ned and I looked at each other. This harangue evidently meant, "If you satisfy my curiosity, perhaps I 'll be your friend ; if not, look out for storms ! "

" Fire away, Ned ! " said I.

So Ned began, and told rapidly our scheme and the most important events of our travels, leaving out all mention of Maggie, Captain Chambers, and José Miguel.

When he had done, the captain rose, and slapped him heartily on the back.

"Now, damn me if I don't like that ! " said he. " You Yankees are plucky. I 'm glad you told me, boys, and I 'll help you all I can. When we reach port, you can have your time on shore, and I won't blow on you. If you come up to the mark, you 'll get an A.B.'s wages. Now tumble up, and report to the mate."

He shook us each by the hand, and we went on deck.

CHAPTER IX.

T was the 17th of May, 1878, when, as foremast hands of the ship "Falcon," we bade a long farewell to the western continent. We realized that now at last we must buckle down to work, — not work with the stimulus and inspiration that alleviates and even glorifies labor undertaken voluntarily and independently, but hard, wretched drudgery, under the orders of a stern master.

A man must be endowed with an unquenchable thirst for romance, to extract much poetry from a sailor's life — after experience. But for a year we had been accustoming ourselves to face this probability in imagination, and we met it now unflinchingly.

And it was not so bad, after all. What if our bunks were dark and cold, and the smell of bilge-water almost overpowering! We consoled ourselves by remembering that at least our bed was not so bad as the ragged edge of a precipice or the heart of a snow-drift. What if we were surrounded and housed with all sorts of rough characters, dirty, foul-mouthed, and uncouth! What if our fare was " dog's-body," " junk," " souse," and " dandy funk," — dishes known only to the *menu* of the toilers of the deep! Still, we were strong, healthy, inured to hardship, and accustomed to make light of it ; and Ned at least, under the coarse exteriors of our companions, knew how to find his way to warm hearts and friendly feelings.

There were Englishmen, Americans, Germans, Swedes, and Spaniards in the crew, but the English element naturally predominated. The foreigners were hailed indiscriminately as " Dutchmen " or " Portagees," — the former title applying to the light, and the latter to the dark type.

We got along well enough after the first breaking-in. As soon as assigned to our watches and shown our quarters, we had to run the gauntlet of a series of petty persecutions and ribald jokes, such as new-comers are almost always subjected to among a lot of old tars ; but we strove to take all in good humor, knowing full well that the slightest symptom of rebellion would bring a tenfold weight of woes upon us.

There was one little Swede named Anson, that made himself particularly obnoxious to us. So long as the rest of the watch were inclined to poke fun at our freshness, he felt secure in the support of numbers, and was always foremost in that tongue valor by which small men often seek to make up for their physical deficiencies ; but one evening something that he said happened to touch the secret spring in Ned's organism, and brought him to his feet as if the chest beneath him were charged with dynamite that some one had exploded. Ned, the good-natured Hercules, the hero of the gymnasium, the master of the hundred-pound dumb-bell, seized the small Anson by the slack of the trousers and the nape of the neck, and held him at arm's length, while he shook him as a terrier would shake a rat. Then with a careless fling over the shoulder he dumped the demoralized offender in a corner and turned to the rest of the watch.

" Messmates," said he, " neither Tom nor I are going to get mad at a good-natured joke now and then. We 're used to rough and tumble, and we don't ask odds of any man. I 'll leave it to you if I did n't serve that dirty little pup right."

" You did that, my hearty ! " said an old sailor, bringing his fist down on the chest ; " you served Dutchy a good un ! Lads, the boys are all right, say I ; let 's give 'em a free course, and not run athwart 'em any more ! "

That was enough. One in authority had spoken, and the rest of the crew easily assented. Ned had conquered ; and under the protection of his strong arm, I came in for my share of good-will.

But there was evidently something about us that our companions failed to comprehend. The second mate, who had been with the captain and heard our conversation on the dock, had told some marvellous stories about us, and it was known that we had had a private confab with the captain as soon as we came on board, and had left guns and other property with him. The story seemed prevalent that we had considerable money with us, and were taking this trip before the mast for some mysterious reason of which the captain was a confidant.

But the captain kept his own counsel, so far as we knew, and we kept ours, and the crew were left to speculate and imagine whatever they chose. It was known that we had expressed a desire to get to Lima, and the boys cudgelled their thick heads to find out why we were going away out across the Pacific in order to reach the capital of Peru.

"It 's a daily conunderum to me how yez will iver rache Leemy this way," said an old Irishman to me one day.

That " conunderum " had bothered both Ned and myself a good deal ; but I shook my head knowingly, and evaded the question, willing to profit by the fictitious importance that a secret always lends to its possessor.

Our thorough gymnastic training, the rough life we had led for the last year, and our practice in the previous trip, soon enabled us to do good work as sailors ; and Ned, after a short time, came to be acknowledged as the best reefer and furler on the vessel. The second mate, in whose watch we were, went aloft as far as the topsails and courses, and was accustomed, from his superior seamanship, to take the post of danger ; but once or twice Ned got ahead of him. This is the privilege of any sailor smart enough, but at the same time it was not at all calculated to win the affection of the mate. The latter was a surly Englishman by the name of Smith, a powerful fellow, but disagreeable and ill-natured, and only respected by the men on account of his ability as a sailor.

One evening during the second dog-watch, from 6 to 8 P. M., when, in fine weather, rough games and practical jokes are allowed among the sailors, some one had carefully balanced a bucket of tar in such a manner that the first one who passed under it would be baptized with its contents.

The second mate happened to be the victim. Purple with rage, his head and face dripping with the nasty mixture, he turned furiously about for some one upon whom to vent his wrath. Ned was standing near, laughing with the others, and toward him the mate sprang.

"You damned Yankee hound!" shouted he, "I'll teach you to play your tricks!" and he seized a rope.

"Keep off!" said Ned, assuming the defensive. "I won't stand that!"

"You won't, won't you? You damned impudent pup!" and more enraged than before he rushed forward.

The rope twined itself around Ned's left arm, while his right fist flew straight out from the shoulder and caught Smith under the eye. There was a sharp crack, and the mate measured his length on the deck. In an instant he was on his feet, and, perfectly blind with rage, he drew a long knife and sprang at Ned again. This time they closed, and I held my breath in dismay ; but the next instant the mate was imprisoned in Ned's long arms, with the knife clutched above his head, helplessly wavering in the air.

A crowd had gathered around, and shouts were heard : " Fair play there ! " " Drop that knife ! " " Squeeze the life out of him ! " " I 'll bet on the Yankee ! " when suddenly the voice of Captain Johnson was heard.

" Stand back there, men ! Let go of him, Markham ! What ! a knife ! You damned murdering dog, I 'll teach you to draw a knife on board my vessel ! Put him in irons ! Markham, report at the cabin ! "

Smith was put in irons and taken below, struggling furiously, and Ned followed the captain to the cabin.

Eight bells struck, we went below, and quiet reigned throughout the vessel.

In a short time Ned appeared in the forecastle, and was at once greeted with a chorus of inquiries : " What 's the news, messmate ? " " Was the old man ugly ? " " Did you tell him how it was ? "

" It 's all right, boys," answered Ned. " Captain Johnson was sitting on the quarter-deck and saw the whole thing."

After being kept in irons for twenty-four hours, Smith was broken, and took the position of a common sailor ; while Ned, as the best seaman on the ship, was promoted to the vacant place of second mate.

There was some little grumbling at a raw recruit being preferred to so many men of experience ; but Ned had become popular with the crew, who called him " the big Yankee," and did not fail to recognize his ability. We were in luck again ; but there was no doubt that we had made at least one bitter enemy on the vessel, who was quite capable of playing us a dirty trick if he had a chance.

This slight diversion in the monotony of the voyage occurred on the 24th of June, when we had been thirty-eight days out from Valparaiso, and were nearing the line. So far we had had fairly good weather ; but now began the calms, light baffling winds, and sudden squalls, that make the neighborhood of the equator so unpleasant for a sailing-vessel.

Under the impetus of a short breeze from the south we ran

across famously on the 28th of June, and a few hours later were rolling helplessly on the long glassy waves, without a breath stirring the sails. It was intensely hot, and Ned and I, who had come aboard with only the rough, heavy clothing we had bought in Buenos Ayres, suffered severely. Now and then, when an opportunity offered, we took a plunge overboard, heedless of sharks, so tempting was the water, and so unbearable the heat of the air.

On the 30th of June, soon after six bells in the evening, the crew were lounging listlessly about the deck, too hot and uncomfortable to indulge in the rough games that usually enlivened this part of the day, when suddenly, without the least warning, a huge black cloud bore down upon us from the southwest. Before any one knew what had happened, the ship was staggering under a full press of canvas before a roaring gale, at every leap plunging her nose into the waves that rapidly mounted higher.

The order was promptly given to take in sail, and in the midst of a deluge of rain, with the vessel pitching before a violent gale, and in a sudden darkness like that of night, we hurried aloft.

I was hanging on with tooth and nail, striving to clutch and secure the flapping canvas, when suddenly the ship gave a tremendous roll, a heavy body whizzed past me with a cry, and in an instant arose that dreadful shout, "A man overboard!" Some one had lost his hold and been pitched far out into the foaming sea.

Even as I clung there desperately, with the yard at one moment rushing down toward the black waves that rose to meet it, and in the next flying far back into the air again, one thought consoled and cheered me. It could not have been Ned that had fallen, for his place was below me, while the unfortunate man had been thrown from some yard higher up.

When at last our work was done, and exhausted and trembling we reached the slippery deck, there was a chorus of exclamations: "Who was it?" "Who's missing?" "How did it happen?" and those old weather-beaten tars were peering anxiously into one another's faces, shaking hands as each recognized a chosen friend or comrade, and speaking hearty words of congratulation and good-will. The instant I touched the deck, Ned grasped my hand in that tremendous grip of his. He said not a word, but his face, in the weird light of the storm, spoke volumes.

It soon transpired that the unfortunate sailor was a Spaniard known as Pedro. Everything had been done that the circumstances would permit, but that was not much. Buoys, spars, and planks had been thrown out, but it was impossible to launch a boat in such a sea, and to attempt to put the ship about and bring her up into the wind would have been madness. We tore through the water at the rate of fifteen knots an hour, and that little spark of human life that had burned and flickered through forty years or more was left leagues and leagues behind, to be quenched forever in the immensity of the ocean.

There were no jokes that evening in the forecastle. The men sat quietly smoking their pipes, and the conversation naturally turned on the poor fellow that had lost the number of his mess.

"A quare divil of a Portagee he was!" said the old Irishman. "So quiet like, and snaky! Seemed loike he was always thrying to dodge a press-gang."

"More like it was a peeler he was afeard of," said another. "They Portagees is mostly murderin' some one when they gets ashore."

"Whist now, lads!" said an old tar, knocking the ashes from his pipe and emphasizing his remarks by striking the bowl upon his hand. "You mark me! No good ever comes of speaking ill of the dead. The poor lad 's gone to Davy Jones. Let him rest! I 'm not the one as wants to see him again."

An approving murmur followed these words. Sailors are proverbially superstitious, and there were probably not more than two or three in the party who did not deem it quite probable that the drowned Pedro would appear in the vessel again.

"Where did he ship from?" inquired I.

"We picked him up at the Canaries, where we put in for water," answered some one. "He was there wid his chest all ready, waitin' for a vessel bound for Melbourne."

"Did he ever mention any friends, or tell where his home was?"

A number of voices replied: "No." "Never mentioned nothing." "Kept a close mouth." "He was a deep un."

One sailor finally said : "Maybe old Smith could say somethin' about him. They used to spin great yarns together."

"It spakes divilish well for the pair of 'em," said the Irishman. "They was a tough crowd, take 'em both togither. And now I bethink me, byes, it was Pedro's knife that Smith drawed on the big Yankee."

When approached the next day, however, Smith swore with a volley of oaths that he knew nothing about the fellow, except that his name was Pedro Nevarro, and that he was bound for Melbourne.

As usual in such cases, the property of the drowned sailor was put up at auction. The chest was brought on deck and its contents offered piece by piece, the steward officiating as auctioneer. Each article was knocked off to the highest bidder, and the amount of his bid charged against his wages.

A light sailor's blouse, packed at the bottom of the chest, and apparently new, was the last thing brought to light. It would have been very acceptable either to Ned or to myself; but Ned could never have got his huge shoulders and long arms into it, so after a few bids it fell to me.

As soon as my watch was over, I repaired to the forecastle to try on my new garment. It was an ordinary sailor's blouse, but the collar was folded in and sewed at some distance down the back. As I put it on, something crackled very much unlike cloth. Upon feeling of the collar, I discovered that there were undoubtedly papers concealed in the enclosed space that I had noticed. There was no one in the forecastle, and to take out my knife and rip up the collar was the work of an instant. Three folded papers fell out, one of them enclosed in a torn envelope, on the remnant of which appeared the letters, "Pedro Nev—," and underneath, "Ca—."

"Cairo, — Canada, — Canton, —Aha ! Cadiz !" thought I. "He was picked up not far from the coast of Spain."

But upon unfolding the papers my curiosity was increased instead of being satisfied. Every one of them was written in cipher, the characters employed being Arabic figures written closely together and separated only by commas, with no date, heading, or signature. One of the papers bore at the bottom the mark of a circular stamp, showing a dagger and pistol crossed over a bag of gold.

The sound of some one approaching disturbed me, and hastily thrusting the papers into my pocket, I put on the blouse and went on deck.

It was a dead calm. The sun poured its vertical rays fiercely on the glassy water. The watch on duty were engaged in little odd jobs about the vessel, — splicing ropes, mending sails, painting, etc., — and the rest of the crew were lounging about in whatever sheltered spots they could find.

I looked about for Ned, and discovered him squatted in front of the mizzen-mast, making a sketch of the forward part of the vessel. After carefully examining my discoveries, he remarked : —

"Figures have a reputation for not lying, Tom, but the truth in them is sometimes not extremely obvious. Where did you find these valuable contributions to mathematics?"

"Sewed into the collar of my recent purchase, the blouse of our modest Pedro," I answered.

"Whew!" said he, with a long-drawn whistle. "Another mystery! Tom, you are evidently intended for a detective. A man who has such blind luck in stumbling upon hidden things would be an invaluable aid to the police force. Do you expect to solve these mathematical puzzles?"

"That 's exactly what I intend to do."

"Well, good luck to you, my boy! By the time you see New York again you may have made a beginning. But recollect one thing. We don't know how many languages our friend Pedro understood, and these ciphers may be composed in something that 's Greek even to your vast linguistic acquirements."

"But I know that the man to whom they were addressed was a Spaniard, and the presumption is that his letters were written in that language. I shall try them on that basis first."

How I toiled over those mysterious ciphers! All my leisure moments were devoted to making different arrangements of the alphabet and numbering the letters. The longest of the cryptograms, and the one over which I labored the most, presented this appearance : —

44,333,6,7,2,22,666,66,5,55,7,4,333,222,2,44,99,444,555,0,
333,44,555,11,5,33,44,2,22,333,6,111,22,99,2,88,88,333,22,333,
99,77,111,0,333,99,2,44,333,2,55,99,1,111,44,111,44,99,6,2,1,

111,44,111,44,99,00,111,444,444, 333,99,111,00.2, 5,11,11, 333,
44,11,77,2,5,4,111,44,99,99, 555,4, 33,2,4, 333,2, 88,444, 555,22,
55,111,44.7,6,111,7,111,55,55,4,111,88,333,4,2,88,111,22,6,111,
555,11,55,333,11,11, 333,22, 555,44, 222,111, 99,555,8, 44,2,11,
55,111,11,333,22,99,333,222,333,1,00,333,22,1, 555, 444, 5,333,
55.

The figures 1,555,444,5,333,55, which came at the end of
this letter, also formed the conclusion of another of the three,
the shorter of the two remaining ones, and the one which bore
the dagger-and-pistol stamp. The presumption was that this

was a signature ; but whether the last name alone, the Christian
and family name, or the family name with initials only, was of
course a matter of mere conjecture.

The mystery had taken entire possession of me. I hardly
thought of anything else. The position of every figure in each
of the three papers became rooted in memory, and even when
I was swinging at the end of a yard, that tantalizing row of
figures danced before my eyes.

It was the 7th of July when we sighted the tall, bare cliffs of

Oahu, and before night we had passed the barrier reef, and were anchored in the harbor of Honolulu. The little town nestles at the base of a semicircle of hills and cliffs, and with its low white houses and beautiful palm-trees, creeping down to the bright blue waters of the Pacific and arched by the cloudless sky, it was a wonderfully attractive picture.

We landed at the foot of a long street where loaded trucks were standing, and dodging the crowd of Kanakas dressed in rainbow-hues, the men in straw hats and the women in "Mother Hubbard" dresses, we walked past warehouses, sample-rooms, and billiard-saloons, where sailors and dock-loafers were smoking and swearing. It really seemed quite like home.

After some research we secured a room for the few days that the vessel was to remain in port, and I at once produced my all-absorbing cipher letters.

"Now, Ned," said I, "life has but one object for me until I solve this mystery. Is your letter ready to mail?"

"It will be in half an hour."

"Then take pity on me, and put mine into shape. There are my notes."

"All right, my boy; whittle away at your mathematics, and I 'll do the literary."

So Ned sat down to his writing, and I to my figuring. I was now at leisure, and could devote my whole attention to the work; and in problems of this sort, that is the chief essential.

Years before, I had read Edgar A. Poe's ingenious story of "The Gold Bug," and now I racked my brains to remember how the cipher in that story was solved.

Taking the longest of the three cryptograms, I counted the number of times each character occurred, and tabulated them thus : —

333 occurs 19 times	6 occurs 5 times	77 occurs 2 times
111 " 17 "	5 " 5 "	666 " 1 "
44 " 14 "	88 " 5 "	66 " 1 "
2 " 13 "	7 " 4 "	0 " 1 "
99 " 11 "	1 " 4 "	33 " 1 "
22 " 9 "	444 " 4 "	8 " 1 "
55 " 8 "	222 " 3 "	
11 " 8 "	00 " 3 "	

Now, in the English language the letter "E" occurs more frequently than any other; but how was it in the Spanish? My knowledge of that language was very limited, and I stopped to recall a list of Spanish words to memory. Then I began to wonder why, after all, the papers might not be written in English. Pedro certainly understood English, and there was no evidence that he knew any language except that and his own. Now, a cipher letter addressed to a person in Spain, as one of these undoubtedly was, would probably not be composed in Spanish if the writer and the person to whom the letter was sent understood any other language. The chances were decidedly against these papers being written in Spanish, and in that case they were probably in English. So with new inspiration I began to work on that basis.

The character "333" was the most frequently employed, being used nineteen times in the letter I was examining. "Let's try that as an 'E,'" thought I. When the substitution was effected, the six characters that I had supposed to form a signature, read, "1,555,444,5,e,55."

This did n't suggest any name in particular, and I began to examine the other five characters. The character "55" appeared eight times on the paper, and I noticed that in one place it was repeated, like a doubled letter. Here, then, was a letter occurring rather frequently, and once doubled. The letter "L" was at once suggested. I substituted "L" for "55" in the signature, and it became, "1,555,444,5,el." With the violence of a sudden blow, with a shock that took away my breath and drew from me a startled exclamation, there rushed into my brain the name "Miguel."

"What is it?" asked Ned, looking up from his writing.

"What is it?" answered I, feverishly writing in the newly found letters in the places of their representatives; "I have solved it! Ned, it is wonderful, wonderful!"

"'And yet again wonderful!'" said he, incredulously; "'and after that out of all whooping.'"

He came and looked over my shoulder, and smiled pityingly as he saw the name "Miguel."

"Tom," said he, "many a better head than yours has come to grief by brooding over one idea."

"Ned," said I, "I tell you I never once thought of it. The

wonder is that I did n't. It has worked itself out logically, and without any guidance from me but the ordinary methods of solving a cryptogram."

The cipher as rewritten appeared thus : —

44,e,6,7,2,22,666,66,u,l,7,4,e,222,2,44,99,g,i,o,e,44, i, 11, u,
33,44,2,22,e,6,111,22,99,2,88, 88,e,22,e,99,77,111,o,e,99,2,44,
e,2,l,99,m,111,44,111,44,99,6,2,m,111,44,111,44,99,oo,111,g,
g,e,99,111,oo,2,u,11,11,e,44,11,77,2,u,4,111,44,99, 99,i,4,33,2,4,
e,2,88,g,i,22,l,111,44,7,6,111,7,111,l,l,4,111,88,e,4,2, 88, 111, 22,
6,111,i,11,l, e,11,11,e,22,i,44,222,111,99, i, 8,44,2,11,l,111,11,e,
22,99,e,222,e,m,e,oo,22,m,i,g,u,e,l.

And now the fever was at its climax. Never in my life have I found fingers so tardy a companion to brain. Suggestions crowded so thick and fast that before I had one set of letters half written in, another set dawned upon me. Ned too became excited, and frequently we fairly shouted in unison a word that the scattered letters suggested.

After the signature, our next clew was at the beginning of the letter. We naturally expected the name of the town and the date. There, not far from the first characters, appeared the letters " u, l." " July," thought I, and immediately seized upon two more letters, " J " and " Y." After the name of the month must come the day of the month. We had only one letter in the word following " July." That was the second one, — " E." It might be July second, seventh, or tenth. The word " second " just fitted the space as far as the letter " G." Again I filled in the letters "s, e, c, o, n," and " d " wherever the characters appeared that represented them, and then the whole thing became clear as daylight. It was only child's play to complete it, and it appeared, without the punctuation marks and spaces : —

" newyorkjulysecondgivenitupnorewardofferedhavedoneoldma
nandwomanandbaggedabouttenthousanddisposeofgirlanywayallsa
fesofarwaitletterincadiznotlaterdecembermiguel."

The reader will have no more difficulty than we did in pointing it off and dividing the words so as to make it read intelligibly.

The letter enclosed in the torn envelope read : —

" Paris, December third, seventy-seven.   By order of chief now in California, report in Melbourne early as possible.   Bring recruit if find one desirable.   Order two hundred in.   Amos."

The third letter, the one which bore the dagger-and-pistol stamp, was as follows : —

" Derwent, Melbourne.   Pay Pedro Nevarro two hundred dollars.   Miguel."

" You notice, Ned," said I, when we had carefully compared the three papers, " that the chief, Miguel, was in California in December, '77.   So were we."

" Yes," said he, " there 's no doubt as to what ' Miguel ' is referred to.   And this order for two hundred dollars was enclosed in the torn envelope with the other letter, which explains the rather condensed phrase, ' order two hundred in.' "

" And who do you think the girl is that 's to be disposed of ' anyway ' ? " I asked.

For a moment Ned started, but recovered himself presently, smiling.

" Don't be alarmed, my dear boy," said I.   " No one would send an order to a man in Europe to dispose of a girl in California.   It probably refers to some child that this precious gang of scoundrels have stolen from the neighborhood of New York. You notice the phrase, ' No reward offered.' "

" And who are the old man and woman that have been ' done,' I wonder," said he.

" And here," remarked I, " our friend Pedro is instructed to ' bring a recruit.'   I wonder if he had found one."

" I believe he had his eye on one, at least," said Ned, " and the recruit tried to practise his future profession on me."

" You mean Smith," I replied.   " It may be so.   They were great cronies, and Smith was very much disturbed at the idea that he knew anything about Pedro.   Well, we must keep an eye on him.   The principal actors in our little drama seem to be rallying to Melbourne.   Something further may transpire when we reach there."

" One thing at least we may count on," said Ned.   " Fate intends us to be ' José Miguel-ed ' to the end of our trip."

Never have I felt so elated, not even after slaughtering the grizzly, as I did after solving those cipher letters. But what a field of hypothesis and conjecture they opened before us! This José Miguel, who had so mysteriously mixed himself with our trip, turned out to be the leader of an organized band of desperadoes, having a secret alphabet, a stamp, and agents, or representatives, perhaps in all the principal cities of the world.

While Ned was putting the finishing touches to a sketch, I took a sheet of paper and covertly wrote the following letter:

HONOLULU, July 7, 1878.

Dr. W. French.

MY DEAR DOCTOR, — You will remember that one evening during the three months that we enjoyed your kind hospitality I was indiscreet enough to mention a name at your table, which to my great regret produced very unpleasant results. Will you pardon me if I refer once more to the person bearing that name? I have no disposition to pry into any matters that concern yourself or your kind family; but circumstances seem to have worked strangely, since we left you, to bring us into contact with this *José Miguel.* We have encountered him once, have heard of him three times, and are likely to meet him again. If, without speaking of matters that you would prefer not to touch upon, you can give me any information about the antecedents of this man, you will greatly oblige one who is already largely your debtor, and who esteems it an honor to call himself

Your friend,

THOS. JACKSON.

P. S. Ned knows nothing of my having written this letter, and I must request you not to mention it to Miss Maggie. Should you be able and inclined to comply with my request, please address me at Melbourne. We expect to reach that city some time in October.

The news of our adventures you have undoubtedly had through Ned's letters to Maggie. Did you ever hear or know of a man calling himself Captain John Chambers, of New York?

T. J.

It was long past midnight when we turned in; but we had written our letters, solved our enigmas, and pulling the bed around to where we could catch the fresh sea-breeze, we slept the sleep of the weary and the just.

The next two days were passed in wandering about the town and its immediate vicinity, and in visiting the cliffs of Nuuanu, from whose heights we looked down upon the bright valley, the busy little town, and the wide expanse of blue water beyond.

We met many of the natives in our rambles, and their pleasant "aloha," or "good-morning," never failed to greet us. We were sorry when on the third day, July 10th, we received word that the "Falcon" was ready to sail. With renewed feelings of responsibility we resumed our places on board, passed through the narrow gateway, and catching the northeast trade-wind, bore steadily away toward the west. Gradually the tall cliffs faded from sight, and before evening we were once more the centre of a vast circle of water whose circumference touched the sky.

At about noon on July 16th we crossed the 180th degree of longitude, and the day became for us July 17th. We had lost one day of our five years, and could never recover it unless circumstances should lead us across the same degree of longitude from the opposite direction.

A few days later a bit of land to the south rose into sight for a few hours and disappeared again. It was one of the group of Caroline Islands. And then for days and days there was always the same unchanging view of sea and sky.

But on the morning of August 10th, when our watch was called, we were thunder-struck to find the ship to all appearances completely land-locked. On one side, about half a mile from where the vessel lay becalmed, rose a steep, rocky shore, mounting rapidly into high volcanic peaks. On the other, and not two hundred yards distant, was a gently-sloping bank, thickly covered with vegetation growing close down to the water's edge. In the midst of the luxuriant undergrowth, tall palm-trees and giant bamboos reared their stately forms. Here and there, half obscured by the thick foliage, appeared little thatched huts. The notes of strange birds came to our ears, and the dreamy morning air was heavy with spicy fragrance.

I leaned over the gunwale and gazed on that beautiful shore, until it seemed as if I could realize the feelings of those early voyagers, when after long and weary struggling with the unknown sea they came suddenly upon strange and beautiful countries where everything was new and wonderful, and the rest and peacefulness that pervaded the air seemed to their longing souls the evidence that they had found at last the "Happy Islands" of their dreams. I felt again the powerful fascination that had possessed me, when, as a boy of eight years, I had read the Life of Columbus and the Hakluyt collection of voyages, had been in imagination the right-hand man of Magellan or of Captain Cook, and had wept for very bitterness that that age of romance and adventure was gone, and all the world was discovered and put down in prosaic atlases.

But my day-dream was rudely disturbed by a call to "Bear a hand there!" A light breeze had sprung up directly ahead, and, tacking and beating up as well as we could, we managed to double the point, and passed into another seeming lake, when the wind dropped and we were becalmed again.

A native village was in sight, and the captain called for his gig and went ashore. Ned accompanied him as second mate, and I, to my great joy, was detailed to take an oar.

The instant we landed, a crowd of natives surrounded us, jabbering and gesticulating, with fruits and game for sale. We made some purchases, and returned to the ship just in time to catch a capful of wind that came over the mountains.

We were four days in working through the straits, — days that to me were full of enjoyment, in spite of the intense heat. On the 15th of August we dropped anchor in the harbor of Manilla.

A wide, circular bay was around us, and on its surface rode vessels of every nationality, from the curious Chinese junk to the English line-of-battle ship. Here and there we saw a *banca*, or native boat made of a hollow log and arched over by a bamboo roof, gliding out of the river and paddling swiftly behind the hull of some ship. The city with its massive churches and convents, and its low, solidly built Spanish houses, looked strangely old and out of place in the midst of the fresh wealth of tropical life and the graceful huts of the natives that surrounded it and clustered without the walls.

The health officer came on board, and after a brief inspection we were allowed to land. The vessel was to remain in port about a week, and Ned and I gladly availed ourselves of the captain's permission to have our time to ourselves.

Nothing had occurred since leaving Honolulu to throw any light on the Miguel matter. Smith had gone about his work much as usual, surly and uncommunicative, and it seemed as if he particularly avoided both Ned and myself. We concluded that if Pedro had taken him into his confidence at all, he had not told him of the cipher letters.

We should have enjoyed a longer stay in the Philippines. The interior of the island of Luzon was well worth a visit, and the tall peaks that rose behind the city drew from Ned many an exclamation of regret.

The people have a quiet, indolent appearance, — the Spaniards, as usual, full of dignity and importance, and the natives grotesquely imitating the manners of their masters.

In pleasant weather, the Prado, or fashionable drive along the shore of the bay, was lively with vehicles of all sorts. Here sauntered the Manilla swell, with checked trousers, stove-pipe hat, and silk overshirt, the inevitable cigar in his mouth and cane in his hand.

But the rainy season was just beginning, and at times the water came down as it never comes except in the tropics. Then we loafed in the hotel, talked over our plans, and smoked Manilla cigars.

On the 23d of August we were on board the "Falcon" again. We had struck off the eighth city from our list, and began to work our way through the network of islands toward the south. We were too early to get the benefit of the northeast monsoons, and our progress was consequently slow and irregular.

In the neighborhood of the Sooloo islands we were on the lookout for native pirates ; but they rarely attack a vessel except when they find one in distress, and we were unmolested. Passing through the Torres Strait, we skirted the eastern coast of Australia, and arrived opposite the city of Melbourne on the 15th of October.

We had a long talk with Captain Johnson, who expressed regret at parting with us, and his best wishes for the success of our undertaking. Comforted by his words and still more by sixty pounds of his English gold, we left the old "Falcon" that had been our home and our prison for five months, and were once more our own masters.

CHAPTER X.

UCH has been written and said on the subject of presentiments. There may be something hidden under the charlatanry of modern clairvoyance, some germ of truth that science has not yet succeeded in bringing under the focus of its microscope ; but the great majority of cases of so-called "presentiments" can be explained without any invoking of the mysterious or the supernatural.

So, after all, it was not strange that in approaching Melbourne I was haunted by a vague dread of some disaster that awaited us. The constant brooding over those cipher letters, the strange working of events that had again and again brought us, random wanderers on the great earth, into relations with one individual of earth's countless inhabitants, impressed me with a conviction which no logic could controvert, that we were destined to meet the same man again, and in Australia.

But these shadows of coming events were quickly dispelled by the bustle and life of the great city of Melbourne, and by the immediate call upon all our mental activities to decide upon a present and a future course.

" Now," said Ned, " we are thoroughly independent. We have taken our last degree, and are masters of the art of roughing it. We can turn up our noses at old Dame Fortune, and sneer at her cuffs or her caresses. How shall we live in Melbourne ? Shall it be soft, luxurious beds, champagne and fine cigars, at five dollars a day, or our old fare of junk washed down

with poor beer in a sailors' boarding-house at three dollars
a week?"

"Leave it to you, my boy," answered I. "I am *ad utrum-
que paratus*, like yourself. I've forgotten what style or luxury
means. If we get hard up, we have an order on our friend
Derwent, whoever he may be."

"Let's flip up!" proposed Ned, taking a coin from his pocket.
"Heads means style, and tails economy; here goes!"

It came down "tails."

"Chance is wiser than we," said he. "Well, we'll have one
square meal first, anyway. I long for steak and mushrooms,
with a glass of Burgundy."

It was foolish to run such a risk. After five months of sailors'
fare our appetites were immoderate, and so was the bill that we
paid when we had "gone through" a first-class Bond Street
restaurant's stock in trade. We were nearly sick for several days.

But gradually equilibrium was restored, and the realities of
life in the shape of beef and potatoes became amply sufficient
for our needs.

An early visit to the magnificent Post-Office repaid us with
four letters, — three for Ned, of course all in the same dainty
handwriting, and one from the doctor for me. There was no
word from Dan. The doctor's letter was as follows : —

MY DEAR TOM, — We have all followed your adventures
with the greatest interest. Your newspaper reports, supplemented by Ned's letters to Maggie, have strengthened our faith
in your ultimate success. Keep up your pluck, and look out for
your health. Fight shy of contagious diseases. Among the
class of people you are sometimes obliged to associate with,
there is always more or less of danger. And remember that to
travellers a bottle of quinine is more valuable than a revolver.

So much for professional advice.

I am at a loss what to write in answer to your letter. I have
known much of the antecedents of the man you speak of, but as
you have surmised, there are family reasons for my dislike to
give the details of my knowledge even to friends whom I esteem
as I do both you and our whole-souled Ned.

Of one thing I can assure you. I am filled with alarm to
hear that you are likely to be thrown in his way. *Avoid him as*

you would the pestilence. He is a man of education and of unusual ability, and when he chooses, can exert a remarkable influence over those whom he meets, — it pains me to add, particularly over women.

Of the past events in his life I will tell you one. Some four years ago he was tried in the criminal court of New York for a cold-blooded, dastardly murder, and was acquitted almost solely on technical grounds. There is not a shadow of doubt, in my mind at least, that he was guilty of the crime. Since then I personally believe that his life has been an unscrupulous but very skilful defiance of all the laws of God and man.

Let me entreat you, my dear boy, as a sincere friend, if you will allow me, even as a father, *beware of that man.* If he cultivates your friendship, turn the cold shoulder. Unless you avoid him, he will inevitably, sooner or later, bring disaster upon you both.

Everything goes on smoothly here at the ranch. The family are all well, and just at present enjoying the unusual pleasure of a visit, from a gentleman of the name of Lieutenant James. He dropped down upon us unexpectedly, much as you did, though his legs appear to be both sound, and he has n't mentioned any recent adventures with grizzlies.

I never heard of him before; but a physician, you know, thinks he can look beneath the surface, and considers it a part of his profession to read character readily. I felt justified in urging him to stay with us a short time, and have had no reason to regret my longing for a little cultivated conversation.

I don't remember to have heard of the Captain John Chambers of whom you inquire. If he has any connection with the other person you ask about, I advise you to look out for him too. " Birds of a feather," you know.

With hearty congratulations on your past success, and earnest hopes for the future, I am, my dear boy,

Your sincere friend,

W. FRENCH.

I studied over this letter for some time, while Ned was devouring his. It was evident that the doctor supposed we had met José Miguel on a friendly basis, and wished to warn us against the fascinations of the man. I should have been more explicit in my letter. As it was, this communication simply confirmed what I already knew as to the man's character.

And here too was new confirmation of my idea as to the family trouble. He exerts a powerful influence, "it pains me to add, particularly over women," wrote the doctor. And then there came back to me that conversation that I had had with Maggie, in which she so warmly expressed her sympathy with men unjustly accused, and subjected to the indignity of a public trial. She was evidently interested in this man, and he had been tried for murder, of course, as she believed, unjustly. She had undoubtedly assured him of her faith, and so a strong bond of sympathy had been created between them. Could it be that Maggie was consciously or unconsciously in love with him ; and if so, what of her feeling for Ned? As I looked back, I could not really persuade myself that she was a heartless flirt. "But then," thought I, "the majority of flirts are not deliberate ones. They are simply thoughtless and fickle, easily forgetting the past in the pleasure and triumph of the present. But Maggie seemed true to her defence of Don José, and yet by no means forgetful of Ned."

"Well," thought I, at last, "of course no man knows what he might do under a given set of circumstances ; but it seems to me I could never have much confidence in the reality of a woman's love, who, at the same time that she protested her entire devotion to me, ran such risks and talked so bravely for another man. I wish Ned felt as I do."

At this point my meditations were interrupted by an exclamation from Ned himself.

"Tom," said he, "this is strange. I believe you were right. Captain John Chambers is on the track of Miguel. He overheard our conversation on board the ' Mary Anne,' and he has gone to California to see what facts he can extract from Maggie. Just listen to this from her last letter."

"What 's the date of the letter ? " asked I.

"July 30."

"Well, what does she say ? "

So Ned began to read, occasionally interspersing remarks of his own, which I have placed in parentheses.

"We are blessed with — what do you think ? — a visitor ! Yes, a living human being has taken up his abode with us for an indefinite time. His name is Lieutenant James. (Substitute Captain Chambers.) He calls himself an idler about the world in search of recreation and amusement. I don't believe he will ever find what he is looking for. Such a smile as he has! I wish he would n't! It makes me nervous. And he is the *most dignified* and pompous creature that ever lived. His English is so precise and elegant that I don't dare to speak in his presence. And then he 's always quoting some horrid Latin that I can't understand. (And you may rest assured that every word of it is from Horace.) And I think he 's a bore; but papa says he 's a very polished, cultivated gentleman, and I suppose he knows.

"But, dear Ned, this creature has taken the strangest fancy to me. Now, please don't be jealous, dear, for you know — (Oh, we 'll skip that. It 's the kernel to me, but I know it 's only the rind to you. Here! here it is again.) Forgive me, dearie, if I speak of something I made you promise never to mention. You know girls are n't reasonable creatures, and I am so miserable that —(Well, never mind that. She just apologizes for speaking of Miguel. Here! This is what I want you to mark.) One day he asked me directly if I ever knew a man by the name of José Miguel. Of course I grew scarlet, — I always do, — and told him 'Yes.' And then he said he did n't want to hurt my feelings or embarrass me, but he wished I would tell him where this man was. And that made me indignant, and I said I did n't know, and I would n't tell him if I did. But he did n't get angry. He just shook his head gravely, and said he was very, very sorry. And then he quoted some more of his abominable Latin, and I ran away and cried. And, dear Ned, what shall I do? I 'm so miserable, and I wish you were here, and — (Well, that 's the whole of it.)" And Ned folded the letter and replaced it tenderly in his pocket.

"I can't see any daylight yet," said I. "It 's evident that Captain Chambers turned straight around from Buenos Ayres and went to California; but why he 's so anxious to find this Miguel probably no one knows unless it 's that gentleman himself. All we can do is to wait further developments."

Melbourne reminded us a little of San Francisco. It is a substantially built city, and the people have the free-and-easy manner and the reckless drive that characterize the Californian.

The river Yarra, bordered by immense warehouses, and spanned by handsome bridges, traverses the city from east to west, bearing innumerable steamers, barges, and small craft of all kinds down to the harbor, about three miles distant.

Several days after the "Falcon" had weighed anchor for England, we were surprised to encounter Smith one evening, in the saloon attached to our boarding-house.

He seemed startled at first, turned as if to avoid recognition, and then advanced in a half-friendly way, extending his hand, and saying, —

"Glad to see ye, messmates. Hope ye 'll let by-gones be by-gones. I don't bear ye no grudge. Come and take a drink."

We declined the invitation, and failed to see the proffered hand.

"I did n't know you 'd left the 'Falcon,'" said Ned. "I see she 's sailed for England."

He was a trifle disconcerted, but mustered grace to say, —

"Well, I was sorry to leave the 'Falcon;' but you see the old man got a little hard on me, and I thought as how maybe 't would be best to look for a new berth. Do you stay long in the country?"

"Don't know," replied Ned, curtly. "We 're looking for a man by the name of Derwent. Ever hear of him?"

Smith actually staggered, and a desperate look of fear and hatred shot into his eyes. He finally stammered, —

"N–o. N–ever heard the name."

"Then you can't help us," said Ned. "Good-day!" and we moved away.

"Now, Ned, you have put your foot in it with a vengeance," said I. "That man belongs to the Miguel gang, there 's no doubt of it; and you 've let him know that we are aware of it. Look out for him, now, that 's all!"

"Nonsense, Tom; there 's no harm done. I could n't resist the temptation to scare the rascal a little."

The next evening, Ned made a most astounding proposition. It was simply that we should purchase a tent, a couple of horses, and such implements as we needed, and go out into the gold-fields.

"Not with the expectation of finding anything, Tom," he said apologetically, "but just so as to see a little of the country. And who knows but we might light on a nugget that would carry us through the rest of our trip with flying colors?"

Of course I used all my arguments against this scheme, and of course I finally gave up the point and agreed to go.

Four days later we had travelled on horseback over some two hundred miles of rolling, cultivated country, through several large towns, had watched the operations of the gold-diggers, and had penetrated far beyond the last settlement, into the primeval wilderness of the mountain region.

"None of those old played-out, crowded fields for us, Tom," said Ned. "We'll try our luck in a new quarter."

It was a wild district that we camped in. On one side lay an immense tract of forest formed of she-oaks, with a filling of the straight low saplings called the *mallee.* Scattered hills and mountains crowded toward the north, and grassy plains, bright with myriad-tinted flowers, were behind us. A little stream came down through a ravine from the mountains, and beside this we pitched our tent for the first night.

The weather was mild and clear, as it was now spring, the most delightful of Australian seasons. There was no lack of supplies, for beside the provisions we had brought with us, game was abundant. We could saunter out and bring down a kangaroo at any time; and a short trip into the mallee would often be rewarded by the whirring flight of a *lowan,* or Australian partridge.

The shrill note of the laughing jackass frequently startled us, as he pounced like a kingfisher upon some snake hidden in the grass; and occasionally we paused in our work to admire the gorgeous plumage and graceful form of the lyre-bird.

For we were working in earnest. We had selected this spot because the general appearance of the soil and vegetation resembled that of the gold-fields, and we dug and shovelled all day long, looking for the pipe-clay subsoil in which the gold deposit might be expected.

But three days' labor brought no pipe-clay and no gold; so we struck tent, and going farther up the stream tried it again, with a similar lack of results. Then we moved across country to the west, and after half a dozen miles of rough travelling, found another little stream, in situation and appearance much like the first.

At two feet in depth the spades began to turn up clay. As the first shovelful of bluish-gray substance came to the surface, we uttered a simultaneous yell. It seemed to me for an instant as if the wealth of a continent were under my feet. With bated breath, and hands that fairly trembled, we washed and re-washed that first spadeful, and at last extracted two shining pellets about the size of peas.

I have no recollection of what either of us said. We must have been fairly mad. I know we embraced each other with our muddy hands, and actually rolled in the mounds of slimy earth that were heaped around; and when the first paroxysm of joy was over, we set to work methodically to clear away a large space of the surface soil, and lay bare the stratum of clay. We toiled like beavers, vying with each other in the size of the spadefuls we threw out, and within a couple of hours had cleared an area about twenty feet square.

"That 'll do for the present," said Ned. "There 's enough to make us independent for the rest of our lives."

So we began to turn up the clay, carefully washing and sifting each handful. Almost every washing showed some traces of gold, varying in amount from a single tiny speck to little nuggets an ounce or more in weight. As each bit of the shining metal came to light, we pounced on it with some exclamation.

"Here 's enough for Calcutta!" said Ned, holding up a piece as large as a marble.

"And here 's Japan!" exclaimed I, hauling out another.

"And here 's Lima!"

"And here 's Teheran!"

So we toiled and shouted for several hours, shovelling out the clay, and hailing each new find with the name of some city or country we had yet to visit.

Almost all the clay in sight had been cleared out, and we had a little pile of dust and lumps, about five pounds in all, spread out on my blouse. Ned was picking over the last shovelful, and I was in the pit, scraping along the edges and working under the sides for more clay.

Suddenly the steel struck something hard and solid. Stooping

"We must have been a strange-looking couple." — *Page 177.*

down, I dropped the shovel and tore away the earth with my hands. A dull yellow gleam caught my eye. Like a dog digging out a rabbit, I pawed the dirt and sticky clay behind me, and at last loosened the monster. Heavens! what a weight! My knees shook with excitement. I could n't get breath enough to speak. Just then Ned called out, —

"Here's Quebec, Tom!"

"And here," yelled I, with a despairing effort, "here's the *world*, my boy, *the whole world!* Look at it! Feel of it!" and I dumped the treasure on a mound of earth, and sank down exhausted beside it.

We must have been a strange-looking couple as we sat one on each side of that precious lump of metal. Our faces were pale through all the mud and dirt that encrusted them. We were fairly drunk, — stupefied with the joy of success.

At last, as the stupor wore off, the whole thing began to appear to me like a remarkable joke. I laughed, and Ned joined me. We laughed harder; laughed till we cried; laughed till I lost my balance and rolled into the pit; and then we fairly shrieked with laughter.

Finally Ned said: "Come, let's brace up, Tom, and be sensible!" and immediately we haw-hawed again, louder than ever. It seemed utterly absurd to talk of being sensible.

But from sheer exhaustion, we were obliged at last to be sober. It was beginning to get dark, and the thought of the treasure we had to guard soon brought us to reason.

The big nugget, as nearly as we could judge, weighed about fifteen pounds. Altogether, we had collected in one day something over twenty pounds of gold. That memorable day was the 2d of November, 1878.

After some consultation we sewed all our findings carefully in a piece of canvas, and buried the bag thus formed inside the tent, just under where we slept at night. Then we washed in the brook, built a fire, and prepared supper.

"How comfortable a man feels when he knows there's a little matter of six thousand dollars ready to his hand!" said Ned, as we lay in front of the tent and smoked.

"And when he feels that by shovelling up a little dirt in front of his house he can find six thousand more!" replied I.

"No more hardship, Tom, old boy! No more junk and

souse! No more 'fore-the-mast! We'll finish our trip like gentlemen, and get home in less than a year."

"Where shall we go first?"

"I'll tell you, Tom, what strikes my fancy. There's a line of steamers running from Melbourne to San Francisco. Let's take passage on one, and go down to the ranch for a week or two. We don't have to economize now, either in time or money. Fancy the sensation we'll create!"

"We'll fool them for a while," said I. "Make them think we've given up. And after a visit we can take passage for Japan, and go round in less than eighty days, if we like."

"It's a kind of nuisance to write any more of those confounded newspaper letters, but I suppose we'll have to do it now, just for the name of the thing."

So we talked and planned, full of happiness and hope, and finally turned in, placing loaded guns and revolvers by our sides.

I lay awake for a long time. It seemed to me the wild dogs never made such a howling. At last, too nervous to sleep, I got up and stood in the door of the tent. The moon, full and round, was just appearing over a low range of hills to the north-east. From the west, a soft, gentle breeze stole across the flowery meadow, heavy with a strange and subtle fragrance. Out on the grassy downs I could see the short, stumpy bodies of wombats moving about near their burrows. The melancholy note of the mopoke, or Australian owl, floated in prolonged cadence on the silent night-air.

Suddenly, from behind a bush not far from our tent came the long, dismal howl of a wild dog. It was answered by another, far away in the mallee.

As I glanced toward the moon, I was petrified for a moment with astonishment. "Here is a peculiarity of the Antipodes that I never heard mentioned," thought I. "How striking that resemblance to the figure of a man!"

Within the circumference of the moon's disk was a human figure, standing erect, with arm outstretched.

In an instant, however, the mystery was dispelled. The arm was lowered and the whole form disappeared. It was easy then to explain the illusion. The lower rim of the moon was just touching the brow of a distant hill, and an actual man had been standing in such a position that his whole figure, viewed from my standpoint, fell within the moon's disk.

"Can it be that we are watched?" thought I. "But no; that hill must be several miles distant, and some shepherd has accidentally wandered to its summit."

So I returned to the tent, and without disturbing Ned was soon sound asleep.

The next day we resumed our digging; but although we uncovered a large surface of clay, repeated washings failed to bring to light any gold. The deposit seemed to be exhausted, and we resolved that night that we would start the next day with what we had already secured, make our way back to Melbourne, and leave Australia before any one was aware of our good luck.

We had become somewhat accustomed to fortune by this time, and the fatigue which excitement had held in check, now began to make itself felt. That night we turned in early, and went to sleep almost instantly.

Some people waken slowly. They open their eyes a wee bit, vaguely wonder where they are for an instant, then close them and are lost again. In a moment they turn over, stretch out an arm or leg, heave a long sigh, sit up slowly, and rub their eyes. Gradually their misty ideas take shape, and in the course of some ten minutes they are fully conscious of their identity and their location; in other words, they are wide awake.

With me it has always been different. I am habitually a light sleeper. The faintest touch, the mere presence of some one at the bedside, is always enough to arouse me, and with the first moment of consciousness the thread of recollection is complete, and I am as fully awake as if sleep were only a name.

So, on this night, when a faint, unusual noise reached my ear, I sat up suddenly and opened my eyes. A flood of moonlight streamed full in my face, revealing a dark figure that bent over me. I heard a click, and felt a sudden pressure of cold steel on my forehead. At the same instant a voice whispered in my ear : —

"The least noise, and I blow out your brains!"

As a matter of course, I sat motionless, and in a moment the voice whispered : —

"Stand up!"

With that cold pressure still on my forehead, I obeyed. A

large piece of canvas had been cut away from the side of the tent close to where we were lying. Ned was still sound asleep, and over him stood another man.

"Step outside," whispered my captor.

I had slept next to the wall of the tent, and the gold was buried under my side of the bed. One step through the open canvas took me into the meadow. Two men instantly seized me, and one of them whispered: —

"If you behave yourself we won't hurt you, but at the least outcry or attempt to escape you and your companion will both be shot."

I glanced at the speaker. He was a powerful man, with a heavy. dark mustache.

"It is he," thought I, — "José Miguel!"

There were five in all, — the two who had remained in the tent, the two who had charge of me, and a fifth, who stood at some distance, holding five horses.

I trembled lest they should search me and discover the cipher letters, which I had carried in the pocket-book with my other papers.

In a few moments the two men emerged from the tent, bearing between them our precious sack of gold. Ned had not been awakened. For that, at least, I was thankful.

The sack was securely fastened to the saddle of one of the horses, and after a brief consultation, one of the men started off across the plain on foot.

The man who appeared to be the leader, and whom I had judged to be Miguel, then turned to me and said : —

"Young man, you will mount one of these horses and come with us. I must remind you once more that your only chance of safety lies in obeying me quietly, and in making no attempt to escape or to give an alarm."

A horse was brought up, which I mounted. The others also got into their saddles, and we set out, one in front, leading the horse which I rode, one on each side of me, and the fourth bringing up the rear. We followed the course of the stream, toward the mountains.

"What can be their object in making me a prisoner?" thought I. "Is it possible they hope to secure a ransom for my valuable carcass?"

My hands were free, and I had been nonchalantly carrying them in the side pockets of my coat.

"Will they search me?" I wondered. "Undoubtedly, when they reach a halting-place."

Our money, about one hundred dollars, I carried in a belt worn around my waist and inside my coat.

"It's a pity to let them have that too," I reflected. "Wonder if I can get rid of it!"

So without taking my hands out of the pockets, I began cautiously to feel through the lining of the coat for the belt. I found it without difficulty, and began to work my hands along to the buckle that fastened it. With some trouble I managed to loosen the strap, and as we were travelling over stony ground where the horses' hoofs made considerable noise, I let the whole belt drop to the ground. At the same time I looked about me and strove to fix the surroundings in memory as well as the uncertain moonlight would permit.

Then it occurred to me that if I could manage to drop something along the ground, like Hop-o'-my-thumb in the fairy-story, it might serve as a trail, either to find my way back if I had a chance, or for Ned to follow.

The pocket-book containing my papers was in the breast-pocket of my coat, and there was no way of getting at it without attracting attention.

But in the outside pocket, and under my very hand, was a little note-book that I had used for keeping a journal. I managed to tear a leaf out of this without much trouble, and lifting it to the edge of the pocket let it flutter to the ground.

Then I continued dropping the leaves of my valuable journal at intervals of about a hundred yards apart.

Suddenly we took an abrupt turn to the left, rode for a short distance over an open down, and paused at the edge of a thick growth of timber.

The man in advance put both hands to his mouth and gave a prolonged and excellent imitation of the howl of a wild dog.

"No wonder," thought I, "that the wild dogs seemed unusually noisy last night."

In a moment an answering howl came from the thicket. A man emerged from behind a bush, spoke a few words with the leader, and disappeared. We took up our march and entered the thicket.

It was intensely dark, but the leader must have been thoroughly familiar with the route, for he rode forward without the least hesitation. The men beside me laid a hand on each of my shoulders to prevent my slipping off in the darkness.

We doubled and twisted to the right and the left, but my journal, more valuable than I had ever hoped to find it, was noiselessly falling, leaf by leaf, behind us.

At last, after a couple of hours' hard riding, we pulled up in a somewhat open space, through which the moonbeams faintly struggled.

"Dismount!" said the leader to me.

I obeyed.

"Search him, *Derwent.*"

There was no doubt then as to who my captors were. If there had been, it would have been dispelled when the leader took a cigar from his pocket and proceeded to light it. As the match flared up close to his face, I saw a long red scar on the cheek, the mark which Ned's bullet had left, in our encounter in the mountains of Mexico.

In the mean time the man named Derwent was quietly going through my pockets by the aid of a dark-lantern. Of course the first thing he drew out was the pocket-book. My heart was in my mouth, but fortunately the chief interposed.

"Be quick, Derwent! Never mind papers! All we want is money or valuables."

" No money, Captain, and no valuables except a jack-knife."

" Well, leave him that to whittle his way out of an Australian bush. Now mount and be off! Farewell, my young friend ! Commend me to your companion — when you see him again."

" Adios, Señor," said I. " Don't ignore me when we meet next time."

It was a foolish bit of bravado. The man turned as if half in doubt whether he had n't better put a bullet through me after all ; but shaking his head with a laugh, he put spurs to his horse, and the whole party sprang into the thicket and disappeared.

I was alone, lost in the bush. There was no use in trying to get out until daylight ; so I sat down on a log and felt about in my pockets for something to smoke. My pipe was hanging up in the tent, but I found a little loose tobacco, and with one of the few remaining leaves of my journal I rolled a ciga- rette, and puffing with great cheerfulness and vigor, tried to be philosophical.

" After all," thought I, " it is n't so bad as it might be. We 've lost our gold, but we might have lost our lives. I shall get back all right in the morning, and then we 'll be no worse off than we were day before yesterday."

But with all my philosophy, that was an exceedingly long and uncomfortable night, and the first rays of light were very welcome.

I waited patiently until there was no difficulty in seeing ob- jects in the thickest part of the forest, and then set out to follow up my paper trail. Fortunately there had been no wind during the night, and the papers lay about where they had fallen.

The first one was only a few yards from the edge of the open- ing, and the second caught my eye very soon. I gathered them up as I went, so as not to get turned about and come back again. The third one bothered me for a long time, but at last I found it clinging to a bush.

Walking slowly and carefully, with eyes wide open, sometimes nonplussed and bewildered for an hour or more, I at last reached the edge of the forest shortly after noon.

I was beginning to be ravenously hungry ; but with no weapon but a jack-knife, there was little chance of my eating anything before I reached camp. So I kept on across the open plain, picking up the papers at a run, until I reached the stream. As

I saw the last piece of paper lying on a rock beside the brook, I was almost as crazy with delight as when I unearthed the great nugget; for now I knew that I was safe. Only a few miles down this very stream was our camp and Ned.

"Poor Ned," thought I, "how he must have suffered! But now to find that bag of gold."

There was no great difficulty. It was lying in plain sight on the stones, and I picked it up with a feeling that we were not quite destitute, after all.

In about an hour I came in sight of the tent, and saw Ned sitting on a pile of dirt, with his face buried in his hands.

How I yelled at him, and how he rushed to meet me !. I know that in the joy of that reunion neither thought for an instant of our paltry six thousand dollars.

In a few words I told Ned of my adventures, and he in return expatiated on his alarm and misery at finding me gone, and the gold with me.

"Of course, Tom," said he, "I knew we had had a call from some gang of highwaymen; but the awful thought that I could n't shake off, was that they had murdered you or carried you away into the mountains."

He had spent the day in wandering about and firing the rifle, and was on the point of starting for the nearest settlement to get help in searching for me.

"Well, now give me something to eat," said I. "I 'd rather have a square meal than all the gold we lost."

I did ample justice to that kangaroo steak, and we slept that night without fear of intruders. We were relieved of the awful responsibility of six thousand dollars worth of gold.

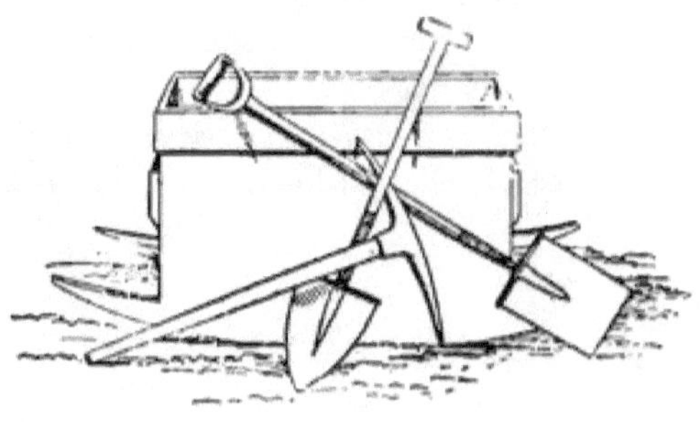

CHAPTER XI.

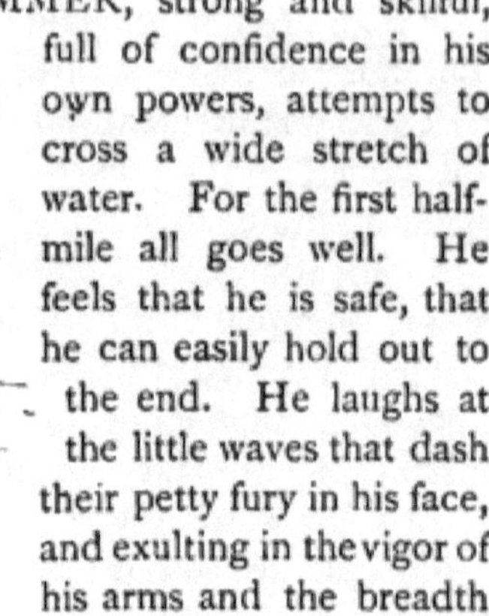

SWIMMER, strong and skilful, full of confidence in his own powers, attempts to cross a wide stretch of water. For the first half-mile all goes well. He feels that he is safe, that he can easily hold out to the end. He laughs at the little waves that dash their petty fury in his face, and exulting in the vigor of his arms and the breadth of his chest, sweeps triumphantly toward the distant shore.

But the waves mount higher; the elements combine against him; Nature has determined to defeat his undertaking. The wind blows keenly in his face, and one after another great volumes of water ingulf him, leaving him at each moment fainter and more exhausted, as he struggles slowly and resolutely to the surface. He is quiet now. That scornful delight with which he first dashed into the water has given place to a dogged determination, and a lurking dread of failure. He economizes strength. His breath is deep and regular, the sweep of his arms slow and steady. No more playful plunging beneath the breakers! No more beating the water in idle bravado! If he can win at all, it is only by employing the last atom of endurance. He strives to hold his head always above the water, to keep his eye ever fixed on that distant shore, which, alas! sometimes appears to be receding.

Suddenly he reaches and grasps a floating plank, and then comes a mighty sense of relief and security. He is safe! With this buoyant support the shore can be easily gained whenever he shall choose. He looks back at his unaided struggles, at that fierce buffeting with the waves, and wonders how he could have endured it so long.

"It was nearly over!" he says to himself. "I could not have held out a half-mile farther!"

And, in an instant, the plank is torn from his grasp by a fierce whirlpool and hurried far beyond his reach, while he, by the merest chance escaping from that resistless force, is left once more alone and unsupported to renew his battle with the deep.

Then is manhood put to the test! Will the weary muscles relax and the helpless wretch give up the now hopeless strife, or will he summon the last resources of that power that is mightier than all the blind forces of Nature, — the power of an unyielding will, — and fight on till he either wins the victory, or sinks, unconquered and still struggling, under the weight of soulless matter that surrounds him?

This was the question that, in various shapes, Ned and I asked ourselves as we journeyed back to Melbourne. After those glorious dreams, that day of sudden fortune, when all our trials and hardships seemed ended forever, it was fearful to be plunged back into the cold waves again. Could we endure it?

"A week ago," said Ned, "we felt as if the hardest part of our trip was over; but to-day what is left for us to do seems a thousand times more difficult than the whole undertaking was at first."

My heart most distinctly echoed this sentiment, but it would never do for both to talk in that strain; so I replied : —

"Where are your logic and philosophy, man? Do you realize that we are only in just the position we occupied three days ago, — neither better nor worse off? We fell asleep one day and dreamed that we found some gold; any fool would know that the dream was an absurdity!"

"Yes, — but sometimes dreams are so vivid and so glorious, that the realities of life become like a horrible nightmare in comparison!"

"Ned, I am astonished that you, the father of our enterprise, the man whom no dangers could frighten and no hardships affect, should be so totally unmanned by that silly distemper, *love.* Confess that you are at this moment thinking of the little California brunette, and that you are mourning the loss of our gold only because you cannot rush straight to her arms. Brace up, my boy! She does n't expect you. She is counting upon welcoming her hero when his task is accomplished. You would be ashamed to go toddling home with your work half done. It always weakens a woman's love to find that she is stronger than her lover!"

"Much you know about a woman's love!" growled Ned. "You cold-blooded analyzer, you miserable, statistical calculator! But after all, Tom," and his mercurial spirits rose once more, "what's the use of being gloomy! We've lots of fun before us. We shall 'swim in a gondola,' climb the Alps, wander in the Schwartz-wald, and float down the mystic Rhine. The sunshine is as warm, and the sea as blue and glorious, as though we had millions in our pockets."

"True!" said I, my spirits falling as his went up. "And kicks are as disagreeable, and offal as unpalatable, and bunks as dirty, as though we were linked in a chain-gang. If fortune only shows us half a smile, I'll be even with the Miguel gang!"

So we went, like boys playing see-saw. When one was up, the other was down.

But before we reached Melbourne, our "second wind" had fairly come. The first exuberance and delight in our adventurous wandering was nearly expended, but in its place was a stern determination to go through to the end, to make the best of everything, hope for no good fortune, but seize all that came in our way. And in my mind, at least, had grown up a second resolution, inspired by revenge, — to discover the secrets of the gang that had plundered us, and to wrest from them our golden spoil.

This last subject was a constant theme for discussion between us. To go to the authorities in Melbourne would be to convict ourselves of having been engaged in mining without paying the government tax, and would also delay us for months in Australia. This would never do.

Upon reaching Melbourne we sold our horses, and then instituted a search for our old enemy, Smith. Through all the sailors' boarding-houses and low dens of the city we prosecuted our inquiries, but all to no purpose. The man was not to be found.

Neither could we hear of any man in the whole city of the name of Derwent.

"Would you know him if we met him?" Ned asked.

"I think so!" I replied. "He held the lantern quite close to his face while my pockets were being rifled, and I noticed that his nose was broken by a blow or a fall."

We occasionally encountered a man with a broken nose, but it was never Derwent.

Still, I was firmly convinced that he was in the city, and further, that he was the regular Melbourne representative of this cosmopolitan band of cut-throats.

In the mean time, however, our precious weeks were gliding away, and we finally, though with reluctance, were forced to abandon the search. It was the 16th of November when we determined to secure berths on the first vessel bound to any port we had yet to visit.

That very evening a man appeared in the saloon where Ned and I were sitting, and addressing the crowd of lounging sailors, shouted : —

"Now then, boys! Three A. B's. wanted for a cruise to Yokohama, Foochow, and home to London! Who wants to go home?"

Ned and I started to our feet, and another man followed our example.

"Here's two of us will ship for Yokohama," said Ned. "Don't want to go to London."

"The whole cruise, or not at all!" said the man. "Here, you!" to the other sailor. "Are you a half-water jake, too?"

"Divil a bit of it, Cap," replied the sailor. "I'm in for the whole trip!"

"Get your chest ready then, and go down to Williamstown and aboard the 'Bonnie Belle' in the morning."

He took down the sailor's name, and then turned again to us.

"Don't you want to go home to London, boys?"

"Never was in London in my life," said I.

"Where you from?"

"New York."

"Oh! Yankees, are you, and want to stop at Yokohama? All right, go aboard!" and he added our names to the list.

To describe in detail our three months' voyage on the "Bonnie Belle" would cover a great deal of paper and be but wearisome repetition of the routine of a sailor's life. It will be sufficient to mention only what has a direct bearing on the network of intrigue that was beginning to graft the plot of a novel upon our simple expedition. During all those weary days I thought almost constantly on the mysterious organization whose members had so cruelly plundered us. Night after night, through the long, quiet watches, Ned and I discussed ways and means of getting even with them. Finally I hit on a scheme, which while it did n't promise very much, offered a bare chance of our obtaining more light on the subject.

"We don't know how large the association is, Ned," said I, "but it seems evident that they have correspondents in several cities in different quarters of the globe. Now, if they are represented in Asia at all, what city would be their probable headquarters?"

"Most likely some place in India, — Calcutta or Bombay."

"Just my idea! Now, after visiting Japan we shall be apt to cruise back along the China coast, take up Peking and Canton on our route, and so work around to Calcutta. If we have good luck we ought to be in India, say in May of next year."

"Well, go on ; develop your scheme!"

For answer, I handed Ned a piece of paper on which I had written the following : —

Brig "Esperanza," at sea, July 30th.

To Derwent, Melbourne:

Lost overboard from ship "Falcon." Picked up by this vessel, bound for Foochow, Hong Kong, and Calcutta. Hand badly hurt. Can't reach Australia at present, as instructed. Order two hundred enclosed. Send money and instructions Calcutta.

Pedro Nevarro.

"Humph!" said Ned, after a moment's reflection. "I suppose you mean to send this to Melbourne. What result do you expect?"

"I intend to put it in cipher, address it to Derwent, Melbourne, enclose the order for two hundred dollars, and mail it at

Hong Kong, where I heard the mate say we should put in for a few days. I believe it will reach Derwent, for he is certainly in Melbourne, and there are few, if any, others of that name in the city. I think Derwent will accept the letter as genuine, for Smith has certainly joined the crowd and has told them of Pedro's fate. It is equally certain that Smith did not know of the cipher letters that Nevarro had, and consequently we shall not be suspected. So, on the whole, I think it likely that Derwent will either send the money and a letter of instructions direct to Pedro Nevarro, Calcutta, or else he will send him an order upon the Calcutta agent and refer to him for instructions. When we receive the letter at Calcutta, we can discuss what to do next."

"Your scheme is gauzy," said Ned. "I can see daylight through it in several places, but I suppose there 's no harm in trying it. Go on with your dark intrigues. This is growing exciting."

On the 27th of December we arrived at Hong Kong, and were in port for three days. Ned and I obtained permission to spend half a day on shore, and our letter, duly constructed in the cipher, was mailed to Derwent.

The few hours passed in the English city of Victoria were not sufficient to enable us to study it in detail. We saw a busy town scattered along the shore of the island and backed by high cliffs and mountains. Good, wholesome English saluted our ears, and we frequently laughed at the curious jargon called "pigeon English," spoken by the Chinese employés. The next morning we were under sail again, beating up the coast against the northeast monsoons.

The weather grew cold as we advanced toward the north. One morning the deck was covered by a light fall of snow, and we had the novel and by no means pleasant experience of going aloft on rigging coated with ice.

On the 25th of January, 1879, we sighted the southern point of the island of Kiusiu, and within five days were at anchor opposite Yokohama, in the great bay of Yeddo.

"Fifteen months ago, Tom," said Ned, "we were in San Francisco, trying to cross the Pacific. We 've reached here at last, but by a deuced long route, — some twenty thousand miles out of the direct course."

"And our return route is likely to be considerably longer," replied I.

We received our discharge from the "Bonnie Belle," and wages amounting to about one hundred and thirty dollars. This, with what we had saved from our Australian disasters, gave us in all two hundred and fifty-five dollars when we landed at Yokohama.

The air was bracing though not very cold, and some snow was to be seen about the city and on the thatched roofs of the houses. The wide street up which we walked was lined on each side by stores and booths, where lacquered ware, bronzes, curiously carved ornaments in ivory, and toys of all descriptions were displayed.

The street was literally roaring with the shouts of the salesmen, who stood before their booths and advertised their wares to the passing crowd.

Here and there we passed Japanese tea-houses, or restaurants; and the winning smiles of the rather good-looking girls who stood before them, reinforced by the calls of appetite, finally induced us to pause and step inside.

For a moderate charge we enjoyed a cup of delicious tea and a breakfast of hard-boiled eggs peeled by the dainty fingers of our waitresses.

"And now for Tokio!" said Ned, as we rose from breakfast. "Shall we go in style on the new railroad?"

"It's only a matter of eighteen miles," said I, "and the weather is just right. Let's walk it!"

So we left our guns and the bulk of our baggage in charge of an American merchant, and set out along the Grand Imperial Highway of Japan.

An innumerable throng were coming and going. Yakoneens, or government police, galloped along with swords poking out awkwardly under their cloaks; now and then we met a norimon bearing the person of some high official, and followed by a long train of coolies with the luggage. Travellers to and from the capital passed us on foot and on horseback; the tea-houses on the route were full of people squatting on the mats within, — beggars, blind, lame, and deformed, pointed out their claims for sympathy, and fell on their faces imploring alms; on one side stretched the wide bay covered with junks and fishing-boats,

with here and there the tall masts and square sails of a western
ship; and away in the distance lay the hills, green even at this
season, and standing out against the high volcanic peaks, white
with the winter snow, that rose behind them.

On the summit of a little rising ground we paused at last to
gaze at the capital of the Japanese empire.   Stretching away in
crescent form around the semicircle of the bay, it spread back
as far as we could see among the hills, a city closely built up
over more than sixty square miles, and numbering a population
of nearly two millions.

A river wound its way through the heart of the city, and
wavy canals or moats, branching off from the stream, encircled
the central portions of the capital.   Scattered here and there
among the buildings we could see high mounds or hills surmounted by the Japanese temples.

The city is full of life and activity, and the Japanese as a
nation seem willing and anxious to reap the benefit of Western
invention and progress.

"We are swinging round with the course of civilization,
Ned," said I, "and we have almost reached the starting-point.
Here on these far eastern islands we are near the source of the
world's intellectual life.   The ball that began ages ago to roll
around the earth in the course of the sun has at last acquired
centrifugal force to throw its first flakes of progress across the
wide Pacific.   Soon it will leap the gulf, and who shall say that
the Asiatic of the future may not be what he once was, — the
highest type of man?"

"That's good, Tom!" replied Ned.   "The idea is a trifle
old, but dress it up and put it in your next letter!"

Returning to Yokohama, we secured berths on the American
ship "Phantom," which was to stop at Chefoo, reaching that
town on the 15th of February.

Chefoo is a miserable, scattered Chinese settlement, and we
were glad of a chance to embark on the steamer the same day,
and proceed up the gulf.

We reached the mouth of the Pei-Ho River early the following morning, steamed past the ruined Taku forts, famous in
the annals of English and French warfare, and toward night
arrived at the great port of Tien-Tsin.

This was our first real experience of a Chinese city.   Tien-

Tsin has been a free port for a great many years, and there were a large number of foreigners, principally sailors and traders, to be seen in the streets; but nevertheless it was thoroughly Chinese in its houses, population, filth, — and above all, in its smells.

"If this is Tien-Tsin in winter," remarked Ned, with his handkerchief to his nose, "how can even Chinese endure it in the summer?"

By the next day we were curled up in a Chinese cart, jolting over a horrible road through a dreary winter landscape toward Peking.

During that three days' journey we scarcely spoke. It was actually dangerous. Our first attempts at conversation resulted in wounded tongues and nearly dislocated jaws, and we lapsed into silence broken only by curses through our set teeth. Never in my life have I experienced anything like the constant and terrific "chugs" of that Chinese cart.

At last, aching in every bone, we dismounted within the Eastern Convenience Gate of the capital, paid our charioteer the stipulated "cash," and were for a time glorified residents of the Celestial City. We supped that night at the lodging-house of one Chang, where we had some kind of roast meat, an extremely sour wine, and the inevitable and ever-welcome tea.

I hasten over our life in China, as this aims to be rather a record of our adventures than a book of travels; and although we met with much that was disgusting, our experience was only that of every foreigner in the Celestial Empire.

Strange as it may seem, China interested us but little. Everything was so utterly unnatural, that it seemed to us like a very bad theatrical burlesque, where the characters were clumsy imitations of men and women, and the whole setting of the piece reflected but a distorted image of that Nature to which it purported to be a mirror.

We were in Peking three days, and our only adventure was not remarkable, but sufficiently disagreeable at the time.

We were pursued in the streets one day by a crowd of boys and men to the number of nearly a hundred, who saluted us with the cry of "Fan kwei" (foreign devils), and assailed us with stones and other less dangerous but more unpleasant missiles. Ned received quite a cut in the head from a stone, and we might have fared very badly indeed, had not a good-natured Chinaman taken pity on us, and beckoned us into his house, whence we escaped by a back door opening on another street.

From Chefoo, on our return, we took passage on a steamer for Shanghai, where good luck gave us berths on the English brig "Welcome," for Hong Kong.　We bowled along merrily before the monsoon, and landed at Victoria for the second time. April 1, 1879.

"We 've no time to lose, Ned," said I.　"There is Canton yet to visit, and we must be in Calcutta in May."

"I really believe you are fool enough to expect to find two hundred dollars waiting for you in Calcutta!" said Ned.

"I don't *expect* anything," I replied; "but all the same I want to be on time in case there should be something that would throw a little light on this business.　Somehow, I am growing to think more about José Miguel than about the whole trip."

"No side issues, my boy!"

"That sounds well from you! You have your fair Margaret; I shall devote myself to her — well, excuse me — her mysterious acquaintance!"

Ned did n't half like that, and he was glum for the next hour.

A fleet of American river steamers ply between Victoria and Canton, and we had arrived just in time to embark on the morning boat bound up.

Puffing across a wide bay dotted with islands, we entered the mouth of the Pearl River, and were soon voyaging between flat, wide fields of rice. The air was soft and warm, and we passed junks and fishing-vessels of all sorts dropping gently down the stream, the fishermen lounging on the decks under their three-cornered sails. Now and then a village or town came in sight, the low, thatched houses crowded close together, with here and there tall towers rising from their midst.

"The captain says those towers are pawnbrokers' establishments," remarked Ned. "Our Chinese uncles must do a thriving business."

"At all events, they are looked up to," I replied.

Toward evening we approached the great city of Canton, and began to discern the residences of the "floating population." Thousands of boats moored to each other, or to the shore, or drifting gently along the stream, covered the river as far as we could see. More than a quarter of a million of human beings are born, spend their lives, and die in these narrow floating homes, many of them not going ashore for years; and yet they seem contented and happy.

"Thank Heaven, you put only two Chinese towns on your list, Ned!" said I, as we hurried up the narrow street, holding our noses, and jostling right and left against the everlasting blue-bloused Chinamen.

"Let 's transact our business and get out!" replied Ned.

So we secured our testimonials, left our letters to be mailed, and hurried back to the dock in time to take the evening steamer down the river.

"Better fifty years in Europe than five minutes in Cathay!" was Ned's exclamation, as we left the metropolis of southern China.

In the morning we were in Victoria, anxiously seeking passage to India.

"Ho! for Calcutta!" said Ned. "Somehow I feel nearly as eager to reach there as you do."

"I don't doubt it!" replied I. "You also will make for the Post-Office. What if Maggie should have eloped with Captain Chambers, or Lieutenant James, as he calls himself?"

"What if Aphrodite should elope with a satyr!" growled Ned.

"Your parallel is unfortunate, my boy. If classic legends are to be believed, Aphrodite was by no means nice in her affections, and frequently chose without regard to much beyond sex."

"Bah! you wield your classic lore very awkwardly sometimes, Tom; but ho! for Calcutta!"

"And for revenge!" added I.

There was no difficulty in securing berths. There are few English sailors who can endure the climate in these waters for any length of time. Most of the vessels are manned by Malays, and an English or American sailor is a prize. We were "gobbled up," so to speak, by the English brig "Alert," and sailed for Calcutta on the 5th of April.

The winds were baffling and uncertain, and we were nearly three weeks in reaching Singapore, where we put in for one day, but Ned and I had no chance to get beyond the docks. The weather had grown very warm, and the rains were beginning. Most of the time we went about our work with nothing on but breeches and thin undershirt, and we gradually grew somewhat inured to the greenhouse atmosphere.

Through the beautiful straits of Malacca we slowly made our way, then across the wide bay of Bengal, and on the 10th of May, entered the Hooghly River and drew near to Calcutta.

Past deep jungles, the home of the tiger, through cultivated meadows lying on each side of the stream, we at last came in sight of the "City of Palaces."

There lay before our eyes the tall masts of hundreds of vessels, the vast warehouses, the temples and mosques, the magnificent esplanade, — all the wealth and grandeur of the East and West combined.

We had reached the thirteenth city, and with it closed the second year of our pilgrimage.

Our records showed that we had travelled during the past

twelve months, in round numbers, about twenty-two thousand miles, and had written twenty-seven of the one hundred letters.

We had begun our year with a capital of $179.15, had received $593.00 and paid out $603.65, so that our balance on hand was $168.50.

Our health was excellent, spirits fairly good, confidence in ultimate success A 1.

With expectant feelings we landed at Calcutta.

CHAPTER XII.

T was a very American-look-
ing pair of tramps that
strolled down the espla-
nade of Calcutta on
the afternoon of May
11, 1879. We wore
the typical tattered,
slouched hats, the
dusty and dilapi-
dated garments, the
grime-incrusted faces
and the neglected
beards, that are so
characteristic of the
independent travel-
ler without means in
our native land. We
did n't "go much" on looks at that time.

Hot! Steaming, — boiling, — baking hot!

"The California desert was n't a circumstance to this!"
remarked Ned, as he mopped his dusty brow with his dustier
handkerchief.

It was a relief even to get into our stifling room in a sailors'
lodging-house, and lay down our arms. How we did hate
those guns!

"Let 's dispose of the things!" said I. "They are a confounded nuisance, and no kind of use to us here!"

"Agreed!" answered Ned; "and the small change we get
for them will be very welcome at this stage of the game."

We waited only until the sun had dropped behind the lofty
buildings, and then, somewhat refreshed by a thorough scrubbing
and a change of underclothes, we made for the Post-Office.

Ned went in first, and returned shortly with several letters; and then, wearing Pedro's blue blouse, and affecting a Spanish accent, and trying my best to look "tough" (needless effort, by the way), I inquired if anything had been received for Pedro Nevarro.

After a short delay a letter was handed out, bearing the Melbourne postmark.

"Victory!" exclaimed I, as I hurried past Ned; and together we scurried back to our den.

For once even Maggie's letter had to wait. When translated, my correspondent's remarks were as follows: —

Apply to Phelim Wylie, Calcutta. Have instructed him in regard to you. DERWENT.

"Brief, and to the point!" said I. "So, Brother Phelim, note my application!" and I seized a piece of paper.

"Now, look here, Tom!" said Ned; "this thing has gone far enough! Usually you are the most cautious of men; but your conceit is absolutely sublime, and when at rare intervals you evolve an idea, its radiance utterly blinds your eyes to the dictates of common-sense. I suppose if I allowed it, you would deliberately walk in among a gang of cut-throats and imagine yourself smart enough to fool the whole lot!"

"Now, don't play the oracle of common-sense, Ned," I replied. "The rôle is out of your line. I'm not going to put myself in the slightest danger, nor 'walk in' among any cut-throats at all; but I am going to follow this thing as far as is safe, and I warn you, for once I shall have my way."

Needless to repeat the long argument that followed. Ned at last gave it up in disgust, and turned sulkily to his own letters, while I constructed the following neat effusion in cipher:

PHELIM WYLIE, CALCUTTA: Derwent instructs me to apply to you for money and orders. PEDRO NEVARRO.

The only fact that interested me in the sixteen pages that Ned devoured was Maggie's remark that Lieutenant James had left the ranch, announcing his intention of sailing for Japan. There was no reference to Miguel in the letter.

A letter from Dan, which had been addressed to Melbourne, and forwarded to us from that city, informed us that a man answering the description of Miguel had sailed from Buenos Ayres for Australia, and advised us to "watch out for the spalpeen."

" 'Thanks for the suggestion, friend Dan," said I ; " unfortunately it comes a trifle late. But never mind, Señor Don José Miguel, we are on your track ! "

To which remark Ned replied only by a grunt that sounded like " Rats ! " and we turned in.

I awoke suddenly from troubled dreams to find Ned sitting bolt upright in bed.

" 'Sh ! Listen ! " he whispered.

The riotous revelry in the saloon below had died away, and the night was still. A moonbeam struggled in through the open window, lighting up a little square patch of flooring.

From far away in the distance came a long, melancholy wail, rising gradually louder for an instant, and then slowly dying away into silence. It was the most unearthly, the most blood-curdling and flesh-creeping sound I ever heard in my life.

Neither Ned nor I spoke or moved, but in spite of the stifling heat in the room I could feel a stream of ice-water trickling slowly down my spine.

Again the sound was repeated, from a different direction, then again from somewhere else, then from two or three quarters at once and louder than before, and then suddenly the air was full of that hideous, fiendish howling, — louder and nearer, from all points of the compass, seeming to converge upon our room, as if all the devils of the air were upon us.

By a simultaneous impulse we sprang out of bed and rushed to the window. I remembered afterward, when my toe pained me, that I kicked the butt of Ned's rifle as I ran across the room. I did n't notice it at the time.

The street, flooded with moonlight, was deserted, but the howling and wailing, the snarling and snapping, were worthy of the most terrific nightmare that ever tortured a poor dyspeptic.

Now and then a long, lank figure, like a good-sized dog, sped down the street at a swinging gallop.

" Oh," said Ned at length, with a long breath, " I have it ! The jackals ! the scavengers of Calcutta ! "

We turned in again, but not to sleep. My hair seemed to

have been permanently stiffened and strengthened so that it actually pricked when I laid my head down.

The next morning I mailed my letter to Phelim Wylie, and we spent the rest of the day in writing our newspaper reports.

Then in the evening we strolled out with our guns in hand to find a purchaser. After some trials we disposed of the two for twenty pounds to an English dealer, and went to saunter in the Maidan with quite an independent air.

This is the place to see the world of Calcutta on a fine afternoon toward nightfall. The drive presents the most brilliant and cosmopolitan appearance imaginable. An endless procession of vehicles of every kind and description occupies the street, while the sidewalk is thronged with Turks, Hindus, Jews, Afghans, Negroes, Chinese, Englishmen, all in their native costumes and preserving their national individuality.

My letter received the next morning read, —

Meet me on steps of Post-Office at six P. M., May 13. Will wear red handkerchief on neck. Say " Esperanza," and I will reply, " Melbourne." PHELIM WYLIE.

" That ends it ! " said Ned. " You don't go ! "

" This begins it ! " replied I. " I *do* go."

So we had it again for a matter of some hours, with the result that toward five o'clock we sallied out together. I had taken nothing with me but my revolver and the cipher letters of Pedro Nevarro.

I wonder now, in looking back, what devil of foolhardiness could have possessed me.

As we drew near the Post-Office, Ned grasped my hand, and with a parting injunction to "keep cool and not be led out of the crowd," paused while I went on.

I ascended the steps of the Post-Office and glanced about. A small man was leaning against the wall in a shaded niche of the building, and my heart gave a little flutter as I noticed a red handkerchief round his neck.

" Now for it ! " said I to myself, and as I passed the man, I glanced under his slouched hat, and said " Esperanza ! "

" Melbourne ! " replied he, promptly, and then added, " Follow me out of this crowd."

I hesitated for a moment ; but glancing at the diminutive

stature of my guide, I felt for the handle of the revolver, and with a shrug of the shoulders, followed him down the steps.

Ned's tall figure loomed up for an instant in the crowd, and I saw him raise his hand warningly, and then the small man dived down an alley and I stepped after him. My blood was up, and I meant to see the matter through.

Wylie paused for a moment to grasp my hand, and then said hurriedly, "We can't talk here. Come to my quarters," and was off again down the alley, and I followed.

For an hour or more we walked rapidly through streets and alleys, till just as it began to grow dusk we entered the Black Town, or native quarter, of Calcutta.

Our roundabout and zigzagging course had somewhat perplexed and alarmed me ; but I satisfied myself with the reflection that Wylie was probably well known to the police, and was obliged to take this measure to throw possible pursuers off the track.

Suddenly my guide paused for a moment, and said apologetically : —

" It 's rather poor quarters I 'm taking you to, but it 's safe ; and there is n't much of the town that 's that for me."

" Go ahead ! " said I.

Low mud huts surrounded us on all sides ; heaps of decaying garbage filled the narrow streets and polluted the air with foul odors ; half-naked women and children squatted in the shaded doorways of their wretched dwellings ; and now and then a jackal could be seen skulking out of sight around a corner.

The courage and confidence had for some time been quietly oozing out of me, and I would n't have been at all sorry to find myself back in our little den, with Ned's stalwart figure at my side. Somehow my scheme did n't seem such a brilliant idea as I had fancied it a few hours before.

It was getting quite dark when Wylie stopped before a building somewhat larger than the huts we had passed. Like them it was built of mud, but with a wooden framework, and a heavy door, on which my guide rapped three times.

An interval of silence followed, and I remember wondering whether my pulse would register a hundred and fifty, or more than that. Suddenly the door flew wide open, and at the same instant a violent push from behind sent me headlong into the building.

Involuntarily my hand grasped the revolver; but before I could draw it, four brawny, naked arms were thrown around me, and in spite of kicks and struggles, I was disarmed, bound hand and foot, gagged, and deposited on a bench by the wall, — all in about two minutes.

The door was closed, and two powerful Hindoos, naked to the waist, took their places before it and stood motionless as statues of bronze.

With the first glance at the room, my heart fairly leaped into my mouth, and then seemed to sink slowly out of me.

At a table in the middle of the long, gloomy room, sat José Miguel himself, Smith of the " Falcon," and a third man whom I did not recognize. They were leaning over the table and examining some papers by the light of a dim lantern. None of the party honored me with the slightest attention.

For a time I did not realize all that the situation implied; but gradually, as the first benumbing effect of the shock wore away, I began to perceive what my headstrong and reckless perversity and conceit had brought me to.

I had carefully prepared a trap for our enemies, and had then complacently walked into it myself. From the time when I wrote the first letter in the name of Pedro Nevarro they had perceived and understood the whole plan, and had simply left me to my own blindness and conceit; and just as they had expected and intended, I had wrought my own destruction, for there was not the slightest chance of my ever leaving that place alive.

The long, melancholy wail of a jackal broke the depressing silence, and there arose in my mind the sickening thought that before another day had dawned, those fierce creatures would be stripping the flesh from my bones.

Where was Ned? Had he followed us? As I remembered our rapid pace and devious route, my heart sank again with the hopelessness of such good fortune.

Poor Ned! What would he do when the night had gone, and the day, and the next night, and still I had not returned?

There was a slight stir among the group at the table. The leader raised his head from the papers he had been examining, and made a gesture. The two half-naked Hindoos left their position by the door and glided silently into the adjoining room.

In a moment they emerged, supporting between them a man dressed in sailors' clothes, bound and gagged like myself. At a second gesture from Miguel the gag was removed from his mouth, and he drew a long breath of relief that ended in a groan. His face was ghastly pale, and the perspiration trickled from his forehead in streams, and ran down his long, matted beard.

In low tones the chief addressed him : —

"James Arling, there is little need of our wasting words with you. You are well aware that in our society there is but one crime and one punishment. That crime you have committed, and that punishment awaits you. Have you anything to say?"

With an effort the man cleared his throat and replied : —

"You forced me blindfold into your accursed gang. I have never tried to betray you, and my only crime was in trying to escape." His voice broke down, and his head sank upon his breast.

Again the Hindoos seized him, and he was removed to the inner apartment. The door was closed, and in the deathly silence that followed, I waited breathless for my time to come.

Minutes that seemed like hours passed away. There was a confused noise from within, a groan, a few strangled gasps, and then again that awful silence.

The long, impatient howl of a hungry jackal, with its final despairing wail, reached my ears and sank deep into my soul.

The door opened, and again the Hindoos emerged, bearing between them the naked body of the man who but a few moments before had walked alive into that room. His head hung helplessly on one side. The face was black, and a small cord was drawn tight around the throat. The outer door was opened, and the men disappeared with their ghastly burden.

Again for ten minutes there was silence, and then the Hindoos returned and quietly resumed their position before the door. At the same time began the jackal howls. Louder, longer, and fiercer, they seemed to gather from all directions, and their snapping and snarling cries could be heard close beside the hut.

At a sign from Miguel I was lifted from my seat and supported before him.

" Remove the gag," said he.

No one who has not suffered from one of these atrocious instruments can realize the exquisite relief of feeling it no longer.

" I must keep cool," thought I, " and seize upon every possible chance of delay."

" These attendants," said Miguel, " have orders to despatch you instantly at the slightest outcry or attempt at escape. Search him ! "

Before leaving my room I had carefully removed everything from my pockets except the two cipher letters. These were soon produced and handed to the chief. He examined them attentively and his brow contracted.

" There are others," said he. Again the search was renewed, but of course without result.

In the mean time I had been reflecting : " So there were other papers ! Could I use this fact in any way ? "

" Strip him," said Miguel, " and search every garment ! "

I was subjected to the humiliating operation of having every article of clothing taken from me.

Summoning all my courage, I said, "You will not find the others."

No answer was returned immediately, but after all my clothes had been examined, the chief said to me, —

" Where are the other papers that you stole from Pedro Nevarro ? "

" The papers you mention," said I, " are in the hands of one who will know how to use them in case I should not return. Did you think me such a fool as to put myself absolutely in your power and surrender all my weapons at the same time ? "

He smiled sarcastically, and inquired, —

" How did you escape from the Australian bush ? "

" By the same knowledge of you and your gang which brought me here to-night," I replied. " You and all your comrades are absolutely in the power of my friends in this city. I am here to treat with you ; and should I not return before morning, they will strike, and you will realize the truth of what I tell you."

For a few moments Miguel consulted with the others.

" Will you send an order which will bring the other papers if I promise to set you free when they are received ? "

" I have no confidence in your promises," I replied. " I did not come here to buy my escape, but to make a proposition to you."

"Name it!" said he with a sneer.

"Restore the six thousand dollars worth of gold which you stole, and I will restore the missing papers, and promise you immunity in the name of my friends."

The scar on Miguel's cheek sprang into a vivid red, and his brow darkened as he replied : —

"Such is your *proposition !* Now hear my answer. If at daylight to-morrow you do not write the letter which I shall dictate, and which you will direct to the proper place, the stranglers will do their work. Remove him."

"One moment," said I. "I am in your power for the time ; but as surely as you injure one hair of my head, you and your gang are utterly lost. Will you permit me to put on my clothes?"

He nodded carelessly, and bracing myself with a tremendous effort to control the trembling which had seized me, I put on my clothes and was led by the guards to the inner room.

The door was closed, and one of the Hindoos pointed to a heap of straw in the corner, on which I sank, utterly worn out.

The room was similar to the first one. Clay walls and floor, with an opening at each end near the roof. A lantern stood upon the floor, and the two Hindoos squatted cross-legged beside it.

The heat and closeness of the atmosphere were stifling, and the thoughts that coursed in rapid succession through my mind were overwhelmingly bitter and hopeless.

I heard the closing of the outer door, and knew that I was alone with the stranglers.

Imagination is powerless to picture the misery of that hour. The physical suffering caused by the heat and closeness of the air, the weird gloom of the apartment, those dark figures, silent and remorseless, their naked, brawny chests reflecting the dim light of the lamp, stealthily watching like tigers about to spring upon their prey, the oppressive stillness within, and the long, melancholy howl of the jackals without, the thought of my awful position and the impossibility of doing anything to alleviate it, — all combined to swell the dread and horror that pressed with leaden weight upon both brain and heart. What writhing in agony on my couch of straw, what bitter memories and unspeakable longings filled the early hours of that night, fortunately for my present happiness, are nearly gone from memory.

Suddenly one of the Hindoos approached, and silently placed by my side a board containing a jug of water and a half-dozen small round cakes. Eagerly I seized the jug and drained it to the bottom.

I had no appetite for food, but feeling that I must support strength by all the means in my power, I ate the cakes, and then sank back again upon the straw.

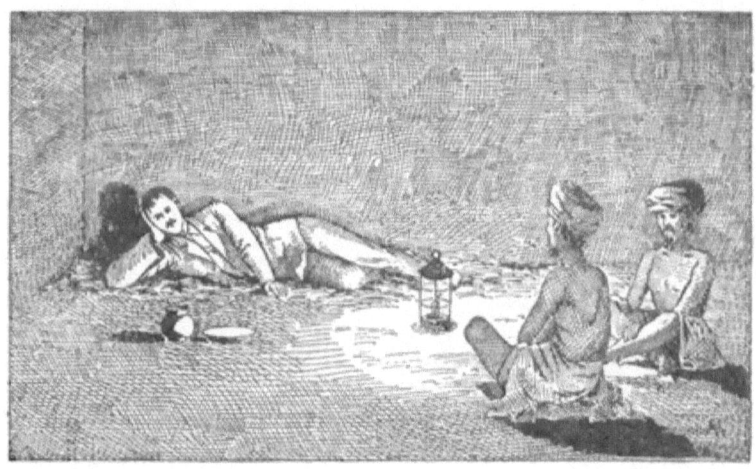

Gradually as I lay there a strange sensation began to creep over me, thrilling to the finger-tips, and slowly lifting from me the weight of suffering and anxiety I had endured so long. The racking headache was all gone, the heat that seemed insupportable became a pleasant, healthful glow, the dangers that menaced me so nearly passed into dim, far-away visions, — things with which I had no connection whatever. Even those grim, mysterious Hindoos, whose voices I had never heard, and whose eyes I had never evaded, lost all their terrors, and became to my exhilarated fancy grotesque caricatures which provoked mirth rather than alarm. As I gazed at them sitting cross-legged side by side, their whole appearance struck me as so amusing that I laughed aloud. I was happy, serenely contented ;

my body was as light as air, my mind free from a shadow of apprehension, and every nerve was quivering with an exquisite unknown sensation.

"Truly," thought I, "those cakes were the very ambrosia of the gods."

For hours and hours, nay, for days and days it seemed to me, I was in this state of absolute and perfect happiness. I was an elysium to myself. The world around was not for me. I had no part nor parcel in it. Danger, hardship, suffering, heat and cold were vague, abstract ideas, as difficult to imagine as eternity or annihilation.

But gradually, as a cloud slowly spreads across the blue sky of June, there arose within me a shadow of distrust, a spectral presentiment, an unspeakable dread, indefinable and formless, but yet growing each moment more real and more appalling. I seemed to shrink as from an impending blow, and yet I felt that what I shrank from was within.

From far away in the distance there came to my ears the muffled beat of a drum. Stroke upon stroke, louder and nearer but never faster, and mysteriously the conviction forced itself upon me that when those drum-beats should cease, life would be extinct. With what agony I listened! Would they stop? Would not the drummer grow weary for an instant, and then — Sometimes the blows were irregular, and with every longer pause a horrible shiver of dread passed through me. At last with a desperate effort I raised my face from the straw in which it was buried. Then, for an instant, perception was cleared, and I realized that the drum-beats I had heard were the terrific throbbings of my own heart.

Leagues and leagues away there appeared a spark of light that slowly rose and grew into a brilliant flame. "It is the sunrise!" thought I. But the flame mounted higher and became a vast beacon light, and around it thronged a crowd of dusky figures. More and more brilliant grew the beacon, the flames rolled and swept upward with ever-increasing volume, and the dark figures prostrated themselves before the raging mountain of fire. "Are they worshipping?" I wondered. But no! those innumerable figures were writhing with dread, not devotion.

The great final day had come. The world was on fire, and I,

too, seemed to share the agony of that frantic crowd, and yet there was no power in my muscles to obey the terrified will. I could not move, but in anguish watched that seething wave of fire slowly rolling nearer and nearer. At last, after ages of suffering, I felt the heat upon my face. I started, and the spell was broken. The mountain of fire that I had watched for so long was the flame of the lantern, and the innumerable crowd were the two Hindoos seated beside it. One of them had risen, and held the lantern close to my face. As I moved, he silently withdrew and took his seat again.

Then began an awful struggle within me. I know not how I shall describe the sensation. No words can possibly reproduce it. The life, the soul, rather the heart, for all seemed one, was striving to rend itself from my body. The will alone retained it, and the will was growing weaker. Long and bitter was the struggle. *My soul left my body.* At least some part of me, which was *myself*, was torn from within with that anguish that a man would feel could he live to have his heart plucked from his breast and to see it still palpitating beside him. And yet more, that heart or soul that went from me was as much *myself*, was as conscious, as individual, as the form that lay prostrate on the straw. I soared aloft into cold, dark regions of limitless space, and yet simultaneously I grovelled on the floor of that wretched room. I was *two*, and yet those two were one, and that divided life was agony intolerable. From my couch of straw I gazed bitterly and fondly after the soaring spirit, and longed in vain to call it back. From those clear, ethereal heights I looked down in anguish on my infirm body, and yearned to raise it to where I floated in space.

Long this bitter suffering endured, and then at last my soul returned to my body, only to prepare it for new horrors.

I was in a gorgeous Indian temple; strange, fantastic carvings surrounded me. Hideous crocodiles leered from the walls, dragons raised their angry crests and dragged their scaly bodies toward me; all the quaint and horrible chimeras of the Orient had become instinct with life, and were writhing and crawling about me. The grotesque idols nodded their triple heads and beckoned me with their multitudinous arms, and mysterious dark-robed priests seized and placed me on a sacrificial altar. The long, keen knives were bared, and I was

powerless to move or to speak. Then suddenly over all rolled
a grand and solemn burst of music. Those mighty organ-tones
swept through the lofty arches, thrilling me with sweet memories, turned to inexpressible bitterness. Through all that wild
and terrible jumble of crawling reptiles and nodding idols and
bloodthirsty priests I heard always the strains of old remembered songs and hymns floating in the air and bringing tears of
bitter recollection to my eyes.

My breast was bared, and the knife was raised to strike.
Slowly — oh, how slowly it descended! I closed my eyes, —
and then for an instant reason returned, and I heard a familiar
air whistled close to the wall of the room.

With a mighty effort I raised myself on the straw and shouted,
" Ned ! "

There was a sound as if all the storms of heaven were let
loose upon the earth. Thousands of dark figures were battling
over my cowering form. My eyes were dazzled with the gleam
of innumerable weapons, and my ears rang with the uproar of
that terrific engagement.

Then came the culmination, — an explosion so tremendous
that it seemed as if the solid earth itself had split into a thousand fragments, and with that final crash my soul sank into utter
darkness and oblivion !

CHAPTER XIII.

"RACE up, and roll out of that, old man! There are more worlds to conquer! Is n't that hashish eliminated yet?"

Such was the salutation that aroused me on the morning of the sixth day after my unpleasant experience related in the last chapter.

We had arrived in Bombay the evening before.

How we reached there has always been more or less of a mystery to me. Ned persists in telling a cock-and-bull story about having rescued me from the two Hindoos, of whom he knocked down one and shot the other, and having dumped me on the railroad-train less than two hours later, since when we had been for five days rolling across the great peninsula of India. Of the truth of his assertions I feel myself incapable of judging. Should I attempt to set down my own recollections of the matter, it would certainly destroy the reader's confidence in this entire narrative. So I simply record Ned's statement as above.

At all events, we were certainly in Bombay, and it was equally certain that our first effort was to get out of it. This we were fortunately enabled to accomplish on the next afternoon after our arrival, by securing a chance to work our passage to Kurrachi on one of the steamers bound up the gulf. Beside our usual certificates, we took with us two mementos of Bombay, — a fine revolver which I purchased to replace the one stolen from me in Calcutta, and a piece of foolishness in the shape of a beautiful box of inlaid work, with a secret spring, which Ned was unable to resist. We steamed rapidly away from the city, and the stately Towers of Silence dropped at last below the horizon. Our personal knowledge of Bombay would not occupy long in the telling.

It was a four days' voyage to Kurrachi, and in spite of the breeze it was a hot voyage. When, on the morning of May 24th, we finally clambered up the miserable ladder to the jetty of the port of Kurrachi, we looked forward with hope, even to the deserts and dangers that lay before us.

"Just imagine," said Ned, "the absolute perfection of gall to which we have attained. Two youthful Yankees with one hundred and twenty-five dollars in their pockets, preparing to penetrate the heart of Asia alone."

"'There 's a divinity that shapes our ends,'" replied I, — "the divinity that watches over drunken men. Blind luck will help us out, — as it has before."

So we toiled along the wide, dusty highway toward the town of Kurrachi.

I think that even the very magnitude of what we were undertaking served to intoxicate us. Certainly we never were in better spirits, and Ned's cheery basso trolling out "Upidee," drew a glance of disgusted amazement from a turbaned Moslem who passed us, and even caused his camel to survey with mild-eyed reproach the reckless individual who could find anything song-worthy in life.

In Kurrachi we elbowed our way through throngs of Turks, Jews, and other infidels, past long trains of camels and mules, and halted at last at the door of a mercantile house whose proprietor was a gentleman named MacDougal.

Honor to the name of Scotchman, and double honors to that noble representative of the title ! Should he by any chance ever see this record of our adventures, let me take this opportunity of reiterating to him the gratitude which Ned and I vainly tried to express, when, worn, exhausted, bracing ourselves by the fictitious courage of desperation, we were received by him, reclothed, hospitably entertained, cheered, and encouraged, aided in our enterprise, forewarned of all that we must expect to encounter, and sped on our way at last, supplied with provisions, and all that true kindness and generosity could furnish for a forlorn hope such as we had determined to undertake.

Long did the worthy Scotchman argue with us that moonlight evening, as we sat on the cool veranda of his bungalow. Many times did his flaxen-haired daughter, the canny Kate, tell us of the nearly insurmountable dangers that lay before us, and beseech us, almost with tears, to abandon our foolhardy design. Ned and I had grown callous to danger, and doggedly and recklessly determined, and for once the Scotch persistence had to succumb to the Yankee determination.

For we had definitely made up our minds and sealed our resolve with a solemn hand-grip, that, blow high, blow low, we would penetrate through the heart of Southern Asia to Herat, thence to Teheran, and from there, if alive, we would struggle on to the Mediterranean coast.

And so the noble old Scotchman, finding that his kind and wise exhortations were wasted on men who had calmly made up their minds to go, with the true spirit of hospitality betook himself to doing all that could be done to enable us to make the perilous trip in safety, and so defeat his gloomy predictions.

With the early morning we were back with him at his office, and he had sent for a guide, a man, as he told us, who better than any other living man could pilot us through the wild region before us. He was a Persian, educated in a Calcutta office in his boyhood, who had learned to speak English fluently, but from the study of classical English had acquired more of the language of Shakespeare and Milton than of the present day. He had travelled repeatedly over the length and breadth of Southern Asia, was a master of the Afghan tongue and of half a dozen of the dialects of the nomadic desert tribes, but as our worthy friend informed us, "kenned o'erweel the taste o' whiskey." Further, he was not altogether to be depended on in the matter of honesty; but as we had no funds to intrust him with, he seemed on the whole to be the very man we wanted.

Abdallah appeared, and after some pompous discussion on his part, and some guying on the part of Ned, was engaged to convoy us to Teheran, *via* Herat, his remuneration to be, his living on the route, and ten pounds on our safe arrival at the capital of Persia.

Then Mr. MacDougal bestirred himself to secure our admission as fellow-travellers with a large caravan which was to set out for the north on the following day ; and this accomplished, with indefatigable ardor he procured for us four sound and stalwart mules, to be delivered to a correspondent in Teheran, to whom he gave us letters, and then proceeded to superintend the packing of one of the mules with a tent, camp equipage, and provisions to the extent of the carrying capacity of the said mule, including a fine rifle and double-barrelled shot-gun.

To all our protestations his reply was, " Hout, mon ! can ye no allow me the privileege of exercising the juties o' hospitality ? "

So, after one more evening of quiet home comfort and jollity, we found ourselves on the morning of May 27th arrayed in Oriental costume, with wide baggy trousers and mighty turbans, seated on our mules and *en route* for the mysterious regions of earliest civilization and latest barbarism.

The caravan to which we were attached consisted of one hundred and thirty camels, fifty mules, and about seventy-five men, mostly Afghan merchants returning to Candahar and neighboring points.

The preparation for the start was a scene of confusion such as could rarely be equalled elsewhere. Our turbaned companions rushed frantically in every direction, kicking and belaboring their mules and camels, and every tongue was wagging without a second's pause. It seemed to us as if the scenes of the Tower of Babel and the confusion of tongues had been reproduced for our especial benefit. The only word we could recognize was the frequently recurring " Allah," often used in a way that recalled the American mule-driver's use of its English equivalent.

Our worthy Abdallah waited with folded arms and calm superiority until, after an hour or more, the excitement had subsided and the long caravan was formed in line. Then he mounted his mule, and with a courtly wave of the hand invited us to fall in. We took our places near the rear, Abdallah leading the pack-mule, and the procession set out.

Our route lay along a barren, sandy plain, with a few withered shrubs scattered over its surface, toward a faint, blue line of mountains, away to the northwest.

"This desert is n't much worse than California," said Ned. "We 're seasoned for something hotter than this."

"Here is not the desert!" said Abdallah. "Later will the Sahib long again for the cool atmosphere of the present."

"If your Oriental eye leads us astray, Ab," said Ned, "we shall produce an atmosphere for your benefit that will make you long again for the hottest desert you ever experienced."

"The Sahib needs no fear, but much patience and endurance," was the reply.

At ten o'clock we had accomplished about fifteen miles, and with new uproar and clamor the caravan halted and went into camp for the noon rest beside a brackish well.

In an hour the dirty, brown tents were pitched in a circle, the camels and mules were contentedly resting within the enclosure thus formed, sentries were posted, and the silence of the noon siesta had fallen upon the camp. The hot sun beat down upon the tents, and Ned and I, after a hasty meal, and dripping with perspiration, fell into a troubled sleep beneath our sheltering roof of canvas.

At four o'clock, with the same uproar, the march was renewed, and at ten o'clock, when the night halt was called, we had made about twenty miles more.

On the morning of the third day we arrived at the Beloochee town of Bela, and camped just outside the mud walls. We had reached the mountains, and the high cliff rose like a wall just behind the little town.

Abdallah pointed out the palace of the Jam, rising above the other dwellings, with its turreted walls of mud.

We had a throng of visitors at camp, — dirty, fierce-looking Beloochees, — from whom we purchased a few supplies in the shape of chickens and eggs.

Keeping the mountains to the left, we travelled on toward Kelat, sometimes over stretches of desert, now and then mounting to cool passes, and rarely skirting the banks of rivers through fertile, tropical valleys.

Only once was there any incident sufficient to cause a moment's excitement or a thought of danger.

We were crossing a wide stretch of desert on the morning

march, when suddenly a cloud of dust appeared away on the western horizon. There was a sudden outcry, a halt, and to my amazement, in less than five minutes the animals were all huddled together in a group, and seventy-five men had dismounted and formed with military precision in a double line, all with guns ready for action, and facing the ominous cloud, which had now lifted sufficiently to disclose a troop of about a hundred horsemen coming on at a swinging gallop.

Suddenly, when just beyond range, the approaching party halted abruptly; a few scattering shots were fired, causing little spurts of dust to spring up where the bullets struck the ground just before us; and then, instantly, the riders wheeled their horses and disappeared again in a cloud.

Not a shot had been fired from our party. Our firm and ready front had proved too much for the stomachs of the gallant sons of the desert.

That noon the sentries were doubled, and Ned and I slept but little.

It was the evening of June 9th, fourteen days after setting out from Kurrachi, that we camped in the neighborhood of Kelat. This was the last of our association with our travelling companions. In the morning the caravan moved placidly on its way toward the northeast, in the direction of Candahar; while we, in obedience to the guidance of Abdallah, turned toward the northwest, and took up our journey alone through a fertile valley, resting on the edge of the desert from 10 o'clock A. M. until 8 o'clock in the evening.

As our guide insisted, we must travel thenceforward only in the night, concealing ourselves as much as possible in the daytime.

Who that has not experienced it, can realize the awful magnificence of a night journey across the desert?

The dry, pure air, intensely hot, but relieved occasionally by light, wandering zephyrs that fainted as they fanned our scorching cheeks; the wide, level plain unbroken in any direction by the slightest elevation, no smallest tree or shrub or living form to relieve the monotony of that sombre waste; above all, the perfect dome of the sky unmarred by even the suggestion of a cloud, but sparkling with stars more brilliant than the moon of other regions, — all combined to keep us silent, almost oppressed by the grandeur of the desert.

For five nights we made forced marches, halting each morning by the side of a desert well, where we rested during the day, taking turns in keeping guard of the camp. We saw no living thing from the night we entered the desert until on the morning of June 21st we reached a fertile valley, and the first settlement in the mysterious and dreaded Afghanistan. We had yet eight hundred miles to travel before reaching Herat.

Following Abdallah, we boldly entered the village, and were at once surrounded by a curious crowd of Afghan peasants, with whom our guide held a long and animated conversation, gesticulating and pointing to us with motions of the deepest respect. At the conclusion of this dialogue, to which we had listened in dignified silence, one of the elders of the village led the way to an immense fig-tree under whose branches all the male population of the village assembled. In a few words Abdallah informed us that he had given us the character of thrice-holy men, — Persians, who had three times made the pilgrimage to Mecca, and who by our holiness and skill were able to cure all diseases. We caught the spirit of the affair, and Ned gravely produced from his pack a small parcel containing a bottle of quinine, a box of pills, a preparation for dysentery, and sundry other remedies. Pipes and tobacco were brought, and for half an hour all hands smoked solemnly in silence.

Then the sick began to be brought on litters or crawl to us on their legs, — some on their hands and knees. We gravely interviewed each through the medium of Abdallah, and then administered such remedies as we thought least harmful, each time going through a series of elaborate gestures and genuflections toward the direction of Mecca, and repeating a charm, consisting of a quotation, — the first that came to our minds. A passage from the Iliad, recited in the original in Ned's sonorous voice, seemed to have a remarkable effect, and the patient was wonderfully improved every time that this passage was employed.

At nightfall we set out once more, escorted to the outskirts of the village by nearly the whole population, and bearing as our fees, chickens, eggs, cakes, and fruit in abundance to last us for many days.

During nearly a month we travelled on toward the north, for

the most part through a pleasant, fertile country, living on fruits, corn, chickens, and black grouse, and playing the rôle of physicians whenever we reached a village. To prevent the speedy exhaustion of our small supply of medicines, we manufactured pills from flour, flavoring them with various bitter herbs, and the effect was probably quite as beneficial.

But a dark day was before us. On the morning of July 20th we encamped by the side of a little stream at the foot of a range of mountains. For the past two days we had been again traversing a desert. Abdallah had led us away from the fertile valley we had for a long time followed, saying that a short cut across the desert would save us many miles in the route to Herat.

It was strange, we afterward thought, that no sentiment of distrust entered our minds at this time. We were so completely dependent on our guide, that we were obliged to yield entirely to his instructions; and when he informed us that two days' climbing through the mountains would bring us in sight of Herat, we felt that our dangers were happily terminated.

" We must journey by sun's light now," said Abdallah. " The dangers are no more by day. Here rest we until the morning."

" And a good scheme ! " replied Ned. " Ab, you 're a trump, a veritable right bower, though not much of a joker."

We arranged our camp, and then Ned and I took a short trip around the neighborhood and succeeded in shooting a hare and a brace of black-legged partridges.

At dark, after a hearty supper, we curled up snugly in our tent, leaving Ab to keep watch outside, and were soon lost in the sleep that only tired wanderers can secure or appreciate.

The bright sunlight streaming through a slit in the tent full into my eyes awoke me. I sat up and punched Ned, who instantly arose and looked out.

" Holloa ! " said he. " Ab ! Something wrong, Tom ! Where 's that infernal Oriental ? Ab ! I say ! "

There was no response. In the mean time I had struggled to my feet, and with the first instinct which had possessed me every morning for two years, felt for my money-belt. It was gone !

There was no sign of our guide, no sign of the mules. The rifle also had disappeared. The shot-gun I found lying almost under me, so that my arm must have been over it as I slept.

"Beat!" said Ned.

"Robbed!" said I.

"By an infernal, solemn-faced, lantern-jawed Oriental!" added Ned.

"What to do?" said I.

"Breakfast," replied Ned.

We set to work, made a fire, cooked and devoured a good breakfast, and then sat down to a council.

"Tom," said Ned, "this is, on the whole, a little the worst deal yet!"

"Agreed!" I replied.

The scoundrel had taken the four mules, the greater part of the cooking utensils, the belt containing all our money, — about $120, — the rifle and the rifle cartridges, and all our stock of provisions except one small bag of corn-meal, the hare we had shot the day before, and the remains of the package of coffee we had brought from Kurrachi, now nearly exhausted.

"Tom," said Ned, "here 's a sheet of paper and a pencil. Write out our situation and let 's take an inventory. Then we will vote as to our future course."

So I wrote (I have the paper now before me) : —

"July 21, 1879. Wilderness of Central Asia, somewhere near Herat probably. Desert on one side, range of mountains on the other.

"Two American youths, — alone. No acquaintance with the country or the languages. No means of conveyance except shank's mare. No money. Possessed at present of the following articles : —

"A suit of clothes apiece, — Persian style of garments, — somewhat worn. A double-barrelled shot-gun. About a hundred rounds of shot cartridges, assorted.

"Two good-sized canteens.

"Two revolvers (seven-shooters).

"Sixty cartridges for same.

"Two leathern haversacks or knapsacks, containing, —

" Two flannel shirts.
" Twelve handkerchiefs.
" Four towels.
" Four pair socks.
" Two tooth-brushes.
" Two flutes.
" Two hundred and fifty sheets paper.
" Ten lead-pencils.
" Four and a half boxes matches.
" One inlaid box with secret spring.
" Package of letters and certificates.
" Contracts (to do something apparently impossible).
" Two small hair-combs.
" Three cakes soap.
" Also, two large knives (style known as Bowie).
" Two small knives.
" One ball strong twine.
" Two papers pins.
" Two packages containing assortment of needles, thread, buttons, etc.
" Package of fish-hooks (sundry sizes).
" Two coils fish-line (different sizes).
" Small bag corn-meal.
" Small bag coffee.
" Two tin cups.
" One small camp-kettle.
" One tin pail.
" Two heavy woollen blankets.
" One roll maps, — India, Central Asia, Persia, Syria, Asia Minor, and Palestine.
" Two brierwood pipes.
" Two pounds tobacco.
" Remains of four pocket blank-books.
" Two long pocket-books.
" Small leather case, containing, —
" One half-pound bottle quinine.
" Four boxes pills.
" One bottle preparation for dysentery (nearly empty).
" One pint flask brandy.
" One tent.

" Above goods, except the tent, can easily be packed and carried on our shoulders.

" Question for discussion, ' What shall we do? ' "

After a prolonged study of the map, we decided that Herat must lie on the other side of the range of mountains, as our absconding guide had asserted.

" Then," said Ned, " the thing to do is to get there. Let 's pack and away."

" For once," said I, " your mountain predilections agree with me."

There was no trail or path before us, — only a wilderness of mountains, with the chance that we might discover a pass. But at least they were neither as high nor as rugged as the Sierras, and a vale opened up before us, down which came the little stream by whose side we had camped.

So we packed and shouldered our earthly possessions, and leaving the tent standing, we set out boldly up the valley.

" Which way can our slippery assistant have gone, I wonder," remarked Ned. " It may be that we are following close on his trail."

" Probably we are near the Persian frontier," replied I, " and he has doubtless friends within a few day's journey, to whom he has betaken himself with our mules and wealth."

" At all events, this is somewhat better than if he had seen fit to abandon us in the desert," said Ned ; and as he spoke, a brace of partridges whirred up before us, and both dropped at the discharge of the shot-gun.

For five days we wandered among the mountains, trying always to work through to the north, often compelled to retrace our steps to seek a new outlet, sometimes baffled and discouraged, but always living well on the abundant game, and sleeping comfortably in our blankets.

On the fifth afternoon we came upon a stream which unquestionably flowed toward the north ; and as the valley seemed to open out for some distance in that direction, we felt sure that we had at last found the outlet, and could readily reach the other side of the range.

But next morning, after we had followed the stream for several miles, it suddenly leaped over a precipice forming a beautiful waterfall; so a couple of hours' hard climbing was necessary to bring us to a point that offered a descent to the lower level. From this point we looked down upon a gentle wooded slope, and beyond, gleaming through the scattering trees, appeared a wide white level surface.

"The sea!" exclaimed Ned in wonder.

"No," said I; "the desert! and there," I continued, suddenly pointing toward the right, "see that smoke rising above the trees! There is a village; and Herat is just beyond. Forward!"

We joyfully descended the rocky slope, and hurried toward the direction of the smoke which we had seen. The wood became more open for a distance, then closer, and as we penetrated through a thick growth of shrubs and bushes, we suddenly came into an open, park-like clearing, and plump into a *camp*.

Thirty or forty black tents were scattered about; fires were smouldering in all directions; cattle, sheep, and horses were browsing all around us; and swarthy-skinned men, women, and children were lounging about the camp or busy with their duties.

A few rods to our left the trees dwindled away, and the great white desert stretched out to the horizon.

All this was taken in at a glance, and we simultaneously uttered a startled exclamation, — "Turcomans!"

It was too late to retreat. We had been seen the instant we broke cover. A shout went up, and before we had time to turn or fly, an eager crowd of fierce-looking men was close upon us.

It was a fearfully trying moment. I remember the thought flashed through my mind, "It is folly to resist!"

Some other thought must have entered Ned's mind, for as the first stalwart savage rushed at him with arms outstretched, as if to be the first to seize the prey, Ned's mighty fist flew straight out from the shoulder, and the powerful assailant was lifted clean off his legs, and dropped on his back six feet away. Then there was a confused rush, a flashing of knives, a *crack! crack! crack!* of revolvers, — in the midst of which I observed my own smoking revolver in my hand, though how it got there I had no idea, — and then suddenly, before I realized what had happened, our assailants had fled from the field, leaving six of their comrades in the dust, and Ned was pulling a long, ugly-looking knife from the fleshy part of his right forearm.

"Quick! Tom!" he shouted, as he thrust the knife into his belt, — "your handkerchief!"

In an instant I had whipped out a handkerchief and knotted it tightly around his arm, from which the blood was running in a stream.

"To the woods!" cried I. "Those devils will be back in five seconds."

We turned for a rush, when Ned seized my arm and shouted, "No, the horses!"

Not twenty feet from our left, and toward the desert, stood four magnificent horses, ready saddled and bridled, and tied to a couple of young trees, as if a party had been ready to start out just before our appearance.

In four seconds, in spite of the luggage which encumbered us, we had mounted two of the horses and cut the ropes that tied them. In two seconds more we had darted through the scattering grove, and were in full gallop straight away into the desert.

A fierce shout arose behind us, and a volley of bullets whistled round our ears, one of them striking with a sounding ring on the iron camp-kettle suspended from my back.

"Aim lower, boys!" shouted Ned.

Another moment, and glancing back, I saw four riders in full pursuit, and a dozen others just emerging from the trees.

"Forward, Ned!" I shouted. "They're after us!"

With voice, hand, and heel we urged our horses on. Ah, but what horses those were! Never had I known what riding was before. We seemed to fly through the air, and the only evidence of our touching the earth was in the quick spurts of dust that sprang around us at each magnificent bound. It was like sitting in a hammock, so far as comfort was concerned; and yet the stride of those grand creatures was the most tremendous motion I had ever dreamed of. The hot air of the desert was cut as a vessel cleaves the waves of the sea.

Close together—neck and neck, almost touching each other —they sped away across the burning plain, and the proudly arched necks and the mighty heave of the flanks told what grand reserve of power was in them.

Now and then a shot whistled past us; but our pursuers

evidently counted upon overtaking us, and did not waste many bullets.

Our course was toward the west, and the afternoon sun had dropped about half-way to the horizon, so that when we glanced behind, our pursuers were in full view, but their sight of us must have been greatly affected by the sun shining directly in their eyes.

We had some three hundred yards the start, and it seemed to me that, barring accidents, *no other* horse could possibly gain on the tremendous pace at which we flew over the ground.

Still, after ten minutes it was evident that one of the pursuers had a steed that was equal if not superior to ours. All the others had been left far behind, but this one was certainly gaining. In another five minutes there was no doubt. He was much nearer to us. Still, our horses were going at their very highest speed.

"Shall we wait for him?" asked Ned.

"No," I replied; "too much risk! The rest would come up before we could start again. Let me try a wing shot!"

The shot-gun was slung across my back, and it would have been useless in any case for this purpose. I loosened the revolver in my belt and waited.

Still we sped onward. No slackening in that fearful pace. No slightest symptom of exhaustion in those noble horses. Still, our pursuer was gaining. He was near. Not seventy-five yards lay between us. I could see the fierce gleam of his eyes. He was already unslinging his rifle for a shot.

I grasped the revolver firmly, leaned back upon my flying horse, aimed low, and fired.

There was a sudden thick cloud of dust where our pursuer had been, and in the next second we saw him standing beside his fallen, struggling horse. At the same instant there was another sharp report, and I felt a bullet graze my shoulder and go singing on beyond.

"Hit?" asked Ned.

"No; scratched!" I replied.

"We 're safe," said Ned; "there is no other horse can reach us!"

His last words faltered a little, and I turned and looked at him. He was white to the lips.

"I grasped the revolver firmly, leaned back upon my flying horse, aimed low, and fired." — *Page* 224.

" Damn that arm ! " said he.

" Hang on for dear life, old man ! " I cried. "In fifteen minutes we 'll stop and dress the arm."

I glanced back ; a faint cloud of dust was just vanishing on the horizon. Our enemies had abandoned the pursuit. Onward, still onward, toward the West. For twenty minutes we rode without speaking or drawing rein. Still the same grand pace. Of what were these horses made? What living being could keep that pace and live? I had never before known what was meant by the desert steed of the Turcoman.

A groan from Ned caused me to turn.

" Must stop, old man ! " said he, faintly.

With some difficulty we reined in our horses and dismounted. They scarcely seemed to breathe heavily. They must have come nearly twenty miles in thirty minutes.

I administered a good drink of brandy to Ned, and then while he held the horses with his left hand I bared the right arm and washed the wound thoroughly with water from my canteen. Then I tore up two of our clean handkerchiefs and bandaged the wound as carefully as my surgical skill and the appliances at hand would permit. Ned felt better.

" Can you ride ? " I asked.

" Of course ! " replied he, and mounted lightly to his seat. The brandy had worked wonders.

The wound was not dangerous, apparently. The knife had entirely pierced the fleshy part of the arm and had let out a quantity of blood, causing considerable faintness and a good deal of pain.

" Now," said I, " we must put as much distance as possible between ourselves and those miscreants before camping."

To the right, in front of us, and behind us, lay the boundless desert. To the left, seven or eight miles distant, stretched the mountain-range from which we had started diagonally across the desert. It was now about four o'clock.

We headed our horses on the other diagonal back toward the mountains, and rode forward at a more moderate gait.

Before sunset we had reached the outlying trees, as we calculated about thirty miles distant from the Turcoman camp. We had probably ridden over forty miles in all.

Half a mile beyond the first open grove we came suddenly

upon a considerable river flowing along the foot of the mountains, — perhaps the stream which we had followed when we
came down the valley that morning. Our horses took to the
water bravely, swam safely across, and we made our camp in a
beautiful grassy grove on the south side of the stream.

CHAPTER XIV

WHEN I awoke, Ned was laughing uproariously. I feared the poor fellow had become delirious from the effects of his wound and the sun.

"It just this moment struck me," said he, "how funny our descent was on that Turcoman camp."

"Did n't strike you so funny at the time, did it?" replied I.

"Right you are! My appreciation of the humorous was n't keenly on the alert at that moment. I was busied with more important matters. But look at it now, at thirty miles distance! Here are two poor forlorn wretches without even a mule

between them, walking straight into the middle of a camp of the terrible Turcomans, shooting down six of the great louts, stealing their best pair of horses before their very eyes, and cantering away with a placid 'Good-afternoon.' Imagine the kicking those fellows are giving themselves! And how the air around that camp must reek with Koranic oaths!"

In spite of Ned's hilarity, I saw with some alarm that he was not quite himself. He was flushed and feverish, and his legs were a trifle shaky. The wound was doing fairly well, considering our long ride under the desert sun; but we finally decided to rest in camp for one day, to study up the situation a little, and lay out a course for the future.

" It strikes me, Ned." said I, " and I have thought of it several times, that our interesting Abdallah must have fooled us completely in regard to the location. I believe he led us away to the northwest and beyond Herat. This desert is the great steppe that stretches to the Caspian Sea, and probably somewhere over to the northeast is Merve, the head-centre of the Turcomans."

" If that 's the case," said Ned, " Persia lies just across these mountains, and we shall soon be able to find one of those passes through which the gentle Turcoman is wont to lead his sportive hunting expeditions."

" Then when we prance gayly through the pass, the inhabitants will flee before us ; for they flee from the Turcomans, and behold, we are greater than they ! "

Our captured horses were nibbling the grass quietly beside us, and we had a chance now to examine them more closely. They were alike in color, — a strong iron-gray, — large and powerfully developed, but not so handsome in shape as either the Arab horse or the English thoroughbred. The neck was a trifle too long, and the head inclined to the shape known as " hammer-headed." But they were kind and gentle, — evidently well trained, — and of their speed and endurance we had had ample experience.

The next morning Ned was better, though still somewhat weak. I had dosed him thoroughly with quinine, not supposing it would be of any special benefit, but on general principles, and he seemed to be thriving, either because or in spite of my treatment.

We determined to move on westward and work through the mountains to the south as soon as we found a passage that appeared feasible. In any case we should be going in the right direction.

It was easy travelling for the first day. We kept along comparatively level ground, with the mountains to the left and the river to the right. The direction varied somewhat, of course, but the general tendency was westward.

On the next day we had ridden perhaps fifteen miles, when the country became more irregular. We lost sight of the desert, and mountains began to rise on the north of the river. Ten miles of very rough travelling brought us to a point where the river took a wide sweep directly toward the north, between two broken ranges of hills, while a stream came in through a gap in the southern mountains, and joined the river. Here, we hoped, was our pass toward the south.

For four days we struggled up this pass, turning now west, now east, laboring over places that would have been difficult for a man to climb, and which seemed almost impassable for a horse.

Yet we got through somehow, and on the morning of the fifth day descended the southern slope of the mountains and halted on the edge of — another desert.

It was truly discouraging. The glaring white sand stretched out before us, for all we knew hundreds of miles in extent ; and yet, far away to the southwest, through the twinkling and blinding sunlight, it seemed as if we could make out something like another range of hills or mountains.

A little spring bubbled out of the hillside near where we had stopped, and ran away to be absorbed by the thirsty sand.

Here we rested for the remainder of the day.

Fortunately we had found plenty of game in the mountains. Hare, partridges, and grouse were abundant, and our larder had been well supplied.

"I think we must chance it, Ned," said I, "and make a break to-night across this bit of sand. It is probably a high desert table-land in the heart of the mountains, and a few miles to the south we shall strike the other wing of the range."

We rested and refreshed ourselves and our horses through the day, and at nightfall, drinking all the water we could, and filling our canteens, we set out boldly, heading a little to the west of south, and taking our course toward a brilliant star that shone in the south high above the horizon.

We rode silently and swiftly, side by side. It was a great risk we were taking, and we both appreciated it. If the sun should rise and find us "out of sight of land," we knew that it would probably mean shipwreck in that vast and arid waste.

The air was hot and still. The sand, scorched by the daily sun, radiated waves of heat about us.

Steadily we rode forward, and the only words spoken were an occasional, " A little more to the right, Tom," or, " Keep to the right, Ned," as we glanced up at our guiding star.

Strange ! we did not realize that as the night advanced our star was moving toward the west, and that in following it we were making our course much more westerly than we had intended.

Only after riding about five hours did the truth dawn upon us, when the star had dropped so low as to be noticeably near the horizon.

In less than half an hour it disappeared altogether, and yet we supposed it was still two hours above the level edge of the desert.

"The mountains !" cried Ned, suddenly. "It has gone behind the mountains !"

We rode forward joyfully. In another hour we were among the first straggling outposts of the forest, and an hour later we had kindled a fire and camped beside a swift little stream that rippled merrily over its stony bed, while before us, and to the east and west, rose the dark shadow of the mountains.

We had a long, sound sleep for the rest of the night and far into the following day, and awoke refreshed and greatly encouraged. We had reached a point that seemed to offer a ready exit from the mountains, with which we had struggled so long.

The hills and ranges lying around us were much less rugged and difficult than those we had traversed, and a wide valley, mounting gradually upward toward the southwest, seemed to offer all that we could desire for a passage.

"But what are we to do, Ned," said I, as we rode easily up the pass, "when we reach the settled and civilized country of Persia, if there is such a region ?"

"Live on the country," replied Ned. "Follow the illustrious example of Xenophon, that friend of our youth. Steal and fight our way through to 'Thalassa,' the Mediterranean."

"You think, then, that two Yankees are equal to ten thousand Greeks. Well, as one Greek was considered equal to ten Persians, we ought to be able to cope with quite a large population. But there 's a rather important point to be considered. We know approximately the direction of Teheran ; but for a man to point at a city five hundred miles distant, and travel to it around mountains, across deserts and rivers, through a country about as familiar to him as soap is to a Turk, would be somewhat of a feat, even for a Yankee."

"Do you know what we 'll do, Tom?"

"Yes; we 'll get there."

"We 'll catch a guide."

"You left your lasso in California."

"Yes, but not my nerve."

"Your assurance, your *cheek*, you mean by that?"

"Shall I tell you something?"

"By all means."

"You left a large part of your nerve in that mud hut in Calcutta. You don't talk so much about getting even with the Miguel gang lately, do you?"

"Don't mention that little episode. No. I 'm not saying anything now, but I 'm keeping up a devil of a thinking."

"Can't offer you a penny for your thoughts, because you are the treasurer, and the funds have been misappropriated."

"And if I gave you the thoughts, you would misappropriate them."

"No, Tom, it would probably be impossible to turn them to any account."

"Doubtless; for you would be unable to grasp them."

Toward the latter part of the afternoon we reached the ridge, and were able to look down to the south. We saw a wide, cultivated valley, running nearly east and west, with broken mountain-chains and hills beyond; something of the semblance of a road lying along the midst of the valley, and close beneath us, not two miles distant, a little Persian village.

We descended cautiously for about a mile, and paused to reconnoitre.

A thick growth of bushes and low trees obscured our view; but turning to the left for a short distance, we found an opening through which we could force our horses, and came suddenly upon an orchard or vineyard, with apricots, grapes, pomegranates, and other fruits ripening on the slope of the hillside. A man was standing at about ten rods distance, with his back toward us, busy at one of the vines.

We glanced about. There was no one else in sight, and the nearest house was about a half-mile distant.

"This is our very opportunity, Tom," whispered Ned. "Follow me and help me out."

We suddenly urged our horses to a run, and came up one

on each side of the startled Persian, and before he realized
that anything had happened, we had thrown ourselves to the
ground, and stood beside him, each with a revolver pointed at
his head.

With a muttered exclamation, the man fell upon his knees
and raised his hands above him, placing his wrists together.

"All right, Tom," said Ned; "he knows the ropes. See if
you can find one."

I produced our ball of stout twine, and twisting four or five
strands together, rapidly produced a short rope with which we

strongly tied the hands of our captive, who all the time offered
not the slightest resistance, evidently considering himself the
spoil of the Turcoman.

"See if he has any weapons," said Ned.

A search only revealed a large knife, possibly a pruning-
knife. This I slipped into my belt.

"Now, get up," said Ned, with a gesture which was doubtless better understood than the words.

The man arose, trembling. Ned mounted his horse, and I
assisted our captive to mount behind him. Then we retraced
our course for about a mile up the pass, and halted at a level
spot that looked attractive for a camp.

Our captive was deposited on the ground, where he sat in a state of sullen apathy.

"How 's that for a Turcoman raid?" said Ned. "Was ever one conducted more quietly and peaceably? Now see me tackle this degenerate descendant of the race of Cyrus."

Ned approached the Persian, who was seated on a log, and to my astonishment began a long harangue from the Iliad, beginning with the Τὸν δ' ἀπαμειβόμενος προσέφη, etc., and ringing in all the odd scraps he could think of, without regard to connection or sense, all delivered in the most pompous and imposing manner, with dramatic gestures.

"That 's just for a starter, Tom," he said; "to get him worked up to the exigencies of the case."

Our captive listened and gazed with an expression of the most stolid indifference on his face.

Then Ned assumed a conversational tone and a confidential manner. He took the Turcoman knife from his belt, at which the Persian crouched and cowered in abject terror.

"Good!" said Ned, in an aside to me. "He has no more nerve than the ordinary Oriental. We can manage him."

He cut the cords that bound the wrists of our new friend, and leaning forward, said confidentially in his ear, "Meshed," and then sprang back with an air of satisfaction, as if he had struck the keynote of the whole matter.

No result.

Then Ned said, "Mashid," then "Mash*eed;*" then he tried seven other pronunciations, with no success.

At this stage I became interested, and turned in and took a whirl at the poor chap, with about eight more pronunciations of the same name. At last something like a ray of intelligence seemed to enliven the expressionless face before us. We seized on the pronunciation that had elicited this gleam, and repeated it several times in an inquiring tone, pointing north, south, east, and west, in succession. The Persian gravely raised his arm and pointed east.

"Capital," said Ned. "We have got to the west of Meshed. The next question is, 'How far?'"

It is unnecessary to go into all the details of our methods of communication with the Persian. We finally learned that we were five days' journey west of Meshed, and nineteen days' east of Teheran. We concluded, rightly or wrongly, that the "day's journey" was about twenty miles, which would give us three hundred and eighty miles to reach Teheran.

"And with these horses, Tom, it will take us about eight days," said Ned; "or rather eight nights, for we must skulk in the daytime, and travel in the dark."

"And what do you propose to do with that poor thing?" asked I.

"Take it along to spy out the land for us, and show us the way to the capital. It's neck or nothing now with us, Tom. Of course it's a little rough on the poor chap; but we won't hurt him, and will turn him loose, when we reach Teheran, to find his way back."

We kindled a fire, gave our guide a hearty supper, and after about two hours' hard labor we succeeded in making him understand that we were going to Teheran, that he must go as our guide, and that we would set him free as soon as we reached there. Further, that at the least symptom of treachery we would blow out his brains, broil him, or treat him to some other pleasant alternative of that character.

As soon as it was fairly dark we set out.

I do not suppose that any one else ever travelled through Persia in precisely the manner in which we journeyed to the capital. We literally lived on the country, and yet the country knew it not. Ned and I had had great experience, in our youthful days, in the felonious appropriation of melons from neighboring gardens; but we never indulged in that pastime so constantly and successfully as during this trip. And the melons were well worth the trouble of securing them. I have never eaten such anywhere else.

Our guide, who called himself Ali, soon became quite reconciled to his lot, and entered into the spirit of the thing with a zest that did credit to his intelligence and his education.

He had a wonderful nose for a fine melon-patch or a vineyard, and the appropriating of the fruit or the sheep of his compatriots seemed to be quite a familiar and enjoyable occupation to him. Ned called him either Ali Baba or The Forty Thieves, and he grew to respond to the latter appellation quite as readily as to the former.

We travelled and foraged only in the night. As soon as the first rays of daylight appeared, we turned aside and hied us to a secure retreat on the mountain-side or in the forest, where we rested through the day, taking turns in sleeping, occasionally getting a shot at a partridge or a hare, and once at a red deer, which proved a delicious roast. Ali always slept placidly and contentedly through the day, except when roused to a meal.

Most of our route was through a beautiful, fertile country, with hills and valleys alternating, while the mountains rose to the north, growing more lofty as we advanced, and occasionally crowned with snow.

It was on the tenth morning, just as day was breaking, that we came in sight of the walls and minarets of Teheran.

We took leave of Ali, giving him to understand that he was free to find his way back to the bosom of his family. With our blessing, which was all we had to bestow, he set out to return on foot, while we moved onward, and passing through the stately Meshed gate, entered Teheran, the fifteenth city of our list. This was Friday, August 15, just eighty days since we had set out from Kurrachi.

The streets of Teheran were thronged with the busy tradesmen going to their booths, and the population of the surrounding country coming in on mules and horses to their daily business. The letters which our Scotch friend MacDougal had given us were addressed to an attaché of the English embassy, and thither we directed our steps in the first instance.

Our reception was as cordial as could be desired ; and when MacDougal's friend had read the letters which we presented, he insisted upon taking us at once to his own residence in one of the suburbs, where nearly all the English people live. As soon as our story was told, we became the heroes of the hour. Englishmen or Americans were not such frequent visitors at the Persian capital as the little English colony could wish, and none had ever come with such an experience as ours. We felt badly over the loss of the mules, which we were to have delivered to MacDougal's friend, and we did our best to make amends for this misfortune, even offering one of our Turcoman horses in their place ; but our new friend would not listen to such a thing.

"I shall do exactly as old MacDougal would do himself," said he. "I shall do everything possible to make your visit pleasant, and see that you leave here properly equipped, and with papers which will perhaps be of assistance to you, if, as you say, you are determined to ride through to Bagdad and Damascus."

We had indeed fallen on our feet again.

It is perhaps a very commonplace and trite remark, — but it was brought home to us very strongly and gratefully in all our travels in foreign lands, — that no one ever appreciates a fellow-countryman (and for this purpose we considered Englishmen as fellow-countrymen) so much as when encountered far away from home and friends, in a strange country, and among a race different in language and customs from one's own.

A load seems lifted from one's shoulders. Amid all the jargon, the strange people, and the bewildering surroundings, you feel as if you had found a bit of home. Here, at least, is something you can understand, some one to whom you can explain your situation, something solid to which you can cling amid the unfamiliar and unreliable people and circumstances among which you are thrown.

For six days we stayed in Teheran, enjoying ourselves hugely after the long months of hardship and dangers through which we had passed. We became familiar with all of the little English colony, and received many kindnesses at their hands. Nothing could have been more hospitable and courteous than their treatment. We really felt that it was worth all it had cost.

But the best of all their kind acts, and the most important to us, was reserved until the close of our visit. Almost every one had heard of our enterprise, and many of the details of our adventures. All had greatly admired our wonderful Turcoman horses. We might have realized a considerable sum, had we been willing to part with them. But there was still over a thousand miles of desert and wilderness lying between us and the Mediterranean, and we felt that no other means of conveyance could take their place. Moreover, we had become greatly attached to the noble brutes, and they had learned to know and understand us. No! we could not part with our horses.

But one evening our friend of the embassy proposed that we should meet a party at one of the neighboring houses and tell them our story in detail.

"The East is a great place for story-telling, you know," said he; "but I believe that very few even of the marvellous tales of the Orient would prove as interesting as yours."

We readily assented, and went with him to a gathering of about forty of the English residents, to whom, as well as I was able, I related the story of our adventures, leaving out the Miguel portion almost entirely.

I was pleased to see that my audience was interested, and still more pleased and surprised when at the conclusion of the story one of the gentlemen presented us with a purse of forty pounds, on the part of the English colony, "as a token of our appreciation of the pleasant evening you have given us, and as a tribute to Anglo-Saxon pluck and enterprise."

Every one knew that we were absolutely without a cent; but the method they took of helping us on our way seemed peculiarly courteous and thoughtful.

It would be easy to write many pages of the interesting sights and pleasant experiences that rendered the Persian capital a delightful reminiscence to us, but time and space are pressing, and much remains to complete the story.

I leave Teheran here as we left it then, — with sincere regret.

Besides our usual letters, our kind friends obtained for us documents from the Persian authorities which might prove of value in our long march through the country, and they also gave us letters to English residents in Bagdad, which insured a cordial welcome there.

I had nearly forgotten to mention what was to Ned the greatest happiness that Teheran offered; namely, a long letter from Maggie. Poor hungry soul! it was the first morsel he had had since Calcutta.

It was the 21st of August when, with two English gentlemen and a long caravan of Persians with camels, mules, and asses, we set out for Bagdad.

Our route was largely through a fertile country, with occasional patches of desert and one or two mountain-passes. Nothing occurred to disturb the well-regulated monotony of a caravan journey. On the morning of Monday, September 8, the eighteenth day, after a wide stretch of desert, we came in sight of the fringe of palms bordering the banks of the Tigris, and soon saw the minarets and domes of the City of the Caliphs rising from the plain before us.

CHAPTER XV.

BAGDAD is a true type of the Oriental city of to-day.

Its associations as the seat of government of the "Good Haroun Alraschid," as the home of all the mystic and marvellous imagery of the "Arabian Nights," as the centre of all that barbaric wealth and splendor celebrated by so many historians and poets, make the name of Bagdad synonymous with the word "Oriental," and with all the vague and gorgeous images which that word suggests.

And the present aspect of the city conveys another idea which history has associated with the word "Oriental," — the idea of a grandeur which is *past*, of a profuse and reckless magnificence whose evidence to-day is seen only in the mosques and palaces and minarets fast falling into decay and ruin.

The calm, indifferent fatalism of the East has been brought into conflict with the progressive, defiant thought and enterprise of the West, and the old man is being forced to the wall.

In the picturesque booths that line the streets of Bagdad, the Arab merchants sit placidly smoking their chibouks, or sipping their black coffee, and they seem to regard with dislike and annoyance the man who ruthlessly disturbs their meditations by attempting to make a purchase.

And yet there is life and movement in Bagdad. The restless foreigner is there. The Turk, the Armenian, the Greek, the omnipresent Englishman, throng the streets in their national costumes, jabbering, bargaining, prying, and inquiring, —

and otherwise disturbing the placid repose of the faithful,—while the solemn silence of the old towers and palaces, brooding over their past magnificence, is broken by the discordant whistle of the western river steamboat.

Five days were pleasantly passed in Bagdad. There are many English people there, and our reception was cordial and hospitable as we could have desired. Ned and I were as brown as Indians from long exposure to the desert sun, and we had become very thoroughly inured to the tremendous heat. Yet when the mercury ranged to 125° and 135° in the shade, we were glad to seek the cool seclusion of the *serdaubs*, or underground apartments, of our friends. The nights were passed on the flat roof, under the brilliant starlight, the usual bed-chamber of the inhabitants of Bagdad.

During our stay in the city we made the acquaintance of a young Englishman called William Morley, a quiet, pleasant fellow, master of a considerable fortune, and a great traveller and hunter. For five years he had been roaming the earth, accompanied only by his servant, the faithful Sam, a type of the old-fashioned English valet and factotum.

Mr. Morley was an enthusiastic hunter, and a crack shot with the rifle. He had killed tigers in India and lions in Africa, and he had the true spirit of adventure and daring which has made the name of Englishman so wide-spread throughout the earth.

He was fascinated with our story, and in the course of a day or two a strong friendship grew up between us. It resulted in his determination to join us, with his inseparable Sam, in our journey across the Syrian desert to the Mediterranean, and perhaps beyond.

We were advised by all our friends in Bagdad to take the long caravan route up the Euphrates and by way of Aleppo to Damascus, as by far the safest route both as regarded the danger from wandering Bedouins, and also the water-supply; but we were anxious to visit the ruins of Palmyra, and decided to take the short, direct route, straight across the desert, taking in Palmyra, or Tadmor, in our way. About once in two weeks a single Arab made this passage on a fast dromedary, carrying the mail; we would go with him. And in this decision our new friend Morley concurred heartily.

"There is no excitement in life, unless we have a spice of danger," said he ; " and I have not yet shot a Syrian lion."

So on Saturday morning, September 13, we said farewell to our Bagdad friends and set out boldly on the last long section of our Asiatic journey.

We were a party of five, — the Arab mail-carrier on his dromedary ; Morley and Sam, mounted on fleet Arab mares, and each equipped with an English rifle and a brace of revolvers ; Ned and I on our Turcoman horses, also with rifles and revolvers.

Morley had at first wished to provide a mule-train with tents, camp equipage, and a good supply of barley for our horses, as well as provisions for ourselves. This was overruled, however, as time was the chief consideration, and we must rely upon the speed of our horses to bring us through the dangerous regions.

We travelled as light as possible, only carrying on each horse a bag of barley and a goat-skin for water, with our simple personal baggage and provisions.

Away from the city we headed a little to the north of west, following a road across the Mesopotamian plain toward the Euphrates. Little Arab villages were scattered about over the plain, and we followed for many miles the ruined course of an ancient canal, which had formerly united the waters of the Tigris and Euphrates. The bed of the canal was high above the level of the surrounding country, drifted half full of sand from the desert. Yet the banks, even ruined as they were, rose for twenty feet above the bed, a tremendous monument of the old civilization that had reared them. We camped that night at an Arab village, and on the next afternoon (Sunday) we reached the bank of the Euphrates, and stretched at full length in a grove of beautiful palms.

"Sam," said Morley, "it's good to be on the war-path, again. You have travelled in style lately, Sam, and you're growing fat and lazy. A little desert life will do us both good."

"Which is what I thought to myself, sir," replied Sam. "You have not been in such good spirits for months before, sir."

"I fancy we shall all need a stock of good spirits for the next two weeks," said I.

Our Arab companion sat quietly smoking his long pipe beside his dromedary, at some distance away.

"Come over here, old Eli!" shouted Ned. "Come and join the group."

So the singular-looking postman brought his precious mail-bag and gravely squatted beside us.

Then for an hour or two we told stories and smoked, and enjoyed a comfortable rest, while our horses cropped the herbage on the river-bank.

For three days we travelled northwest along the bank of the Euphrates, then crossed the stream and headed due west into the desert.

Ten days, our guide said, should bring us to Palmyra, and our successfully arriving there depended on three contingencies, — the finding a supply of water and fodder at the usual places, our endurance of the heat and the sand-storms of the desert, and the avoidance of hostile parties of Bedouins.

"I believe the Bedouins would have some labor to catch us," said Ned, "except for our dromedary friend."

"And for the heat," said I, "we can stand it."

"And for the water," said Morley, "we must take our chances."

The first day's journey was over rolling ground scantily covered by thin shrubs, with here and there a withered palm-tree struggling bravely to support itself and the reputation of the soil. At night we reached a little spring and a grove of palms, at the foot of the range of hills that formed the western edge of the Euphrates valley.

"Now the trouble begins!" cried Ned, as we launched ourselves bravely the next morning on the great rolling desert that stretched before us to the western horizon.

There was one peculiarity about our horses, both the Arab and the Turcoman, — they had but two gaits; they must travel either at a walk or a gallop. The dromedary, on the contrary, had one gait, a long, swinging, ambling trot, constantly the same, and covering the ground with amazing rapidity. So, as we must not part with our guide, we fell into the habit of walking our horses until the dromedary was a mile or two in advance, when we would overtake him at a run and drop behind again.

The ground was a soft, yielding sand, here and there thrown up into ridges, mounds, and hillocks by the wind. The plain was a billowy ocean of sand.

An American or English horse would have labored hard over such ground ; but our animals were at home, and to them it seemed as firm and springy as the softest turf road.

There was something wonderfully grand and terrible about the sun as it looked down on the desert. When the great round orb rose red and lurid out of the sand behind us, and we looked at the wide expanse of sky through which he was to pass, with never a sign of cloud to dim his searching rays, we could readily appreciate and understand the Gheber creed. To fall down and worship that awful majesty, to implore on bended knees some mercy from that all-devouring, scorching fire, seemed the only and the natural recourse.

During the middle of the day we halted and formed a kind of tent with our blankets, under which we crowded as much of our bodies as was practicable, keeping our heads at least sheltered from the direct sunlight. The poor horses stood patiently beside us, holding their heads drooped as low as possible, almost between their legs.

The first day brought us to a brackish desert well, and a few stunted palm-trees, where we found a small camp of friendly Bedouins. We rested until midnight, refreshing ourselves and our horses, and obtaining a supply of barley and bread from the Bedouins at an exorbitant price.

Then, well loaded, we set out again, and made thirty miles before halting.

The third and fourth days we found no water. Our supply was carefully husbanded, but we suffered considerably, and on the fifth morning, when we halted in a little valley between two low rocky ridges and found the spring dry, we were nearly on the verge of despair. But by digging in a moist spot of sand we succeeded in finding a limited supply of water, which kept us alive and revived our courage. The sixth morning we camped beside a genuine spring forming a little stream which made a patch of green a few rods in extent, and then disappeared in the immensity of the sandy ocean.

Three days more, and Palmyra ! We were elated and confident. The Arab assured us that we should find water every night.

We had seen no wild animals as yet, nor any hostile Bedouins. At night the hyenas howled around our camp, but the roar of the desert lion had not yet aroused us.

On the afternoon of the following day we were walking our horses quietly over the sand, listening to one of Morley's tiger-stories. Our Arab, on his dromedary, had gone on in advance, as usual, and had for some time been out of sight beyond a little hillock of sand and rock that lay across our route a half-mile away.

" We will walk to the brow of the hill," said Ned, " and then overtake him."

Morley finished his story, and his mare, a fast walker, forged on a little ahead of the party, so that he reached the crest a few rods in advance.

Suddenly we saw him wheel about and gallop back. He dismounted, threw the bridle to Sam, and motioned us to do the same.

" Bedouins !" was all he said.

Hastily dismounting, we ran forward with him to the hill, and keeping our bodies out of sight, peered over.

Away out a mile distant on the plain we could see our poor Arab flying toward us with all the speed that his dromedary could put forth.

Cutting down from the north, so as to head him off, came a wild troop of a hundred or more Bedouins, their horses flying like the wind, their spears and muskets in the air. In two minutes, as we gazed, they had closed down upon and surrounded him at about half a mile from where we stood.

" Poor old postmaster !" said Ned.

" Damn the scoundrels !" hissed Morley. " If we were only a dozen, we could drive off the whole crowd ; but four, — the odds are too big."

" It 's too bad," said I ; " but discretion is the best thing for us. We can't help the poor Arab, but we can get out of this ourselves."

We turned and ran back to our horses, and heading them to the south, sped away at full gallop, keeping the low ridge between us and the west. When at last, after an hour's hard riding, we crossed the hill, there was neither Bedouin nor dromedary to be seen. The boundless plain showed no trace of a living being beside ourselves.

"Shall we go back and give the poor chap a decent burial?" I inquired.

"Nonsense!" said Morley. "Those fellows have n't killed him. All they wanted was the dromedary, and they will carry off the Arab and probably give him a chance to get back to Bagdad, or somewhere else."

"I hope so," said Ned. "It hurt me to have to abandon the poor chap. All the same, it was mighty lucky for us that we let him ride ahead."

"In the mean time," said I, "what are we to do without a guide to show us where the water lies? We ought to be about two days' ride from Palmyra; but we may travel a month in this desert without finding it."

"It's a bad case!" said Morley, gravely. "We have come at least fifteen miles out of our course, and we don't know exactly what our course was. I believe the best thing we can do is to ride straight west and keep a lookout for signs of water. We can't stay here, at all events."

We turned our faces once more toward the west and rode until midnight. The character of the soil had changed. It was no longer soft, sinking sand, but a comparatively hard, smooth surface, strewn with small pebbles.

At midnight we halted, gave our horses a little sip of the water that we carried in our goat-skin bags, and a few handfuls of barley, and lay down to rest beneath the stars.

The next morning, after five hours' hard riding, there was still no sign of water, or of any change in the dismal, fiery landscape that surrounded us. We were obliged to call a halt at ten o'clock, and we exhausted the last drop of our precious goat-skin supply.

The hours wore on as we rested beneath our blanket tent. Scarcely a word was spoken. For my part, the only thing I could bring myself to think of was the sensation of a draught of cold water trickling down my throat.

At one o'clock, Morley stood up. "We must go on, boys," said he. "Our only chance is in pushing forward. So long as our horses can go, we must ride without rest till we find water."

We packed and mounted without more words. The horses were not themselves, especially the Arab mares. Ned's horse and mine appeared a little worn, but struck out at a gallop with nearly as much spirit as ever. But we had to wait for the mares.

"Those Turcomans are better than the Arabs," said Morley. "If we get out of this, I want them, at your own price."

"You can have mine to-day for a cup of cold water," said I, with a ghostly attempt at a smile.

About three o'clock in the afternoon, a low rocky ridge rose before us, and a dome-shaped hillock of sand appeared just above the crest. We hurried on, and in another hour had reached what proved to be a long outcropping of limestone rock, forming the farther side of a channel which may once have been the bed of a stream, but which was now dry and half filled with the desert. The round sand-hill rose just above the bank, almost a perfect dome in shape, twenty feet in height by about fifty in diameter at the base.

"Remarkable shape!" said Ned. "I suppose the whirling desert storms have gradually worked up that dome."

"Think so?" said Morley. "I don't. But we must find water first, and then we'll examine your sand-heap."

In a deep depression of the valley we at last discovered a spot where the sand was moist. With hands, knives, and every implement at command we all set to work to dig. The horses crowded close beside us, reaching their heads forward and sniffing eagerly for the first drop.

Finally it came. After a hole six feet deep had been excavated, the moisture began slowly to trickle down the sides and ooze up from the bottom, forming a little pool. It took two hours to satisfy our own thirst and our horses'. The water was really as poor as could be imagined, but it was wet, and to us was the sweetest drop ever tasted. It had saved our lives for the present. The sun had disappeared, and it was growing dark when we spread out our blankets and camped in the little hollow formed by the two banks of the ancient stream, if such it had been.

It was my watch. My companions were sleeping soundly on their blankets, and the horses stood close together, now and then moving a little, and rubbing their noses over each other in

friendly congratulations on that last delicious draught of water.
The full moon had risen above the bluff behind us and flooded
the valley with its clear soft light.

The round dome of sand rose straight in front, every separate
particle on its surface sparkling with the brilliancy of the white
light.

Moonlight always inclines me to dreaming, and now I began
to go back in memory to all the different plights that old moon
had seen me in.

It seemed hard to realize that the same old round face had
looked down upon me struggling in the snow-drifts of the Andes,
floating on the bosom of the broad ocean, digging in the plains
of Australia, lost in the desert of Syria. And then recollection
went back still farther, and I thought of the time when I used
to sit far into the night with both feet on the veranda-railing
of my old New England home, and smoke my pipe and gaze
at that same moon, and dream, not of the past, but of the
future.

And now the moon seemed laughing at me, and I could almost fancy her saying : " My boy, I have seen pretty much all
the world, and a great many times, and I know no place quite
so comfortable and pleasant as that same old veranda."

And just then I was not inclined to quarrel with her opinion.

Suddenly there was a movement among the horses. They
crowded close together and edged up to where I was sitting,
and my own horse, Timour, came and put his nose on my
shoulder, trembling all over. And then on the silent desert
air there broke forth one tremendous, awful roar. The very
moonbeams seemed to shiver with the horror of that sound.

I turned quickly to arouse the sleepers. There was no need.
Morley was close at my elbow, and Sam was beside him.

" Which way, Tom ? " whispered Morley, as he held his rifle
in readiness, then added quickly, " Sam, take care of the horses ! "
There was need of the latter injunction, for the poor beasts were
plunging and dancing in a frenzy of terror.

Ned instantly joined us, and with our three rifles cocked we
gazed up and down the narrow valley, now completely revealed
by the moonlight.

Again came that thrilling roar, followed by Sam's soothing
expostulations to the horses, and at the same moment a huge

lion and lioness appeared on the brow of the bank and slowly made their way into the channel some half-dozen rods to the north. They turned, and walked directly toward us, lashing their tails, and occasionally pausing to crouch like cats at play.

"Keep cool!" whispered Morley, "and wait till I give the word. Tom, you will take the female; Ned and I will both fire at the lion."

In a moment he added quietly, "Are you both perfectly ready?"

"Ready!" we both whispered.

"Oh!" slowly. "Well then — aim low — and — let them have it!"

The three rifles cracked almost simultaneously; and as the smoke cleared, we saw the old lion rolling and pawing in the sand, while the lioness scurried up the bank and disappeared.

"Never mind, Tom," said Morley, coolly, as he slipped a fresh cartridge into his rifle, "you hit her. She will not go far. Sam," he continued, "would you like to go and give the *coup de grace* to our struggling friend there?"

"I think not, sir," replied Sam. "The horses are very restless, sir."

"Prudent youth you are, Sam. Well, let's go and see the king of beasts, boys." But before we reached our game, the struggles were over, and the mighty form was silent in death, with one bullet through the head and another just back of the shoulder.

"Either would have done," said Morley.

We returned to our camp, and passed the rest of the night in smoking and telling stories.

At daybreak our little well was half full of water, and after a hearty draught and a light breakfast, we went to examine the dead lion. He was a glorious fellow. What a rug he would have made! But regretfully we were forced to leave the greater part of him, and content ourselves with the heavy tuft on the end of the tail, and a few of the terrible claws.

"And now," said Morley, "it will not hurt us to rest for half a day and examine Ned's sand-hill. I think we may find something curious."

We climbed the bank and approached the mound. It was

not quite so perfect a dome as appeared at a distance. One side was somewhat irregular, showing a large hollow, into which the sand had drifted, forming rough, uneven piles.

Ned and I were certainly much astonished to find stone appearing through the sand, and still more amazed to find that the stone consisted of large blocks of limestone accurately cut and fitted close together and laid up in courses, forming what must have been originally a nearly perfect dome.

" It is as I thought," said Morley. " An old ruin ; probably a tomb."

" And how old ? " asked I.

" Probably as old as the Pyramids, or older," was the reply. " Look at those massive stones, fitted together without mortar, and yet forming a perfect circle. That style of building dates way back of the Christian era, and points to a time when perhaps this whole region was a fertile, settled country, and this little ridge on which we stand marked the bank of a wide river. This was probably a dismal ruin, centuries old, when the Greeks were besieging Troy, and when Herodotus was wandering about, picking up scraps of information to form the ground of innumerable learned arguments in our day."

" But why has this never been discovered and explored? " asked Ned.

" Simply because it is out of the track of all present travel and investigation, in the midst of a frightful desert, and unknown except perhaps to a few wandering Bedouins."

" But it shall not remain unknown to us," said Ned. " I mean to see the inside of that tomb, or whatever it is, if I have to take out every stone from the top down."

We all set to work with a will to clear out the sand from the opening on the ruined side. Several large stones had broken and crumbled away, letting the ones above fall down, and the opening thus made was filled up with the débris of the crumbling stones, and with the sand of the desert, which had drifted into the hollow for centuries.

We had worked for about two hours, when Sam, who was tugging and pushing at a large fragment of stone, suddenly disappeared from view, following the stone, which had yielded to a vigorous shove and gone inward, leaving a wide black opening where Sam had just stood.

We all sprang forward in time to hear a strange confused sound of scraping and bumping. Then there was silence.

"Sam!" called Morley.

His voice sounded strange and hollow, as if he were speaking into a huge kettle.

"Here, sir!" came the answer from away below us.

"Are you hurt?"

"I think not much, sir."

"How far did you fall?"

"I did n't fall, sir, I slid."

"What did you slide on?"

"I slid on my face and hands, sir. It would have been pleasanter to slide on the other side of me."

We could n't help laughing at the doleful sound of Sam's voice as he made this observation.

"Are you comfortable where you are, Sam?" shouted Ned.

"Yes, sir. I am sitting here quite comfortable. It is cool here, but very dark."

"Can you see us?" I asked.

"Yes, sir; you seem away above me at the small end of a spy-glass."

"How far above you are we?"

"I can't tell, sir; I came here very swiftly, but it seemed a long time."

"Have you a match in your pocket, Sam?" asked Morley.

"Yes, sir."

"Scratch it, and hold it up."

In a moment a faint spark of light appeared far below us and some distance away.

"All right, Sam!" shouted Morley. "Don't move, and we will join you in a moment."

Morley hurried to his pack and returned presently with a small folding-lantern, which he prepared and lighted. Then stepping inside the opening and holding up the lantern, he disclosed an inclined plane of sand, nearly as firm as the bed of the desert outside, and sloping at an angle of about 45° into the darkness below.

"Here goes, boys!" said Morley. "We must follow Sam's method, but we'll try the 'other side' of us;" and with a shout, "Look out, Sam!" he seated himself and shot down the slide. Ned and I followed, and we all brought up safely at the bottom, where we found Sam sitting contentedly on the piece of stone which had beguiled him into his involuntary descent.

Morley trimmed the lantern and held it up. We were in a vaulted apartment, standing on a stone floor or pavement. Our inclined plane had probably been formed by the sand drifting in for countless generations through the ruined walls above.

"Probably," said Morley, "this was the ground level once, but the outside soil has risen some fifteen feet since the building was erected."

A faint ray of light struggled in from an opening directly above us. One or two large stones lay about, evidently fallen in from some part of the wall or roof. Moving along the sides of the chamber, we found by the light of Morley's lantern that the walls, except where covered by the immense sand-heap, were faced with huge stones, on whose once smooth surfaces we traced the remains of innumerable carved hieroglyphics, extending all around the building and up toward the vaulted dome as high as we could see. The characters were nearly obliterated by the slow crumbling of the face of the stone, but where discernible, they were totally different from any we had ever seen or heard of before.

"They are not Egyptian," said Morley. "They are certainly not Chaldaic or Assyrian. They probably belong to a civilization many centuries earlier than that of the Pyramids, and whose crumbling ruins are perhaps all about here, buried from twenty to fifty feet under the sand of the desert."

"How tremendously thick these walls must be!" said I. "On the outside, the building certainly measures fifty feet in diameter. This chamber is not over twenty feet wide. The walls must be fifteen feet thick."

"Those old fellows built for keeps," remarked Ned.

There was absolutely nothing to be discovered in the room. The floor was of immense solid slabs of stone, and entirely bare, except for the sand-heap and the few blocks of stone that lay where they had fallen.

"It must have been merely a sort of record-chamber," said Morley; "but how the devil did they get into it? We can't suppose the recorders slid in the way we did."

We had followed clear around the wall of the chamber from one side of the sand-heap to the other, when suddenly, in taking a step close to the edge of the sand, my foot went through, and I sank to the knee, barking my shin against the edge of the stone pavement. I was speedily seized and pulled out by the others, while the sand, set in motion by the undermining hole punched by my foot, began slowly sliding downward and pouring into the hole in the floor, as in an hour-glass.

For some time we watched it, until we began to be afraid that our whole inclined plane, which offered the only means of exit, would disappear into the hole.

Finally the movement stopped, and still there was a black hole yawning close to the great bank of sand.

"We must get down there some way," said Ned. "There is another chamber below this."

With the utmost caution Morley worked himself into the hole, and found a footing about twelve inches below the level of the floor. Then working carefully onward, he reached a footing still lower, and as he did so, the noise of sand was heard, sliding and grinding far down below.

"It's a flight of stone stairs," he cried. "It follows the curve of the wall, and I have just started a lot of sand over the side of the steps."

"Look out you don't start a lot over your head!" shouted Ned suddenly; and Morley sprang back just in time to avoid a perfect avalanche from above.

A large part of the side of the heap fell away, leaving a nearly vertical wall of sand which the slightest touch would bring down. But that which fell had all gone into the hole, and left us ample room to work without endangering the pile above. We cleared away what lay on the upper steps, pushing it downward until we had reached the fourth step and were clear of the lower line of the stone floor, when we pushed the sand off sideways into the room beneath, and descended easily down a flight of fifteen stone steps, winding with the curve of the wall into the room below. The steps were about three feet in length, and built up with solid stonework beneath.

The room was similar to the one above, except that the ceiling was flat, formed of immense single stones more than twenty feet in length and nearly three feet thick.

On the side of the room opposite to the stairs loomed an arched entrance-way, closed far within its portals by a single solid stone.

"There's the door," said Morley. "Think of it, — thirty feet below the present level of the ground outside!"

We examined the doorway. The stone was as solid and immovable as any part of the wall. As we stood near the door, the delightful sound of running water caught our ears. A part of the stone flooring had crumbled away, close to the wall, and a spring of water oozed up, forming a little pool in the broken flooring, and then trickled away under the walls. We eagerly stooped and drank, finding the water cool and delicious.

"That," said Morley, "is probably all that remains of a river that once carried the fleets of a powerful and prosperous nation. This is where the water came from that we dug for so long last night."

In the centre of the room stood a massive stone coffer or casket. It was about eight feet long, three feet deep, and the same in width. The top was a single stone a foot in thickness. Our united efforts could not stir it.

"We must get it off some way," said Ned.

We looked carefully all around the coffer, and discovered a place where the under side of the stone cover had decayed a little and fallen away, leaving a wide crack. With our heavy knives we soon dug out the rotten and crumbling stone, and made quite an opening, not sufficiently deep, however, to reach the interior.

Then Morley produced a small powder-flask and nearly filled the opening with powder, ramming it hard with the handle of his knife. A long strip of paper was twisted up for a fuse, thrust into the opening and lighted. We retired behind the end of the stone stairway and waited.

The explosion was tremendous, and the room was instantly filled with a dense, stifling smoke, but we rushed to the coffer. The stone lid was broken into six fragments. We easily pushed off these pieces, and the whole interior was exposed.

There lay before us a mummy, the form of a woman, wrapped closely in numerous folds of cloth, but with face and hands exposed. A long, heavy coil of black hair fell over her shoulders and partly concealed the upper half of the body. She was nearly seven feet tall, and the whole figure was powerfully built, the hands large, but beautifully shaped. The face must have been handsome, rather of the Semitic type, with nose somewhat prominent. Three heavy bracelets of gold encircled each arm, and a narrow, plain band of gold was around the head.

On one side of the body lay the curiously carved gold hilt of a sword. The blade was indicated only by a line of red rust where it had been. On the other side was the remains of what may have been a sceptre, — the gold handle and a small gold head, with three points like a trident. The space between the handle and the head was occupied only by dust.

For several moments we stood and gazed in silence. In me it produced a very weird sensation. As we stood there in the darkness of that underground chamber, peering through the smoky atmosphere by the flickering light of a pocket lantern, the thoughts that came over me were too swift and complex to be analyzed.

Five, six, perhaps eight thousand years ago, that stately queen had been laid away to her last rest. A long procession of mourners had followed her to this silent mausoleum. A nation had attended at her obsequies and mourned for their queen. And since that day so long ago, what had happened? The face of continents had been changed. Egypt, Chaldea, Assyria, Persia, Greece, Carthage, Rome, had all sprung into life, endured their time, and hastened down the path to decay and oblivion. Barbarian after barbarian had swept over Asia and Europe. A new civilization had sprung up in the west. A new world had grown into life; a new era had dawned upon mankind.

And through all those changes this mighty Amazon queen had slept quietly, unchanged and undisturbed.

And where was the powerful people who had laid her here? Where its cities, its broad rivers, its fertile valleys?

Gone! Utterly and absolutely disappeared from the face of the earth. Their recollection was buried beneath the sifting sands of time, as they and their cities, their rivers, and their civilization were buried beneath the sands of the desert.

And in the year 1879 of an era which began ages after they had been forgotten, four strangers had penetrated into a fearful wilderness, known only to the Bedouin and the wild beast, and had uncovered the face of their queen for the first time since she was laid to rest.

Sam, I think, had no respect for antiquity, or for anything, indeed, except his master. He was the first to break the silence, with a stifled cough and the following remark : —

"I think, sir, we had better take what we want, and get out-doors. It is very close in here, sir, and the smoke of the powder does n't go away, sir."

We all started at the first sound of a voice.

"You 're a reverent chap, Sam," said Ned, with a laugh, "but I guess your head is all right! We 've no time, boys, to be sentimental. This is an ancient piece of femininity, and I presume the relatives will not make a fuss if we plunder the remains."

So saying, he leaned forward and lifted the gold fillet from the brow of the mummy. As he did so, the long black hair crumbled instantly into dust, leaving the head as bald as a skull.

The ice was broken now, so to speak; and we all fell to with a will, plundering the royal corpse. With some tugging the heavy gold bracelets were stripped from her arms, but a massive seal ring, stamped with a strange hieroglyphic, which was worn on the third finger of the left hand, resisted all my efforts to withdraw it.

"Alexander had a neat way out of such difficulties," said

Morley; and with his bowie-knife he calmly hacked through the wrist, and presented me with the severed hand bearing the ring. That hand now lies on the table before me as I write, with the ring still on the finger. It is a novel and convenient paper-weight. "To such base uses do we come at last."

We took the gold sword-hilt and the handle and crest of the sceptre. These, with the bracelets and the crown, were all the valuables we could discover. There was nothing else in the coffer but the mummy — and dust.

Then we climbed the stone stairway and cautiously ascended the long slope of sand, keeping as far as possible from the caved-in side.

We all reached the top in safety; but Sam, who was the last, chanced to step near the broken side just before he reached the outlet. In an instant the sand gave way, and Sam, sinking rapidly, was seized by the collar and pulled through the opening. In five minutes there was a yawning gulf where our inclined plane had been.

"The next man that goes in will need a rope to get out with," said Ned.

The light was blinding as we came out on the desert once more, and the heat seemed at first unendurable. Our horses were standing close to the western bank of the gulley, with heads hanging low. It was long past noon.

We filled our goat-skins at the pool, and after a long draught and a feed of barley to our horses, and a hasty lunch for ourselves, we mounted, and once more galloped out toward the west.

It was a long and terrible journey. Not the prospect of another discovery, even of a coffer full of gold and diamonds, would induce me to take that ride again. For three days we were in the desert, — for the first two days without water, except what we had carried in our goat-skins.

On the morning of the third day we found a well, with the remains of a Bedouin camp scattered about it, and three dismal, withered palm-trees.

Two hours afterward, as we had just started again, a single Bedouin appeared on foot, toiling along with a pack on his back, toward the north.

He waited for us, and begged a drink of water, — a plea which we could not resist. The poor fellow drank with a gusto from one of our goat-skins.

By a few words of Arabic which Morley understood, and by signs, the Bedouin told us that a fertile country and a city lay about a day's journey to the northwest. We hurried on in the direction indicated, leaving him toiling slowly after us.

In less than an hour we began to see the blue outline of hills and mountains, and the next morning we had reached a grove of palm-trees in a cultivated valley, with the mountains rising just beyond us, and a town nestling at their feet, a few miles away.

CHAPTER XVI.

WE had arrived at the confines of the settled country of Syria, about fifty miles south of Damascus, and near the caravan route to Mecca.

Our desert dangers were over. We had missed Palmyra, having strayed nearly a hundred miles south of our intended course, but even the attractions of the ruined city of Zenobia were not sufficient to make us willing to return one mile to the eastward.

Two days of easy travelling among mountains and valleys, across wadies and hollows, with now and then a reminiscence of the desert, brought us in sight of the grand old city of Damascus. As we looked down from the hills upon the "bowery loveliness," the sparkling streams, the white walls and houses of the city, and the snow-clad range of Anti-Lebanon towering beyond, it seemed to our hungry and thirsty souls the very paradise which it appeared to Mohammed, and to many another traveller.

We installed ourselves comfortably in Demetri's hotel, and Morley — fortunate man — went off to present a letter of credit.

"All expenses in Damascus will be borne by me," said he. "Let that be understood at the outset."

To this proposition Ned and I could only return our thankful acceptance.

We wandered out into the "street which is called Straight," and investigating the contents of the booths, succeeded in replacing our Oriental costumes, now in a sad state of decadence, by something reminding us a little of the clothes we had been wont to wear. We retained our cork helmets, the badge of the English tourist, which we had worn only since leaving Bagdad.

"Now, Ned," said I, that evening, "Damascus makes sixteen and leaves twenty-four. What next, and how?"

"Jerusalem next, then Cairo," was Ned's reply. "After Cairo, Constantinople and Europe."

"Will you join us, Morley?" I inquired.

After some reflection Morley replied: "I believe not. Sam and I spent six months in Eygpt about two years ago, and there is a large region in this neighborhood that I want to explore. I don't propose to be fooled out of Palmyra. Think we'll make our headquarters here at Damascus for a couple of months, and then travel north through Turkey and overland to Constantinople. May meet you there, perhaps. But I want your horses. Name the price."

"Well," said Ned, "I suppose we can't use them much more. We shall be afloat on the Mediterranean for a time. What do you say, Tom?"

"I hate to let the old fellows go," I replied; "but as we must part with them, I'd rather resign them to Morley than to any man living."

"Thanks!" said Morley. "And what do you think of a hundred pounds for the pair?"

"I think it's more by a good deal than any one else would offer us."

"All right, if you're satisfied! When you get ready to go, we'll all ride over to Beyrout together, and Sam and I will see you safely off on the steamer; for I take it you don't want to go back to Jerusalem by land."

So that was settled, and Ned and I felt more wealthy than at any time since we left New York, except for one memorable evening in Australia.

"And now for the division of our desert spoils," said Ned, — "those little personal adornments of which we relieved her six-thousand-year-old-Majesty."

"Let Morley select what he wants," said I, "and we will each take a memento only. The hand and the ring is all I care for."

"That's generous!" replied Morley. "I confess I should like very much to possess those relics, not by any means for the intrinsic value of the gold, but to put in my trophy cabinet in England. But I will not accept more than my share without giving you something like a cash equivalent."

We discussed this matter at some length, Morley kindly insisting upon paying us a large sum for the relics. We finally compromised by my keeping the hand with the ring, Ned taking one of the bracelets, and Morley accepting the rest of the spoil, for which he paid us fifty pounds. This, with the balance of what we had received at Teheran, made us the happy possessors of about seven hundred and fifty dollars.

"Our Asiatic experience, Tom, was the most dreaded, the hardest, and the most profitable of our whole trip, so far," said Ned.

"And we can do Egypt and the Mediterranean in style, which is what we need for a change," I replied.

So we settled ourselves to write our newspaper letters, the forty-seventh of the series.

"Nearly half done, Ned," said I cheerfully, as we completed our writing, "and by far the hardest part of the work is finished."

"But — Lima!" replied Ned, ominously.

"Yes. Confound Lima! Lima is our *bête noir*. It bids fair to knock us out in the end."

"We have everything else almost in our grip. But Lima! It makes me feel tired to think of working our way before the mast clear round to the other side of that cursed South America!"

"We must trust to luck, as usual, and watch for our opportunity; and I think we should both have learned by this time not to cross a river before we reach it."

On the morning of Thursday, 2d of October, we all four set out for Beyrout, along the fine road that winds over and among the mountains to the coast. The scenery was grand and beautiful, and as we reached the summit of the Anti-Lebanon range, away to the southwest through a break in the opposing mountains, there was the glimmer and the blue sheen of the most famous water in the world, — the storied Mediterranean.

"Thalassa!" shouted Ned, joyfully; and I doubt if even those old Greeks themselves felt more delight than we.

But when we stood on the grand summit of Lebanon, there lay before us the broad, beautiful sea, stretching away to the horizon, rich with that brilliant deep blue that seems to belong to no other body of water.

And below us was the picturesque city of Beyrout, and the sun, dropping down between the far distant Pillars of Hercules, lit up the strange sails of a dozen vessels in the harbor, and seemed to look lovingly on that sea where it had witnessed so much that has been potent in the world's history.

Away to the northwest we could make out a steamer puffing along toward the harbor.

No scene in all our wanderings had looked to us so exquisitely beautiful.

This was the third day of our ride from Damascus.

At Beyrout the steamer arrived shortly before we did, and with a hearty English hand-grip from Morley and Sam, and a hasty farewell of the noble horses that had borne us so bravely through the dangers of the desert, we went on board, and were soon on our course for Jaffa.

There were about a dozen Americans on the steamer, and it seemed to us like being at home again. It was delightful to have so many about us talking our native tongue with the true American inflection, and to hear all the news, some of it more than a year old, and yet new to us.

And we became again the heroes of the group, and it was by no means unpleasant to hear the words of admiration and encouragement, and to see the manifest pride with which our countrymen regarded us.

And then we told bits of our story, and I produced my severed hand, whereat the ladies screamed as though it had been a mouse, and yet peered at it from a safe distance with an interested horror in their pretty American eyes, and we had a very pleasant trip on that steamer.

At Jaffa, from the open roadstead, we were pulled ashore by howling, "backsheeshing" Arabs, and set out the next morning, after a direful night-struggle with the fleas, *en route* for the Holy City.

We rode donkeys, and formed a part of a long cavalcade of

pilgrims, travelling in the regular approved fashion. How we missed our noble desert steeds !

What can I say of Jerusalem that has not been better said many times before? There was nothing in the way of adventure to enliven the pilgrimage. Let me spare the reader and myself an attempt to put into words what we saw, and more especially what we felt. We visited Jerusalem ; saw the same sights, suffered the same impositions, listened to the same time-honored lies, that have aroused the enthusiasm or the shame of so many travellers before us.

In a week we were back at Jaffa, waiting for the steamer to Alexandria. We were done with the continent of Asia. We embarked at nightfall, and reached Alexandria the following evening, touching at Port Said on the route.

And then began the Babel, the frantic clamoring cries of the Arab boatmen, fighting and struggling for the possession of every passenger that appeared on deck. By some means or other we reached the shore, and after the Custom-House formalities, found our way through the narrow streets to the Peninsular and Oriental Hotel.

We had scarcely entered the hotel, when a familiar, courtly voice saluted us.

"Am I mistaken? Gentlemen, do you not recognize me?"

We turned, to find ourselves confronted by the veritable old Captain Chambers.

In spite of my surmises and suspicions in regard to the honorable captain, I felt a throb of genuine delight as I grasped his outstretched hand.

"Upon my word, gentlemen," said he, "this is a very agreeably small world. We part from friends in South America, and we meet them in Egypt. This is to me a very pleasant accident."

"And equally pleasant to us," I replied. "But you know, captain, there is no such thing as an accident. Probably if all the facts were known, it would seem quite the natural and inevitable thing that we should meet you here."

It was a random shot, a feeler, but I fear it missed the mark.

The captain's face never changed.

"What recondite theory are you evolving now, my friend?" answered he, with the same pleasant smile.

"Nothing particularly deep, captain," I replied. "You are from inclination a great traveller. We are, from our vows, compelled to be wanderers for a few years; what more natural than that we should encounter each other somewhere? It happened to be in Egypt. If not here, it would probably have been somewhere else."

"You convict your theory at the outset, my friend," said the captain. "You say there is no such thing as *accident*, and yet it *happened* to be in Egypt."

"It strikes me," broke in Ned, "that you are a very extraordinary pair of fellows, — beginning to discuss the theory of cause and effect at your first meeting after nearly two years' separation. I am 'of the earth, earthy,' and I suggest that you join me in a cock-tail and a cigar, and discuss mundane subjects."

So saying, he linked an arm in each of ours and escorted us to a comparatively cool retreat, where we seated ourselves and lit our cigars.

"Now, captain," said Ned, "where do you come from?"

"'From going to and fro in the earth, and from walking up and down in it,'" replied the captain.

"I trust not on the same errand as the other fellow," said I.

"Why not?" replied the captain. "He was merely looking for something that would interest or amuse him, and such, I regret to say, has been my only occupation for some years. But seriously, gentlemen, I came this morning from Cairo. Previous to Cairo, I have been in Australia, in Japan, and in Calcutta, since I parted from you in Buenos Ayres."

"So have we," said I; "which seems to make it remarkable, not that we met you here in Egypt, but that we did not meet you before."

"I have been always just a little too late," said the captain; and he uttered this in a solemn and serious tone, quite different from his previous conversation.

Then quickly recovering himself, he added, "But at last we have 'made connection,' as they say in America, and you must tell me of all your adventures in detail. Your faces show me that you have been either at sea or in the desert."

"They are truthful faces," said Ned, "and they reflect both the ocean and the desert."

We went to dinner together, and then over the coffee and cigars we related the principal incidents in our travels, — by a common instinct studiously avoiding the name of José Miguel. And the captain applauded and encouraged us in his genial, polished way, and at the end of our story he rose and held out his hand.

"I have unfortunately taken passage on the early morning steamer," said he, "and must bid you good-by as well as good-night."

"No sooner met than parted!" said I. "Where shall we next *happen* against each other, captain?"

"From here I am going direct to London," replied he. "My course after that will depend upon the result of some business transactions. I may go home to New York and be one of the enthusiastic crowd to welcome your glorious arrival there."

"'Business'!" said I. "That word sounds strangely from your lips, captain."

"And it is strange to my habits," replied he. "But we all find it a disagreeable necessity at times. I bid you good-by once more, gentlemen, and once more assure you of the pleasure I have had in meeting you, and of my most earnest wishes for your success."

With which elaborate peroration the captain shook hands cordially with us both, and withdrew his stately form to his room.

Ned and I sat looking at each other for several moments.

"Well?" said he.

"Well?" said I.

"What of it?" said he.

"Exactly!" replied I.

"The captain is not himself."

"He never was, so far as I know."

"He did n't quote one line of Horace."

"He looks ten years older than when we last saw him."

"What is your theory about that most extraordinary personage, Tom?"

"I have n't sufficient facts on which to base a theory. One

thing I will say, however. We have seen Captain Chambers. Look out for traces of José Miguel."

"You don't mean to say that you believe he is in any way connected with that gang!"

"I mean to say only what I did say: 'Look out for Miguel!' Captain Chambers is pursuing Miguel, or else Miguel is pursuing him, or they are both pursuing us, or we are both pursuing them."

"And it 's a mighty unprofitable pursuit all round."

"So far," said I.

"And *ad infinitum*," replied he.

"Let 's go to bed!"

Which we did.

In the morning, when we arose, the captain, after his customary manner, had disappeared.

At about nine o'clock Ned and I took the train for Cairo.

The country through which we travelled was flat and monotonous. The Nile was nearly at its highest point, and much of the region resembled an immense lake.

At three o'clock we came in sight of the Pyramids, and a few moments later arrived at Cairo.

Chartering two small donkeys, two small boys, and two large cudgels, by their combined assistance we arrived at the Hôtel d'Europe.

"We 'll stay here to-morrow, Tom," said Ned, "and make the Pyramid trip the day after."

There were quite a number of Englishmen and Americans at the hotel, and we were soon in conversation with two Americans from Cincinnati. As we were talking, a man approached us and said, —

"Pardon me, gentlemen, but I am sure I have met you somewhere. Are you not Messrs. Markham and Jackson, — the Americans who are becoming so celebrated?"

"You have the names correctly, sir," said Ned. "As to our being celebrated, that is something we had not yet discovered. But you must excuse us," he continued, as he glanced at me and saw me studying the stranger's face with a puzzled expression; "I am entirely unable to recall your name, and I can see, from Tom's face, that he is in the same predicament."

"That is a natural difficulty for gentlemen who have met so

many people as you must have encountered in your travels," replied the stranger, "but it is one which is easily remedied ; " and he handed us a card, — "Mr. John Lowrie, Edinburgh."

"I must apologize also," said Mr. Lowrie, "as I find myself at a loss to make sure where it was that I met you. It was in Buenos Ayres, Melbourne, or London ; but for the life of me, I can't tell which."

"It was certainly not in London," said I, "as we have never been there. It may have been in one of the other cities you name."

"Well, what matter anyway ! " said he. "I am sure I have seen you somewhere ; and in a strange land, you know, we are always anxious to claim every possible acquaintance."

I had been studying Mr. Lowrie's face ever since he joined us. I have a fairly good memory for faces, and it seemed to me that his was not entirely strange ; but in spite of my efforts I could not connect it with his name, or with any circumstances in our travels. Ned and he were talking of Buenos Ayres, and I finally came to the conclusion that he must be some one of the many people we had talked with for half an hour in some quarter of the globe, and who had faded from our memory like most of the others.

He was well dressed, in the ordinary costume of the English tourist, smooth-shaven, apparently a man about forty years old, and a pleasant and ready talker. There was something about his face, however,—I think in the expression of the eyes, — which affected me unpleasantly. Still, under the influence of the fine cigars which he offered us, the pleasant, cooling drinks which he ordered, and his agreeable and complimentary conversation, I soon made up my mind that I was hypercritical, and that Lowrie was altogether a very nice fellow indeed.

"Of course you will visit the Pyramids," said he, after an hour or more of conversation.

"Yes," said Ned. "We expect to go over there the day after to-morrow."

"By Jove ! " said he, "you 'll be badly scorched. I climbed the Great Pyramid a week ago to-day, and I assure you the sun is something dreadful. It is almost directly overhead now, you know, and if you leave here in the morning, you get there about noon. By the way," continued he suddenly, "a friend of mine told me the other day that the view by moonlight from the top of that Pyramid was the grandest thing he ever witnessed. I have been wanting to try it ever since, but did not like to go without some company besides these miserable Arabs. What do you say, gentlemen? Do you feel like making a night expedition?"

"That's a novelty, at least!" replied Ned, after a moment, "I'm inclined to favor it, Tom."

"I see no objections," said I, "and if we want the daylight view, we can easily go up again in the morning."

"Consider it agreed, then," said Lowrie. "I know a couple of splendid Arabs who will furnish us mules and go with us to the very top of the Pyramid, without our having to employ those lazy fellows that get you half-way up and then sit down and demand 'Backsheesh.' We should start from here about two o'clock in the afternoon, as we have ten or twelve miles to go. I'll have everything ready at two o'clock to-morrow."

"All right!" said Ned. "You can count on us, Mr. Lowrie."

So we said good-night and went to our room. We discussed our new friend for some time, but finally agreed that we must have met him somewhere, as he said, though Ned had no recollection of his face or name.

In the morning, with donkeys and cudgel-boys as usual. we made an excursion through the narrow streets to the United States Consulate, where we obtained our certificates and spent a half-hour in pleasant chat. As we rode back, I said, " Ned, I don't half like that Englishman, Lowrie."

"Why? He seems to be a pleasant, harmless sort of chap."

"Possibly; but I shall keep one eye on him, and I advise you to do the same."

At two o'clock Lowrie called for us.

"My Arabs and mules are waiting a few blocks away." said he. "I am staying at the New Hotel, and as the Hôtel d'Europe was a little out of the route, I left them down ' below."

I was inclined to be suspicious, I knew not why, and this seemed a singular freak, — to leave his means of conveyance "a few blocks away." We said nothing, however, but proceeded with him on foot for about half a mile, where we found five donkeys and two Arabs.

We mounted the donkeys, and rode on our way through old Cairo and on to the bank of the Nile opposite to Gizeh.

Passing through the town of Gizeh, we made our way along the elevated causeway toward the Pyramids. The water lay on each side of us, as the river was now nearly at its highest point, and almost the entire country was flooded.

"We have one advantage," said Lowrie, "in arriving at night; we shall not be beset with the usual crowd of howling Arabs. We can make our trip to the top undisturbed. I presume you, gentlemen, after your experience in mountain-climbing, will make light of getting up the Pyramid. For myself, I like to have one of these fellows on each side of me."

It was nearly dark when we arrived at the base of the Great Pyramid. Away to the east the moon was just rising, and the tremendous monument loomed up before us like a mountain, misty, and vaguely immense in the uncertain light.

We left our mules and began the ascent on the north side. It was far from being a joke. The rough, broken projections, or steps, were from two to three feet in height and about a foot and a half in width. The two Arabs sprang up each step and pulled Lowrie up, grasping him by both arms. Ned and I struggled up as bravely as possible, now and then aided by a timely pull from the Arabs. Several times we sat down to rest. I counted two hundred and two steps to the top. It was the hardest of all the hard climbs we had accomplished. The two Arabs, contrary to the custom of their race, scarcely uttered an exclamation, and the ascent was made almost in silence.

Finally we reached the summit, — a level space about thirty feet square, — and in spite of our exhaustion, we felt repaid.

The moon was now high in the cloudless Egyptian sky. The broad stream — rather lake — of Father Nile lay glistening below us to the east. The figures of the other Pyramids could be dimly discerned, rising like giant spectres from the plain. To the west stretched out the wild and strange vastness of the desert, in which the struggling moonbeams were lost. With what vague and fearful phantoms imagination could people that mysterious waste !

We had all gathered close to the eastern side of the summit.

Ned stood nearest to the edge, Lowrie close beside Ned, I by Lowrie's side, and the two Arabs just behind me.

Ned was gazing off over the moonlit waters of the Nile; Lowrie seemed to be doing the same; I was looking at Lowrie.

Presently, without turning his head, Ned said, —

"This is wonderfully fascinating, Tom! I could stand here and dream for hours."

"Yes!" said Lowrie. "It is a grand scene, and there is no better hour to see it than — *NOW!*"

The last word was uttered with a shout, and simultaneously the hand in Lowrie's pocket was withdrawn with a revolver,

which he fired point-blank at Ned's head, three feet away. But as the revolver appeared, by a sudden, quick movement forward, I struck up the arm that held it, and the bullet flew harmlessly over Ned. At the same moment I shouted, "Treason!"

That sudden motion of mine probably saved my own life, for at the instant that Lowrie drew his pistol, one of the Arabs close behind me made a tremendous lunge with a knife. My movement carried me out of his range, and, overbalanced by the vigor of his thrust, he sprawled past me and stumbled over the edge of the Pyramid, down to the second step below. I turned again in time to seize the arm of the second Arab, and grappled with him in a desperate embrace. In turning, I caught a glance of Lowrie, as Ned picked him up bodily and by a quick back-hand fling of his tremendous arms threw him straight out over the edge of the Pyramid. There was a fearful shriek, a dull, heavy blow and a groan, and I was wrestling with the Arab.

But Ned was at my side; his hands were gripped like a vise around the Arab's throat. In a moment I felt myself free. I took the knife from the nerveless hand of my late opponent, and the Arab lay flat on his back, gasping and feebly struggling, while Ned knelt over him, still encircling his throat with that crushing clasp. The struggles grew less violent, then stopped. Still, Ned was immovable.

I drew my revolver.

"Let go, Ned!" I said. "He is safe now. The other has cleared out."

Still, Ned never moved or relaxed his hold. His face was set and rigid, and his eyes protruded like those of the man he was strangling. The very devil of rage had taken possession of him, and his terrible strength had been put forth to its very utmost in those few moments.

"Ned!" I shouted, and seized him by the arm. "Let go! the man is dead!"

Slowly, with a shiver, Ned relaxed his hold and stood up. The Arab lay motionless. Even in the moonlight I could see on his neck the marks of those tremendous fingers.

In a moment Ned was himself again. "That's the second time in my life, Tom, that I lost my temper," said he.

We knelt beside the Arab and raised him up. He was still alive, but unconscious.

With my knife I pried open his set teeth, while Ned poured a drink of brandy down his throat. He gasped, spluttered, drew a long breath, and looked about with an idiotic, vacant stare.

"Ha–ah!" said he presently. "Much big chokee!" and he put his hand to his throat.

"You damned scoundrel!" said Ned. "I ought to have finished you. What made you try to murder us?"

The Arab reflected. "Ha–ah!" he gasped again. "English, he give much backsheesh kill Yankees."

"Do you know where your Englishman is?" asked I.

"Dead!" said he. "Big man throw over — chokee Arab."

"Get up," said Ned, "and come down with us. If you try to run away, I'll throw you clear out onto the desert."

With shaking limbs the Arab arose, and we all clambered down the east side. On the tenth step we found the body of Lowrie, his head and arms hanging over the edge. He was quite dead and horribly mangled, his skull smashed in on one side. He had been thrown upward and outward about seven or eight feet, and had probably rolled down several steps after striking.

The other Arab had disappeared entirely. After stumbling over the edge of the Pyramid, and then seeing Lowrie flying out over his head, he had probably scurried down the steps and made the best of his way off.

"This is a bad business, Tom!" said Ned.

"I fail to see it," replied I. "Three men tried to murder us, and one of them lost his life in the attempt. That must have been a fearful fling you gave him, Ned."

"It was the only thing I could do," said Ned. "There were two of them on you, and I had to dispose of this scoundrel without loss of time. But what does it mean? Who is he, and why this conspiracy to murder us?"

"We shall soon find out," I replied, as I gazed at the face of the dead man. "I have an idea now where I have seen him."

We carefully examined all Lowrie's pockets. There was a five-pound note, a little loose change, three cigars, and a half-dozen cards. No letter or paper of any sort that would throw any light on the mystery.

At last, however, from the bottom of an inside vest-pocket, I drew out a small scrap of paper, folded into a space as big as a postage-stamp. As I unfolded and held it up to the brilliant moonlight, we could see that it was covered with a series of figures.

"There you have the mystery," said I. "The trail of the serpent! And now I'll tell you about Mr. Lowrie. He is the man who sat with Miguel and Smith in that hut in Calcutta when I was brought before their august presence. He wore a heavy beard then, which he has shaved off, and he had on a different suit; but he is the identical man, and now that I have been able to recall his face, I wonder at my not recognizing him the moment he approached us."

" So, then, they are on our track, are they?" said Ned. "We must fool them in some way. Can you translate the paper?"

" Not by this light," I replied. "It will keep until we reach Cairo."

" But we don't want to be delayed and bothered by any investigations," said Ned. "What can we do with this body? He may be known and recognized as the English tourist Lowrie, and it will be shown that we took this trip with him to-night. We can't leave the body here."

After some further talk we directed the Arab to pull the corpse down to the foot of the Pyramid, while we followed. Four or five steps below where he lay I picked up the revolver, which had been jerked from his grasp when Ned gave him that back-handed fling.

At the foot of the Pyramid we made the Arab scoop out a hole in the sand, in which we laid the body of our treacherous assailant.

" We have done unto him as he would have done to us," said Ned ; and we covered him with the desert sand.

Then we rode back to Cairo, leading the two unmounted donkeys. Arrived at the outskirts of the city, we dismounted and gave up our donkeys to the Arab.

" Now," said Ned, " get out ! If you're found within the limits of Cairo or Alexandria in the next week, you'll be shot for a treacherous, murdering dog, as you are."

The Arab needed no second bidding. In less than a minute he was out of sight, — donkeys and all.

Ned and I walked to our room in the hotel, reaching there a little after noon.

The cipher paper which we had found in Lowrie's pocket read as follows : —

" The two in Cairo in October. Look out. Must be disposed of."

" Now, how in the world did they learn that we would be here this month?" said I.

" We may have been spotted by some one of the gang in Damascus or in Jerusalem," said Ned. "They couldn't have received their information before that, for we did n't know ourselves where we should be."

I had been examining the revolver that we had picked up on the Pyramid.

"Here is another discovery, Ned," said I. "This is my identical revolver that they stole in Calcutta. See that long scratch on the handle. I did that trying to break a stone in the Sierras."

"We must keep our eyes open for the varmints hereafter, Tom. They may pursue us all over Europe," said Ned.

"Then we had better travel by some special conveyance. Take a sailing-vessel from Alexandria and avoid the steamers."

At Cairo we found a letter from our old friend Dan O'Connor. He was getting along famously in Buenos Ayres, and hoped to join us in Dublin if we could arrange to be there some time the following year.

"At all events, Tom," said Ned, " we must get out of Egypt as soon as possible."

I wrote a short note to Dan, and Ned wrote to Maggie, telling them that our movements were uncertain, but to address us in Vienna. Then we took the train to Alexandria.

After some inquiries and discussion we went aboard a Greek brigantine bound for Smyrna, whose captain, Nicearchus Kalopticus, agreed to transport us for fifty dollars, — not, however, guaranteeing anything in regard to time of arrival.

"It may be a month," said he in his mixture of Greek, English, and Italian. "It will depend on the wind which the good Saint Nicholas sends us."

"*N'importe*, Ned," said I ; "we need a rest, and this voyage will be a pleasant way of securing it."

So the little Greek trader spread her sails, and before a fair southerly wind we made our way out of the harbor and into the broad Mediterranean.

"Farewell to Egypt !" said Ned, as we watched the low shores recede. "Farewell to the Pyramids and the Sphinx and the mummies, and all the other musty memorials of the dead past !"

"And hurrah for Europe and the West, and life and action and the future !" added I ; and we lit our cigars and lounged on the deck under the swelling sails, and watched the blue waves dancing past, and felt very reasonably contented and comfortable. And the great palace of the Pasha dwindled into a speck, and the forts of Alexandria became a blot on the horizon, and the windmills disappeared ; and by four o'clock on the afternoon of Saturday, October 18th, we could see nothing but the bright blue Mediterranean all about us.

CHAPTER XVII.

W E were quite a classic company on board that little Greek brigantine. There was Alcibiades the cook, a clever fellow from Syra, accounted quite an important personage on board, being owner of one fourth of the vessel and cargo. He was not, however, exactly calculated to recall our early impressions of the handsome Athenian profligate. He was negligent in his attire, and his person was as greasy as his soups. We had also Socrates, a 'fore-the-mast hand, but far from being a philosopher. He was the worst grumbler, the sourest-tempered and most disagreeable man on board. It seemed as if he were striving to emulate — not his illustrious namesake — but rather his namesake's illustrious spouse, Xantippe. We would have cheerfully administered a cup of hemlock to the surly dog on several occasions.

Xenophon was a dapper little Cretan, and he went far to verify the old saying: "All the Cretans are liars." The yarns which he spun were astounding even in a Greek. The old friend of our college days, the Xenophon of the Anabasis and the Memorabilia, was a poor man at a story compared with his modern namesake. This later Xenophon evidently meant to show that if Greeks had degenerated in some respects, the art of narrative and the unfettered freedom of imagination were at least unimpaired. They had shaken off the shackles, and

had risen superior to the grovelling slavery of facts. He was the recognized "rhapsodist" of the party. When the wind was light and fair, and no immediate anxieties vexed the minds and disturbed the content of these valorous Grecians, they were wont to gather around the poetic Xenophon, while seated on a coil of rope he temporarily laid aside his unclassic pipe and turned his imagination loose, pouring out a continuous roll of sonorous Greek that entranced his hearers, and caused even Socrates to forget his latest grievance.

Of course, much of this eloquence was lost on Ned and myself; but after a few weeks we gradually began to catch the words, and to receive faint glimmerings from the blinding glare of lies which he evolved.

They were a remarkable crew, these hardy Greek mariners. I suppose they were not very different from their ancestors of twenty-five centuries ago. Of course they persisted in hugging the shore all the way around the eastern Mediterranean, skipping from island to island where possible. Not they the reckless tempters of the saint, to venture out across that broad, mysterious sea and endanger their precious lives! Not they the fools to fly in the face of Providence by trying to beat up against the wind! Time was of no more importance to them than it was to their worthy fathers who besieged Troy for ten years. If the wind did not blow in the right direction, they either ran before it until it changed, or made for a snug harbor and waited the pleasure of Heaven.

Ned and I spent several hours one day in showing the captain how he could trim his vessel to lie close to the wind, and we even induced him to try it; but the experiment was no sooner attempted than abandoned, for the crew positively refused to allow such unholy manœuvring. So the captain, poor man, was obliged to submit. He was only captain by the will of the crew, "clad in a little brief authority," which he held at the pleasure of his constituents. And the helm was put up, and away we flew to the westward.

When the wind blew strong, and the sea rose in angry waves, then these valiant Greeks proceeded to pacify the elements after the manner of their ancestors, only instead of offering a sacrifice to Poseidon, they burned incense before Saint Nicholas. And we drifted pleasantly about all over the eastern Mediterranean, north, south, east, and west, largely at the mercy of the wind.

"If the 'gang' are on our track, Tom," said Ned one day, "they will be bothered to hold the trail."

But we had a good time, — a pleasant, lazy, free-and-easy time; and we did gradually work on our way, although the progress was much like that of the frog in the well, who jumped up three feet in the daytime and slipped back two feet in the night. We lounged about the deck, wrote up our notes, made sketches, prepared our newspaper letters, and played the flute for the enjoyment of the crew, which they highly appreciated. We even bade fair to become rivals of the story-telling Xenophon, and were nearly ready to pose as modern Arions.

On the 22d of November we saw the eastern shore of the island of Cyprus. The weather had been rather dirty for a day or two, and the vessel had run before an east wind, while the sacrifices and vows to Saint Nicholas had been frequent and fervent.

We ran into the harbor of Larnecca, and waited for two days for the wind to change. Ned and I spent much of the time ashore, wandering about the town and the immediate neighborhood.

"Here is the home of beauty, Ned," said I ; "the very birthplace of its queen. Don't be beguiled into forgetfulness of little California."

We saw many pretty girls, graceful and slender, with the true classic face and the dark liquid eyes (I believe that is the correct expression) that —

> "launched a thousand ships,
> And burnt the topless towers of Ilium."

Finally, however, the wind blew fair, and our gallant mariners spread their sails once more, and flitted past the long extremity of the island, and made their way, with dread forebodings, straight across to the coast of Asia Minor. Then, skirting the land, we worked our course to the westward.

It was not altogether unlike the Odyssey. There was quite as much superstitious dread, and as many direful dangers in the imagination of these Greek traders, as were encountered in the belated voyage of the wise Odysseus and his followers.

The season was getting late, and the north-winds off shore were sometimes rather chilling. But by perseverance and prudence, and countless promises to the good Saint Nicholas, the dangers were overcome, and we entered the beautiful harbor of Smyrna on December 22d, sixty-five days after we had left Alexandria.

"Time enough," said Ned, "to have gone round the world !"

It had been growing steadily colder for the past few weeks, and the north-winds, sweeping down from the snow-covered plains of Russia, were keen and cutting enough to make us forget that we had ever felt the scorching desert sun. But we found the air of Smyrna soft and balmy, much like the winter climate of Southern California.

The city lies at the base of an encircling amphitheatre of hills, and is sheltered completely from the cold northern blasts.

We passed two days pleasantly, strolling about the city and climbing the surrounding hills, admiring with Western freedom the beautiful girls that looked down on us from their hanging windows, and on the 24th we took passage on a Russian steamer for Constantinople.

" This is our third Christmas, Tom ! " said Ned, as we faced the frosty north-wind next morning. " The first was on the California desert just north of Fort Yuma ! Where was the second ? "

" On board the ' Bonnie Belle,' " I replied, " in the Pacific Ocean."

" And the third," continued he, " is at the mouth of the Hellespont ! Wonder where the fourth will find us ! "

" On deck — somewhere ! " I replied.

We passed the famous Hellespont, steamed swiftly across the Sea of Marmora, and soon came in sight of the most beautiful city in the world — when glorified by the enchantment of distance.

At the mouth of the " Golden Horn " our steamer came to rest. With a motley crowd of travellers of all nationalities we landed on the northern side of the " Horn," and made our way up the steep and narrow streets into Pera, and to the Hôtel d'Europe. We were actually for the first time on European soil, though it seemed still under Asiatic dominion.

" Rather too early to hope to find Morley," said I. " We left him at Damascus in October, and he is probably just about setting out for his journey on horseback."

" Yes," said Ned ; " we should be in Paris when he reaches here."

The weather was quite cold, but pleasant. A bracing, crisp air and a tingling north-wind, but the most glorious sunshine, and an invigorating atmosphere that made new men of us in a short time.

We formed many pleasant acquaintances among the Europeans and Americans in Pera, the great head-centre of all the representatives of foreign governments, and through the kind influence of attachés we obtained firmans to see all that any foreigner can see of the Turkish capital.

The second day after our arrival, when our letters were written and our credentials secured, we went from Pera down through Galata, and over the Galata bridge into Stamboul.

How different is the aspect of Constantinople in detail, and the effect of the *tout ensemble* when viewed from a distance ! The shabby, tumble-down, wooden shanties, the rough, white-washed walls, the coarse and decaying masonry, all become the very ideal of the picturesque and magnificent, if only mellowed and tinted by the magic of the Eastern sunlight, and seen through the glamour of distance, and perhaps also the idealism of associations.

But a close inspection too often destroys illusions. Ned and I found it so in this case. The town of Stamboul, which is Constantinople proper, was vilely filthy, far worse than even Havana, (although possibly distance lent enchantment also to our reminiscences of the Cuban city).

But the interior — only the interior — of St. Sophia was grand and impressive beyond all that we had dreamed of. The awful feeling of immensity, of the vastness of space, seemed forced into our minds, brought nearer to realization than even when we gazed up at the dome of the sky itself. It was the arousing of the æsthetic feeling, of the sense of the sublime, which by many so-called " religions " is mistaken for the religious feeling.

But what a lapse it was to come out of that silent, awful immensity into the narrow, dirty streets of Stamboul, crowded with yelping curs and scowling, swarthy Turks ! It was worse than from the sublime to the ridiculous.

We visited the other mosques, the Top-Hané, the Seraglio as far as the outer apartments, and we passed many hours in wandering among the countless booths and bazaars.

In no city that we visited did I so long for unlimited funds as in those booths of Stamboul.

We were nearly three weeks in and around Constantinople. It was hard to tear ourselves away, and there was so much to interest and occupy us that the days fled almost unnoticed.

Moreover, we were in doubt as to the best course to follow in advancing on the continent of Europe. Ned, having in mind the chances of a letter from Maggie, wished to take the most direct route to Vienna, while I did my best to persuade him to employ the winter months in visiting Greece, Italy, and Spain, leaving the interior for the warmer weather. But there are certain states of the minds of certain — I might even say most — men which render the unfortunate victims not quite answerable to reason. It is unnecessary to add that Ned's mind at this time was in one of these conditions. And after some reflection I became convinced that, even viewed from a purely selfish standpoint, it would be better for me to go to Vienna at once, than to spend several months on the balmy Mediterranean with a man who was constantly hankering after the Vienna post-office. So I gracefully yielded the point, and we prepared to set out for the capital of Austria.

"And as to the route?" I inquired. "Do you propose to go in the lordly style we have been following lately, or will you condescend to roughing it again?"

"We'll have luxury whenever we can afford it, Tom; and when forced to the roughing, we'll consider it luxury. How are the funds?"

"Cash, forty pounds, odd shillings."

"And two rifles on which we can realize."

"Leaving only our revolvers to defend us against Bulgarians, bandits, and gypsies."

"If they were enough for Turcomans, they should be sufficient for the mild ruffians of civilized Europe."

So we sold our rifles, obtaining five pounds for the two.

Then, leaving a letter for Morley, we took the steamer for Varna on January 23d, and thence proceeded by rail through Bulgaria and Roumania, and alighted at the Saxon town of Kronstadt, in Transylvania.

"This meets my ideal, Ned!" said I as we walked to our inn through the quaint old town. And indeed there was something very satisfying to my imagination in the strong walls of the city, half ruined though they were, in the queer old German houses, the church, the old-fashioned market-place, and especially in the grand mountain scenery that surrounded the town, and the ancient castles and fortresses that frowned down upon us from their commanding heights.

"These bold Saxon squatters have had to fight hard to keep their grip here," said Ned. "Many a time have the trade guilds turned out to man those old walls against the Turk."

It was a pleasure to hear a language that sounded like something familiar. Neither Ned nor I boasted of our knowledge of German, but we could understand it readily, and could make known our few wants without difficulty.

Although it was the middle of the winter season, and in this mountain country the snow lay deep on the ground, yet the air was clear and bracing, and the sun was so warm that after a day spent in Kronstadt we determined to resume our original means of locomotion and tramp to Hermannstadt, which lies nearly a hundred miles west of Kronstadt. And so we did it ; but really it reminded me of nothing so much as of the passage of the Andes from Mendoza to San Felipe. It required six days to make the trip. The roads were rough and wild, often heavily drifted with snow, and though the weather was clear and bright for the most part, we sometimes suffered considerably from the cold.

Each night we rested in some little village, and as we sat by the good log-fire and drank the delicious Transylvanian wines, we enjoyed our life more than we had done for many months.

"We are away from the 'gang,' at least," said Ned. "We have beaten them at all points. You can't make me believe that even with all their outfit of spies and agents they could locate us to-night."

"But I am sure we shall hear from them again somewhere," said I. "And that reminds me of Captain Chambers. What a truly Horatian opportunity he would have here to-night, sitting by this fire and sipping this wine. 'Dissolve frigus ligna super foco, large reponens,' etc."

> "' When round the lonely cottage roars loud the tempest's din,
> And the good logs of Algidus roar louder yet within,'"

quoted Ned, in a sleepy way. "Tom, this is nice, but do you know, I don't feel quite up to the mark. There is something brewing within me, and for the first time I fairly dread to-morrow's tramp."

"Quinine, my boy !" said I ; and I adminstered a big dose that night. In the morning Ned seemed to be himself again, and we bravely breasted the few remaining miles that lay between us and Hermannstadt.

But by the time we reached our destination in the afternoon, he was exhausted, and more discouraged than I had ever seen him. He was thoroughly blue and dispirited.

"I fear it's a failure!" said he. "Three years nearly gone, and think of all that lies before us! Think of Lima, and St. Petersburg, and Edinburgh, and — "

"Pshaw!" said I. "Don't talk nonsense! Think of what we have done! What remains for two years is very much less than two thirds of what we have done in three."

But in spite of arguments and quinine I could not rouse him from his dejection. Ned was one of those fellows who concentrate their fits of blues into periods occurring only once in two or three years, making up at such times for all that they have lacked since the last seizure. I suppose the blues in such cases are cumulative, and gather in the system unobserved until they force an outlet, often at times when we wonder what there is to be blue about.

But it seemed to me that Ned was not well; and dreading a serious illness more than anything else, especially in this remote country, I strongly urged our going by rail direct to Vienna, although the funds would scarcely justify it under ordinary circumstances.

Ned assented with the utmost indifference, and we took the train for Vienna the very evening of our arrival at Hermannstadt. My fears were soon realized. Poor Ned grew worse so rapidly that I became seriously alarmed within two hours after leaving Hermannstadt. His head ached furiously, his back ached, his face became flushed, hands hot and dry, pulse ninety and on the increase, spirits zero. He was evidently in for a fever. Knowing the effect of the imagination on men of Ned's temperament, I did my utmost, though my own heart was sinking, to rouse and brace him up.

"To think that after traversing fever countries, deserts, swamps, and Calcuttas for three years, you should take it upon you to have a fever in Hungary in mid-winter is utterly absurd!" said I. "Brace up and be a man, as you have been. Remember the letter that waits for you at Vienna!"

"I shall never read it, Tom," said he, dolefully. "I am clean knocked out!"

I believe that ride from Hermannstadt was to me the most utterly miserable and discouraging part of our whole trip. Like most physically strong and usually healthy men, Ned was entirely demoralized by this first serious illness; and I, having no advice and no experience, was nearly distracted by my ignorance and my fears.

After a sleepless night for us both, Ned was so much worse that I gave the guard a handsome tip and sent him through the train to inquire in all the languages at his command for a physician. His efforts were successful, and a dapper little French doctor appeared, who flitted about Ned nervously for a few moments, asking questions and making his diagnosis, and who then took me aside and informed me that the patient showed dangerous symptoms of typhoid fever, and that if I valued his life I must stop at the first large town and put him under proper treatment. In the mean time he left me a soothing dose to keep Ned reasonably quiet for the journey. Then the little doctor bowed himself out, courteously declining my offered fee, and leaving me plunged in the depths of despair.

And we rolled on our way through beautiful Hungary, and to

this day, in my mind, the recollection of those picturesque scenes brings only a shuddering pain. Ned grew worse so rapidly, that at Buda-Pesth, with the help of the guard, I took him from the train and drove straight to the hospital.

And then began a weary time. It was typhoid fever; and the next morning Ned was delirious, raving of Maggie, of the old college days.— now suffering under the scorching desert sun and calling for " Water, water !" as he never called in those real days of privation that we had passed through. Again he was fighting with the Hindoos in Calcutta, crying and groaning that Tom was lost and they had murdered him ; and then it needed four strong men to hold him in his bed. And day after day and night after night I sat by him, suffering, it seemed to me. all that he could possibly be enduring.

I telegraphed to Maggie and to Ned's father simply that Ned was dangerously ill. I don't know what benefit I hoped to derive from sending these cable messages, but I was distracted, and scarcely knew what I did or why I did it.

From Dr. French a cable message came, telling me to keep him advised of Ned's condition, and to spare no expense to give him the best treatment. Needless advice ! I would have sold myself into a life of slavery, I believe, could that have guaranteed Ned's recovery.

It was very bitter to me to sit by his side through the long night-watches and think of all the magnificent courage, the splendid physique, the warm, self-sacrificing friendship, the light-hearted generosity, that had so gloriously withstood the severe tests of the past three years, now wasting and yielding to the fell disease that I was powerless to aid him in resisting.

For many days the doctors could give me no encouragement. Ned's life seemed to hang in the balance ; and when after nearly a month of watching and waiting the crisis was past, and there was no longer a reasonable doubt of his recovery, worn out and exhausted as I was, I am afraid I had something like an attack of feminine hysterics.

I had also sent a cable message to Ned's newspaper in New York, and long afterward we came across an issue of the said paper, with the head-lines : " Will he still be victorious? The conqueror of the desert, the mountains, and the sea, now battling with typhoid fever in Hungary."

But as soon as the turning-point was fairly past, Ned began to recover with the same industry he had shown in getting sick. In ten days I had him out of the hospital, and comfortably located in a quiet lodging,, where we had a pleasant room with a fine view of the river, and fairly good meals.

Then, as I knew it would be many weeks before we could set forth on our route again, and as funds were getting low, I nosed about the town till by the help of a German friend I secured a position as second flute in an orchestra in one of the small theatres. This helped our finances a little ; and Ned, being cheered by a long letter from Maggie, improved so that in two weeks he was able to walk out, leaning on my arm, an emaciated creature on whose huge frame the skin seemed to hang as loosely as the clothes.

But as the days passed we began to take longer walks, crossing the river by the suspension bridge or the iron Margarenthenbrucke, and wandering up among the straggling streets of the old town of Buda.

We made many pleasant acquaintances, Germans, Hungarians, and an occasional Englishman. We visited the National Museum, the Houses of Parliament, the Public Gardens, etc. ; and as the spring gradually displaced the chilly winter blasts, and the sun waxed warm and invigorating, the old feeling began to steal over us both, the spring restlessness, when " longen folk to gon on pilgrimages."

Ned especially grew more and more restless each day as he gained flesh and strength. I resisted him as far as was possible, feeling that the rest should be as long as we could stand ; but one night I came home from the theatre and found Ned, with all our small appurtenances spread out around him, writing a letter to his newspaper.

" I 've been taking stock, Tom," said he, " and finishing letter No. 65. Here is a sentence from the letter : ' We leave here to-morrow for Vienna. The fever has gone, but like an absconding cashier it has taken the funds with it ; so we shall resume our primitive system, and trust to legs and luck to reach Vienna.' "

" And how are your legs now ? " asked I. " Do they feel any shakiness ? Can you walk twenty-five miles to-morrow and feel no more used up than you did three years ago in the New Jersey barn ? "

"I feel better and stronger to-day, Tom, than I have in all the three years since then. And I should leave this town to-morrow, even if I had to crawl out on all fours."

"Well," said I, "when you talk that way I believe the sand has got into your system again, and I'm with you."

So at eight o'clock the next morning, being the 18th day of May, 1880, as on the 1st of May, 1877, we again set out westward on foot, with cash amounting to $25, and equipments about the same as when we left New York.

We took as short a cut as was possible, heading for Raab, which lay on the other side of the great Bakony forest. Ned, after his long-enforced idleness, was as full of spirits as he was when our campaign was only on paper, and it did seem like a new beginning, a new lease of life to our expedition. Ned was glorying in his new-found strength and health; I was supremely happy as I remembered the dark days of a few weeks before; and the bright, warm spring sun flooding the valleys and lighting up each picturesque scene with its genial glow lent a very substantial aid to our exuberant feelings, and made the world a pleasant place to be in, the past a success, and the future full of promise.

We were like two prisoners just turned loose into the fields, two boys who had been kept after school-hours and had at last earned their freedom; and the stern old crags and frowning fortresses of Hungary listened in solemn amazement to the unfamiliar sound of New England college songs as we trudged merrily on our way.

The first day we contented ourselves with only about ten miles walk, stopping at a little village in the mountains, and the next morning we plunged into the great *Bakonyer Wald*, following the narrow road up steep heights and down rocky declivities, everywhere surrounded by the old beech-trees fresh with their spring foliage.

"Great country for bears, Tom!" said Ned. "We might find some good sport if we had anything to shoot with besides revolvers."

"And a great country for brigands," said I. "We might lose some cash if we had any to lose."

We had intended to reach a village about twenty-five miles distant, but the roads were rough and in some places very steep, and when the evening shadows began to gather we were still in the heart of the forest.

"Looks as if we should have to camp," said I. "Fortunately the night is fine, and a good fire will make us comfortable."

"But a supper is much more important to me than a bed," replied Ned. "Let's push on, at least so long as we can see the road."

Suddenly, as the road wound around a jutting rock, we saw through the gathering gloom the twinkle of firelight among the trees, and at the same moment a strain of music met our ears. We stopped to listen. It was a Hungarian melody, such as we had heard occasionally played by the orchestras in our own country, but never with such an abandon, such a fierce intensity of feeling, as inspired these unseen musicians.

"We 're in for it," said I, — "a camp of brigands!"

"Nonsense!" said Ned. "They 're gypsies. The woods are full of them, and the orchestra is rehearsing for its performance at the next village tavern. This means a good supper and an evening's entertainment for us, my boy. Come on!" And he strode boldly through the woods in the direction of the fire.

After a few moments of stumbling over logs and scratching our hands with bushes, we emerged into a small clearing revealing a wonderfully picturesque scene.

Around the edge of the open space were ranged a dozen or more small tents. A huge log-fire was burning in the middle, and men, women, and children were scattered about, the brilliant colors of their costumes and their black hair and eyes gleaming and flashing in the firelight as they listened intently to the music of a half-dozen performers seated in a little group together; and the thick forest of beech-trees, rising like a wall of blackness, formed the background of the scene.

For several moments we were unnoticed. Then a half-naked child suddenly gave a quick cry and pointed at us. Instantly the music ceased and all sprang to their feet, and as we slowly advanced, a stalwart gypsy, apparently the leader, stepped out to meet us. Ned addressed him in German, stating that we were travellers who had lost our way in the forest, and attracted by the firelight had come to seek hospitality at their hands.

The man turned to the crowd and said something in their own language, and then with quite a courtly bow and a lordly wave of the hand motioned us to a seat on a blanket spread out near the fire. Meantime, some of the women bustled about, and in fifteen minutes Ned and I were enjoying a delicious meal of broiled mutton and red Hungarian wine, while the orchestra resumed their music, and the children and young girls gathered about us, laughing and casting shy glances from their dark eyes.

The men lay stretched out on the ground, leaning on their elbows and occasionally talking among themselves. Some of them were fierce-looking fellows, and I could not help reflecting that a gold piece would be sufficient temptation for any one of them to cut our throats.

However, we were treated with distinguished courtesy, and as we took great pains to express interest in all that we saw, the most friendly footing was soon established. Nearly all the gypsies spoke German, with peculiar idioms and pronunciation; but still we understood them quite as readily, I think, as they did us.

We soon had our fortunes told by dark-eyed maidens, beautiful in face and figure, but rather unwashed in appearance, and I produced a few small coins which, scattered among the children, seemed to add greatly to our importance. The men were not very communicative, but we had some conversation with the leader, and by telling him that we were Englishmen, and that we had a great desire to see a genuine gypsy dance, we at last induced him to grant us the privilege.

A wide space was cleared, and the young girls and children took their places, the orchestra struck up a wild, plaintive melody, and the dance began.

"Tom," said Ned suddenly in English, "look at that little blonde! I did n't notice her before. What a contrast to the others!"

The little girl was about ten years old, as graceful as a sylph, with long, flowing golden hair, clear complexion, and blue eyes. All the others were as dark as night. We watched this little one with much interest. She was the best dancer as far as ease and grace were concerned, though she had not quite the fire and vivacity of some of her dark sisters.

"She is no gypsy!" said Ned, in a few moments. Then he added in a lower voice, "She has been stolen."

"Nonsense!" said I. "I suppose those peculiar types sometimes appear even among the gypsies. I don't believe the old nursery stories about gypsies stealing children. They have more of their own than they can take care of."

The little girl was quite near us during this conversation, and seemed aware that she was the subject of it. She watched us as closely as we looked at her. She became nervous and apparently distressed, grew confused and made several mistakes in the figure, throwing the rest into some disorder, and at last suddenly stopped and withdrew from the dance, seating herself at a little distance from the party.

A dark, villanous-looking fellow, who had been stretched at full length with his chin resting on his hands, instantly got up, and stepping to our little blonde seized her roughly by the shoulder and spoke to her in a harsh and threatening tone. The child shook her head and looked up pleadingly. Then the man picked up a stout stick and again spoke to the child. Ned and I rose involuntarily to our feet. "Damn the scoundrel!" said Ned, "he is n't going to strike her!"

"Keep cool, Ned," said I; and I glanced about at the others. No one had moved. They were all indolently watching the scene, but without any apparent interest. The dance had stopped with the music.

We walked to where the man stood, and I said to him in my best German, and in as pleasant a tone as I could assume, "We have enjoyed the dance very much, but the child is tired and frightened now. Do not be severe with her."

The man scowled at me for an instant, then turned again to the girl. Once more he spoke to her more fiercely than before. The poor child cast one imploring glance at him, then turned to us with a look that went to my heart, and then she sank on her knees, covering her face with her hands and sobbing violently. The scoundrel raised the heavy stick, but Ned stepped quickly in front of him, his lips set and his face white as death. I knew the old rage was on him, and I trembled for the end.

"Don't strike that child!" said he, fiercely.

The blow descended across the poor little one's bare shoulders, and with a faint cry she fell flat on her face. But at the same instant Ned's fist flew out like lightning, straight from the shoulder, in the good old-fashioned way, and the burly ruffian measured his length on the ground.

Every man was on his feet in an instant, and with a hoarse cry the one whom Ned had struck bounded up like a rubber ball, and made a dash at us with a knife, only to pause as he found himself looking down into the muzzles of two revolvers. Instantly the chief stepped forward, and seizing the man by one shoulder swung him round unceremoniously against the crowd that had gathered behind him. A few sharp words of command he spoke to the men, and they sullenly withdrew, and seated themselves around the fire again.

To us he said in German, " Put up your weapons. You are my guests." Then lifting the sobbing child to her feet, he quietly motioned with his arm, and she at once disappeared in one of the tents.

I began to apologize to the chief for the trouble we had caused, but he interrupted me, saying, " It is right ! "

Then he gave some further orders to the party, and they withdrew into the different tents, all except one man, who took his seat by the fire apparently to keep watch. At a gesture from the chief we followed him to a small tent that stood somewhat apart from the others, near the edge of the woods.

" Enter," said he ; " it is for you. May you rest sweetly."

" Not very likely," remarked I in English as we sat down within the tent. " I shall imagine that pirate's knife between my shoulders every fifteen minutes."

" I was reckless as usual," said Ned ; " but my blood would n't stand it to see that pretty little girl struck with a club ; neither would yours, Tom. But I guess we 're safe enough. The old chief is a trump, and the rest are afraid of him."

" But remember, there 's no more treacherous dog in the world than a gypsy," said I.

Then we sat smoking our pipes in silence. We had brought our blankets and other belongings into the tent, but we had no thought of unrolling the blankets or making any attempt to sleep. The fire burned low in the opening, and we could see the guard sitting with his back toward us.

So the night wore slowly on, and we smoked and talked in low tones for several hours.

Suddenly a faint rustling sound in the rear of the tent attracted my attention. I grasped Ned by the arm, and we both drew our revolvers. I glanced through the door of the tent. The fire was nearly dead. The moon was looking down from above the dark trees that formed the edge of the clearing. The guard, with his head bent over nearly to his knees, was sound asleep.

Again came the rustling sound as of some one crawling toward the tent. We held our breaths and listened. Almost immediately there was a scratching on the wall of the tent, and then the canvas flapped as if some one were shaking it from the lower edge. Moving close to the rear of the tent and holding his revolver in readiness, Ned said in a low tone, and in German, " Who is it ? "

From the other side of the canvas came a thin, childish voice, " It is I, Marcsa."

" And who is Marcsa ? " asked Ned.

" The little girl whom you saved. Let me in quickly, for I must tell you."

We raised the canvas, and our little fair-haired protegée crawled in and crouched down on the ground.

" You must go away at once," said she, speaking in a breath-less way. " I waited so long to come and tell you, for Matyi was not asleep. He will kill you. I hate him."

" Who is Matyi ? " asked Ned. " Is he the scoundrel that was going to beat you ? "

" Yes," said she. " And you struck him, and a gypsy never forgives. He will kill you."

" But are not you a gypsy, little one ? " asked Ned.

" No," said she. " I was brought here long ago, when I was a little girl, and I hate them all, — all but old Tara. She was kind to me, but she is dead ; and the rest hate me and beat me."

" Don't you know who brought you here, my child ? " said Ned.

" No, it is long since. I have forgotten. But you must go at once. Matyi may come, and he will kill you and beat me."

"Tom," said Ned in English, "I have a scheme. It's a wild one, like yours, but don't make an outcry. You'll agree with it when you reflect."

The little girl was listening intently.

"I have heard words like those," said she. "I almost know that."

"Little Marcsa," said Ned, in German, "we will go away to-night, but you must go with us. We will take you home to the land that you came from, to your friends, away from cruel Matyi and all the people that hate you. No one shall ever beat you any more."

This was a wild scheme, truly. My head recognized the utter foolishness of it, but my heart silenced my head for once, and I said: "Yes, little girl, come with us, and we will take care of you. We will be kind to you, and take you away across the water to a pleasant home. Will you come?"

For a moment the little one was silent. Then she said slowly: "Across the water. Yes, I remember, the great water, and all the people, and how I cried!" Then suddenly she leaned forward and clasped Ned around the knees. "Oh, will you take me?" she sobbed. "I will be so good. I will dance for you; I will beg for you. I can sing; I can walk far; I can show you the way through the woods. I know all the woods, and all the paths, and the houses, and the villages; and you will not beat me. Oh, you are so good—" and the sobs choked her.

"There, little one," said Ned, lifting her up in his arms; "don't cry. Come, we must go, and you shall show us the way. Be brave, and help us."

In a moment the child became the woman. She stepped stealthily to the door of the tent and peered out.

"Pali is asleep," said she in a whisper. "Come!" Then lifting the canvas she glided under it, and Ned and I followed, with our blankets and haversacks. Quietly and swiftly picking her way among the trees and bushes, the child led us on. In ten minutes we had emerged upon the road, a quarter of a mile below the gypsy camp. Then she walked swiftly on in the moonlight, her little bare feet treading fearlessly over sharp rocks and through deep mud, and Ned and I trudged silently behind.

Looking back we could see, far away in the distance, the faint glimmer of the gypsy camp-fire, but no sound reached our ears. The trusty sentinel was still placidly keeping watch — in dreamland.

At a bend of the road we lost the twinkle of the fire, and felt that we had made good our escape.

"The Gypsy Sentinel."

CHAPTER XVIII.

THE road was rough, and the dense forest made it almost impossible to see where we were treading. Only now and then a moonbeam, struggling through the leafy branches, showed us for an instant the little white figure flitting on before us, and still we stumbled after.

"It's a big undertaking, Ned," said I, after a time.

"I know it, Tom," replied he. "But we had to do it, and we must meet the emergency in some way."

Then we relapsed into silence and thought, "What shall we do with this child?" I reflected over and over again. We had no money to put her under proper care, or to help her to find her home, if she had one; and to take her with us through all the rough life we still must undergo seemed too absurd for consideration. I presume Ned arrived at no better conclusion than I, for he said nothing.

After two hours' walking, the woods began to open and break away, and as we reached the summit of a steep hill, suddenly a valley lay before us, and a little village sleeping in the soft moonlight.

"We must not go there," said Marcsa. "To-morrow Matyi and all will be there. We will go this way;" and she suddenly turned aside into a narrow path that led off to the left of the road.

"But look here, little one," called I, "it is dark, and we can't see the road."

The child laughed, and turning back, took me by the hand. "I can go through the woods at night as well as day!" said she. So we struggled on in the dark, till Ned began to lose patience, and suddenly called a halt.

"I say, Marcsa," he exclaimed, "we have gone far enough to-night. Your little feet are tired. We will lie down here and rest, and in the morning we can go faster. We are safe from the gypsies here."

We unrolled our blankets and wrapped the little girl in one of them, spite of her protests, and then Ned and I curled up together under the other.

We were both very tired, and had grown accustomed to sleeping anywhere at short notice, and in less than a minute the wind, that was sighing through the branches over my head, had passed with its soft murmur into my dreams.

When I awoke, it was daylight. Marcsa was sleeping quietly, looking wonderfully pretty and innocent, with her sweet, childish face and golden hair just showing above the rough blanket.

I awoke Ned to look at her.

"It's a pretty picture," said I; "but what are we to do with it?"

"We must take her with us, Tom, — at least until we reach some place where she can be properly cared for. In Vienna we will get her some clothes."

"We have twenty-three dollars, my boy. You don't propose a very elaborate wardrobe, I trust. We must also get her something to eat, and it seems to me now that I should enjoy sharing a meal with her."

As if she had heard me, the child suddenly opened her eyes, and in an instant sprang lightly to her feet, emerging from the blanket like Aphrodite from the sea.

"You are hungry," said she in her curious German. "Come! I will get you some breakfast."

"Where will you get us breakfast, little one?" asked Ned.

"You shall see," she replied with a smile, as she rolled up the blanket.

In a few moments we were following her quickly along the narrow trail. After a half-mile the woods were passed, and we looked down into a wide cultivated valley dotted with here and there a peasant's cottage, a village in the distance, and cattle browsing over the plain.

It was a beautiful scene in the bright morning sunlight.

Just below us, and around a low projecting hill, a thin column of smoke was rising.

"You shall wait for me," said the child with a pretty air of command; "I will come again soon." And she sprang lightly down the steep path and disappeared from our sight.

Presently from below us came the sound of singing. It was a single child's voice, without accompaniment, but the notes rose sweet and pure and strong on the still morning air, and with a tenderness that made me almost fear to breathe lest one tone should escape me.

We listened enraptured. It was a quaint, pathetic gypsy melody, and the words were in an unknown language; but those full, thrilling notes that seemed to float in the air around us and blend with the exquisite rural beauty of the scene affected me as no music had ever done before.

Verse after verse rose to our ears, and when at last the song ceased, I involuntarily drew a long breath of delight.

"Tom," said Ned, "we have found a treasure in that child. She will help us far more than we can help her."

"A voice like that," said I, "seems to me a help to all nature."

Presently the little one appeared, and climbed swiftly up the path; and, joyful to behold, she carried a large pail of milk in her hand, and several small loaves of brown bread under her arm.

We sprang to meet her.

"See!" she said triumphantly. "They are good people. They know me, and they will always give me what they have, if I sing."

We all sat down together around the pail and broke the bread, dipping it in the milk. Never was bread and milk so delicious!

Then Marcsa returned the pail, and we set out across the valley, the child still leading.

"With this accession, Ned," said I, "we can do a little of

the strolling-minstrel business, and eke out our travelling expenses. We can blow on our flutes, Marcsa can sing and dance, and we can all sing together. Could any 'rude Carinthian boor' resist such a combination of talent?"

"I've been revolving that very scheme in my mind," said Ned. "It's worth trying. We may be able to travel all over Europe that way. But we must practise together."

At noon we stopped at a peasant's cottage not far from Raab, and by politeness and a little music secured a meal.

In the afternoon, having passed Raab at some distance to our right, we halted in a little wood and spent several hours in practising all our old flute duets and songs, teaching Marcsa the English words and the melodies, which she acquired with wonderful rapidity, and with the greatest delight. The words seemed to affect her strangely; and in fact whenever Ned and I talked English she listened with a puzzled expression, as if trying to recall something.

"That is my language," said she. "I can remember the sound but not quite the meaning;" and she learned English and pronounced it with a readiness that seemed to prove the truth of what she said. There was no doubt that she was an English child.

Then we talked with her long and persistently, trying to awaken some recollections of what had happened before she knew the gypsies, and gradually we drew nearer to the facts.

She traced back her life with the gypsies, step by step, for five or perhaps six years, telling us of all their wanderings, of the different members of the tribe, the towns and villages they had visited, the death and burial of old Tara, who had been her best friend among them, and back of all we reached substantially this : —

She remembered a great ship and a long voyage, and that she was sick and cried, and a dark man scolded and frightened her, and a woman tried to soothe her ; and she had vague recollections, still farther back, of a grave, kind man, who used to take her on his knee in a large room, and let her look from the window at the carriages and people going by, and a sweet, tender lady who sang to her, and who undressed her at night and dressed her in the morning.

And Ned and I helped her memory as much as we could by suggestions, — describing all the little details of a child's life in a comfortable American home ; and often she would suddenly clap her hands with delight, as something we described awakened a long silent memory. And we recited all the old nursery rhymes, and she remembered nearly all of them ; and when Ned began, "Ride a cock-horse to Banbury Cross," she fairly took the words out of his mouth, and screamed with delight the *English* words, "To see an old woman ride on a white horse," but with the pronunciation of a child just learning to speak plainly.

"There 's no possibility of doubt, Tom," said Ned. "She is an American girl, and she was stolen from her home in New York, or some other American city, when she was four or five years old."

"Don't you remember what they called you then?" I asked. "Marcsa is only the name the gypsies gave you."

"Yes, that is my gypsy name," she said. "I had another once. They called me, — oh! I can almost remember."

"Was it Mamie?" asked Ned.

The child shook her head, still studying.

"Was it Alice, Bessie, Lizzie, Gertie, Maud, Sallie, Maggie, Jenny, Kittie, Edith," and so forth. We repeated every English or foreign girl's name that we could recall; but the little head still shook denial, and the sweet face grew more and more perplexed and intense.

"Give it up, Ned," said I. "I believe the name will come to her. Her mind is at work, and so intensely that unconscious cerebration, as Prof. T—— used to call it, will work out the result, and the name will suddenly flash into her mind when she is thinking of something else."

So we dropped the subject for the present, and wandered on our way toward Vienna, across the wide meadow country of the Danube, sometimes sleeping in the woods, sometimes in a peasant's cottage or shed, managing to earn our meals and such lodging as we had, by our little store of musical accomplishments. Those were happy days, in spite of the occasional privations. The little girl that we had rescued was like perpetual sunshine to us. Her gypsy education had made her capable of exertions and endurance that often shamed Ned and myself, hardy veterans as we considered ourselves, and she was never discouraged or sad, — always bright, playful, and as full of life as a kitten.

One sunny afternoon we rested under the shade of a fine old beech-tree, and sang a little, to get our voices in trim for our supper performance.

We tried several of the old college songs, most of which Marcsa had already learned.

"Ned," said I, "we have n't tried 'Integer Vitæ.' It 's properly a quartet, but when Marcsa learns the soprano we can easily arrange it for a trio. Come, little one, stand by me and listen while I sing the air and Ned growls the bass."

So we began. As we sang, the child drew closer and closer to me, clasping her hands round my arm and listening with an eagerness that was unusual even in her. When we reached the last lines, —

> "Dulce ridentem *Lalagen* amabo
> Dulce loquentem,"

she suddenly let go my arm and screamed, "Lalage! Lalage! That is it! That's my name!" and began to dance about us in a whirlwind of delight.

The song stopped abruptly, and we looked at her in astonishment.

"Well," said Ned, presently, "that 's a piece of luck!"

"It 's no wonder we could n't suggest it to her before," said I.

"Let me tell you, Tom," said Ned, "that name will prove the clew by which we trace her family. Girls named Lalage are not as thick as blackberries."

"Lalage! Lalage!" sang the child. "Now I can see my papa. He always called me Lalage."

"Do you remember how he looked?" asked Ned. "Would you know him if you saw him?"

"Oh, yes! I would know him! Now I can see him, — just as he sat in the great chair and held out his arms to me."

"Come, then!" said Ned. "We will find him. You must be patient, little one, but some day we will find him. And now we shall call you Lalage, and not Marcsa."

Then we went on our way with a new happiness inspiring the child, and a new satisfaction in the minds of Ned and myself.

We entered Vienna on the 6th of June, having made the whole journey from Pesth at an expense of only about two dollars, which we had spent on the first day.

After securing a quiet lodging for the few days of our stay, and leaving Lalage in charge, we visited the Post-Office. Ned found the long-delayed letter from Maggie, which seemed to interest him as much as if he had not received several later editions of the same story.

More important, at least in my opinion, was a letter from Morley, dated at Constantinople, January 27th, four days after we had left there.

Following a brief account of his overland journey from Damascus, he stated that he found letters which would make it necessary for him to go to England at once.

"There is a scheme on foot," he wrote, "which will interest you, and I am anxious to see you. Hope this letter will reach Vienna in time to find you. I know you have much to do in Europe. Try to arrange your route so as to meet me in Trieste, July 15th. I shall be there from the 15th until about the 20th. Shall have my steam yacht, the 'Rover.' You will easily find her in the harbor. I cannot be more definite now, but I assure you it may solve the *most difficult part* of your problem if you meet me. Make every endeavor to be in Trieste before 20th July."

"The most difficult part of our problem!" commented Ned. "That must be Lima! What can Morley be up to?"

"Peru is just now having a bad time with Chili," said I. "If the war ends as it threatens, there may be no Lima for us to visit. At all events, we must meet Morley and find out."

"And we have just about time to tramp comfortably from here to Trieste before July 15th," said Ned.

"And Lalage?"

"She goes with us, of course."

"To Lima?"

"Yes, if necessary; but we can settle that when we see Morley."

So we hurriedly finished our business in Vienna, purchased some good strong clothes and stout shoes for the little girl, and set out toward the south on June 8th.

We were a jolly party of three. We had but three dollars left, but we had splendid health, effervescent spirits, cheering prospects, and one of the most beautiful countries of the world to wander leisurely through at the finest time of the year.

The first twenty-five miles of our route were over a fine highway, through a level, fertile country, abounding with vineyards and thriving villages.

Then we followed the road up over the first range of the mountains, at one point reaching nearly three thousand feet of elevation. Down again into the rich, green valleys of Styria, along winding streams, through the town of Brück, on again to Grätz, over new mountains, and through new valleys to Laibach and Idria, everywhere in the midst of the most varied and beautiful scenery, and without a day or an hour of discouragement or regret. Thousands of tourists and travellers have passed through this beautiful region. Many have written full and glowing accounts of its charms. I do not believe that one of them made that trip with more complete enjoyment than the three strolling adventurers who loitered along the road in the summer of 1880, singing and playing their way clear through the country with but three dollars in their pockets.

A farm-house, a peasant's cottage, or a village tavern furnished us our meals and lodging readily enough as the payment for our concerts. Our audiences were not musical critics, and we seemed to please them.

At one village, however, a German theatrical manager who happened to be staying overnight at the tavern heard little Lalage sing one of her gypsy solos. He was as much delighted as we had been, and did his utmost to persuade us to let him take her to educate for the stage, promising her the best of advantages and a brilliant future; but the child only laughed at him.

We scarcely ever walked more than ten miles in a day, often much less, and we not unfrequently spent the whole afternoon in some picturesque mountain village, enjoying our lordly leisure without price.

At last, on the 14th of July, from the top of the last range of hills we looked far down upon the blue Adriatic below us, and upon Trieste with its clustering buildings and tall masts in the distance.

On the morning of the 16th we entered the city and went at once to the docks.

An hour's research, and a dozen attempts to gain information in English, French, Spanish, or German (our Italian was weak), at last unearthed a boatman who spoke German, and who could take us to where the "Rover" lay at anchor.

The fee we paid the boatman was actually our first expense since leaving Vienna. I believe if we had not been so impatient, and Lalage had taken the time to sing one song, he would have rowed us out to the vessel free of charge.

As we drew near the yacht, we recognized the honest, placid countenance of Sam, gazing at us from the deck. We cheered him lustily, and presently a faint look of surprise began to creep over his face, much like that which he had shown when the sand-heap so suddenly gave way under his feet as he climbed out of the Syrian tomb.

It soon passed, however, and he welcomed us on board with a smile that beamed in spite of his efforts to preserve the fitting dignity of a trusted retainer.

"Sam, old boy! how are you?" shouted Ned, as he grasped the honest fellow's hand and slapped him on the back. "I'm mighty glad to see you! Where's Morley?"

"Mr. Morley is in the city, sir," replied Sam; then with a subdued cough and a side glance at Lalage, "might I ask, sir, who is the young party, sir?"

"'Sh, Sam!" replied Ned in an impressive tone. "She's a Bulgarian princess travelling in disguise. She has heard of Morley, and wants to interview him about taking command of her armies."

From that time forward Lalage had no more devoted attendant and admirer than Sam.

In the course of an hour Morley arrived on board, and greeted us with the heartiest of hearty English welcomes. When we told him of our rescue of the little girl, and our determination to find her family or to provide a home for her, he joined most warmly in our feelings, and promised to assist us and her by every means in his power, especially as Lalage, with her sweet, innocent face and charming manner, was an argument that no man could resist.

We all sat together in the main cabin of the yacht, cosey and delightful, fitted up with every luxury and convenience that wealth could procure; and we sipped the fine liquors from Morley's sideboard and smoked his choice Havanas, while he told us of his ride from Damascus to Constantinople.

"And how are our old desert steeds, Morley?" I inquired. "Where is Timour?"

"They are both safe in England," he replied, "at the old home in Kent; and my sister thinks more of Timour than of all the rest of the family, I believe."

Then we told of all our adventures and Ned's illness, and Lalage sang a gypsy song for us, and at last, as the morning was well spent, we had a sumptuous yacht dinner served in the cabin, which was to us more like a return to civilization than anything we had known for years. And when the coffee had been served, Morley said, —

"Sam, will you kindly take the Princess Lalage and show her all over the yacht and explain everything that can interest her? And then, Sam, you will arrange my private stateroom for her exclusive use hereafter. I shall occupy one of the three berths in the large stateroom with my friends."

And the youthful princess, who now understood English quite well, blushed and looked at us; and Ned said, —

"May I ask you, Commodore Morley, what you propose to do with your humble servants and their royal charge?"

"All in good time, my friend," replied Morley, with a smile. "I am about to explain matters to you. At all events, you will go to England with me in this yacht. Beyond that it will depend on yourselves. Sam, the princess is bored. Do the honors of the yacht and entertain her, while I talk with these gentlemen."

So Sam, with the greatest deference imaginable, escorted the young lady on deck, and Morley closed the door and drew his chair nearer to us.

"I imagine," said he, "that you know to what I referred when I wrote of the most difficult part of your problem."

"We imagined that you referred to Lima," said I.

"Exactly!" he replied; "and you know, of course, that there is war between Peru and Chili."

"Yes."

"Very well! Now, I feel that I can trust you with all my plans, and I know you will go with me and help me out when

I have explained." Then he lit a cigar and continued : "The Peruvian government is in a bad way. Their navy is practically ruined. The capture of the ' Huascar ' has left them almost defenceless at sea. The only possibility of their preventing an absolute conquest of the country is in the management of their land forces. They are hard pressed, — short of men, short of ready money, and short of armaments and war supplies. An agent of their government has been in England and has interviewed a wealthy friend of mine.

"The upshot of the whole matter is this," continued Morley, leaning forward over the table and lowering his voice. " There is to-day, in a certain English harbor, a small, fast-sailing steamer, well armed and nearly loaded with a cargo of arms and munitions of war. She will sail for Callao probably within two months. The Peruvian government agent of whom I spoke will be a passenger. There will also be a Peruvian engineer, familiar with the position of every torpedo which has been placed in the vicinity of Callao, and who knows every foot of the shore thirty miles north and south of that port. The vessel and its cargo are owned by six Englishmen, and my interest is one fourth. We shall man her with a picked crew, sail her to the Pacific coast, dodge the Chilian cruisers and land our cargo at Callao, receiving Peruvian government bonds in exchange. I shall be in command of the vessel. The scheme pleased me because it smacks of excitement and adventure, and will be a novelty. I am here with my yacht for two purposes, — first, to purchase certain Austrian goods to complete my Peruvian cargo ; second, to meet you. This yacht is now loaded with what will help to equip several Peruvian companies. I know that both you fellows are good seamen, that you are familiar with Spanish, — which I am not ; I know that you want to visit Lima, and from personal experience I know that you are the men that I want for this expedition. On the part of the owners of the steamer ' Alliance ' I have the honor to offer to you, Ned, the position of second officer, and to you, Tom, the position of third officer on said steamer, for a cruise to Callao and return. The remuneration will be satisfactory to you, and will be in cash, not in Peruvian bonds. There you have the whole story, boys, and I have n't said so much at a stretch for a year."

And Morley poured out a pony of brandy which he swallowed at a gulp, relit his cigar and tipped back his chair, looking at us expectantly through a cloud of smoke.

Both Ned and I had listened intently through this whole business. I had anticipated the general drift from the beginning; but the final proposition was so unexpected that it fairly took the oxygen out of my lungs.

Ned was the first to speak. He rose, and extended his hand.

"Morley," said he, "you 're a trump!"

"Then you 'll go?" said Morley, grasping his hand.

"Go!" replied Ned. "I would go if you only allowed me to work my passage before the mast."

"And you, Tom?" said Morley.

"Is thy servant an ass, that he should reject this thing?" replied I. "If we had already been to Lima, I would still risk six months time rather than lose this trip with you, Morley?"

"Good!" said he. "That settles it. I knew you 'd both go; and now we 'll say no more about it. There will be another load of stuff out from the city to-night, which will finish my cargo, and to-morrow we will leave Trieste."

"But what about little Lalage, Tom?" said Ned.

"I 've thought of her," said Morley. "We will all go together to my place in Kent, and the little girl will stay there as a guest until we return from Peru. My sister will be delighted to have her there, and will devote herself to educating her, and trying to awaken her recollections. When we return, we shall be ready to begin the search for her family."

Then we went on deck, and rejoined Sam and Lalage. The child was radiant with delight. Everything on the yacht interested her, and she could not express her happiness at the thought of having such a charming little stateroom all to herself. She had evidently made a great impression on Sam. That worthy confided to me, — "She be a remarkable child, sir; and she 's as good as she is handsome."

"Now," said Morley, "we are so near Venice that I think we will take a run over there to-morrow, and from there we will cruise to England, stopping only at Marseilles."

So Ned and I retired to the cabin, and prepared our letters

to be mailed at Venice. They were the sixty-eighth letters of the series, and Venice was the twenty-first city.

In the evening a mysterious launch came out from the city, and its cargo was quietly transferred to the hold of the " Rover."

We sat late that night on deck, talking over all the old times, and discussing the future with Morley, and turned into our comfortable bunks at last, full of confidence in our final success.

At daylight, when we came on deck, we were steaming across the Adriatic, with the towers of Venice just appearing above the horizon.

We spent but one day in Venice. Ned mailed a letter to Maggie, telling her to address him at London, as Morley assured us that it would be at least six weeks before our steamer would be ready to sail.

Then we continued our voyage, down the Adriatic and the Mediterranean, spending a half-day at Marseilles, — our twenty-second city, — through the straits, and around to London, arriving on the 20th of August. There is no pleasure in life like a voyage on a well-appointed yacht with a good company.

At London, Morley drew up papers for our signature as the second and third officers of the " Alliance," and then advanced us forty pounds apiece on account ; so we were in high feather. We took Lalage to a dressmaker's establishment, and surrendered her to the proprietress, to be dressed in the costume of civilized life, while Ned and I went through the same process at a tailor's.

Then Morley and Ned took the train north, to visit the steamer and inspect the preparations, while Lalage and I amused ourselves in London till they came back.

"They 're infernally slow," said Morley, when he returned. " It looks as if we could n't possibly be ready to sail before November 1st, so we may as well go home and rest in the mean time."

So we all went down to Elmhurst, Morley's home in Kent, and were right royally welcomed.

A younger married brother of Morley was manager for him, as his own roving disposition made him unwilling to settle down at home. The other members of the family were the mother, Madam Morley, — a genial, courtly old lady, whose only unhappiness in life was the restlessness of her eldest son, — and a sister of Morley, a charming girl of twenty, who at once fell in love with our little Lalage, as indeed all the family did.

Once more I mounted my glorious Turcoman, old Timour. I fancied that the noble fellow recognized me, and was as glad to greet me as I to see him again.

For two months our life was the *dolce far niente* of a welcome guest at a fine English country-house. We made occasional visits to London, and often to our steamer. Preparations were hurried to the utmost. A crew of fine-looking, resolute seamen was engaged, and all was promising well, though Morley and the Peruvian agent, Señor Garcias, chafed continually at the delay.

In the mean time, at Elmhurst, little Lalage was becoming the pet of the entire household, from old Madam Morley to the stable-boys.

Her story alone attracted every one; but her beauty, her bright cheerful disposition, and her wonderful voice endeared her more and more each day.

A little English pony was placed at her disposal, and under the skilful and devoted instructions of Sam she soon became an expert horsewoman. Many a delightful morning we all spent together in the saddle, Ned and I on the Turcomans, Lalage on her pony, and the others on thoroughbred English horses.

One day, toward the end of September, Ned returned from a trip to London in a state of extravagant joy. He had received a letter from Maggie, and she announced that Dr. French had promised to take her abroad in the spring. They would be in Paris probably in March.

"And I shall be there too," said Ned. emphatically.

"Of which there is no doubt," replied I.

On the 20th of October the steamer was ready to sail. We bade farewell to the kind family who had entertained us so long, and commended Lalage to their care. The little girl cried bitterly when we left her, — the first tears I had seen her shed since the night when we rescued her from the brutal gypsy.

She had grown very dear to us both, — how dear we did not realize until we had to part from her. But we consoled ourselves by remembering that no place could be better for the child than the delightful home in which we left her.

Two days later we were on the deck of the steamer, making our way rapidly down the Irish Sea.

CHAPTER XIX.

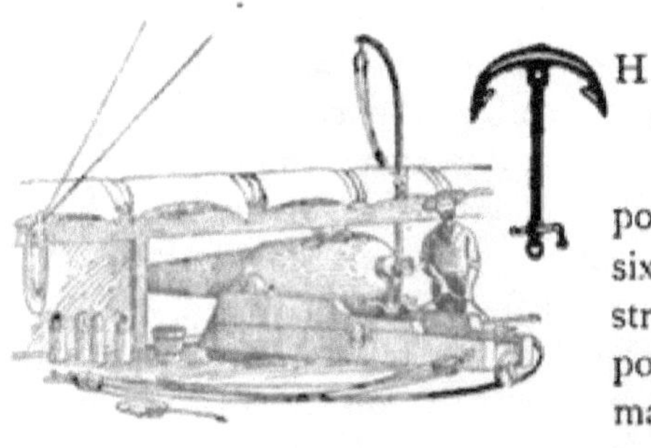

HE "Alliance" was a double-screw vessel of 700 tons, 680 horse-power. She was armed with six 40-pound B. L. Armstrong guns, with concealed port-holes. Her papers and manifests showed her to be a merchant steamer, with a cargo of various manufactures, consigned to parties in San Francisco. This fiction was further corroborated by an assortment of boxes of cutlery, etc., which were stowed on top of the actual cargo.

The speed of the vessel was from fifteen to seventeen knots. She was manned by a crew of adventurous English sailors, all of them picked men, drawing good pay, and whom Morley felt he could depend upon to fight the ship if the occasion should demand, — men who would ask no questions, but obey orders.

No one on board, except the officers, the two Peruvian passengers, and Sam, knew the real destination of the vessel.

"With plenty of sea-room," said Morley, "we can outrun any Chilian cruiser. The only trouble will be in dodging their blockade and getting into Callao."

Señor Garcias was anxious and moody during the whole trip. He was a genuine patriot, and he suffered deeply under the reverses which his country had sustained. Again and again, glad to find a sympathizer who could understand his Spanish, he described to Ned and myself the causes of the war, — the arrogant, unjust claims of Chili, and her savage persistence in continuing the war after she had possession of the miserable nitrate-fields which had been the bone of contention.

"With us, gentlemen," he said, "it is no longer a war over a piece of disputed territory. It has become a war of defence. We are striving to protect our homes and families from a cruel and insatiable invader. We would gladly make terms of peace, ceding more than was claimed at the outset, and paying a large war indemnity; but we will defend our homes and our honor against Chili, as we did against Spain, and as I trust we shall always do against every enemy."

Señor Varela, the Peruvian engineer, who spoke English quite readily, was equally patriotic, and their earnestness and intensity of feeling soon had a decided effect on us. We had gone into the enterprise purely as adventurers, with not much interest beyond the fact that the expedition served our own purposes. Before we reached the Straits of Magellan, the cause had become our own, and we felt identified with it, and ready to sacrifice almost anything to promote its success.

Our voyage to the straits was uneventful. On the 12th of November we put in at Punta Arenas for coal. Although this is a port belonging to Chili, Morley ran out his guns, and boldly venturing in, succeeded in obtaining the needed supplies. They appeared to be glad to get rid of us.

After passing the straits we kept well out to the westward, to avoid any possible cruisers. One vessel was seen at nine o'clock on the morning of November 18th, which evidently desired to overtake and interview us; but we preferred to keep our own counsel, and our legs proved too long for our pursuer. Though we saw her smoke on the horizon throughout that day, she had disappeared by the next morning.

On the afternoon of December 4th we arrived in the latitude of Callao, some fifty miles to the westward. Here we waited for night.

"And now," said Morley, "the fun begins."

He called all hands aft, and made a short address.

"Boys," said he, "we 're about fifty miles west of Callao, the port of Lima. The harbor is blockaded by a fleet of Chilian gunboats. We 're going to dodge in to Callao to-night. If the gunboats catch sight of us they 'll try to make it warm; but I know we can get through if you mean it. There 's ten pounds apiece for every man of you if we get into Callao before day-light to-morrow. Are you ready for the job?"

"Ay, ay, sir!" came the chorus in cheerful tones.

"All right," said Morley. "Let every man look sharp, and attend to his duty promptly. All lights will be extinguished, and no noise or loud talking permitted. Remember, we must try to avoid a fight, and trust to our speed and the darkness to get in. If the gunboats tackle us, we'll make a running fight and get away from them. All depends on you, and the way you obey orders. Now, go to your quarters. Every man will have his special work assigned to him, and an extra ration of grog."

With a rousing cheer the men retired.

Morley smiled as he turned to us.

"Those fellows would rather have a fight than not," said he.

At sunset the steamer was headed due east, and under easy steam made her way toward the coast.

Morley, Ned, the two Peruvians, and I sat together on deck and scanned the horizon with our glasses.

"The night promises well," said Morley. "There is no moon, and the clouds are enough to shut out the stars. It depends on luck more than anything. We may run alongside of an ironclad that could blow us out of the water."

The sea was like a mill-pond, — the surface unruffled; only the long swell rolled slowly under us. We were making about eight knots.

Gradually the shadows grew deeper, the horizon became dim and indistinct. Soon we were rushing forward into the heart of absolute darkness, our vessel as dark as the surrounding night.

Morley consulted his watch.

"We should be now twenty miles from the island of San Lorenzo," said he. "We shall soon see signs of these block-aders."

Full head of steam was put on, and we began to walk through the water at a tremendous pace. The guns had been shotted and run out, and the men were at their places, ready for action.

The night was dark and cloudy, and for another hour no sign of any vessel appeared. Then the lookout reported, "Light on the starboard bow!"

Away to the southeast a faint glimmer was seen, close down

on the water, alternately appearing and disappearing with the swell of the sea.

Presently another light gleamed out to the northeast, moving down so as to cross our course, then another one dead ahead, and momentarily growing brighter, as if a vessel were approaching us.

Our course was changed to the northeast, so as to pass in rear of the vessel that was moving south. At this time Morley and the Peruvian engineer calculated that we were ten miles east of San Lorenzo.

We steamed on our new course unmolested for over half an hour, working a little more toward the east as the lights that we had seen began to fade out to the south.

"Listen!" said Morley, suddenly. From across the water dead ahead of us came the regular beat of machinery.

"It 's a vessel coming straight at us," said Ned. "If we can hear them, they must be able to hear us."

The course of the "Alliance" was promptly altered to due north. At that instant a rocket shot into the air from a point to the east, apparently three or four miles distant. In a moment it was answered by another from the north and two from the south.

"They 're onto us!" said Ned. "It 's neck or nothing now!"

"Yes," said Morley; "we must make a break and squeeze in

between the jaws;" and he ordered the vessel's head several points east.

Suddenly a blue light lit up the horizon to the south, dimly showing a turreted ship about two miles distant.

"Santa Maria!" exclaimed Garcias; "it is the 'Huascar'!"

Morley blew a long whistle.

"One of her 300-pound shots would be a bad pill for us," said he; and again we headed north, crowding the steamer to her utmost speed.

In a few moments a bright red light flashed out directly ahead of us, succeeded swiftly by a green light, then again by the red.

"It's one of the new torpedo-boats, with her revolving signal," said Señor Varela.

"The devil!" exclaimed Morley. "Those boats are the fastest things afloat!"

As he spoke, another revolving light appeared to the west.

"And there's the other," said Ned. "By Jove! this is the most exciting game of hide-and-seek I ever played."

Again we headed due east. And now from over the water came the sound of the rapid pounding of machinery. It was the first torpedo-boat bearing swiftly down upon us, and from the south we heard the slower, heavier beat of another engine.

"That's the 'Huascar,'" said Morley below his breath.

Still we sped on straight toward the east.

The signal lights flashed once more from the north, — this time quite near, — and a moment later a blinding flash appeared from the same direction, revealing a vessel about a thousand yards away and headed diagonally across our course. Then the thick darkness fell again like a blanket, and simultaneously came the report, and a shell went screaming over our heads and exploded three or four hundred yards beyond us.

It was an exciting moment. Morley was the coolest man of the party. Only by a little knitting of his eyebrows and an unusual glitter in his eyes did he show the slightest trace of feeling. With his mouth at the speaking-tube and his hand on the bell, he delivered order after order as coolly as though no enemy were within a hundred miles.

In the next fifteen minutes our course was changed to the northwest, then to the northeast, so as if possible to pass in the rear of the torpedo-boat we had seen.

Signals appeared to the south, southeast, and southwest, and from several points we heard the sound of approaching vessels. The shot of the torpedo-boat had aroused the squadron, and they were all on the hunt for us.

We turned east again, then southeast, then south.

As the last order was given, Ned said, "You 'll run right into the thick of it, captain!"

"No," said Morley, quietly, "we shall pass most of them. We must get down to San Lorenzo and signal the batteries on shore. That shot has put them on the watch, and they will be expecting us."

A signal appeared to the right, and the quick thump of machinery indicated an approaching torpedo-boat.

"There 's the same fellow," said Morley. "Just discovered his mistake. If he gets too close we must give him a broadside."

Nearer and nearer came the sound. Straining my eyes, I fancied I could discern the form of the approaching vessel. Still, Morley kept steadily on his course. The seconds seemed to lengthen into hours.

Then suddenly through one tube went the order, "Hard a' port!" Then through the other tube, "Port guns, *ready!*"

Swiftly the vessel swung around through a half-circle from south to north.

Then came the order, "Port guns, *fire!*" followed instantly by three bells to the engineer, — "Full speed ahead!" A bright blaze lit up the water, showing the torpedo-vessel coming head on and not two hundred yards distant. Simultaneously came the reports of three of our 40-pounders, and the "Alliance" reeled under our feet. A crash told us that at least one of our shots had taken effect, but there was no telling how serious the damage was. The sudden darkness after the flash of the guns seemed deeper than before.

Instantly our vessel was again headed east. Too late, however. The enemy fired a single gun, and a solid shot flew right through our midst, striking Señor Garcias and carrying him overboard. Not a word was spoken. Morley only gave one quick glance at the group, then seized the tube and headed the vessel south.

In two minutes the lookout reported! "Land dead ahead!"

Straining our eyes, we made out a high, barren cliff rising like a mountain through the gloom, and about a quarter of a mile distant.

"It is the northern point of San Lorenzo," said Señor Varela.

Our course was altered so as to leave the land on our right, and Morley said : —

"Señor Varela, all now depends on you. The enemy will not venture into the channel, and you must work us through your torpedoes. Will you take my place and direct the vessel?"

So Varela took the tube and began to issue orders, while Ned and I displayed the preconcerted signals.

Presently an answering light appeared from the shore, and we began to work our way slowly through the channel. A report sounded from behind, and a shell from the torpedo-boat exploded in our rear. In a moment came a flash and a sullen boom from the shore, and a shot from one of the batteries went whistling above us.

Then the blockading squadron, disappointed at the loss of their prey, began to open fire upon the batteries. From all along the coast and the forts above, the guns of the Peruvians responded. Shot and shell flew screeching over our heads from all directions. But in less than an hour we had made our perilous passage and were moored safe inside the Darsena. Gradually the firing ceased. The squadron withdrew to their stations out of range of the heavy guns of the batteries, and our work was accomplished.

"The only thing I regret," said Morley, as we stepped ashore, "is the loss of poor Garcias."

We were met by quite a gathering of officers, who greeted Varela effusively, and congratulated Morley warmly on his successful run.

Then a large force of men was set at work unloading the steamer. The cargo was duly checked off, and transferred at once to a train of cars for transportation to Lima.

"We never needed supplies more than now," said one of the officers. "If you could have brought us five thousand trained soldiers, Señor Morley, we might retrieve our disasters. As it is, we can only make a desperate defence. The enemy are preparing for a final assault on the capital, and our army is practically destroyed."

By daylight the entire cargo had been unloaded, and Morley took a receipt duly signed and acknowledged.

As we looked out from the batteries over the harbor and the roadstead beyond, we could see the blockading squadron moving in to their daily quarters near San Lorenzo. We counted seven or eight vessels.

"There 's the 'Huascar,'" said Ned, "and there 's our friend the torpedo-boat. I wonder what damage our broadside did."

We went at once to Lima by rail, accompanied by Señor Varela. The distance is about eight miles, up a considerable grade, through rich cultivated fields and past smiling villas.

Arrived at the city, Morley, Ned, and Varela went to the palace, while Sam and I looked up a hotel. Everything was in confusion, — all places of business closed; no traffic in the streets; only groups of citizens — mechanics, students, business men — discussing the imminent danger that threatened their beloved city.

One division of the enemy had landed, and occupied the town of Yca; others were reported on the way, and all were concentrating for a march on Lima. To oppose them the Peruvians had only some two thousand veterans, the remains of their army, and a motley crowd of the citizens of Lima, untrained and badly armed. The whole force at their command did not exceed seventeen thousand men, and against this promiscuous mob the Chilians were bringing an army of over twenty-five thousand veterans, flushed with success and eager for conquest. The result could not be doubtful. All that the Peruvians could hope for now was to save their honor and die bravely in defence of their country.

It was a sad sight to look upon those groups of young men, — students, sons of wealthy parents, mechanics, and artists, so full of promise, and in whom rested all the hopes for the future of Peru, and to think that the greatest service they could now render their country was to form a frail rampart with their bodies, through which the cruel enemy must cut its way.

Ned and Morley soon returned with their business satisfactorily transacted, but they were both affected by the universal gloom.

"Tom," said Ned, with his usual impetuosity, "it 's hard for me to be a spectator here.   I have half a mind to take a Winchester and fall into line with these brave fellows."

Morley interfered. " I sympathize with your feelings, Ned, but you will kindly remember that at present you are in my employ, engaged for a certain enterprise, and until you return to England or are discharged by me, you are not at liberty to make any engagements."

" All right, Morley !" said Ned. "Your head is the oldest, but I know your heart is urging you to go in with these fellows yourself."

" Never mind !" said Morley.   "In the mean time, I have work for you both. It seems probable that Lima will be captured.   I do not choose to lose my vessel, nor do I wish to return without a cargo. There are large quantities of sugar, rice, and other products stored in and about Lima, which can be bought for cash at a considerable reduction from the usual market ; and I have the cash, — I brought it with me. The owners realize that their property will probably be destroyed or seized by the Chilians in a few weeks, and they will be glad to change it for gold even at a large sacrifice. I intend to secure a cargo and get away from here in time to avoid the final catastrophe. Ned, I shall want you to help me look up the stuff and negotiate for it ; and you, Tom, will take command of the ' Alliance,' and receive the goods and see them properly loaded. You can take Sam with you."

So we spent that evening in writing letters, and the next day Sam and I went down to Callao and took charge of the " Alliance."

Our cargo came in somewhat slowly, and we had an opportunity to see much of the excitement of the blockade.

On one day, about the 5th or 6th of December, a small Peruvian steamer, the " Arno," was cruising along just outside of the harbor, when two torpedo-boats made a rush at her. She showed fight with her 40-pound Armstrongs, and her assailants scurried off. The batteries on shore took a hand, and presently the whole blockading squadron moved up and opened fire at the forts from about three miles distance.

One of the Chilian torpedo-boats, the " Fresia," the very one which had given us such a chase, was struck by a shell from the batteries and sunk.

" Blast her eyes ! That 's good ! It serves her right, sir ! " re-marked Sam, as we looked at the fight. But the Chilians afterward raised the " Fresia " and put her on her legs again ; and her legs were longer than those of any vessel on the coast.

Another redoubtable craft was the " Angamos." She had but one gun, an 8-inch Armstrong throwing a 180-pound shot, but she could send a ball effectively from over five miles distance.

One afternoon she amused herself by pelting at the "Union," the only war vessel the Peruvians had left, and after ten or twelve trials succeeded in sending a ball clean through her upper deck, while there was not a gun in the shore batteries that could reach within a mile of the " Angamos's " position.

Morley and Ned came down every day or two to see how we were getting on, and to bring us the news.

Since it was known that the advance of the Chilian army would be from the south, the Peruvians had hastily thrown up two lines of fortifications. The first or outer line extended from Chorillos, a seaport about ten miles from Lima, back into the country some six miles. Just to the south of Chorillos a rocky promontory called the Morro Solar rises some five or six hundred feet. The southern base of this hill was occupied by the Peruvians' right wing, about five thousand strong, under command of Iglesias.

About three miles to the east, at the hill of San Juan, was the centre, held by Caceres, with three or four thousand men, while the extreme left was commanded by Davila, with four thousand men.

The fortifications were merely sand-heaps, thrown up hur-riedly, and behind them the untrained citizens of Lima, ignorant but brave, grimly held their guns and waited the attack, deter-mined to drive back the invader or to die at their post.

Some few of the old 500-pound Rodman guns, brought up from the batteries at Callao, and quite a number of poorly made, short-range field-pieces, constituted the only available artillery.

Some distance in the rear General Suarez was posted, with a reserve force of three thousand men.

The second line of defence extended about four miles inward from Miraflores, a summer resort on the coast, six miles south of Lima.

"The Chilian army is well officered and well equipped," said Morley. "Lynch, who has been ravaging the coast in true buccaneering style, has command of their left, with eight thousand men. The centre and right will number at least eighteen thousand more. They have the best arms, and long-range field-guns. They will carry one position after the other without trouble, and will be in Lima within a week after they make the first assault."

"And when will they begin?" asked I.

"Quien sabe?" said Morley. "They are encamped some ten miles south of Chorillos, across the desert, getting everything in readiness, and apparently reconnoitring our lines. The Lima students and citizens will make it warm while they and their ammunition last."

"And when shall we have a cargo?"

"At present appearances, about the 5th of January."

We were loaded and ready to sail January 7th, but Morley said, "Wait! When the attack fairly begins, the blockading fleet will be diverted and we shall have a better chance. In the mean time we may as well go down and see the fun."

So we secured horses and rode to Chorillos. Pierola, the supreme chief, had his headquarters here, and was busy every day, riding along the lines, encouraging every one, and apparently confident of repulsing the enemy.

On the morning of January 13th, at daybreak, we were awakened by the sound of firing. We rose at once, mounted our horses, and rode along the highway leading over the eastern spur of the Morro, to a position from which we could get a view of the combat.

The firing had increased to a roll of musketry as rapid as a drum-beat, and the boom of field-pieces and siege guns was more and more frequent.

Below us floated a dense cloud of smoke, through which flashed constantly the blaze of cannon and small arms. Occasionally, as the pall lifted, we could see the solid ranks of the enemy charging up the slope, only to be met by the unflinching front and withering fire of the brave Peruvians.

It was a decided novelty to all of us. Ned was hoarse with yelling; and when we saw a line of the enemy broken and scattered, flying headlong down the hill, I chimed in with him and used up my lungs. Even Morley seemed to forget his usual coolness.

"God!" he exclaimed. "If we only had our six Armstrongs right here we could pepper those ruffians well!"

But in spite of the brave resistance, the odds were too great. In vain the defenders, urged to their utmost by the kindling words of Iglesias, and of Pierola, the brother of the chief, again and again drove back the enemy. Fresh forces advanced to the attack. The Peruvians were falling by hundreds. Chilian gunboats stationed opposite the Morro threw shot and shell into their midst. Field batteries played upon them from in front. Step by step, fighting every inch of ground, they began to fall back around the base of the Morro.

"The game is up!" said Morley. "Holloa! Yes, I should say so! Look there!"

From the east, a body of Chilian troops was moving up rapidly to attack the Peruvians in flank.

"They have driven in the centre," continued Morley, "and are swinging round to catch these poor fellows between the devil and the deep sea. This is no place for us, boys."

We turned our horses and galloped back to Chorillos. The town was filled with fugitives, women and children hurrying from their homes, weeping and distracted, turning their steps toward Lima. The centre and the left had been carried, and the enemy was reported in full march upon the capital.

In the mean time the right wing, the gallant defenders of the Morro, hemmed in on all sides, were driven out to the extremity of a narrow point projecting into the sea. Here they were raked by the fire of the gunboats, and slaughtered by the long-range field-guns in front, until Iglesias, seeing the hopelessness of further resistance, surrendered his command, fifteen hundred men remaining of the five thousand who had begun the defence four hours before.

"Unless we move quickly, boys," said Morley, "we shall never see the 'Alliance.' These Chilians are no respecters of persons."

We set off at a gallop for Lima, arriving in time to see the remains of the population — old men and boys — flocking out to man the last line of defences and die in the last ditch.

In Lima we learned that the foreign representatives were attempting to arbitrate and adjust a settlement between the combatants. In the mean time the remnant of the Peruvian army, reinforced by about two thousand nearly useless citizens, had taken up their stand at Miraflores and eastward along the second and last line of defence.

The next morning an armistice was agreed to, and representatives of the Peruvian and Chilian commands met the foreign ministers to discuss the terms of peace. But on the afternoon of the 15th, even while the conference was in session, the Chilians broke the armistice, and began an advance upon the Peruvian lines. The Peruvians opened fire upon them, and the battle of Miraflores, the last battle of the war, began.

Morley should have been the commander of an army. I believe he had better information of the enemy's movements, and better judgment as to the result, than any general in the Peruvian forces. The moment we heard the firing on the afternoon of the 15th he said, —

"Boys! we sail to-night. This is our chance."

We hurried down to Callao, went on board the "Alliance," and got up steam at once. All the heavy vessels of the blockading squadron were down at Miraflores, throwing their shot and shell into the Peruvian lines. Only some three or four gunboats, including our old friend the "Fresia," kept up the semblance of a blockade.

When it was fairly dark, we slipped out from behind the "Darsena," ran stealthily along the coast for fifteen miles north, and then steamed straight out into the Pacific. At daybreak, we were out of sight of land and vessel.

Of the result of the battle of Miraflores and the occupation of Lima we learned only upon our arrival at London.

Our voyage was a rapid one, and we encountered no mishaps or adventures, arriving safely on the 25th of February.

We were several days in London, where Morley disposed of his cargo to good advantage, and Ned found a letter from Maggie, announcing that she would be in Paris with Dr. French on the 5th of March.

When all the business of the expedition was duly settled, Morley turned over to us three hundred pounds as balance in full for our services, and insisted upon our going down to Elmhurst for a few days before continuing our course.

As we rode comfortably down to Kent, we felt very well satisfied with our achievements thus far.

" We 're safe, Tom, my boy," said Ned. " We 've had a long four years' fight ; but thanks to Morley, here, we 've reached the end of it."

" Yes," I replied ; " with fifteen hundred dollars we can make the run around Europe and be in New York in four months."

" There 's only one thing more I 'd like to do," said Ned.

" And that is ? "

" To have money and time enough to track that Miguel crowd, recover our gold, and bring the scoundrels up with a round turn."

" Very well ! " said I. " When we get back to New York, we can start out again with that special end in view."

" Not much ! " was the answer. " When I get back to New York, I am a staid and respectable member of society. No more wanderings ! "

" Except a trip to California by the most direct route ; and then — exit, Ned ! The world knows him no more ! "

" I 'm sorry for you, Tom ! I really thought you would find your fate. But you are too cold-blooded. You will be a lonely bachelor all your life. Well, come out to our ranch and make your home with us."

" Yes ; and see the friend of my bosom daily estranged by woman's wiles. I know all about it. Thanks, kindly ! "

What a greeting we had at Elmhurst ! Morley's brother and sister were at the station to meet us ; and a beautiful little girl, with bright, dancing blue eyes, and heavy golden hair that no art could confine, sprang into my arms and nearly smothered me with kisses. Our little Lalage was as glad to see us as we to see her.

After a week's rest and enjoyment, we set out for Paris, taking Lalage with us. Both Maggie and Dr. French had written, urging us to bring the little girl, and begging permission to adopt her until we all returned to America, and could begin the search for her family.

The child had not yet quite recovered from the roving propensities which her years of gypsy education had inculcated, and although she had been very happy at Elmhurst, she was delighted at the thought of new travels.

" Only," she said, " I wish we could walk and sing together as we used to do.   It 's so much nicer than being respectable."

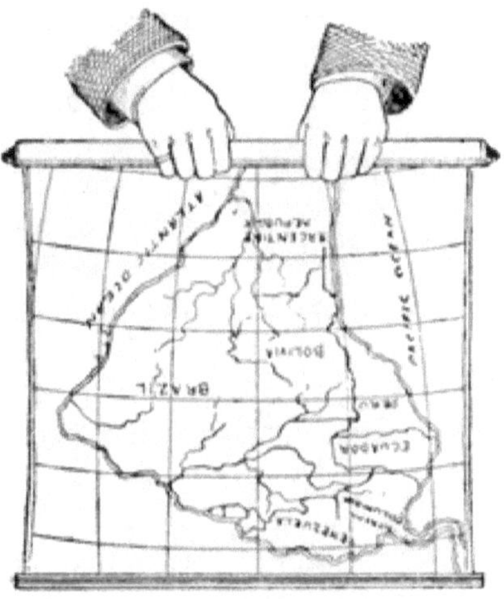

CHAPTER XX.

THAT was a great day for the lovers, when they met in Paris, March 6, 1881, after more than three years' separation; and I could n't find it in my heart to blame Ned, as I gazed again upon the object of his devotion. She was more beautiful than ever; and when in the enthusiasm of her welcome she gave me one of those kisses that Ned seemed to enjoy so highly, I confess I felt more than ever her friend, and that little unexplained affair which had worried me in California lost all its importance in my mind.

Dr. French was equally cordial, and greeted us as warmly though in not quite so demonstrative a manner as his daughter. And Lalage was received with a kindness and tenderness which made us happy in the assurance that however our search for her family might result, she would never be in want of a happy home.

Then of course we all sat down and talked steadily for the rest of the day; and Maggie had to tell us all about her journey from California, — just as if we cared to hear about any more journeys; and the doctor had to have a full and detailed account of Ned's illness; and the Turcoman knife and the scar

of its wound on Ned's arm came in for a large share of attention; and the mummy's hand sustained its reputation; and
finally, when we went to bed at midnight, I believe we felt as
tired as on any day for four years.

For a week we "did" Paris together; and then the doctor,
claiming that he had some business in the south of France, insisted on taking Maggie and Lalage with him, leaving Ned and
me to our own devices for a time.

"We shall be back in a week," he said, "and then we will lay
out a tour together, and visit some few of your remaining cities
in a jolly party."

So Ned and I took a lodging, and loafed and smoked, and
laid plans for our last victorious campaign.

It was a few days after the doctor and party had left us that
we made the acquaintance of Seldom.

In search of amusement or adventure, we one evening strolled
into a café in the Latin Quarter. A convivial party of seven or
eight young men was seated around a table listening to the full-
voiced declamation of one of their number, who had risen to the
occasion, and with glass in one hand and cigar in the other, was
throwing his whole soul and body into his words.

He was a striking figure. An enormous head, covered with a
shock of tangled black hair; a strong, rugged face, black with
luxuriant and unkempt whiskers; dark, piercing eyes, deep set
under shaggy eyebrows; broad shoulders, deep chest, short and
compact figure, and a voice like the roar of a bull of Bashan, —
such was our friend Seldom, as we first saw him.

We discovered that Seldom was an American, a twenty-year
resident of Paris, an artist philosopher, — poor, of course, —
a genuine Bohemian, with some ability, but no power of con-
centration, and at once the amusement and the admiration of
the little circle of gay and careless artist students who surrounded him.

After a short acquaintance we grew to like him. His philosophy, as he called his crude and exuberant vaporings, sometimes became a bore, and he was inordinately conceited, but
withal in so good-natured a way that one could not feel greatly
annoyed by his self-glorification. It was so extravagant as to be
amusing; and he accepted snubs and ridicule with a smiling
serenity that disarmed them.

He took us to his room one evening, — a bare, bleak apartment in the top of a rickety old building in the Latin Quarter. It was a veritable type, — an old straw mattress with a blanket in one corner; four cheap chairs, not one of them in sound condition ; a plain deal table, piled a foot high with a miscellaneous assortment of old papers, books, broken penholders, pencils, loose paints and brushes, cigar and cigarette stubs, pipes

and scattered tobacco, dust and ashes. bottles and broken glasses. Paintings and sketches of all sorts and sizes, in various stages of completion, covered the walls and some half-dozen uneasy easels.

"Here is my domain, gentlemen," said he. "Here is the environment of genius. Here are continually evolving ideas and principles which destiny is slowly weaving into the great warp of the future. The generations to come will forever consecrate this dingy apartment as the birthplace of a new era in the world's progress, the spot which marks the conception of the true, all-absorbing, all-acomplishing philosophy, — the key to all wisdom, the solver of all problems, the ameliator of humanity, the panacea for all ills!"

"Cures colds, catarrh, rheumatism, nervous diseases; restores the hair, lights the fire, blacks the stove, pays the butcher's bill, and tends the baby, — all for fifteen cents," was Ned's comment.

"Yes," replied Seldom, unflinchingly, "and far more! You speak in jest, but you know not the truth of what you say. When this grand philosophy is fully evolved, when all its outlines, now dim and shadowy, are brought into clear and bold relief, when that towering and awful conception is fully revealed to me in all the transcendent majesty of its being, then the human race can lay down every burden, then the path will be smooth and easy before it, — the path which will lead swift and straight to that absolute perfection, that supreme happiness, which is the ultimate aim and destiny of humanity."

"Whew!" whistled Ned. "Draw it easy, old man. Have you named this promising infant, this shadowy immensity, this triple-refined extract of the essence of totality, this what not?"

Rash question! This was Seldom's opportunity, and he seized it. A glow of inspiration lit up his face, his chest expanded, he rose to his feet, and stretched forth his arm as if to still a vast audience. Ned and I subsided, and resigned ourselves with a sigh, and the orator began: —

"Deep hidden under myriad effects humanity gropes darkly for the cause, — the one eternal, ever-present what, the third essential of the great Triune. Matter and force we know, and vainly strive to make a unit of two thirds alone; but the eternal Truth, the perfect Whole, still veils her face and waits the talisman, the magic thought, the missing link of mind, the one ingredient beneath whose touch the cold and lifeless facts of human lore will flash into a brilliant beacon-light which shall irradiate the universe, and cause even Truth herself to stand revealed.

"A great gulf lies before us. With slow toil and strenuous endeavor Science strives to throw her bridge out from the hither shore.   Block after block is tried and cast away, till one is found which seems to fit the place and stand secure. So, slowly, step by step, the work progresses, till the builder finds, by his own laws, his limit is attained.   Then Science calmly folds her hands, and calls the gulf that lies beyond ' Unknowable.'   Religion, fluttering on her waxen wings, the ' wings of faith ' she fondly dares to say, drops deep and deeper into the abyss, and growing blinder in the nether gloom, im- agines darkness light, and is content."

At this point Ned broke in, —

" Look here, Seldom, if you 're going to talk blank-verse, let us get our flutes and play an accompaniment."

" Ned," said I, " you 're near the table ; scoop up some of that loose tobacco in your fist and pass it over here.   Observe, Seldom, the pipe, the tobacco, and now the third ingredient, the match.   See the beacon-light flash out, and observe the grand result — smoke."

Seldom descended from his pedestal at once.

" Oh, well ! " said he, " I see you are still crude, — material only.   Intensity of thought and brilliancy of expression are be- yond your range.   We will have some wine.   That will touch you more nearly."

" Excellent ! " said Ned.   " You know, Seldom, I admired that discourse immensely, but it made me a little dry."

" But tell us, Seldom," said I, " what have you got in your head?   What does all that beastly rubbish mean?   Now, don't go off into a rhapsody again, but try and put your ideas, if you have any, into common-sense English."

It was hard work for poor Seldom, but he tried it.

" The great idea, the magnificent secret which I have dis- covered," said he, " and which I am striving to elaborate and follow out into all its details, is this : The principle, the cause, the mystery, which lies back of all the universe, and through which all Nature (and by Nature I mean not only the physical, apparent world, but also the mind, the soul, the life of humanity in all its aspects) works out its evolution and progress, is the Triune, the Trinity, the three factors combining to form a per- fect unit, varying as the factors vary, but ever preserving the principle of triple combination as the essential of an efficient cause, without which combination no effects would result, nothing could exist; matter and force, mind and body, soul and substance, would be annihilated.

" The number *three* is the sacred and mysterious number. It appears everywhere. In the material world we have the three great classes of phenomena, — animal, vegetable, mineral. In the functions of mind we have intellect, feeling, will. Corresponding to these, and as products of their action, we have philosophy (embracing science), art, conduct; or, as Emerson puts it, ' culture, beauty, behavior.'

" Every unit of organic life involves the necessity of the three sets of functions, — nutrition, reproduction, correlation; and throughout the details of the evolution of forms in the natural world we find always the principle of triple arrangement, triple combination, prevailing."

" Why do we happen to have five senses instead of three? " inquired I, feebly.

" Philosophy," replied Seldom severely, " does not talk with idle, popular words, or depend upon the classifications of children. Your five senses are but one, — the sense of touch. All physical sense is but the perception of the impact of the external upon the variously constituted nerves of sense, — simply varieties of the sense of touch."

" Squelched, Tom ! " said Ned. " Seldom, why don't you get married? How you could silence a curtain lecture with a shaft of your philosophy ! "

" I cannot marry." replied Seldom. " I love three girls; I have named them Intellect, Feeling, and Will " (the last with a sigh).

" I 'll venture the unphilosophical remark that these three do not harmonize and combine to form a unit," said I.

" Yes," replied Seldom, " they are one — in their devotion to me."

" Well, Philosopher." said Ned, " your system appears to me to contain one grain of sense and three bushels of nonsense."

" Sense ! Nonsense ! " was the quick retort. " Yes, you are right. What is *sense?* That which the common herd of mankind accepts as truth. And *Nonsense! The Not Sense* — that which has not yet received a *majority* vote — is not yet duly and properly elected. And from the working of the *Not Sense* upon the *Sense* is evolved the truth as accepted by the future, and so the race progresses."

"That's the time you got it, Ned," said I.

"We'll have another bottle!" remarked Seldom.

"No more!" said Ned. "Wine and philosophy require a third factor to make the perfect unit."

"But we have had but two bottles, and the mystic three must be maintained."

After this evening, in Seldom's den, we were with our new friend almost continuously. He was a true Parisian, and there was little in the great city to which he did not introduce us. His attachment to us, I think, was largely due to our being willing to act as an audience, to a certain extent. When his philosophy became too harassingly pertinacious, we could always shut it off abruptly, and with no danger of injuring the works. The elasticity of his temper was only equalled by that of his philosophy.

One evening, shortly after the visit just described, we were all three strolling along the Boulevard Haussmann, when some one proposed refreshments. We entered a café and ascended to one of the private rooms in the second story.

As we stepped into the room a voice from the adjoining apartment caught my ear. Instinctively I turned to the others with a warning gesture, and in a whisper directed the waiter to bring us some wine, slipping a coin into his hand and advising him that we wished for no noise, as the next room was occupied by parties whom we were trying to avoid. The waiter, undoubtedly accustomed to such instructions, smiled and bowed, and noiselessly disappeared. We quietly took our seats.

Ned leaned toward me and whispered, "What is it?"

"José Miguel!" replied I, in the same tone.

To Seldom I whispered, "You are a philosopher, and above all a man of Paris. Keep your mouth shut and your ears open, and hereafter tell us what the third factor is combining with those two actions to produce the result I am looking for."

There were apparently two men in the adjoining room, and every word of their conversation could be distinctly heard. They were talking in Spanish.

Without being absolutely positive, I felt a strong conviction that the voice of one of them was that of our old enemy, José Miguel.

This is about what we heard : —

Unknown voice. "And so you think yourself safe, Señor?"

Miguel. "Entirely so! my investments have been carefully made; the profits have been all drawn out, and are in my possession in the shape of cash. There is no one in the company or out of it who knows my whereabouts. The company has gone to pieces, and I alone gather the spoil."

At this point Seldom leaned toward me and whispered, "If we were in Canada I could understand the drift of this."

The conversation continued : —

Unknown. "How much spoil have you gathered, captain?"

Miguel. "I have in cash always at my hand three hundred thousand francs, — about sixty thousand dollars, as you and I used to reckon. And besides that amount I have safely invested under my Parisian name five hundred thousand francs additional. So you can realize, Amos, that the proposition I have made you is safe for you to accept, so far as my resources are concerned."

Unknown. "I have no hesitation on that score, Señor; the only thing I think of is the rest of the company with which we were formerly associated."

Miguel. "Have no fears on that point. The body is powerless without the head, — and you remember that I was the head. I have been in Paris six months, and have been undisturbed, nor have I seen or heard of any of my former subordinates except yourself."

Unknown. "And are you willing to tell me what *dangerous* investments have been engaged in since I last saw you, three years ago, so that I may know what to guard against?"

Miguel. "There is only one possible chance of danger, and that is so slight as to be not worth considering. Two Americans caused us a slight annoyance a few years since by accidentally learning of some of our investments and our methods of transacting business. Twice we nearly silenced them, but each time they managed to escape. That danger has long passed, and when last heard from they had gone to Peru. They doubtless lost their lives in the attack on Lima."

Ned gripped my arm so tightly that I could scarcely refrain from an exclamation.

Seldom was looking from Ned to me with an expression of

utter bewilderment, but listening with the alertness of the Parisian who scents an intrigue or a mystery.

Unknown. " I think I may accept your offer, chief, if you will make the advance payment two thousand francs instead of a thousand."

Miguel. " I will do so. Come with me to my apartments, and we will close the bargain at once."

There was a sound of the moving of chairs, and our neighbors were evidently preparing to leave. We all rose to our feet.

" We must keep them in sight," whispered I.

Silently opening the door so as to look through the crack, I waited. In a moment, two men emerged from the adjoining room and went toward the stairway. In spite of his shaven face, in spite of his different clothing, I knew that one of those men was José Miguel, — the man who had held a revolver to my head in Australia, who had been my judge and examiner and nearly my executioner in Calcutta, the man of all men with whom I longed to " get even."

We three quietly followed the two down the stairs, out upon the boulevard, and saw them get into a cab.

I called another cab.

" The old trick," said I to my companions ; then to the driver, " Keep that cab in sight, and double your fare ! "

We crowded into the conveyance, and were whirled rapidly over the pavement. In the mean time I told Seldom of our acquaintance with Miguel, dating from the time of the encounter in Mexico. He listened without a comment until the story was told.

Then he rubbed his hands together.

" This is immense ! " said he. " A delightful diversion ! Until we catch this Miguel, humanity will suffer, and you two individuals will be the gainers. I shall give my mind to this matter exclusively."

I expressed the highest appreciation of this sacrifice of the many to the few ; and indeed, since we began to hear the conversation in the café, I had been making up my mind that Seldom would be an invaluable aid to us, and that he must be taken into our confidence to the fullest extent. Underneath all his philosophical and rhetorical bombast, I fancied could be detected the sharp, shrewd *Parisien ;* and in the vague schemes which flitted through my mind, such a man would be a necessity.

Suddenly the cab made a sharp turn and abruptly stopped. I opened the door and looked out. We were in a narrow street just around the corner from the boulevard.

"Cab has just stopped at the end of next block on boulevard," said the driver. "I turned in here to avoid being seen."

Then Seldom justified my estimate of him. He quickly stepped out and said to the driver, in French, "Wait here until I return;" then to us, in English, "Stay inside. I know this business. Leave it to me, and I will report in a few moments."

Then he disappeared around the corner. Ned and I sat in the cab and waited.

"I beg you to recollect, Tom," said Ned, "that you crossed swords with this gang once before now. Do you recall the circumstances?"

To which I replied, "Ned, I think you have some cigarettes in your pocket. Will you hand me one?"

In about twenty minutes, Seldom returned. He directed the cabman to drive to his room in the Latin Quarter, and then got in with us.

"I have located the enemy," said he, "which is all we could do to-night. Your friend Miguel occupies apartments in the building No. —— Boulevard Haussmann. I observed the cab until the small man came out of the building, got in, and drove away. Miguel remained. It is an apartment building of the first class. We will go to my room and lay out a plan of the campaign."

Of the matters which were discussed that night until the first rays of dawn found us still smoking our pipes and plotting, I will say nothing now. The sequel will show what our scheme was, and how it succeeded. Seldom was at once the organizer, manager, and head of the enterprise. His philosophy was laid on the shelf, and he became the cool, clear-headed, practical and far-seeing man of the world that I had hoped to find him.

"Seldom," said I, "you should have been with us for the past four years. We would have done better."

"What!" said he. "Out of Paris? No! I should be a helpless infant crying for its mother; a useless encumbrance."

Our plan did not aim at the arrest of Miguel and his trial

before the courts. We had no time or inclination for that sort of revenge, besides that we were doubtful of our ability to convict him. We meant to use our knowledge of his crimes and his own admission of his present position and resources, which we had overheard, to compel him by intimidation, and force if necessary, to restore the money of which he had despoiled us.

It was arranged that Seldom should go alone to the apartment building which Miguel occupied, interview the concierge, and by bribes or other means learn everything that could be ascertained in regard to the lodger. We were to meet him at noon, and discuss our further arrangements in the light of his report.

Though very tired, Ned and I slept but little that forenoon, and at tewlve o'clock we repaired once more to the scene of our consultations, to find Seldom waiting for us.

"Gentlemen," said he, "in laying aside my studies I have also temporarily laid aside the name which will one day be famous. To the concierge of No. —— Boulevard Haussmann I am known as Monsieur Frequent, a wealthy American gentleman, who with two friends desires to find a comfortable suite of apartments for a short residence in Paris. The concierge has exactly the suite which will please Monsieur. It is on the second floor, elegantly furnished, and at a very moderate rent. 'Who are the other tenants in the building?' They are all of the highest order of respectability, — a French gentleman nearly related to the Marquis of What-do-you-call-it; a wealthy English family with a very attractive daughter; a retired Spanish banker extremely wealthy and of most polished and agreeable manners, etc. Will Monsieur examine the apartments? Yes, they are undoubtedly the finest rooms in Paris for the price. The suite opposite is occupied by Señor Don Enrique, the Spanish banker. No! Monsieur need fear no disturbance or annoyance of any kind. This is the quietest and best regulated house in Paris. Don Enrique is the only tenant at present on this floor, and he is invariably absent the greater part of the day. He has few friends in Paris. He has occupied the apartments for two months. A few gentlemen call upon him, and now and then a lady.

"Monsieur is much pleased with the rooms, and having obtained the information he desired, departs to consult with his two friends in regard to securing the apartments."

"And the two American gentlemen," said I, "being much pleased with the report of their friend Monsieur Frequent, instruct him to take the apartments at once — for a month — on trial."

"All right!" said Ned. "I agree to that, and we will move in to-night, after dark."

"Good!" said Seldom. "We should lose no time."

At ten o'clock that evening we were in possession of quarters directly opposite the rooms of our old enemy. Ned's name, printed in large letters on the end of a trunk packed with rubbish from Seldom's philosophical warehouse, was "J. G. Smith, Philadelphia, U. S. A." A similar trunk bore my name, — "P. D. Q. Osborne, New York."

The enemy's outposts were in our possession without a blow, and we were preparing for an attack on his stronghold.

The next morning we remained in our rooms until Seldom had made a reconnoissance and reported that Miguel had gone out. Then we sallied out also, leaving Seldom in command of the position.

We went to the hotel, and found the doctor, Maggie, and Lalage returned from their trip.

"And as you are probably tired of Paris by this time," said the doctor, "what say you to taking the train to-morrow for an Italian tour? And perhaps we may all go as far as Athens together."

It was rather a hard position for us to escape from, but to my surprise Maggie came to our rescue.

"You are a miserable travelling companion, papa," said she, "for a week you have kept us on the move, and we no sooner reach Paris again than you wish to start. I like Paris, and I have n't seen half enough of it. A week from now we 'll talk about travelling."

"And I should like to know, Mademoiselle," replied her father, "who it was that was on the rush until we reached Paris first? I would have been glad to stay two days in Chicago and a week in New York; but you made me secure staterooms by telegraph from San Francisco on the first steamer we could catch."

I saw Ned looking at Maggie with a curious expression that almost seemed like suspicion. I wondered what he was thinking of, but he did n't tell me. However, it was finally agreed that we should stay in Paris for at least three or four days more, and after an hour or two Ned and I returned to the Boulevard Haussmann. Seldom met us at the corner as agreed, and reported the coast clear; so we went to our rooms.

Ned was gloomy and silent. The next morning, as we left the house, he said, —

"We won't go to the hotel this morning, Tom. If we mean to do anything in this business, let 's make or break it at once; I want to get it over with. To-day is as good as any day will be."

"All right, my boy," said I. Then I added, "Cheer up, Ned, and don't be suspicious; it 's all right." But he gave me no answer.

We spent the forenoon in roaming around the city, and returned at two P. M.

"He went out about two hours ago," said Seldom, "and left word with the concierge that he would return at half-past two. I have been here on the boulevard for the past hour."

"We are just in time," replied I. "This afternoon is the time, Seldom."

"None better," said he.

We went to our room, and leaving the door partly open, waited behind it in silence. Every man knew his part of the programme.

In fifteen minutes, steps were heard ascending the stairs. Seldom, who had the handle of our door in his fingers, slowly closed it except the tiniest crack. We listened in breathless silence. The footsteps paused. We heard a key inserted in the lock of the door opposite to us; then the door swung on its hinges.

Instantly Seldom opened our door, and stepped quickly across the hall and into the doorway opposite, so that the door could not be closed. Miguel turned and faced him.

"Excuse me!" said Seldom blandly in French. "Is this Señor Don Enrique?"

"That is my name, sir," replied Miguel, stepping into the room.

"A thousand pardons for intruding," continued Seldom, coolly. "We have tried many times to find you in, but without success heretofore.   Would you kindly allow us five minutes of your time on a matter of business interest to yourself?"

At this instant Ned and I walked into the room, and Seldom stepped quickly to a front window looking on the boulevard, which he instantly raised.   I closed the door, and stood in front of it.   Ned stepped to the table in the centre of the room, quite near where Miguel was standing.

For perhaps five seconds there was silence.   I felt that Miguel was eying me.   I glanced rapidly around the room; it was a large apartment, handsomely furnished.   Three windows opened upon the boulevard.   Near the raised window stood Seldom, with a whistle conspicuously held in his hand.   A doorway and portière at the left seemed to give access to some adjoining room.

Then Miguel spoke very quietly in French to Seldom, —

"Monsieur, will you have the kindness to close the window? May I ask to what business I owe the honor of this extraordinary visit?"

With equal quietness Seldom replied in English, —

"Señor, the answer to your question involves the greatest principle of philosophy.   We are *three*, and you are *one*.   I beg you to bear this in mind from the outset.   For the window, I opened it for a purpose, and this whistle which I hold in my hand also conduces to the same purpose.   In the street below, concealed behind the adjoining building, are located three policemen. Should I blow upon this whistle, they will at once mount the stairs, enter this apartment, and arrest you.   Should you attempt to escape, they will meet you on the stairs.   Your only hope of safety is in retaining your admirable composure, and listening quietly to what we have the honor to propose to you.   I might further add that every man of us is fully armed, and accustomed to use his weapons on very slight provocation."

To this harangue Miguel listened with scarcely a change of feature.   I noticed, however, that he looked at me more and more intently, whether because he recognized me or because I stood before the door, I could not decide.

At the conclusion of Seldom's remarks Miguel quietly drew up an arm-chair and seated himself.   With a motion of his arm, he said in English, —

" Kindly be seated, gentlemen."

Ned took a chair; Seldom and I kept our positions. Ned said, —

" You do not seem to recognize me, Señor Don José Miguel, and yet that scar on your cheek was made by a bullet from my revolver."

For an instant Miguel lost his coolness. He instinctively put his hand to his face, and muttered a Spanish oath. Recovering himself, he said, " I seemed to recognize your companion," indicating me, "and now fully recall the company who have honored me to-day. If I remember correctly, sir," — to me, — " I twice made serious mistakes in my hospitality to you."

" Apologies are unnecessary, Señor Miguel," said I. " I have duly appreciated the consideration you showed me both in Australia and in Calcutta."

" But the third gentleman," said Miguel, " who I fear will take cold at that open window, is a stranger to me."

" Allow me to introduce myself, Señor Miguel," said Seldom. " My name is Peter J. Frequent. I am a private detective, of New York. Two years ago I was employed by these gentlemen to look you up, owing to some slight irregularities in your business relations with them. I have been quite earnestly engaged in prosecuting my researches; and although much time has been consumed, it has not been wasted, as I have accumulated incontrovertible evidence of enough of those eccentricities called *crimes* in your past history, to hang about seven men. This evidence is not as yet offered to the authorities, as my employers preferred to use it in their own way; however, should you decline to accept the proposition which they will make you, I am instructed to cause your immediate arrest, and let the law take its course. Our witnesses will be forthcoming when required; they are all of good standing and undoubted veracity, and even your own large resources will not approach the wealth which will be brought to bear to secure your conviction."

For a few moments there was silence; Miguel appeared to be reflecting.

" And suppose," said he, " that I should bring evidence which would entirely refute all that you could produce. Suppose I should show that every crime with which I might be charged was committed by others, without even my knowledge ; that — "

Ned had been growing restless ; his temper was rising. At this point he could control himself no longer. He broke in, in a loud voice : —

"Such suppositions are useless and absurd, Señor Miguel. We *know* of your crimes ; we have seen and experienced them. Can any of your suppositions make us doubt that we saw you and your miserable accomplices murder an inoffensive traveller in Mexico, and steal the savings of years of his life? Can you make us doubt that you entered our tent in Australia, and plundered us of all we had, and left Tom in the bush, intending him to die a miserable death?

" Did not Tom see you order a poor wretch to be strangled in that hut in Calcutta? Does he, or any of us, doubt that you intended the same fate for him? Can you bring *evidence* to persuade us that one of your gang did not, at your orders, attempt to murder us in Egypt? Have we not had the best of evidence for years that you were the head of an association of professional murderers, highwaymen, and criminals of the worst type?

" Do we not all know that you are even now engaged in a dastardly crime, and that less than a week ago you paid the advance money to the scoundrel who does the dirty work for you? Do you pretend to tell us — "

Ned suddenly stopped in his fierce denunciation and sat like a statue, his lips parted, his look fixed straight before him, while the blood vanished from his cheeks, leaving his face like marble.

I looked quickly in the direction he was gazing. In the doorway of the adjoining room stood Maggie French. Her dark eyes glowed with excitement, and her face was as white as Ned's.

With a voice that was a groan, Ned slowly said, " Maggie — you *here!* My God!" then bowed his head and looked straight at the floor.

She quietly entered the room and stood directly in front of Ned.

" Ned," said she, "look me in the face and tell me if what I have just heard you say of this man is the *truth.*"

"In the doorway of the adjoining room stood Maggie French." — *Page* 342.

Ned instantly stood up and looked straight into her eyes.

"Every word of it is true," said he, "and very much more which I did not say." Then he deliberately turned his back upon her.

For an instant Maggie tottered. I stepped forward, fearing she would faint. But she rested one hand on the table, and said slowly, —

"Ned — you do not believe in me, but I *must* believe you; and you have caused me — the greatest suffering I have ever known. That man — this Miguel — this man whom you have proved to be the vilest wretch in the world — Ned — he is — my —*father!*"

Here she at last broke down in sobs and fell upon her knees, covering her face with her hands.

Ned turned slowly about with a wild, incredulous, and yet half-hopeful look in his eyes, and said, —

"Your *father!* Your — And who is Dr. French, then?"

Through her sobs Maggie managed to say, "He is — only my step-father. This man was — divorced from — my mother, because every one — thought him — a — criminal — and I — I believed in him — and loved him — all the more — because I thought he had been wronged; and now — Oh, Ned! don't you understand? Pity me! Take me away from him — I will tell you everything — not now — I can't!"

By this time she was in Ned's arms, sobbing on his breast.

This was all a mystery to poor Seldom; but he never lost his presence of mind, and at this moment he said, —

"Señor Miguel, be kind enough to take your seat again, or I shall be obliged to blow my whistle."

I had left my position at the door, and Miguel had quietly risen and was on the point of leaving the room, when Seldom spoke. He hesitated an instant, then with a muttered oath, resumed his seat.

"Mr. Markham," said Seldom, gently. "it will be better if you take the young lady away. Mr. Jackson and I can finish this business."

Ned looked about for a moment. "Well," said he, "we will go. Tom, you'll forgive me for running away?"

"I shall not forgive you if you stay," said I. So I opened the door, and the unhappy lovers passed out.

"And now, Señor Miguel," said Seldom, "we will come at once to business. In Mexico you took from two poor Irishmen four thousand dollars, — say twenty thousand francs; we will call the interest ten thousand francs, making thirty thousand francs. You also murdered one of those Irishmen. We will estimate the money value of his life to his aged mother at twenty-five thousand francs. In Australia you stole from these two American gentlemen, say thirty-five thousand francs' worth of gold. Call the interest fifteen thousand francs, or a total of fifty thousand francs. Thirty thousand francs plus twenty-five thousand francs plus fifty thousand francs equals one hundred and five thousand francs. The costs of the work of bringing you to time, namely, my professional services, I modestly estimate at ten thousand francs. If within fifteen minutes you do not pay one hundred and fifteen thousand francs into the hands of my friend and employer, Mr. Jackson, I shall blow my whistle and surrender you to the hands of justice."

Miguel gave a short, forced laugh.

"And do you imagine," said he, "that I can put my hands on one hundred and fifteen thousand francs in fifteen minutes?"

"We imagine nothing," replied Seldom. "We *know* that you have in these apartments nearly three hundred thousand francs, ready to use for any emergency like the present."

Miguel appeared confused for a moment.

"And if I comply with this demand," said he, "what assurance of safety have I?"

"We will give you our promise that you shall have twenty-four hours to escape. At the end of that time we shall put the evidence in the hands of the police."

"And if I should be captured, the evidence would show that you had been guilty of compounding a felony and assisting a criminal to escape, receiving a round sum of money for your silence."

"That is a risk which we will assume."

Silence for some moments; then Miguel said abruptly, —

"I will accept your proposal. As you are such expert sneak-thieves and blackmailers, you are of course aware that my money is in a vault in the adjoining room."

"You are quite right in your judgment of our perspicacity," replied Seldom. "Mr. Jackson, will you step to the adjoining room with Señor Miguel while he counts out the money he owes you. Have your revolver in readiness. At the first sign of treachery I will blow the whistle."

I followed Miguel into the next room. He opened the safe, — an iron vault set in the masonry walls of the building, — took out a long box, and actually and without a word or a tremor counted into my hands one hundred and fifteen thousand francs in bills of large denomination. I could not help reflecting on the difference between our relative positions now, and on that night when I lay in the hut in Calcutta.

We returned to the main room.

"Is all right, Mr. Jackson?" asked Seldom.

"All correct," replied I.   ·

"You have the money?"

"One hundred and fifteen thousand francs!"

Miguel sat down with an air of indifference. Seldom looked at his watch.

"It is now," said he, "4.30 P. M.   At 4.30 P. M. to-morrow, Señor Miguel, we shall notify the police of sufficient facts to make them exceedingly anxious to meet you.   And now I think we may bid you good-afternoon.   Mr. Jackson, will you open the door?   Señor Miguel will excuse me if I leave the window raised until our departure."

But the end was not yet. Steps were heard in the passage, and as I threw open the door, a man pushed against me and entered the room. I stepped back in astonishment, and exclaimed, "Captain Chambers!"

He seemed neither to hear or notice me. He stood erect in the room, looking straight at Miguel. The latter, for the first time, entirely lost his self-control. He positively cowered back in his chair. His face became livid with fear. His lips trembled, and he muttered inarticulately.

"You do not seem pleased to meet me, Señor Don José Miguel," said Captain Chambers, "and yet I am *very* glad to see you. I have been longing for this pleasure for the past five years."

Miguel neither moved nor spoke. After a moment Captain Chambers turned to me

"Ah!" said he, "Mr. Jackson!" and he extended his hand. "So you also have had business with this Spanish *gentle-*

man. I fancied it. And where is your comrade, my good friend Mr. Markham?"

" He left here but a short time ago," said I.

" So you have done the world, and at last arrived in Paris, the Mecca of all travellers. Where are you staying?"

" We shall be for a few days at the Hôtel Meurice. There are also two other friends of yours there, — Dr. French and his daughter Maggie."

"Oh!" said the captain; "so you guessed at my identity with Lieutenant James. I shall be very glad to see the doctor again and his charming daughter, and especially your brave comrade Ned. Kindly give my regards to them all. I shall try to call upon you to-morrow afternoon. I judge that you had completed your business with Señor Miguel, as you seemed about to withdraw. If such is the case will you excuse me if I ask you to leave me with him, as my business is of a very private nature."

I bowed, shook hands with the captain, and Seldom and I left the room and the house.

We walked quickly down the boulevard and turned in at the first café. I was beginning to feel desperately sick and faint. A glass of brandy revived me somewhat.

Seldom was as gay as a lark. He whistled and chatted, and would have danced a fandango on the street had I not held on to his arm.

" Do you know," said I, "that we are running a tremendous risk in this performance?"

" Risk!" said he. " Did you think me ass enough to say anything to the police? What I told that scoundrel was only to frighten him and drive him out of the country."

" And possibly he so understood it," replied I. " At all events, Ned and I will make an offing by to-morrow night; and you must go with us, Seldom."

" What! I! Leave Paris! Never, my friend. With the ten thousand francs which my astuteness secured, Paris will become my elysium."

We took a cab to the hotel, where we found Ned anxiously awaiting us.

" A complete victory, my boy!" said Seldom, embracing him. " ' Veni, vidi,' etc. 'We have met the enemy and he is ours.' One hundred and fifteen thousand francs indemnity; paid up at once without our opening fire. The size of our guns frightened him."

Ned did not seem hilarious, but rather quietly happy.

"How is Maggie?" I asked.

"She is very much overcome!" he replied. "I understand the whole matter now. What a fool and a brute I have been, Tom, ever to doubt that girl! To think of turning my back on her! But — it was an awful moment, Tom!"

"I know it, Ned," said I.

"She has had a long talk with the doctor," continued Ned, "and has gone to bed feeling more quiet; but it has been a terrible shock to the poor girl."

"Still, it had to come some time," said I; "and she will soon recover."

"And without being too *Frequent*, might I ask something about this affair?" said Seldom.

So we told Seldom of our first acquaintance with Maggie, and the mystery which had connected her with Miguel, now strangely but happily explained. Then Ned reported the doctor's explanation.

More than twenty years ago Miguel, then a Spanish banker in New York, had married Maggie's mother. Some years after the birth of their daughter the irregularities, cruelty, and more than probable criminal practices of the Spaniard became too much for his wife, and she finally secured a divorce, and went with her daughter, then about seven years old, to live with friends in the country. But her divorced husband continued his persecutions. He managed to obtain frequent interviews with his little daughter, and used all his authority and his winning eloquence to persuade her that he was a wronged and outraged man. His kindness to the little girl, and the sympathy he had instilled into her mind at that early age, had had their effect through all her life, in spite of the arguments of her friends, until Ned's bold denunciation and clear statement of facts the afternoon before had shattered her idol at one blow. Fourteen years ago Maggie's mother had married Dr. French.

"We have had a full and complete understanding at last, and once for all," said Ned. "She has promised me not to speak or write to that man again, and we have agreed never to refer to the matter."

Then we speculated on the sudden appearance of Captain Chambers, and everything seemed to indicate that his final encounter with the man he had been pursuing so long boded no good to Miguel.

"The clouds are clearing away," said I. "If Captain Chambers calls here to-morrow we may discover the solution of other mysteries."

"And now to reach our old friend Dan," said Ned. "He is a sharer in our good fortune."

"A cable message!" said I. "Expense is no longer an item of consideration." After some study we despatched a message as follows:—

To DANIEL O'CONNOR, Cattle-Dealer, Buenos Ayres:—

Have met Miguel. Recovered your money. Meet us in Dublin within three months. Name place and time. Answer to Hôtel Meurice. NED, TOM.

For this little message we cheerfully paid a toll of one hundred and fifty francs.

"If it finds him," said Ned, "we shall have an answer by to-morrow night at the latest."

This appeared enough for the day, as it does for the chapter.

THE next morning we went early to the apartment building on the Boulevard Haussmann. A handsome fee to the concierge greatly mollified his feelings at our abrupt decision to give up the rooms.

He informed us that Señor Enrique had gone out the evening before with a strange gentleman, and had not yet returned.

"Captain Chambers, undoubtedly!" said I. "Worse luck for Miguel!"

Our pretentious trunks were transferred to their former quarters in Seldom's attic, and we returned to the hotel.

Maggie and the doctor were waiting for us, the former still very pale and unusually quiet, but pleasant and self-possessed.

Little Lalage ran to meet us, and twined her arm in mine in the old way.

"Where have you been so long, Tom?" said she. "I was here in these great rooms all alone yesterday. The doctor was gone, and Maggie went shopping, and she would n't take me, and I went to sleep."

"Never mind, little one!" said I. "Business kept us out. But now we are all here, and we 'll arrange our trip together."

"Tom," said the doctor, "I 'm afraid we 'll have to give up our little jaunt and leave you to hustle over your course alone. Maggie is not well, and I think it best to take her home at once. We will go to New York and wait for you there. And my other little daughter will go with us, won't you, Lalage? Tom and Ned will meet us there."

"Will you come soon, Tom?" said the child.

"Very soon, dear," replied I; "and the doctor and Maggie will be with you, and when we come back we will all try to find your own father."

So it was finally decided that the doctor, Maggie, and Lalage should take the steamer from Havre, leaving three days later. After which Ned and I would hurry over our round of remaining cities, and rejoin them in New York as soon as possible.

In the afternoon a card was brought up, — "Captain John Chambers." Maggie at first seemed inclined to withdraw, but finally decided to remain.

Captain Chambers walked into the room as dignified and polite and unruffled as we had always known him. He greeted each one of us cordially, and smilingly apologized to the doctor for his assumed name, — Lieutenant James. Lalage had taken refuge in the window, and partly concealed by the curtains, was looking out into the street.

At the first sound of Captain Chambers's voice she crept down from her seat and stole quietly toward the group, then stood looking straight at the captain, the same puzzled expression in her eyes which I had noticed when she was trying to recall her name.

In a moment the captain saw her. He stopped in the midst of an elaborate remark about the attractions of Paris, and began to tremble. Presently he cleared his throat with an effort, and said, —

"Who is that child?"

"She is a little girl whom we rescued from the gypsies in Hungary," said I, breathlessly.

"And her name is — "

"Lalage!"

He turned upon me fiercely, —

"You would not dare to lie to me! But — Forgive me! It is true. My little Lalage!"

He opened his arms to the child, who crept to his side, whispering, "Papa!"

By a common impulse we all rose and went into the adjoining room, closing the door, and leaving the father and daughter together.

Maggie, poor girl, doubtless remembering her own affliction, was in tears.

Seldom rubbed his eyes and remarked, —

"I like excitement, but you fellows would wear me out in a month."

Then every one began to talk at once.

"Why did n't we think of it, Tom?" said Ned; "Remember that first cipher letter."

"And why did n't the name Lalage suggest the man that so persistently quoted Horace?" replied I, etc. It would have puzzled a stenographer or a phonograph to report that conversation.

In half an hour I quietly opened the door. The captain was still sitting where we had left him, the child in his lap, her arms about his neck. Lalage had been crying, and there was moisture in the captain's eyes as well.

"Come in, friends," said he. "My little Lalage has told me

all the story." Then he extended one hand to Ned and gave me the other.

"You know I cannot thank you, gentlemen," said he. "Words are very unsatisfactory things at such a time. I must see you alone this evening."

"Last night," continued the captain, "I learned for the first time that my long-lost little girl was in the hands of the gypsies. I should have left here for Hungary to-night."

Just then a telegram was handed to Ned. He opened it and read aloud : —

To Ned Markham, **Hôtel** Meurice, Paris :

Glory to God ! Will meet you at Gresham, Dublin, June 1st. Hooray ! Dan.

"He cheerfully paid a dollar or more to put in that ' Hooray ! ' " said Ned.

That evening we sat alone with the captain in his room.

"Gentlemen," said he, "I asked you to meet me that I might tell you of some events in my life which I had once resolved that no man should ever know. But an explanation is due to you, and it will give you an understanding of what must have seemed to you extraordinary in my past actions. The story and the reminiscences connected with it are very painful to me. I shall be as brief as possible, and having once given you this explanation, I must beg of you as my friends not to question me further, and never to allude to the subject again. It is now, thank God ! wholly past, and the remainder of my life, with the aid of my little daughter, will be spent in trying to forget it."

As this preamble seemed to demand no answer, Ned and I simply bowed, and the captain began.

During all the narrative he never moved from his position or showed the slightest feeling. He sat with his eyes fixed on vacancy, and spoke steadily and slowly in a perfectly monotonous tone, as if he were simply compelling himself to utter a series of words, but would not permit himself to think of their meaning.

"Ten years ago," said he, "I was engaged in the practice of criminal law in New York. I was a successful lawyer, and besides the income derived from my profession I had considerable inherited property. My true name is Lawrence Weldon — "

Both Ned and I started slightly and glanced at each other. We remembered that name in the newspapers some time before our departure, in connection with a mysterious murder and robbery which had baffled the police of New York. I remembered also the strange disappearance of Mr. Weldon after his recovery from the murderous attack which had been fatal to his wife.

The speaker continued : —

" A man arrested on the charge of murder sent for me to defend him. The evidence against him was very strong, although almost wholly circumstantial ; still, he told so plausible a story, and impressed me so favorably, that I became firmly convinced of his innocence. There were some unpleasant rumors in circulation regarding his character previous to the arrest ; but after a long and careful investigation I came to the conclusion that they were utterly without foundation. At the trial, I succeeded in securing his acquittal. I had seen so much of the man, and had been so much pleased with him, that I invited him to my house, desiring to show society that I considered him an innocent and wronged man. That man was José Miguel. He became a frequent guest.

" I was then residing on Fifth Avenue, with my wife and little girl.

" One afternoon in November, 1876, my little Lalage, then five years old, went out to walk with her nurse. They never returned. Everything was done to discover them, but without success. They had both utterly disappeared.

" In the days of unhappiness that followed, Miguel was our constant companion, showing his sympathy in every conceivable way, apparently doing all in his power to assist us in our search.

" In January, 1877, a sudden scream from my wife awoke me at midnight. She had been a nervous, sleepless invalid ever since the loss of our child.

" I instantly pressed the electric button at the head of the bed, lighting one of the gas-burners on the chandelier. The flash of light was just in time to show me a club descending with crushing force upon the head of my wife. As I tried to spring from the bed, another blow fell upon me, and

I sank back insensible. In that instant I had recognized Miguel as our assailant.

"Three months later I recovered consciousness in the hospital, to learn that my wife had been long buried, and that the authorities had practically given up the search for the criminal.

"In those days of slow recovery to health and reason I formed a resolution, — that my life and my entire fortune, if necessary, should be devoted to the discovery and punishment of Miguel; that the work should be done by me alone; that I would keep my secret and accept assistance from no one. To those who asked if I could describe my assailant, I replied that I only saw a masked man with a club.

"As soon as my health would permit, I turned all my property into available funds, and left New York under the name of Captain John Chambers.

"From that day until last night I have been steadily in pursuit of Miguel. I have visited every quarter of the globe, often travelling thousands of miles on the strength of a clew which proved false, often arriving just too late. But the account is at last settled, and justice is satisfied. The man José Miguel is dead."

We involuntarily started.

"He is dead," repeated the captain, unmoved. "I did not kill him. I am not an executioner. Neither did I employ others to kill him; and yet he is dead. More than this I shall never tell to any one, nor shall I ever mention his name after to-night. As all his property was in the form of funds invested in the name of Don Enrique, and as Don Enrique had no relatives or heirs, it will doubtless revert at last to the French government.

"And now, gentlemen, I have said all that I wished to say to you, or that I shall ever say to any one in regard to this matter. To your friends you may tell as much of it as you think necessary or desirable. I shall still retain my assumed name of Chambers. I have no living relatives except my daughter, and the name Weldon is hateful to me. I shall not go to New York, but probably to Southern California to live, and it is not likely that I shall ever be known. Should any one accidentally discover my identity, it will matter little. I have already told my daughter that her mother died shortly after her disappearance. More than this she will not learn from me until she reads the record which will be given to her after my death."

The captain stopped, rose from his chair, and brought a flask of brandy with glasses. He filled the glasses, and resuming his seat, became himself again.

" Now, gentlemen," said he, " what of your prospects? You must have no more adventures and hairbreadth escapes. The greatest kindness I can ask of you is to allow me to furnish you with abundant means to complete your enterprise."

We assured the captain that we already had much more than enough.

Then we talked for a time of what would be done after our return, and the captain insisted upon advancing a large amount of capital to assist Ned in buying and stocking his proposed farm in Southern California. At last we adjourned to find our friends.

The next day we told Seldom the captain's story. He listened with great interest, and remarked at the close, —

" The only thing I regret is, that I did not value my professional services at four times what I did."

To the others we told nothing of the matter.

Two days later the doctor and Maggie sailed from Havre for New York. The captain and Lalage went with them, intending to go direct to San Francisco, from which point the captain would settle upon a desirable location for his new residence in Southern California.

After seeing them safely afloat, Ned and I returned to Paris and made preparations for our own departure, to finish our tour.

This record of adventures is now practically complete. It is true that fifteen of our forty cities were still unvisited, but our contract in regard to these places was fulfilled in such a rapid way as to leave no opportunity for adventure, and not much for even ordinary observation. We were heartily tired of travelling, and we flew over the ground, growling at every unavoidable delay, and staying in each city only long enough to secure our credentials and mail our letters.

We first went south, through Portugal and Spain, visiting Lisbon, Madrid, and Granada; thence to Athens by steamer; then back to Naples, Rome, and Florence; then north by rail to Cologne and Berlin; then to Dublin, Ireland, arriving on the 31st of May, where we found Dan awaiting us.

That was a grand reunion. Our old friend was well and prosperous, and riotously jubilant over our success, not so much for the recovery of the money, as to think that we " got aven wid that spalpeen."

We had to go with Dan away out across the country to the little hamlet where his own mother and the mother of his dead partner lived, and then we were overwhelmed by the blessings of the two good old ladies, which they showered upon us in the purest of native Erse.

We were two weeks in Ireland, and we left Dan at last still urging the ancient dames to go with him to the sunny South.

Thence we hurried to Edinburgh, and without delay made our way to Copenhagen and St. Petersburg, returning to England for a week's visit with Morley and his family.

Soon we were once more on the broad Atlantic, and this time every quiver of the machinery thrilled us with the thought that we were nearing home at last.

We landed at Halifax, went by rail to Quebec, and thence direct to New York, arriving there August 31, 1881, just four years and four months after we had trudged out from Jersey City, with our faces to the west.

Of the receptions, the greetings, the banquets, the speeches to which we were subjected for the ensuing week, it wearies me now to write.

At last, when calmness was once more restored, and after a short visit to Boston, Ned and I sat down alone one evening to a little reunion of two in the same room at Delmonico's in which we had eaten the memorable repast described in the first chapter.

It was our last night in New York. On the morrow, the doctor, Maggie, Ned, and myself were to take the train for California.

The room looked practically the same, and yet, as I tried to recall my feelings the last time I sat there, it seemed to me that the narrow four walls had expanded so as to take in the four quarters of the globe.

We were very quiet that evening, a little tired, inclined to contemplation, but very happy in the thoughts of the past and the hopes of the future.

"So you will not stay with us in California?" said Ned.

"No, Ned," replied I. "I 'll go out and say good-by to you; and after you are safely launched on the perilous sea of matrimony, I shall return to New York to spend a quiet year in the pleasures of rest, and in writing up our adventures."

"Well, the adventures were all right; but the hardest part of the task to me was the writing. Heaven forbid that I should have to write them over again."

Presently, as we sat idly smoking our cigars and sipping our coffee, Ned took a sheet of paper and began to scrawl something on it with his pencil.

"What were our total receipts in cash on the route, Tom?" he asked.

"Eleven thousand seven hundred and eighty-seven dollars, sixty-five cents," I replied.

"And our total expenditures up to the date of our arrival in New York?"

"Three thousand five hundred and sixteen dollars, fifteen cents."

"At what damages do you assess your broken leg?"

"At nothing. It 's better than ever. But what under heaven are you driving at?"

"Wait a moment. I always hated figures, even in cipher letters."

He continued scribbling away for some minutes, then threw me the paper.

"There !" said he. "You remember I threw my contract over this very table to you more than four years ago. There's the result of it in your true book-keeping style. Does n't it make you homesick for your old Boston ledgers?"

This is Ned's statement : —

"That 's all right, Ned," said I ; "but you forgot one credit item."

"What's that?"

"Credit: By the affections of one California brunette! What do you estimate the item?"

"Money couldn't state it, my lad; and besides, I'd have you understand that that is not a partnership account. It's an individual credit — mine exclusively."

"And she'd be a credit to any man, Ned. I might insist upon a certain clause in our contract which distinctly specifies that all gains of either shall be in common, and shall be divided equally; but I waive the point."

The wedding in San Francisco was very simple — and pleasing, at least to some concerned. A few family friends, Captain Chambers and Lalage, all the doctor's family, and I were the only witnesses. Lalage was bridesmaid, and I had to see Ned through this last adventure by standing up also. I could hardly decide which looked the prettier, — the dark-haired bride, or the sweet-faced little blonde who stood at my side.

Then we all went down to the hospitable ranch together.

"No wedding-tour for me," said Ned. "I've had travelling enough."

Ned at once began negotiations for a large tract of land near the doctor's ranch, and Captain Chambers insisted on supplying half the capital. The captain had decided upon locating at Santa Barbara, and after a few weeks' visit I took up my lonely grip-sack and returned to New York.

And now more than a year has passed since I settled down here in my cosey bachelor quarters. I am growing tired of inaction. The old restless spirit has returned. I long for the ocean breeze, the quick stride of the desert steed, the cool, bracing air of the mountains, the excitement, even the hardships, of a life of adventure.

I have two letters before me. One is from Morley. He writes : —

"Am getting very rusty, Tom, and have devised a scheme to wear it off. Want you with me. No use to ask Ned any more. Say the word, and I'll come to New York and talk it over with you."

Ned writes : —

"You miserable scribbler! Are you going to spend the rest of your life in scrawling that rubbish to bore an inoffensive public? I have tried for six months to get you out here. Now you *must* come. There is a fat, lusty boy here (weight nine pounds) who cries for you night and morning, and will not be comforted. He is named 'Thomas Jackson Markham.' Come at once, and bring the usual silver cup, with a proper inscription; a quotation from Horace will do. Lalage, too, is very anxious to see you, and in fact we all are."

To Morley I have just cabled, —

"Come by first steamer. Will go with you anywhere. Advise arrival!"

To Ned I telegraph, —

"Hurrah for you, old boy! Cup will be on hand. Am waiting for Morley. Will bring him with me."

As an inscription for that cup I have selected —

www.ingramcontent.com/pod-product-compliance
Lightning Source LLC
Chambersburg PA
CBHW051117120726
47905CB00005B/1318